THE LIGHT AFTER EARTH

KATE HALEY

ISBN: 978-1-99-118823-6 (paperback)
978-1-99-118822-9 (kindle)

Cover design by Jared Haley

*This book is for anyone who has experienced an existential crisis. For anyone who has struggled with themselves, the world, and their place in it.
The lost, the confused, the uncertain.*

The determined.

*Give us a shot.
I promise, we will take it.*

CONTENTS

Visit **www.katehaleyauthor.com** for deals and current news from the author.

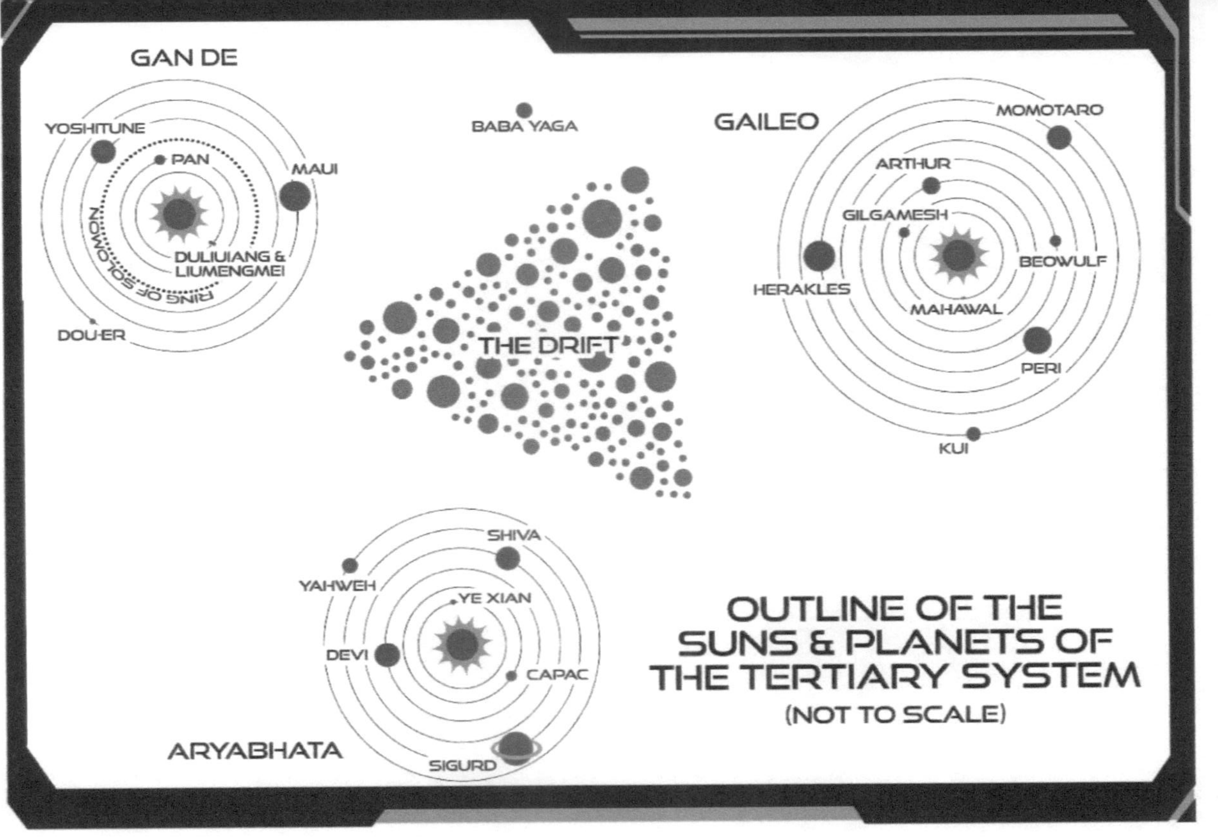
OUTLINE OF THE
SUNS & PLANETS OF
THE TERTIARY SYSTEM
(NOT TO SCALE)
GAN DE
YOSHITUNE
PAN
MAUI
RING OF SOLOMON
DULIUIANG &
LIUMENGMEI
DOU-ER
BABA YAGA
THE DRIFT
GAILEO
MOMOTARO
ARTHUR
GILGAMESH
BEOWULF
HERAKLES
MAHAWAL
PERI
KUI
ARYABHATA
SHIVA
YAHWEH
YE XIAN
DEVI
CAPAC
SIGURD

THE LIGHT AFTER EARTH

CHAPTER ONE

The landing was rough. Al had lived through significantly worse landings, but this was a public shuttle. He wasn't used to flying public. There were kids on this ship. Every jolt and bump was making half of them panic and cry. They were panicking because their parents were panicking, because there's nothing like bringing kids into the world to make you worry about every little thing. Luckily, he'd dodged that bullet.

Humanity had gotten landing spacecraft down to a fine art. Accidents were few. You were more likely to perish in a hover crash or choking on a sandwich than burn up entering atmosphere on a terraformed moon. Still, there was always the freak accident. Al relaxed back in his seat, his whole body vibrating with turbulence, and listened to the anxious noises of the people who thought they were about to become part of a rare and special set of statistics.

Crashing now would solve a lot of his problems. Actually, it would solve all his problems, so there was no chance he could be so lucky. The moon Titania was filling the view out the window and they hadn't broken up yet. There weren't even bits flying off the ship. Practically luxury. Half of him had a painful urge to be the one at the controls, to know exactly what was happening, but he was an average pilot and this shuttle was huge. Nearly as big as they came. His skills were many, specific, and elite, but landing a public shuttle was not one of them. If there had been someone to bet with he would have laid money down that he could do it. If Eric were here Al would have bet him, but Eric probably would have shot out his knees and left.

Al wasn't going to risk drawing attention to himself for the sake of distraction. It wasn't worth it. He could already identify the city of Fika out the window. Coming in hot. Landing wasn't far. He closed his eyes and relaxed.

The shuttle hit the port so hard Al felt it in his bones. He wasn't the only one, but his brain was kindly drowning out the startled cries of others. They were background noise here. Expected. It was the quiet ones you needed to watch for. He was abruptly aware that he was one of those ones. But he'd kept his eye on the passengers across the journey, and none of them seemed like people he needed to watch for. That meant no one was watching him. Or so he thought.

When he opened his eyes again someone was staring at him. A little girl. Her black hair was plaited to one side and her big eyes were staring straight at him. One small hand was clutched in her mother's grasp, and the other pulled at her lip, but the action had clearly been distracted by his face. She wasn't blinking. He shook his head to dissuade her. She kept staring. Fuck, she was about to start pointing. Very casually, Al moved his coat to expose his holstered gun, and stared her straight in the eye as he put a finger to his lips. She blinked. Well, that was something. He needed her to take the hint. Everyone said kids had great imaginations, hopefully the girl did too. Hopefully she was imagining he was on some exciting mission and she shouldn't blow his cover.

The radio above them crackled into life, welcoming them to New Pacifika and informing them that it was now safe to disembark, please remember your belongings, fly with us again, etc, etc. Al was unbuckled and on his feet in an instant. In one fluid movement his rucksack was pulled from under his chair as he stood and strode away. He needed to put some distance between him and that kid before she made a fuss. Blow his cover… what fucking cover? He hadn't been this naked in public for more than half his life. Depending on your definition of naked. He'd shown more skin than this in public, but it wasn't the same thing, not by a long way.

He was out the door as fast as decency would allow. The hot air of the city hit him as he left the cool air-conditioning, but it was only the breaches in the bridge. At the other end he passed back into the terminal and into the customs queue. Fika's security was weak, but they tried hard. Al could see a dozen different ways to cheat it just waiting in line. No wonder they had such a smuggling problem. The gate scanner was old. Really old. The kind of tech that beeped loudly and screamed the name of everyone going through. Shit.

Al grimaced as he watched, drawing ever closer to the dreaded gate. Lin had ordered him to travel under his real name. Bullshit. He hadn't done that for as long as he could remember. All his protests had fallen on deaf ears. He could still see her clearly in his memory, standing in her red and gold office, looking up at him from behind her desk, her dark eyes piercing him like an infrared laser.

"Did I fucking stutter?" she demanded, her strong voice always so alarming from the mouth of such a tiny old woman. "We don't know what this is, Al. We don't know what is happening, and we don't know how to stop it, but we do know that we can't have you running around until the problem is solved. That's why I'm suspending you with pay until we work out our next move. Go home. Go back to your family, go back to reality while we deal with this mess. I will call you as soon as I know more, but you can't help with this one. It's too public. You're too public."

The words stung. He understood them, but he hated everything about them. He was amazing at what he did. Investigation was his business, but he was being told he couldn't research his own problem. No. Go home. Sit around and wait. He wanted to smash things, and the queue was growing dangerously shorter. The guard at the gate raised a hand and bid him wait while the person ahead went through. Beep! Green light. Clear.

He should have defied Lin. He should have kept his scrambler and loaded his chip and bolted for the Aryabhata orbit. Everyone was expecting him to head for Galileo. He wanted to head for Galileo. He wanted to find out what was going on. But at least if he went to Aryabhata no one would know where to find him. He could hide there until all this blew over. Instead, here he was on a rock circling Pan, orbiting the light of Gan De. He stepped up to the gate and held out his wrist. The Gate scanned his chip. Beep! *Al-Amir Akiyama!* Al winced as the robotic voice yelled his name. Green light. Clear.

Everyone was looking at him. He gritted his teeth. Security gave him a nervous glance. They didn't even scan him. So much for cheating the system. Now he felt cheated for not getting the opportunity to cheat. He hoisted his rucksack on his shoulder and barged through. No one stopped him. No one said anything. He could feel the eyes on him all the way through the terminal. People would glance. Then double take. Fuck this. He stormed from the terminal as fast as his long legs would carry him.

The traffic outside was frantic. It was late afternoon now but days were short here. Titania turned fast. A chunk of her sky was taken up by the ball of green she orbited. The super terrestrial Pan had a curve of shadow over him. The sun known as Gan De was hot and bright and close. Al missed Oberon already. Sure, the radiation shields on Titania were just as good as her twin moon, but the heat filter wasn't quite as strong. Lots of people loved it. They said the weather was better here. Those people were wrong. The air was too humid to be comfortable.

He stood in the heat and watched the docks of Fika pass him by. Home. What a dropkick of a city. Now he was here he had no idea where to go or what to do. He hadn't been Al Akiyama for seventeen years. The person he had been when he left had been erased.

Rebuilt. What in all shit was he even doing here?

Standing around was just going to get him noticed again, so he took off for the old neighbourhood. It was like visiting somewhere from a dream. Everything was familiar, but strange. He kept his head down as he left the docks and headed into the depths of Fika. The old neighbourhood wasn't far. This was the part of town he'd grown up in, down in the trade section. Days of his childhood had once flown by scampering around these old docks, hanging with the girls, dodging trouble, watching the ships come and go and dreaming of a life far from here.

He'd made it. He'd skipped town at sixteen and worked hard and run harder to get away from here. Military for a few years until he'd caught Lin's eye, then Specialist Training. Back then Dawa Lin had been Councillor, now she was President. He'd helped make that happen. Sure, if she hadn't hired him she would have found someone else. There would always be others, but Lin wouldn't be sitting behind that desk without the hard work Al had done for her over the years. Now she was President of Titania and she'd just fired him. He was trying not to think about it that way, but every angle he turned it in his head made him feel like he'd just been fired.

That called for a drink. He'd been too young to drink when he'd left town, but he had been back for the occasional visit. He owed his parents that much, even if it was always fleeting visits. Always a brief hello, under an assumed name, with a casual flaunt of newfound prosperity. He was a peacock and he knew it. That was alright with him. But a peacock stripped of its feathers was just a hideous naked chicken, and the shame of it was suffocating. He stalked into an old bar and moved straight to the counter, pulling up a scratched stool and dumping his bag at his feet.

The heavy bartender gave him a familiar friendly nod. The guy looked at him with that expression that knew he'd seen Al before, but couldn't quite remember where. Given his profession it wasn't all that surprising. Except Al was getting really sick of that look from everybody. Not that this guy was at fault. That was half the problem, no one really seemed to be at fault.

"Talofa," the barman greeted him. "What can I get you, friend?"

Al decided it might be safer to avoid speaking and signed for a double ele'vai. The barman gave him a grin and a nod and signed back. He tapped the light-up menu in the counter, flicking through the order and firing it down the bar to Al. Al held his wrist above the reader by his seat and charged the drink to his chip as the barman poured it out. The man made the drink and slid it down the bar to Al, a perfect skid that didn't spill a drop. Now that was an art. One Al had learnt how to do himself. He gave a smile and a nod to convey his appreciation of the man's talent. The man grinned back and signed the bell icon that Al should ring if he needed anything.

He couldn't imagine needing anything but refills. After the first sip he wasn't sure he needed that. The wince didn't show on his face, but he felt it all the way to his toes. He always forgot how nasty dock piss could be. Still, it would get him drunk. Drunk was what he needed to be after two weeks of watching his entire life go up in an irrevocable, radioactive flaming mess.

Like speaking of the devil, he was barely down his first drink when the giant projection behind the bar flickered into his worst nightmare. It had been sports. Who didn't love shuttle races? Who would dare interrupt the post-race analysis for this garbage? The newsreader was talking about him. His name appeared on the scroll. Worse. His face. A bad photo of him from an event six months ago. Sweet Allah, he looked like a woman in that wig. Although, that had been half the idea. He'd been calling himself 'Nat' for that job. Lin's advice, go soft, go pretty. He was good at that.

"Ever since the dreams began two weeks ago, investigators have been digging furiously to find out everything they can about the strange figure we've all been seeing in our sleep," the broadcaster announced.

Al wanted to climb through the screen and throttle her into silence, but he couldn't, so he buried his face in his arms on the bar. He could already feel the bartender staring at him. Yep, that's where you know me from, buddy, Al sighed internally. I'm the man of your dreams. Of everyone's fucking dreams.

"Communications across the three stars haven't been able to find anyone in the entire tertiary system who hasn't dreamt of the mysterious person we are able to confirm as Al-Amir Akiyama, a resident of Titania who supposedly works for Titania's President Dawa Lin."

Now there was a photo of Lin up beside him on the

screen. The tiny lady had a round, lined face with short dark grey hair. The salt and pepper effect was still more pepper, as though age had attempted to take root and was finding the battle more difficult than anticipated. She wore a deep red qipao that matched her crimson lipstick and ruby jewellery. Despite looking like the galaxy's best-dressed grandmother, there was something about her dark smoky eyes that was so shrewd Al was certain Allah himself would think twice before taking her on.

"The United Planetary Systems has ordered an official inquiry into the matter. However, information has been scarce," the newsreader continued, the scroll filling out her words below just in case there was anyone who couldn't hear her. "But our investigators inside President Lin's office are certain that no one knows how or why these dreams have begun. Akiyama's exact role in Lin's government is unknown, but evidence suggests our mysterious stranger works in intelligence."

Al held back a deep groan. Yes, please, just fucking tell everyone I'm a spy. Sure. That's great. Fucking journalists. He could feel a deep breath trembling his lungs. A strange sensation. Not something he was familiar with. What was that? A deep… despair? Well, fair enough. He wasn't just a spy. He was an excellent spy. The best goddamn spy Titania had. At least, he had been, right before everyone orbiting the three suns had started having that weird dream. That messed up flicker of the destruction of Gilgamesh with a static message about Al. The image of his face and a voice insisting he would save everyone from the Goo that destroyed the Milky Way some two hundred years ago.

"No one has been able to determine if Akiyama's investigations have yielded any information into what happened twenty years ago when the alien substance known only as the Goo – thought to have been escaped by humanity – appeared and swallowed the planet Gilgamesh in the Galileo orbit. Despite the floods of terror brought about by the obliteration of Gilgamesh, the Goo appeared to settle after devouring the planet and has remained dormant since. Now, with these strange new dreams no one can explain, people are beginning to fear what the future holds. Immigration from the Galileo orbit has increased in the last two weeks as those fearing their planet will be next look for safer harbours. However, scientists report no indication that anywhere is in immediate danger from the Goo. President Lin's office has officially stated that they cannot link Akiyama to the Goo in any capacity beyond these dreams, but want to assure the public they are doing everything they can to look into it."

"Bite me," Al muttered to the bar, his breath steaming the glazed top. Lin was doing everything she could. Okay, sure, but she had no fucking idea what was going on. No one did. Not even Al, and he was the one parading through humanity's collective subconscious. Now he was benched because being a spy was downright impossible if you couldn't even take a piss without everyone in the bathroom going 'hey, you're that guy!'. Speaking of which…

"Hey! Hey, you!" A drunk grabbed his shoulder and

tried to pull him back, attempting to expose his face. Al yanked his shoulder from the man's grasp.

"Tuu pea o ia," the bartender gently bid the drunk to leave Al alone.

Unfortunately, the man was either too drunk or too obnoxious to take the hint. He grabbed Al again and hauled him off the bar, forcing him to face the room.

"It's you!" the drunk insisted. "You're the guy! What are you doing here?!"

That was a damn fine question and Al wished he could answer it. He wished he had the vaguest clue what he was doing. There was nothing he could say. He couldn't tell the truth, it was all classified. If he followed his sarcastic instinct to mess with people, Lin would have him assassinated for scaremongering.

"You got me confused with someone else," he muttered, trying to wave the man off.

"No, you're the news guy!" The man pointed. It was really hard to talk him down when Al was sitting next to a display of his own face. "You're supposed to be saving us from the Goo! What are you doing in Fika?"

"I'm waiting for intel," Al answered with the bitterest truth he could manage. "Get lost. You're blowing my cover." He wished he hadn't said that as soon as the words passed his lips. Blowing his cover? Seriously? Who was he kidding?

"You like a spy then?" the drunk demanded. "You a spy for that Lin bitch?"

Oh this was going to go so well…

"Get. Lost." Al grated. He waved the man off. "Waiho ahau."

The man shoved him hard enough to knock the bar stool. Al stayed on, but he grabbed the bench to keep from falling. If he turned this into an event the idiot was liable to end up dead. Al wanted to hit him, but he couldn't risk getting into trouble. Not now. Not when the entire galaxy was watching him. But the drunk was starting something, and someone was going to have to finish it. The man was looking for a fight, his body language demanded violence. He opened his mouth to start screaming something. His head hit the top of the bar hard enough to crack it. Al jerked back. He tilted his eyes up a thick multicoloured tree trunk, which was apparently the tattooed arm of a giant.

The giant wore a baggy singlet that exposed his massive, heavily muscled arms and their ink sleeves. His hand could easily wrap around the skull of the drunk, which he held pressed to the bar. Above shoulders that looked like they could have belonged to Atlas, was the face of an impassive yet earnest man.

"Man said 'get lost'," the giant reminded politely. "I don't wanna hurt you, nakama. Please don't make me."

The drunk tried to rip himself free, but the giant kept his head pressed against the bar.

"Don't do that," the giant advised. He held the man down patiently, seemingly waiting for him to tire. The drunk kicked him in the leg. The giant thumped his head again and the drunk's eyes glazed.

"That's enough, Adam," a woman's voice soothed. A tiny hand rested on the giant's free arm. He dropped the stunned drunk with the other.

Al stared at the newcomers. Holy shit. He'd

forgotten how huge Adam was. To be fair, he barely knew him as an adult. The lady he knew well – as well as Al really knew anyone. Her brother might have been chasing seven foot and built like Maui, but she was barely scraping over five foot. Her thick shiny dark hair was woven across the top of her head into a wide braid that trailed into a point at the nape of her neck. She had the widest, friendliest smile in the whole galaxy and thirty years on she still dressed like a little kid. She wore a black compressor t-shirt with grey overalls that had cute animal patches. Al could see a little green snail, a fluffy rabbit, and a teddy bear. She'd always been eccentric, even when they were kids, which was part of how she had ended up with such an unusual nickname.

"Slug?!" he exclaimed.

"Knew I'd find you here eventually," she grinned, ribbing him with her elbow. "We've been waiting for you to show up. Took your sweet time, shin'yū."

Al very suddenly had her arms around his waist and her face buried in his chest. She was so short and warm and loving. He didn't know what to do with that. At first he floundered, not sure how to hug her back or where to put his hands, but looking around meant seeing Adam. Adam Tanaka took up most of Al's field of vision. His face was completely impassive, but it looked like it had been chiselled from stained mahogany and his dark eyes were curious. Except curious on Adam had an underlying level of threat in it that the giant probably didn't realise he exuded. Al felt himself pull Slug in protectively around the shoulders, hugging her back. He wasn't sure which one of them he was protecting, but she nuzzled into it. Adam seemed content with this outcome. Al couldn't take his eyes off him, but that meant the guy was holding his gaze.

"Adam," he swallowed nervously and greeted him with a polite nod, still hugging the man's sister.

"Hey Al," Adam smiled at him. It was a friendly smile. Merciful Mohammad, that was just as bad as a glare. With a glare you knew to watch yourself. The smile set a false ease, you still had to watch yourself just as carefully when Adam smiled, no matter how approachable it seemed.

Slug untangled herself from Al's arms, beaming up at him. She still kept one arm tucked around his waist as she turned him towards the door.

"Come on, Al. Let's get you home," she encouraged.

Home was somewhere he had been deliberately avoiding, but he knew that was his pride calling the shots. Besides, he was used to following orders. It was what he was good at. Having someone else making the decision right now was a relief, and he didn't mind getting manhandled by Slug. He snatched his bag up as she guided him from the bar. Adam followed them out closely, throwing a short glance back in case anyone was looking to follow them. No one who met his eye was going out that door in a hurry.

CHAPTER TWO

Al hadn't been home in three years. It wasn't something he'd made a priority in his life. A visit every couple of years had always felt adequate. Say hi to the folks. Catch up with Slug and her cousins. It was good enough. But things had changed three years ago. He'd been reluctant to come home since. He wasn't prepared to say that to anyone though, least of all Slug. Her real name was Simone. Simone Tanaka. Everyone who knew her called her Slug. She insisted on it. He couldn't think of her any other way. She was his best friend. The only one he'd ever had.

"So what you been doing, huh?" she pestered him as they strolled arm-in-arm down the hot pavement. "You been off saving the galaxy?"

"Not exactly," Al smiled. "Not that anyone believes me these days."

"Eh, they'll come right," she insisted. "Everyone's just spooked. You gotta admit it's odd. No one wants that Goo to start moving again, yeah? It's terrifying the way it can just swallow whole planets… whole systems. The idea of a saviour? Very old-fashioned. Very romantic." She ribbed him teasingly again.

He grinned despite himself. "Lots of things are romantic until you get hit with them."

"Lots of things are still romantic when you get hit with them," Adam chipped in from behind them. "Depends what you're into."

Al shot a glance over his shoulder at the looming titan. "That's... not romance, Adam," he stated apprehensively, concerned that he had to clarify it.

Adam just shrugged at him. Odds were they weren't on the same page. That was one of the many things that made Al nervous about Adam. He never knew what the big lug was thinking. He could seem so vacant, yet only a fool believed that. Adam was clever... the kind of clever that made Al's skin crawl. Still, the giant had been home with his family for three years and no disasters had occurred. Slug doted on him. She believed the sun shone from her baby brother, and Al did not want to be the person who tried to persuade her otherwise, even if he was convinced Adam was little more than a killing machine wrapped in human skin.

"It's so good to have you back," Slug glowed, clinging to Al's arm. "Everyone's missed you something crazy. I was starting to worry when you hadn't shown up on the gates. Expected you days ago."

"What do you mean shown up on the gates...?" he asked.

She let go of him to pull her data communicator from her pocket. The clear display screen lit up like a casino as she opened her lock screen to an unhealthy quantity of running apps. Her nimble fingers flicked the odd few closed, but swiped open a dark image with steadily growing lists of names. Dock immigration. Everyone coming through the port. She'd hacked passport control.

"That's… very illegal…" Al commented.

"Only if you get caught," Slug grinned, closing, disconnecting, and wiping the app. "Lin contacted me and asked me to keep an eye out for you, make sure you got home safe and the like. She's the President. I couldn't say no."

"That bitch did what?" Al exclaimed.

"Al!" Slug smacked his shoulder. "You can't talk about the old lady like that!"

"I can talk about her however I want," Al retorted. "I've said worse to her face. She agrees with me. You should have heard what I said to her when she told me I had to travel here under my own name."

"Well, I wouldn't have been able to find you if you didn't," Slug pointed out. "Unless I'm allowed access to your confidential special covert list of super-classified top-secret identities…?" Her smirk was mocking as she rattled off too many adjectives. Al grinned at her. He wasn't even sure he minded the sarcasm.

"I imagine she wasn't prepared to hand that over," he sighed. "Here I was thinking that she wanted me flying under my own name to keep some distance between us. Figured she wanted me getting busted on an identity that couldn't trace its creation back to her office." He grimaced. "No reason it couldn't be both."

"Na, don't be so sour, shin'yū," Slug bid him, pocketing her communicator again and linking her arm back in his. "These are unprecedented times and Dawa Lin herself called us to try and look out for you. The President cares and she's trying."

Al didn't argue the point. One of the things he had always loved about Slug was her endless optimism and her ability to see the good in everyone. She believed Lin was a good woman trying to do the right thing. It was possible there was a seed of truth in there, but Al knew the woman. She was a career politician. You didn't become President by feeding puppies and kissing babies.

The sun beat down as they walked to the house. He could feel sweat sticking uncomfortably to his back. No place like home. He could smell it before he saw it. Someone had organised a hangi. The delicious smoky scent filled the neighbourhood. The family always knew how to put on a feed. Slug led him through the circular gate out the front of her family home. Adam followed close behind. They strolled through the yard and down the path along the side of the house to the shared space out the back.

Ten large houses, including the family homes of Slug and Al, surrounded the shared backyard that was basically a small park. They had communal gardens and play areas for the kids. There was even a marae that Slug's uncle Tamati had built. At least seventy people were gathered in and around the building, talking, laughing, and eating.

"Ae tina!" Slug called as they came through the gate. "Look who we found!"

Her mother Mele looked over, beaming, and began to call inside. Al didn't know why he wasn't looking forward to this, but he wasn't. A sick dread was weighing on him. It didn't make sense. He didn't usually feel this way, but perhaps nothing was usual anymore.

More people than normal came out to see him arrive, for obvious reasons. They didn't rush, hanging back to let Al's father lead the way. He burst out, hurrying over to Al and the Tanaka siblings as they continued their trajectory towards the marae. His arms were outstretched before he reached them. Al collided bashfully with his father's crushing embrace. Takashi was half a foot shorter than his son, and he caught him around the ribs like a bear.

"Okaerinasai, musuko," he exclaimed, squeezing tightly. "It's so good to have you home safe."

"Arigatō otōsan," Al hugged him back.

"Your mother is at mosque," Takashi informed him, letting go but keeping a guiding arm around his back as they walked forward again. "But she should be back in the next hour or so. She has been going every day since the dreams started."

Al cursed under his breath at the reminder. Takashi gave him a sly sideways glance at the language. Slug was still holding onto his hand on one side, while his father kept an arm around him from the other. They were firmly guiding him toward the meeting house, like they knew he wanted to run away. He should have been grateful he was so loved, but he couldn't be. Not anymore. His job had required him to feign detachment so long that now the cold soul was real. He didn't want to care. He had trained himself not to care. He wanted to hide under his bed and drink until the storm passed.

Slug's parents were the next to greet him. They

always treated him like he was their own. His chest tightened as her father Sato embraced him familiarly. He was so much warmer now, stabler than Al remembered him being. Sato and Takashi weren't biological brothers, but from the way they came up from the street together they might as well have been. They'd been scrapper junkies, but they had built a courier empire from the trash. Al knew he walked in social circles that would have called his background and his family simple, maybe that was why he stayed so far away, but these people were the salt of the earth. Every single one of them was a better person than he was. Well, nearly every single one. Adam was still standing behind him.

"Oh, talofa lo'u atalii!" Mele pulled him in tightly and planted a big kiss on his cheek as soon as he was free of her husband's arms.

"Talofa auntie Mele," he kissed her cheek in return, bracing himself for the onslaught that was about to descend. This was what it was like, visiting the family. Dozens of aunties and uncles and cousins everywhere, an endless barrage of intensely personal questions, too much food coupled with comments about how he could never put enough meat on his bones, and usually some well-meaning light crime and treason – depending on whether the girls could convince him to go scrapping.

"Ay sexy!" a voice crowed through the crowd.

Al knew that sound. He turned to see a tall woman with smouldering dark eyes saunter over. She wore her racing stripes on her shirt, and even had them shaved into the sides of her hair. She flicked a hand at his appearance.

"You off your meds, Ally? You're getting prettier every day," she smirked.

Al raised his middle finger at her pointedly, but kept his tone civil. "Kia ora Lani."

"Kia ora, cuz," she laughed, catching him in a bone-crushing hug.

He met her embrace like-for-like. It was the only way to deal with Lani. The two of them grabbed each other like they were trying to rupture the other's lungs. Al felt confidant he gave as good as he got, but merciful Allah she was so much stronger than him. It wasn't fair. His ribs creaked painfully. It was worth it for the respect in her eyes when she let him go, arm still around his shoulders as she turned back to the crowd.

"Aro, whanau! Meet the man of my dreams," she chortled.

"Fuck you, Lani," Al told her as politely as he could manage.

Her big grin widened. Everyone else chuckled.

"Ae, Lani, leave him be," Slug waved her off. "Come on."

"Aw, Slug," Lani grinned at her. "Is that hands off the boyfriend today?"

Lani smacked Al on the ass so hard he flinched. Should have seen it coming. Careless. These people made him sloppy. A gruff voice barked at Lani sharply.

"Hokulani! Taofi! You keep your hands to yourself, girl!" the order came firm.

Lani rolled her eyes as her dads barged over. They were both a head shorter than her, but the only person around who was noticeably taller than her was Adam. Al couldn't help but smile as Sione and Tamati took turns greeting him and warningly cussing out their youngest daughter. Al had never met nicer men than Lani's fathers. Sione was Mele's brother and a doctor, his husband was a teacher. They were calm and gentle souls, and somehow had three daughters who were chaos incarnate. Well, they used to be. Apparently, only Lani refused to grow out of it. Slug's cousins were slightly older than her, and she and Al had looked up to them and run with them as children, back when they'd all been aspiring wannabe scrappers.

Al pressed his nose to Tamati's in greeting as the older man took him by the shoulders. Tamati's grip was firm and he squeezed Al's arms reassuringly before he let him go.

"It's good to have you back, boy," he said. "Come have some kai, you look like they been starving you, ae."

Al resisted the urge to roll his eyes. He could hear his father laughing behind him. Takashi knew how his son felt about family gatherings. He wasn't the only one. Everyone knew Al was the quiet one. They knew what that meant.

Sione laughed and patted Al on the back. "Don't let him mother you," he ordered. "Whetu is eight months and my aroha here has gone full grandfather mode. He's feeding the village."

"If her children are anything like ours, we're all in trouble!" Tamati exclaimed.

Sione gave him a wink as the group began to usher

Al inside. More and more of the family gathered around. He still had his father at his shoulder, but he looked around for Slug. She was who he needed right now. He realised with a sudden onset of clarity that there was a reason Lin had contacted her to look out for him. Slug was his safety blanket in social situations where he was forced to be himself. In the ocean of whanau he was uncomfortably out of his depth. She found him. Just as he looked around for her, a tiny hand slipped back into his. She was dwarfed by the crowd, but she wasn't going anywhere.

CHAPTER THREE

Al let himself be led inside and fed. He had no real objections, and the family would have firmly ignored them if he had. The food was good, the company was pleasant – especially when Lani and Adam were distracting each other – it was almost enough to make him forget the last two weeks. Almost, but then someone had to bring it up.

"The family's been so worried about you, kid," Sione patted him on the shoulder during a break between conversations. "I know your father don't wanna say nothing, but everyone been asking him about you, wanting to make sure you okay. When those dreams started up everyone panicked. No one knew where you were, if you were off getting yourself killed around Galileo… it's real good to see you home safe."

"Fa'afetai, uncle Sione," Al nodded to him, grimacing slightly. "I'm sorry about it all. I never meant to worry anyone."

"We know you didn't," Takashi assured. He was passing by where Al sat and caught the end of the apology, kissing the top of his son's head.

"I don't know what it is…" Al admitted weakly. "I… I don't know why it's happening or how to stop it. Believe me, if I knew…"

"Well, we can head out in the morning and find out," Sione assured. "President Lin said Slug's ship is up to scratch and it's all signed off."

Takashi had one arm around Al's chest and gave him another loving squeeze at Sione's statement, but Al just looked at them in confusion. He turned his gaze to Slug. She was sitting by him, spooning smoked haiu and saipo into her mouth from a bowl. She raised her eyebrows in innocent speculation, her big eyes guiltless of any crime, and filled her mouth with soft veges and rice. She couldn't speak even if she wanted to.

"You got a ship?" Al asked anyway, prepared to wait.

"Does she what!" Lani crowed, crashing down beside them and catching Slug with one arm. "Lil scrapper here's been salvaging an old ex-military bird. Ancient model, wouldn't win a war, but it looks like she'll fly pretty good. Old lady Lin's cash injection ain't too bad neither. When we get back we'll have to see if she'll cough up to get my racer flying again."

"I don't think President Lin's gonna hand out money for me to fix your racer, cuz," Slug grinned, swallowing her food.

"I don't understand..." Al started slowly, looking around everyone. "What's...?"

"We're the crew taking you to Gilgamesh," Lani grinned.

"Gilgamesh is a fucking Goo bubble," Al objected.

"You didn't tell him?" Lani turned on Slug.

"Didn't tell me what?" Al demanded. His father's arm tightened on him again, cautioning him to settle.

"Well…" Slug wiped her mouth nervously with the back of her hand. "When President Lin called… she… well, she had a lot of specifics that she wanted, yeah? She already knew I was trying to do up an 02-model G.O. Otashii, so she bought me the last few parts I needed to make it safe for travel between stars… I was gonna tell you, Al! I just wanted to wait a bit…"

"Lin ordered you to get a ship to sail me out to Gilgamesh?" Al checked, feeling his blood ice over in the hot room.

"She didn't order me, she asked," Slug defended. "She was super good about it. Said she wanted it secret, kept in the family, like. Of course, the 02 Otashiis are real little, quite cramped, so we're just going skeleton crew, but it's a great plan! Lani's going to fly us, Adam and I will crew 'cos we built her, and uncle Sione's coming to make sure we don't hurt ourselves. Nip out there in a week and check it out — we're going to help you save the galaxy!"

The hope that sparkled in her eyes hurt him. He'd been shot before, and it kinda felt the same. Sweet little Slug, she believed every word of that. Al didn't know what to say. He could feel his jaw clenching. Finally, after some slow calming breaths, he managed to grate out six words.

"I need to make a call." He stood up, untangling himself from his father's arm and striding from the room. He didn't look back. If he met someone's eye he was going to snap. He wasn't sure he wouldn't snap anyway. He strode away from the marae, heading for the quiet area by the back door of his parents' house; it was sheltered from the garden by several trellises for different vegetables. He pulled out his communicator and dialled Lin, the private number he had for emergencies. She didn't answer. Of course. He dialled again. No answer. He wasn't going to stop until she picked up. He wasn't going to settle for leaving a message.

Footsteps sounded behind him. Al paused and turned. Adam. The hulking giant loomed over him, his impassive face serious and a deep and detached flavour of crazy in his brown eyes.

"You upset Slug," Adam stated in a matter of fact tone.

"I didn't mean to," Al assured. "I have to make a call right now, Adam. Slug's going to have to wait."

"She likes you," Adam stated. "She worked hard on that ship. Why're you mad at her?"

"I'm not mad at her," Al replied patiently, trying keep his tone even. His communicator began to ring. Lin's number. "I have to take this. I'll talk to Slug after."

"We ain't done–" Adam started.

"We're done, Adam, or I'm putting you in the ground right now and feeding you to these plants," Al warned.

Adam was silent, contemplative. The phone kept ringing, just a faint buzz. Al stared Adam down. Sweet merciful Allah, this was going to get messy. He needed that kid to back off.

"No…" Adam said finally. "You won't." The giant's body language relaxed and he settled back. "People who are gonna kill you like that don't bother threatening to do it first." He gave Al a polite nod. "Take your call, but you gotta come talk to Slug after." He turned and walked away through the garden again.

Al watched him go, his knuckles going white around his communicator. Adam was right, and Al didn't like Adam being right. No one around here ever asked how Adam knew shit like that. No one wanted to know the answers. Al swiped the call open and Lin's soft round face appeared on the screen. He could feel a muscle in his jaw twitching with frustration. Two weeks off the job and he'd forgotten everything. It had been so easy to fall back into himself, and he was hating every second of it.

"It's good to see you home safely, Al," Lin smiled at him.

"Give me one good reason not to fly back to Oberon and shove my foot so far up your ass it's declared a national emergency," Al growled.

"I'm doing well, thank you, Akiyama," she continued the conversation without him.

"So far up your ass, old lady, that the government thinks our moon is going to explode!" he grated between clenched teeth.

"Kill the melodrama, Al," Lin sighed wearily. "You knew there would be a plan, and you knew you would be brought in on it when you needed to know."

"You dragged my family into this!" he accused.

"Actually, you dragged your family into this," she corrected. "Three years ago, when you used my resources to try and find out about the strange missing boy that showed up. I'm just collecting from an old debt."

"That was my debt to pay," Al challenged.

"It was," Lin smiled. "And now you're paying it." She sighed and drummed her nails on something in front of her that Al couldn't see. "Don't beat yourself up that you didn't see this one coming. After all, I haven't been entirely honest with you."

"Wow, a real first..." Al drawled sarcastically.

"Are we going to talk about this or are you going to keep behaving like a fucking child?" Lin quipped. "You're part of an unprecedented event in human history, Akiyama. This isn't about you, it's about all of us, the entire post-Earth civilisation. Grow up."

Al stayed sullenly silent.

Lin sighed again. Her tiny nimble fingers reached up and began tapping her monitor. Another image appeared on Al's screen. Scans of Gilgamesh. The Goo. It almost looked like a small star, pale and glowy. A beacon of sickly white light.

"We have been trying to stave off any public panic," Lin admitted. "But things aren't quite as simple as we wanted to believe they were. The moons of Arthur have been keeping an eye on Gilgamesh for us, and they found this." She zoomed the image out so far the remains of the glowing planet were pushed off the screen. Something small and indistinct appeared.

"What is that?" Al asked.

"We don't know," Lin admitted. "It looks like it might be a space station."

"A space station...?" Al echoed.

"Yes," Lin sighed. "But it's flying, somehow, out of

Gilgamesh's orbit. It came out of the Goo two weeks ago."

Al stayed silent, but he gave her a look. She nodded.

"It showed up at exactly the same time the dreams started," she confirmed. "And it is broadcasting a signal. We don't know how, but we think that is where all this started, and we need you to investigate it. You are the one it has singled out. It has to be you."

"Why involve my family?" Al demanded. "Why not just send me two weeks ago?"

"Because we have been trying to gather intelligence," Lin said. "We don't want to rush in blind. Now we know more, we know we have to investigate further, and you are going to need help. You can't do this alone."

"I cou—" Al barely got out.

"You're a fucking spy, Akiyama!" Lin exclaimed exasperatedly. "You don't play well with others, you start fights everywhere you go, even half the people we're allied with want to kill you. These are the only people in the entire system you trust. Humanity needs this, and, as much as I like you, you would not have been my first pick for this job. I need a hero, and I got an assassin. Your family are good for you, Al. You love these people. You wouldn't have done what you did three years ago if you didn't. Let them help you."

Al pursed his lips sourly. "I don't want to sail them near the Goo."

"I don't want to sail anyone near that shit," Lin agreed. "But we have to do something, and everyone knows who you are now. We can't control that, so we have to spin it. Al, the Goo is starting to move again. People are terrified, and we are struggling to keep it covered up. Ever since that station appeared, ever since that beacon began, the Goo has been rippling and everyone orbiting the three suns is dreaming the same dream. Aren't you curious?"

"And you want me to say it's worth the risk?"

"Of course it fucking is," Lin huffed. "You've been playing this game with me for fifteen years; don't pretend you suddenly don't know the rules. I've been playing it much longer. Al, I wouldn't be sending you if I thought it was just a sacrifice into the mouth of a lion. You can fight me about this if you want, but we both know you're going to do it anyway. You want answers as badly as the rest of us, and this is how we get them." She sat back and neatly adjusted her crimson scarf.

Al continued to watch her with a sour expression. "I'm not travelling under my real name again."

"You'll do as you're fucking told, young man," Lin snapped.

"Either this is a secret mission you're not disclosing, which means I can use whatever identity I damn well please, or it's a fucking peace envoy to a planet made of solar-eating slime, in which case why not send an actual team of trained professionals to make it look like you're taking the matter seriously?" he retorted.

Now it was Lin's turn to look sour. "Fine. If it will make you feel better about the mission, you have my blessing to play dress-up. I can have someone bring you whatever you need."

"I have everything I need," he replied. "I've got

some scramblers stashed here."

"Of course you fucking do," Lin huffed, rolling her eyes.

Al smiled. He nearly made a quip about sticking her on the flight to Gilgamesh, but he thought better of it. If she wanted to send him with people he was close to, she was smudging the facts to keep her own name off the list. Lin had been his boss for nearly half his life. No one in the galaxy knew as much about him as she did. She was like the grandmother he'd never had, if his grandmother had been a foul-mouthed tyrant who was prepared to raze whole moons in the name of peace. He'd never known his biological grandparents, just this tough-ass old lady who could stare him down like she was going to drag him over her knee and spank him with her shoe if he messed up. He felt like he was on the receiving end of that look now.

"I'll find out what's happening on Gilgamesh," he relented.

"You're damn right you will," she replied. "Oberon is watching me like a goddamn hawk, and all I can do is say I'm working on it. That means my people will be watching you. You can tell that little girlfriend of yours she knows how to put a ship together from nothing. I've seen the specs. She's impressive. A real – what do you call it down there? A real scrapper?"

"She's not my girlfriend, but I'll tell her you said so," Al smiled.

"Sure," Lin scoffed at him. "The only time in your life I've seen you drop everything for someone else was when she called, but sure."

"That was a legitimate family emergency," Al insisted.

"Because she's legitimately family?" Lin smirked.

"Fuck you," Al finished.

The old lady laughed, her scarlet lips stretching into a beaming grin that softened her smoky eyes. She shook her head slightly, helplessly, as though his obscenities were somehow endearing.

"Find out what's going on, Akiyama, and put a stop to it," she ordered. "I want to be able to get a good night's sleep again without dreaming about your pretty face."

"Yes Ma'am," he nodded.

"And come home safe," she added. "I think I might actually miss you if something happened."

"You're going soft, Lin," he teased.

"When you get old, Akiyama, you'll find that sentimentality is a treat you can't help but afford on occasion."

He watched her fingers reaching for the screen again. There was no victory in trying to get the last word in. He waited for her to end the call. She tapped her side. The screen went blank. A message came through as he held the device in front of him. He flicked it open. Their intel on Gilgamesh and the station. He gave the files a brief scan. The station was moving, barely. Drifting more than anything. Didn't look like it had engines firing, but something was happening. Anyone who wanted to know more was going to have to get closer. He sighed, flicking everything closed and pocketing the communicator.

For a moment he stood in the peace and stillness of the garden, listening to the sounds of the family across the way. The noise mixed into indistinct chatter and music and laughter of happy people who knew they had things to live for, and didn't dwell on the existential crisis of what those things might be.

Al weighed up what he knew. Slug wasn't wrong. If her ship was built to spec then it should be able to make the trip to Arthur in about a week, and Arthur was about as close to Gilgamesh as anyone got these days. She was coming too, but she was bringing Adam and Lani. Oh sweet merciful baby Jesus and Mohammed, that was a recipe for disaster. It made a certain amount of sense. Lani was an excellent pilot. She could get them there faster than anyone else they knew. Adam was stronger than an ox, and he did anything and everything Slug said, so hopefully that was a short enough leash to keep them safe. Sione was a stroke of genius. It soothed Al's nerves to think that they would have at least one certified adult travelling with them.

THE LIGHT AFTER EARTH

CHAPTER FOUR

Al was still dwelling on the situation when the back door of the house opened near him. He looked up. The woman in the doorway started slightly, but her surprise was short lived. She smiled at him with a warmth that dwarfed the heat of the city. He couldn't help but smile back. His mother hurried down the few stairs and caught him in a tight embrace. Her hands squeezed the back of his shirt and her silky hijab pressed tight and smooth to his cheek. He hugged her back, breathing in her spiced perfume and wondering if everything would be alright after all.

"I've been praying for you, my darling," she breathed.

"Thanks mum," he sighed. "It sounds like I'm really going to need it."

She pulled away from the embrace, instead cupping his face with her hands, her smile radiating love and wonder.

"I knew…" she smiled. "I always knew. Back when I carried you under my heart, I knew Allah had a great plan for you."

"I would have been just as happy if he didn't," Al grimaced.

His mother, Rajiya, pulled a face and patted his

cheek. "Don't lie, Al. You ran away to adventure as soon as you were able. Don't pretend you would ever have been happy with a normal life."

There was too much truth in her statement to protest it, even if he wanted to. More footsteps hurried their way, and Takashi joined them behind the vines.

"There you are," he sighed, reaching them and placing a hand on each of their shoulders. Rajiya turned into the gesture and kissed her husband.

Al looked between his parents. "You both knew about this plan with Slug's ship?" he asked.

"We did," Rajiya nodded. "She's been so excited about it. All her off-world travel has been for salvage missions, so this is her first trip to another star. The President has been very supportive."

"And you?" Al asked. "What do you two think?"

Takashi and Rajiya shared a look. Rajiya smiled broadly.

"I think Allah has chosen you for something big, my love," she answered. "I think there are questions in the universe that must be answered, and I think he has chosen you to answer them."

Takashi smiled at her, standing with an arm around her and rubbed her back supportively.

"My opinions are not as profound as your mother's," he said. "I don't know what to think. I know that there are a great many things in this universe that I don't understand, and I don't expect to, but I know that you have always been the kind of man to forge your own path, and I'm sure that is exactly what you will do. The Tanakas are family, they will stand beside you, whatever you choose."

"So it's my decision?" Al said.

"Wasn't it always?" Rajiya smiled. "Dreams are Allah's way of guiding us, but we are never forced upon our path. There is always a choice."

Al rolled his eyes. "I can always refuse the call, huh?"

"You can," Takashi nodded. "And we would still be here for you, but President Lin would fire you. You would have to drive couriers for us, wash dishes at the marae, answer to the family about your choices... oh, and Slug will probably kick you in the knees."

"Well, we can't have that," Al sighed. "I need my knees, and I've seen the caps on her boots."

They all chuckled softly. It seemed strange to be making light of the situation, but it was impossible to stare down the full gravity of it. Al had been living with the dilemma for two weeks, and he still didn't feel like he understood it. Billions of people across the system were dreaming of him, of some prophecy he didn't understand, about a substance/creature/entity that had eaten the Milky Way, stalked humanity through a portal, and swallowed a planet. Gilgamesh, their first new Earth. The situation was too big. The whole concept was too massive to comprehend properly. Al barely knew the history. He couldn't be expected to fix the problem. But he was, and there was no escaping it now. Not really. Lin had made sure of that.

His parents looked at him like they understood, and he felt they probably did as much as anyone could. They shared a nod with him, their expressions full of support.

There was nothing else to give. He knew his mission now – fly to the station coming out of Gilgamesh and find out how and why it was transmitting a dream of him. Easy enough. Going places and finding things was his business. The fact that they knew so little this time around… sure it made the job harder, but staying out of it, staying ignorant, would be worse.

The three of them left the cordoned section of the garden and headed back to the marae. Adam was still waiting outside, and Al had a strong urge to cut and run, but the giant was standing with Slug and not even Adam could make Al run away from his friend. She saw him coming, and her big eyes perked up hopefully. He beelined for her, and she walked to meet him.

"Hey, you okay?" she asked as she neared.

He nodded and held his arms out. She hurried into the hug, clutching him around the waist as they collided, mid-stride. He held her around the shoulders, squeezing reassuringly.

"Just had to go tell the old lady I need a reason not to shove my boot up her ass," he muttered.

"You didn't!" Slug protested from somewhere down near his heart, like a new conscience.

"Word-for-word," Al promised. "Told her exactly how far I would shove it for getting my family involved without telling me."

"You do not actually get to talk to the President like that," Slug insisted, still holding on tightly.

"I absolutely do," Al replied, shuffling them both out of the way as others passed by. "I get away with doing bad things because she likes me."

Slug giggled into his chest and Al had to resist the urge to squeeze her even tighter and bury his face in her hair. He sighed.

"I don't know what she told you, but what you signed up for… it's dangerous," he whispered, trying to find the words to explain his problem. "You don't have to do this, Slug. I know you want to help, but Lin is a conniving, manipulative sociopath who will say anything to get what she wants. I don't want you throwing yourself and the family in danger just because she's worked out what to say to make you jump. I can get myself to Gilgamesh, you don't have to do this."

Slug stayed silent for a moment, and Al wondered if he was about to get his knees kicked. She wormed her way from his embrace, not letting him go, but getting free enough to meet his eye.

"What I'm hearing…" she said slowly, "…is that you're allowed to sign up to work for her at age eighteen on missions that were definitely dangerous, but I'm not allowed to sign up to work a mission for her in my thirties that might be dangerous."

"Don't say it like that," Al requested.

"Why?" Slug grinned. "Does it make you sound like an idiot?"

"I'm just trying to look out for you," Al insisted.

"Aw… Al… how completely not-at-all patronising," Slug drawled. "You know, this sounds a bit like the kind of stuff I said to you when you signed up for the military at sixteen…"

"Point taken…" he conceded reluctantly.

She stepped on his feet, tiptoeing up and bunting her

nose gently against his. He grimaced.

"Point definitely taken..." he finished, amping the reluctance.

Slug grinned at him. She let go of him and stepped off his toes, planting her feet in the dirt. "Then it's decided. We set sail in the morning. Glad we got that sorted." One of her small hands stayed tangled in his, and she set about dragging him around for the rest of the evening. He didn't mind. He didn't want to fight with her. He wanted things to feel normal and safe, but it felt like there was a dark cloud hanging over their home now. It wasn't just him. It wasn't just the drama of the last two weeks that he had brought to the door. Home hadn't felt safe for a few years now.

As Slug dragged him around, talking to different people and making preparations for the morning, Al met Adam's eye across the garden. Adam gave him a friendly nod. As far as he was concerned, they were good now. Al had put things right, just like he said he would, and Adam respected him for that. It was not a two-way street. As far as Al was concerned, Adam had walked into their lives three years ago like an incarnation of the grim reaper. He was never going to be able to make anyone else see that, and he had come to terms with that fact, but he didn't like having to share a roof with it. At least for tonight he wouldn't have to.

Al had a room at his parents' house. One last safe haven before shipping out. Still, dusk found him sitting on a bench in the Tanakas' backyard with Slug. There was a walled section of garden with a round gate, down where the plants grew thicker and untamed. A stone bench backed up against the wall, and the two of them had hidden and played down there a lot as kids. Now they sat while Slug explained enthusiastically about all the research she had done for the trip and the course she had plotted. Al smiled and listened. Slug flicked through files on her communicator before closing the screen and pocketing the device.

"There," she pointed up. "That's where we're going."

Al followed the path of her finger to the brightest star in the sky. Galileo. Aryabhata was just as bright, but wouldn't rise for another couple of hours at least. Gan De was somewhere on the other side of Titania.

"I should have unpacked the tent," Slug sighed, kicking her heels against the bottom of the bench as she gazed at the stars. "You know, the one with the clear patch in the ceiling? We could have slept out here tonight looking at the stars, like old times."

"I don't think I'd fit in my sleeping bag anymore," Al smiled.

"It's summer, you don't need one," Slug grinned. "As long as you still wear pyjamas."

Al pinched his lips together to suppress his grin.

"Probably be fine if you don't too, but the whanau will get very curious," Slug added.

Al grimaced but half of him was still trying to hold back a laugh. Slug elbowed him in the ribs, grinning cheekily. It was strange how he struggled to meet her eye in the half-dark. The past didn't seem so far away when there was no sunlight to stretch its shadow. They had a lot of memories of this bench. So many years of hiding away down here. This was where he'd found her hiding so many times after her family had lost Adam, where he'd sat with her and helped her hide from reality, where she'd found him after his transition surgery, where he'd said goodbye to her before he left for the army. Some of those memories felt so close now, like a hand tightening around his throat. Slug sighed with the freedom of someone who had nothing haunting them, and Al felt his heart stir gratefully for her sake, even if he was a touch envious for his own.

"I suppose we should probably head in and get a decent rest before the morning," she contemplated, kicking her heels against the bench again with a thudding sound.

"Probably," Al agreed. He stood and stretched his back out, turning away from the bad decisions he knew he could be making. "If you think you'll actually do any sleeping tonight."

"Oh yeah?" She arched an eyebrow. "You got a better suggestion?"

"What?" he started, turning back to her. Their eyes met. He flushed. "Wha– no– I– no– it– wha– I– I meant with the thing–" he gestured awkwardly to her pocket. "The stuff you were showing me. You seem way too excited to sleep." He hadn't floundered like that since they were teenagers.

Slug had a hand over her mouth to try and stifle her laughter. She was hysterical over his stammering. A small snort escaped as she tried to stop laughing and failed. Al scuffed the toe of his boot in the dirt, grimacing, his hot blush barely hidden by nightfall.

"Fuck you, Slug…" he muttered bashfully.

She laughed harder, bouncing up and planting an affectionate kiss at the corner of his lips.

"You're such an idiot," she praised lovingly.

"Only in front of you," Al shook his head. "You bring it out in me."

"Good," she grinned, turning him around forcefully and marching him from her garden. "Let's get you safely back home before you do anything else stupid."

He wasn't going to argue with that, but he was strangely sorry to kiss her cheek goodbye at the gate and head home without her. Still, that ship had sailed. He'd messed it up a long time ago. All the more cheery thoughts to keep him company until they set off in the morning. Not like he already had the weight of the tertiary system on his shoulders.

CHAPTER FIVE

Goodbyes the next morning were an affair Al would just as soon have avoided. Usually it was easier to get away. Usually he drew less attention. Usually he wasn't taking what felt like half the family with him. Slug spent nearly an hour farewelling everyone and making foolish promises as she embraced everybody at least once. Al waited patiently, trying not to begrudge her this or think about the unknown dangers he was about to drag her and her family into.

He farewelled his own parents several times over the course of Slug's goodbyes, trying not to look at the others and their deep expressions of love. It stirred a tsunami of guilt in him. Foolish, really. There was nothing he could do. All the decisions had been made over his head. Still, the dreams were about him. The mission was his. He felt responsible.

Eventually they were away, and Tamati drove them down to the docks. It felt like a slow drive, hovering safely in the main laneways in the van. Al's own driving would probably have been considered maniacal by his elders. They were in a rush, weren't they? Not that the extended family were suckers for punctuality. Still, the day was already starting to get hot, and he didn't want to stick around longer than he had to. His disguise was weak; large dark glasses and hair loose across his face. He was relying on the new name to do most of the heavy lifting, but it wasn't worth the effort of a full disguise just to get away. Besides, he could do without the judgement from the family. Someone would have commented if he'd gone hard.

When they parked up Al felt another flare of guilt, watching Tamati kiss his husband and daughter goodbye. Allah be gentle, it felt like getting stabbed in the back. It felt almost exactly like getting stabbed in the back. He turned away, stretching out his spine and gently rubbing an old scar, just in case the twinge was all it was. He couldn't watch anymore farewells. If he had to think about it much longer he was going to call the whole thing off. What if they never came back? He couldn't do that. Not to these people.

"Al?" Tamati's voice started him from his thoughts. He turned. The older man took him by the shoulders and pressed their noses together. "Be safe, yeah?"

"Yeah," Al conceded. "Don't worry. I'll look after them."

Tamati stood back, smiling, and clapped both his shoulders. "I know. They'll look after you too, ae."

Al nodded. Tamati clapped him on the shoulders once more and let him go. Al tried to give him a reassuring look, tried to let him know he would do everything in his power to keep everyone safe, but he didn't know if the man before him could see anything but the child who had grown up scrapping with his daughters. It was re-enforced when Tamati turned to Sione again, embracing him once more with a final instruction.

"You don't let these kids do nothing stupid, ae?"

"Ae, good luck to me," Sione joked, squeezing his husband tightly.

Al turned to the docks, dragging his feet as he walked away. It was the only thing stopping him from sprinting. Was it too late to steal the ship from Slug, take off without them, and not have to worry? Fuck, what if he got someone killed?!

A small and familiar hand touched his back.

"Al?" Slug looked at him like she was worried.

"We don't have to do this," he said automatically, like a reflex action.

"Yeah we do," she smiled gently. "But we'll take it slow and we'll be careful. It's okay. Come on."

She slipped her hand into his and held on all the way down to the customs station. The others followed close behind. Al could feel Sione and Lani looking back. Adam loomed like a mountain at his shoulder.

The section of the docks they were heading to was mostly deserted, and Al was grateful to be away from the crowds. This was scrapper territory, and people didn't walk this way unless they belonged. People out of place in this area were easy to spot. You could tell who should be stepping up by the way they walked. That scrapper swagger. He still remembered how to do it. For the rest of the family it came easy. Lani did it best. She was a champion racer, and she stepped like the whole galaxy oughtta know. Slug had a softer stride. There was nothing aggressive about her, but there was also nothing uncertain. Al contained a rueful smile as she let go of his hand and led the way to the customs terminal like a woman on a mission.

The agent at the gate glanced over them. Slug signalled everyone to drop their bags in the scanner as she talked to the agent. His Fika slang was so thick Al felt like he was getting a reality check. There had been a time in his life when he wanted to talk like that, but now he barely understood it. Language evolved so fast. The new slang Fika spat now was not what they had been spitting seventeen years ago. Even the languages he considered commonplace were the result of two hundred years of bastardised Earth languages and cultures evolving on a terraformed moon.

He followed Lani and Sione, dropping his bag and letting the gate scan him. At least it wasn't his name this time. Standing by Adam there was every chance he could borrow some of the kid's menace. On his own, Al's dark glasses, long coat, and 'fight me' expression wouldn't have gotten him far, but standing next to Adam's bared Yakuza sleeves he was hoping to generate a strong disinterest.

It seemed to be working. Unfortunately, Al didn't like the consequences. It wasn't so much that he wasn't interesting, but more that Slug was. Her smile was starting to slip. That meant something was wrong. The guard had taken one look at them and decided she needed some light searching. Al was already moving back. As soon as the agent made a move he was seeing red. Adam got there first. Al froze as the giant grabbed the uniformed man, twisted his arm back, and broke his fingers.

"Adam!" Slug yelled.

The agent shrieked as his hand was broken. Guards descended on them, weapons drawn. Al dove between them all. He raised his hands cooperatively, hoping to deescalate the situation, while mentally cursing the entire plan.

"That wasn't security," Adam stated coolly. "That was inappropriate."

"Let him go!" one of the armed agents ordered, weapon raised.

Adam ignored the guns. Al placed himself in the line of fire, trying to meet the guard's eye.

"We don't want any trouble," he assured.

"Adam!" Slug hissed at her brother.

"That was bad," Adam insisted like he was talking to a child, indifferent to the danger closing in. "You don't touch ladies like that. It's wrong." His grip tightened. "Say you're sorry."

"Jesus Christ, Adam!" Slug hissed at him again, tugging at his arm.

"I'm sorry!" the guard whimpered, trembling in Adam's grasp.

"Good." Adam let the man go. The guard tumbled from his grip, snatching painfully at his broken hand and grimacing. Adam patted the guard's shoulder like they'd just had a friendly chat. "You should get some medi-gel on that, should heal in a couple of hours." He turned to everyone else, addressing the guards and pointing at the man he'd just injured. "You guys should keep your friend supervised. Don't let him assault anyone else."

The irony was so thick Al had to turn to address it, but he just came face-to-face with the grotesque oni mask inked on Adam's massive shoulder. The sakura branches around it did little to soften the monstrous face, and Al felt himself pause bleakly. The demon stared back. Something deep inside him flinched.

"We're sorry," Slug apologised, trying to wave the guards down and pull Adam away. "We're really sorry."

"Don't apologise to them," Adam insisted. "You didn't do nothing wrong."

"Yes, we did, Adam," Slug explained carefully. She touched his chest, trying to focus him. "Adam, sweetie, look at me. We did. What you just did, that was wrong."

"What he did was wrong," Adam contested, pointing at the guard.

"Yeah, yeah that's true," Slug nodded. "But what you did was also wrong. Doing something else wrong doesn't make it right."

"Yeah, it does," Adam disagreed slowly. "He's going to think twice before he pulls that shit again. That does make it better."

Slug looked like she had no idea how to respond to that. Al did not blame her. It was those fundamentals Adam was missing – two wrongs don't make a right. They'd been taught that as kids. But not Adam. He'd been taken by then. Gone too young. Hadn't learnt what wrong was. Gone to the gangs. Come back a walking death machine.

Al could see the guards around him thinking it too. Fingers had slipped nervously from triggers. A couple of guards whispered between each other, eyeing Adam's sleeves. They were seeing exactly what Al had seen three years ago, even if Adam's family refused to see it. It wasn't even the kid's size, or his fearlessness, or his obvious indifference to violence that made him utterly terrifying, but the combination of all of it settling into a calm look that would just as easily kill you as serve you a cup of tea, and it was up to you which way it went.

"I'm sorry, man, I didn't realise she was your girl..." the guard muttered.

"She's my sister," Adam stated. His tone was cool, but the chill that settled over everyone at his words was cooler. Discomfort hung in the air. It was a small miracle they hadn't been arrested yet, and if they wanted to keep it that way Al knew he had to play on the guards' fears.

"Adam," he addressed the giant sharply. "We're leaving now." His voice gave no room to argue, and Adam reacted accordingly.

"Hai, Oyabun," Adam nodded curtly.

No one was pointing guns at them anymore. Good. Al gave the guards one last glance through his sunglasses. They looked terrified. Also good. Al signalled and Adam obediently ushered his family through and grabbed the bags. Al followed behind. At least the kid had been raised to follow orders, even if he hadn't been trained not to pick fights he couldn't win. Except, of course, Al had a horrible feeling Adam didn't think there was any fight he couldn't win.

They weren't even off the planet yet and already

they were trying to get themselves killed.

No one else bothered them as they headed for their dock. Al didn't know if that was because someone had radioed ahead, or if they just looked like trouble. Maybe they were just through security, heading to a private ship, and they weren't anyone else's business. Whatever the reason, he was grateful. Adam might have been strolling at his side like nothing had happened, but the rest of Al's crew were so nervous he could feel it. They didn't get guns pointed at them everyday, and they were shaken.

"I cannot believe we didn't just get arrested, cuz," Lani hissed, ribbing Adam as soon as they were safely away. "You are out of your fucking mind!"

"Na, they're just dock security," Adam shrugged nonchalantly, as though he'd had run-ins like that many times before.

"I don't care who they are, boy," Sione warned. "You don't pull any more stunts like that. You hear me? None."

"Sorry uncle," Adam dipped his head respectfully. "I didn't mean to scare you."

Sione shared a look with Slug. Al watched their eyes meet. Sione knew Adam was apologising for the wrong thing, but there was no easy way to make the kid understand what had just happened. Slug knew it too. Her expression begged for patience with her brother, but what were they going to do with him otherwise? The thought made Al's spine sweat. They were about to be locked in a tin can in the cold vacuum of space with Adam Tanaka. At least he didn't have to wonder how he was going to die anymore. Knowing the root of his demise brought some peace. The tin can wasn't too bad either.

Al wandered up to the Otashii, glancing over the top of his sunglasses as he checked out the ship. She was sleek, black, old parts but not a hint of shoddy work. He caught sight of the decal on her side, and raised an eyebrow as he scanned the kanji marking her name.

"*Hotaru*?" he read aloud. "Isn't that a little… on the nose?"

"Na," Slug smiled at him, a little bit of her confidence coming back. "I think it's just perfect."

Al grinned at her. He couldn't help himself. Slug grinned back. Her eyes were still haunted, shaken by the security incident. For a moment, Al didn't begrudge Adam for breaking that man's hand. He was a little bit jealous. But there was a right and a wrong way to go about things, and being an adult meant you couldn't always do what you wanted to do. He wasn't allowed to break bones just because he felt like it. There had been a way to stop the guard groping Slug without turning to violence. Still, the prick got what he deserved. Hopefully they weren't going to get shot out of the sky in return.

Slug keyed in the code on the docking dial and unlocked the *Hotaru*. The ship cracked and hissed as she opened, the gangplank descending to meet them. A wave of cold air hit them with a sterile metallic scent. Military ship alright. The real smell and feel of home. It was a nice change from Fika. Al wasn't sorry to leave the city behind.

"Welcome aboard," Slug invited them.

Al gave her another smile. Before anyone else could move, Lani gave a wicked chuckle and bolted up the ramp.

"Aw yeah, I'm gonna rattle this bucket of bolts," she cackled.

"You hurt my baby, Lani, I'll put you in the med-bay!" Slug yelled after her, chasing her inside.

"You can try, cuz!" Lani laughed. "Don't hurt yourself."

"Nobody put anybody in the med-bay…" Sione sighed wearily.

Al gave the old doctor a look as Adam followed the girls inside. Sione gave him a half-smile.

"The hard part's over, ae?" Sione teased.

"What? Fika security?" Al replied.

"Yeah, just three more security stations to go and then we only got that big planet of Goo and the ghosts of Gilgamesh to deal with," he joked.

"Allah lend me your sense of humour, Sione," Al sighed.

"Ah, one of us got to be the adult, boy," the doctor smiled. "Here's hoping it's you, ae?"

Al did not smile. He knew Sione was nervous and trying to hide it, jesting with him, smacking his shoulder and striding off into the ship. That was a man who hadn't done much flying, who had been roped into this because his family were in danger, because his daughter and his sister's kids were putting themselves on the line. Aw fuck… hopefully there was a ring of truth to his joke. Hopefully the hard part was over.

CHAPTER SIX

The *Hotaru* had come a long way from the long-range marine assault ship she'd been in her last life. Al had to admit he was impressed with the refurbishments. They entered into a large cargo hold flanked with stairs to the upper deck. Another time he was sure Slug would have wanted to take him on a tour through engineering out the back, but he could still hear her yelling at Lani above him.

He followed Sione up one of the flights of stairs. They came up into the area that had once been given over to the central command console. It had been repurposed into a shared living space with a multi-purpose console and kitchenette. The blue light from the console bathed the room and gave the space a quiet, dark atmosphere; something Al was sure they could effectively slaughter by turning on the lights and making themselves at home. Doors surrounded them in every direction, all with stencilled nameplates that declared their purpose.

Al strode towards the front of the ship, down the corridor lined with doors that assured him they were private cabins. He could hear Slug's heated protests and Lani's laughter coming from the bridge. Sure enough, the women were making the room their own. Lani was getting comfortable in the pilot's chair, and Slug was chewing her out.

"If you wreck my ship, Lani, you have to fucking pay to fix it!" Slug swore. "I am not getting stranded in space just because you wanna see how many bits you can shake off her!"

"Chill, cuz," Lani chuckled, strapping in and flicking the console alive. "I don't wanna die out there anymore than you. Your lady needs to be taken gently…" Lani ran her hands up the sides of the steering controls, "… I can cater to that."

Slug did not look pleased. Al reached her side and placed a comforting hand on her shoulder. She had picked Lani for a reason, now they just had to trust her. Slug's cousin could be brash, but she wasn't suicidal. The real question was how was breakfast sitting in everyone's stomachs, because that was something their pilot might take liberty with. Lani radioed flight control to check they were clear to depart. Al half expected them to be grounded after what had happened on the dock, but it sounded like security wanted them gone as much as anyone.

Footsteps clunked on the metal floor behind them, and Adam ducked through the doorway. His big brown eyes looked around everyone earnestly.

"Stashed the bags away," he announced, taking in Lani's conversation. "You wanna head off now?"

"Not much to wait around for," Sione shrugged.

"Buckle up, buttercups," Lani smirked. "We've gotta race gravity."

"You only put four seats in, aroha," Sione

commented, gesturing to the seating on the bridge.

"There's more space for Adam and I down in engineering," Slug sighed, stepping away from Al and motioning towards the back of the ship. "That's where you'll need us anyway, with this pōrangi at the controls."

Lani cackled. "You know every insult is just a challenge accepted, ae?"

"You should stay up here," Adam told Slug, placing a hand on her shoulder the same way Al had done before. "It's her first real take-off. You oughtta be up here for it. I can manage out back. Besides... Lani's all talk," he smirked at the pilot's chair.

"You wanna go, big boy?" Lani demanded, twisting in the seat to round on him.

"Come at me, cuz," Adam taunted.

"You better get that fine ass down to engineering, chuckles," she warned, turning back. "Before I gotta come back there and smack it."

Slug stood between them, rolling her eyes and shaking her head. Al had not forgotten the family dynamic, but he had blocked the memory of how it felt to be caught in the middle of them all. You never quite knew if it was about to escalate into a group-hug or a throw-down.

"Do not aggravate her, Adam," Sione begged. "I would like to at least take off from Fika in one piece."

"You ain't gonna die, old man," Lani sighed dramatically. "Everyone park your big-baby asses and I'll get us off this rock."

"You sure you'll be okay on your own?" Slug asked

Adam.

"Hai," Adam nodded. "All G, sis. I got you. I ain't gonna break her on her first outing."

Slug gave him a comforting nod and patted his shoulder, which was probably about as high as she could reach. He gave her a one-armed hug and then glanced at Al. Even after three years it was weird seeing them so close.

"You need anything, Oyabun?" he asked.

Al shook his head. Shit, that name was gonna stick. Adam dipped his head respectfully at Al and Sione and vanished back out the door. Al listened to him clomp his way down the metal corridor. At least he probably wasn't going to sneak up on anyone. Unless the heavy footfalls were just to lull everyone into a false sense of security…

Adam was probably very good at balancing his loud rough-and-tumble persona with his silent and deadly one. It was something he would have been forced to practice growing up. Once he was out of earshot, Lani turned in her chair to face Al.

"Why the does he call you that?" she asked.

"Beats me," Al lied.

"It's just a term of respect," Slug shrugged. "He's used it with me before too, when we were down here working on *Hotaru*. I figure it's a habit from his time away, y'know. He grew up working salvage crews and scrapping… that was just the name they would use for the boss."

Al watched her as she said it, rattling off casual facts as she buckled herself into the co-pilot's chair and shrugging the words off like they meant nothing. She really believed that. Of course, there was almost certainly a seed of truth in it... but the family knew better. They had to know better. Her father would know better.

"You ever talk to him about it...?" Al asked softly. He and Sione took the seats behind Lani and Slug, sitting carefully and strapping in.

"Adam doesn't really open up about his time away," Slug admitted. "He always says he doesn't want to talk about it, and I can't say I blame him."

"Adam doesn't have serious conversations," Lani drawled. "You'd have as much luck getting him to explain the shit he pulled back at customs."

"He was just being protective," Slug sighed.

"Someone like Adam getting protective can result in people dying," Al commented carefully.

"He'd never kill anyone," Slug defended.

Al felt his heart sink. She really believed that.

"Oyabun is a Yakuza term," he added before he could stop himself.

"What are you trying to say?" Slug demanded.

"Ae, now, Slug..." Sione cautioned, motioning calmly at the room.

"I mean the reason we didn't just get shot or arrested is because the guards thought we were Yakuza," Al answered honestly. "And you don't get mix-ups like that by accident."

"Adam isn't a gangster!" Slug argued.

"Not anymore..." Al muttered.

"Ae, Adam?" Lani called through the comms. "You

there?"

"I'm here, cuz," his voice crackled back through the speaker. "Just strapping in and I'll give you a buzz."

"Chur," Lani called, releasing the button and relaxing back in her chair.

Silence hung about the room. Al didn't want to start a fight. It was half the reason he'd walked away when Adam came home. He knew things the family didn't, things he didn't know how to tell them. How do you tell someone their son or brother, who was abducted at the age of five, had been sold off to the Yakuza? That he'd been filtered through a child slavery ring. I mean, they had to know. They had to know a little. Adam still had the barcode tatted on his inner left wrist. None of his new ink had gone over it. He had kept the childhood mark. The symbol of his abduction and slavery.

They'd only been kids, but Al still remembered when that circle had been busted. It had been a huge news story on Titania. The child trafficking ring that the law had come down on like the hammer of a god, smashing it open and scattering the pieces. They'd been barcoding the kids they stole and selling them off-world. Adam hadn't been found in the wreckage of that, nearly quarter of a century ago. He'd already been sold on. Not that any of them knew he'd been through the ring at the time. The records had been wiped and hundreds of kids remained unaccounted for. Adam must have passed through quickly.

"Good to go, Lani," Adam's voice came through the speaker again.

"Chur, cuz, starting her up," Lani called back. She

hummed a couple of bars to herself as she ran through the controls and flipped switches. Not one to be taken for a fool, she gave the room a sharp side-eye, measuring the tension and weighing Slug's temper. "You're just salty at your boyfriend 'cos you know he's right," she commented, and started the engine.

The *Hotaru* roared into life, engine screaming as she was born. Her maiden voyage. The whole ship began to vibrate. Al relaxed back in his seat. The sound and the turbulence of take-off was like being caught in a storm. Merciful Allah, it was so soothing. Would he have preferred Lani hadn't snuck that last jab in before take-off? Absolutely. Still, it was nice to be back on a ship.

Al had missed space. He hadn't realised how badly, but there was something about being weightless, out in the darkness, watching the stars spin by, listening to the silence… there wasn't a peace like it. Not that there was all that much silence to be had on this ship, but the last two weeks had been hard. Even as different as this mission was proving, it was still nice to feel like he was out doing something useful again. Out travelling the system again.

They pushed off towards the stars. The *Hotaru* bumped and rattled in protest of Lani's treatment. Al couldn't hear what Slug was yelling over the sound of the *Hotaru* clanking, but his friend was definitely yelling. Al had been on the receiving end of that tone and expression before. The difference between him and Lani was that he cared. Lani was a skilled pilot, but she was a racing pilot, and her dad was not keen on her technique. Slug clearly wasn't either. Al could almost watch them turning green. Personally, he had survived much rougher trips, usually when he was flying. He didn't mind the corkscrews. He liked to watch the stars spin.

They cleared atmosphere and blasted away from Titania. That first moment of freedom, when everything shifted and the pressure eased from his bones, was divine. Like a deep breath of peace. Like everything else melted away. Then Lani had activated the artificial gravity and shot towards Tupua, one of Maui's moons. He didn't begrudge her. They were in a hurry. Still, it had been nice.

Once they were safely away, Slug was the first to unbuckle and activate her mag boots. The *Hotaru* had decent A-grav but Slug was a scrapper, and scrappers never relied on A-grav alone. She stood and doubled over, groaning weakly. She wasn't a first timer, but those shifts in gravity could be unkind to the inexperienced stomach. Now that the *Hotaru* had settled quietly into a gentle purr, there was a lot less to yell about. Al stood hurriedly to check on her. He placed a gentle hand on her back and rubbed soothingly.

"I'm okay," Slug gasped. "How's engineering?"

Lani pressed the comms. "You still alive back there, boy?"

"Woohoo!" Adam crowed down the line.

Lani grinned at the speaker. "'Atta boy!"

"Spin her again!" Adam yelled.

"Do not spin her again!" Sione ordered weakly.

Lani laughed. "You doing okay, old man?"

"Humans are not meant to fire themselves through

space…" he muttered.

"What's it you always say, dad?" Lani smirked. "If you can complain, you must be just fine?"

"Ungrateful child…" he muttered.

She laughed.

Slug was starting to come right. Al hovered about her. She seemed half inclined to wave him off, but enough of her must have liked having him around, even fussing like a useless mother duck.

"I'm alright," she assured, more confidently this time, although she didn't move away from his touch. She straightened up, leaning into his arm and letting him comfort her.

"Let me know if you need anything," he said. "She was a bit rough."

"You're fine though," Slug looked him up and down. "I imagine you've had it a lot worse."

"Practice makes perfect," he smiled. He wasn't about to start listing some of the wild things he'd survived, and this didn't make any list. It barely qualified as a jitter. However, he didn't expect them to be used to it. "I'm… I'm sorry, Slug… about before…"

She shook her head at him and he stopped trying to apologise. It hadn't felt like a particularly good one anyway. Apologising was not something he had enough practice with, and this one was harder than most.

"We all know Adam has been through some terrible stuff," Slug assured softly. "But he doesn't want to talk about it, and we need to respect that. He is trying to rebuild his life with us, and he is doing the best he can, so it's our job to guide and support him, not to judge or victimise him, yeah?"

"Yeah," Al nodded, swallowing back any and all hesitations. He rested his lips against her slicked hair, holding her close and trying to find the words to justify why he said what he said. "You're the wisest person I know, Slug."

"You're damn right," she nuzzled into him.

"I'm just worried about you," he attempted to explain.

She chuckled and looked up at him, hitting him full-beam with that smile like sunshine.

"I ain't the one you need to be worried about, hero," she replied, patting him on the back.

Her response left him speechless, and he froze helplessly as she flashed him with that wide smile and clomped off to engineering.

CHAPTER SEVEN

There was a weird hum… like static. It was constant, pervasive… not just the engine. More than that. More than noise. A song of loss in a language before words. Al shivered as he listened to it. It felt like it was coming out of his bones. He saw his own face, like he was looking in a mirror. A voice called to him. A woman's voice. She called him by name. She begged him to come save her, to save everyone. The light was shifting. A giant planet, robbed of life. An explosion. Ooze. The black goo had burst through the rift gate, tearing it apart. It had spread, faster than humanity could escape. It had coated Gilgamesh, their first new Earth, and everything had been lost. Then it had shifted, turning from an oily black into a soft white glow… a tiny pale star of death.

Al-Amir Akiyama, find me. Stop this from happening again.

Al woke with a start. He groaned in the dim light of his cabin and rubbed his face. For some reason he had held on to the hope that if he started this mission the dreams might stop. It didn't make any sense, but it would have been nice. There was nothing he could do to get to Gilgamesh faster. He was hurrying to answer the call, but with such vague instructions there was little more he could do, and they had to get to an entirely different sun. That meant the dreams would keep plaguing him.

They had survived their first day on the *Hotaru*. With any luck they would soon be passing through the Ring of Solomon and only another day from Tupua. There, they could stop for fuel and supplies before leaping the orbit of Gan De and heading for Galileo.

He regretted falling asleep. The rest was probably needed, but the dreams just made him feel lost. There was something about them. The feeling of drifting through space, cold and alone. Waking up like this did nothing to help the sensation. The bunk was comfortable enough, as ship bunks went. A single military unit set into the wall of a sparse and sterile cabin. It was almost like being back in the service, except lonelier. Soldiers shared quarters. Spies did too, quite frequently, in a different way.

Al drummed his fingers against his sternum, staring at the ceiling. The dim blue light reflected off the metal in streaks like jet streams. He was still thinking about Slug and Adam. He hadn't had to be around them since Adam had come back. Here he was, trying to judge Adam for everything that neither Al nor the police could prove the kid had done. Slug was right. She was always right. They needed to support him. Besides, the law had been keeping an eye on the family. They had promised they would. If Adam had been committing crimes near Slug he would have been caught by now.

Instead, Al just had to live with the fact that he'd been avoiding everyone for three years, and Adam had been there for the family. Been there for Slug. Her life had changed having her little brother back, and Al had just spied on the situation from afar and not even bothered to visit.

His last visit, before this dramatic reunion, had been the only time in his life he'd requested emergency family leave. When Adam had shown up. It had been the strangest call Al had ever received, and he worked in espionage. There was an address his family could send messages to, an inbox he checked between jobs. Three years ago, a message from Slug had come through with the most amazing news. Adam had been found. Al still remembered the cold dread he had felt watching her delirious message. Adam had come home. Everything about it had screamed 'Trap!'. Kid had been missing for twenty-two years. He was long presumed dead. Suddenly, the hulk was standing right as rain on the doorstep. What the fuck.

Al had told Lin everything. She knew about his family, or whatever his family's relationship with the community they lived with was. He and Slug had only been seven when her little brother Adam had been kidnapped. He still remembered how hard it had hit the family. Everyone had been shaken. Al's parents had done everything they could to help as Slug's father had sunk all available resources into finding his son. The years had passed. People had started to make assumptions, none of them pleasant.

Lin knew the story. When Adam had shown up again she knew why Al needed to go. She even sent help. They didn't want to destroy his family's hope, but they didn't want them to get conned either. When a Yakuza-tatted thug showed up on their doorstep claiming to know them, it was more than a touch suspicious. Obviously his chip had been scrubbed more times than a surgeon's hands, and it had read blank when they'd tried to scan him for identity. So the cops had run DNA on him, and it came back affirmative. He really was Adam Tanaka.

Then came the real questions. Where had he been for twenty-two years? Unfortunately, answers hadn't been forthcoming. Adam wouldn't tell them anything. It was possible he really couldn't. There were heated debates from the consulting psychologists with regards to his intelligence. Some of them seemed to think he was simple, some were convinced he was bright enough to know what he was hiding. Al had read the situation and concluded that Adam was a few screws short of a hardware store, and they were the really important screws that stopped the building from collapsing and killing everyone. No wonder the Yakuza had sunk their claws into him. He hadn't rolled though. Not a single name had passed his lips.

He claimed to have little to no memories from his childhood. Didn't remember much before the warehouse. Then 'the family' had taken him in. That was what he called them. No names. Just 'kazoku'. He had worked for them. That had been his whole life. Warehouse work. Ship work. Salvage. Repairs. Cargo. No specifics. The cops knew that something had gone down between the gangs. A huge shakeup. They tried to press Adam for information. Nothing. According to

Adam 'Oyabun' had handed him a ticket for a ship, told him to head to the east docks of Fika, and never go back.

Adam had done what his boss had ordered. He had been wandering around that part of town for two days before he had seen a gate he claimed he recognised. Apparently, looking at the house had been like seeing somewhere from a dream. He had knocked on the door, and told the woman who opened it that he remembered her house. After a second he had decided he remembered her too. Understandably, Mele had gone to pieces, realising that the strange man at her door could be her missing son. Adam claimed not to know anything else. Any attempts to press him for names had been met with a glare so immovable Al still lay awake sometimes thinking about it.

Al had watched from behind mirrors as detectives had grilled Adam. He never told Slug he had helped with the interrogations of her brother. He was fairly sure none of the family knew. That was for the best. After all, once everyone had been satisfied the giant really was who he claimed, he was let back out to his family. No harm, no foul.

Was he probably an unbelievably dangerous gangster who had been bought or stolen by the Yakuza as a child and raised into a life of deadly crime? Odds were pretty favourable. Al would have bet his savings on them. He had personally traced Adam back to the gang after the boy conveniently had no idea what ship he had come to Fika on. Bullshit of the highest order. Adam had been covering his tracks after a shakeup in the gang had left his side dead.

Al truly believed that the leader of the branch of Yakuza Adam had been running with had given him a ticket and told him to leave before the fighting started. The man's head had been found a day before Adam had. If he'd known there was about to be an uprising he couldn't beat, and he'd been fond enough of the child he'd taken in – a boy who would otherwise have stayed and died beside him – then there was a chance he decided one last honourable move would be to send the kid back to his real family.

But this was all speculation. Al couldn't prove a damn thing. Neither could the cops. Adam walked, and Al decided it was safer to stay the fuck away. He could almost hear Slug's voice ringing in his ears – *what a spectacularly selfish decision.*

"Yeah, fuck you too…" he muttered to the ceiling, rubbing his face with both hands.

Now he was starting an imaginary fight with his only real friend, and he hadn't even made it to breakfast on their first full day. Why hadn't Lin just let him take a ship on his own?

He rose and dressed stiffly, trying to ignore the voice in the back of his head that wanted to start fights with everyone – including himself. All the cabins faced out into the communal space in the centre of the ship. It was impossible to enter or exit surreptitiously. The *Hotaru* wasn't that big. When Al left his room he was abruptly not alone. Sione was sitting at the counter in the centre of the room having breakfast. He had his communicator propped up on the bench in front of him, recording.

"– we got safely away from Fika, and Lani is

behaving herself – as much as she ever does," he giggled. "Everything is going smoothly. You can tell Mele that her kids built a good ship. Miss you already, aroha. Will message again from Tupua. Should get there tomorrow. Oh, Al is here!" He turned the camera and waved Al over. "Come say morena!"

Al grimaced. "Morena Tamati," he addressed the screen.

"Someone doesn't like mornings no matter where we are in the system," Sione grinned, turning the camera back on himself. "I see you again soon. Looking forward to hearing from you. Ka nui taku aroha ki a koe." He shut off the recording and pressed send.

Al smiled to himself as he moved around the bench making coffee. It hadn't been until he was a teenager in the army that he had learnt how different families could be, and how lucky he'd gotten with his. Maybe a life like that wasn't on the cards for him, but he was grateful he had grown up around it. It always warmed his heart to see good people in love. Sione finished going through his messages and then clicked the corners of his communicator to shrink the screen back to pocket size. He gave Al a sly look across the counter.

"Oh, now he smiles, ae?" Sione grinned.

"Now he does," Al agreed softly, sipping from his mug. "Once the camera's away."

"Ae, ae, of course," Sione chuckled. "O le ala lena. You never change, Al. Just like humanity. Always predictable."

"That bad, huh?" Al smiled over his mug.

Sione gave him a cheeky frown and scratched

noncommittally at his short grey beard. He looked up through the windows in the ceiling. The blast shades were pulled back to expose the view as they sailed through the Ring of Solomon, a vast and rich asteroid belt. It was usually heavy with mining ships, but if you could catch it in the right time and place, it could fool you into believing it was an empty ring of shiny rocks. Not to mention one of the biggest junkyards outside of the Drift.

Al followed Sione's gaze through the window to the skeleton of an old ship, floating listlessly among the asteroids. It was huge. As big as their home moon. It hung patchy and half-lit in the void. A solemn reminder. One of the ark ships. Old before either of them was born. The giant ships that had brought humanity through the gate, fled Earth for Gilgamesh, and then ventured out into this new system.

"They don't build 'em like they used to," Sione commented.

"They do not," Al agreed, sipping his drink.

"We used to build for adventure, for survival," Sione reminisced. "Once we got out here, once we realised we could thrive, that we could build our civilisations again from new undiscovered resources... we did what we always do. We abandoned the old, harvested it for scrap, discarded the lessons that had brought us here, divided into tribes, and began to build our forts and our war machines."

"We were protecting ourselves," Al replied. "That shit ate our solar system and destroyed Earth. We were right to prepare."

"We weren't preparing," Sione scoffed. "We prepared nothing. When that great Goo came for us there was nothing to stop it. It swallowed the new Earth and we screamed and cried and prayed. Mercy was it held to Gilgamesh without eating us all. We came out here, found new worlds to dominate, took what we wanted, and turned our eyes on each other, same as we always do. Don't try to school me, boy. I married a history teacher. If there is one thing humanity is good at, it's picking fights we don't know how to finish."

"Are you trying to tell me something?" Al asked.

"I don't know." Sione raised an eyebrow. "Do you need to be told?"

Al shook his head.

"Then no, I'm not trying to teach you a lesson," the old doctor smiled.

"We're not just good at picking fights," Al disagreed. "We're creative and versatile – masters of invention."

"Not arguing," Sione conceded. "But which necessities do we choose to direct our inventions towards?"

The look he gave Al was so sharp Al could feel himself start to blush. There was no point pretending he wasn't waving the flag of military invention. He was a military invention. Titania needed to protect herself from threats near and far, and Al was one of the preventative measures their government had created. He missed it. He missed his old work and his old life so desperately. The knowledge that he would probably never be able to go back even if he survived this mission was beginning to swallow him. He was trying to think of other things, but that had just led him to dwelling on Adam. Maybe Sione was right, maybe he only knew how to start fights.

Another cabin door opened and Al braced himself, but the tiny figure that stumbled out was a sight for sore eyes. Slug was rubbing her sleepy face and trying to buckle her overalls at the same time. She looked like a confused dormouse.

"Morning," she yawned at them. "If you can call it that."

"Your body thinks it's morning," Sione told her. "That's what matters."

"Time means nothing when you're hurtling through the void of space in a tin can," she muttered. "The spin of Titania is irrelevant here."

"Still prone to pre-breakfast melodrama?" Al grinned at her.

"Feed me before I bite someone!" Slug pulled her cheeks down like a sad basset hound.

Al and Sione both laughed at her, but Al kissed her hair fondly and started preparing breakfast. Slug sank onto one of the stools around the bench, drooping wearily. The excitement of yesterday had already worn off, but that was to be expected. Just because she'd built the ship didn't mean she was prepared for the claustrophobia of living on it. The least Al could do was make her breakfast. Maybe he could be good for more than just starting fights.

CHAPTER EIGHT

Several hours later, Al found himself back on the bridge. His cabin was starting to feel cramped, but Slug was down in engineering with Adam, so it seemed safer to steer clear of that too. Besides, the view from the bridge was worth a look. They were sailing out of the Ring and towards the massive gas giant that was Maui. The planet looked like a marbled baseball of blues and golds and greens. From this distance they couldn't even see any of the moons yet. Luckily, the computer system knew where Tupua was — not that Al was in any mood to insult Lani's driving to her face.

He lounged beside her in the co-pilot's chair, with his feet resting on the dash, watching the system drift by. They were running on autopilot, but this deep in mining territory it wasn't a bad idea to have someone at the controls, just in case. If anything, it was nice to see Lani taking her job seriously. Al missed responsibility and feeling useful; he wasn't going to begrudge her what he had lost.

She lounged at her own controls, swivelling her chair back and forth slowly, and snacking on saipo crackers. The stereo was playing, but she kept it at a surprisingly respectful volume.

"Y'know," she mused, popping a cracker, "this ship

is way too small for you to keep avoiding Adam."

"I'm not avoiding Adam," Al replied.

Lani snorted. Al gave her a look. She just smirked at him. There was a smug cockiness to her expression at the best of times. Moments like this just exacerbated it.

"That obvious, huh?" he muttered.

"You gotta do you, man," she advised, popping another cracker. "But that shit ain't sustainable." Lani tapped a button on her screen to skip a song and lounged back in her chair, bouncing it comfortably. "Wild about him being Yakuza though. Can't imagine a lot of those purists being crazy about a big brown boy in their gang."

"It was half a world away," Al muttered, tapping his fingers on his leg. "Different city. Other side of Titania."

"Oh shit, you mean for real?" Lani perked up. "Like you actually found him with your spy shit? Is that why he came home?"

Al shook his head. "I didn't find him. Once he got home I used my resources to back-track where he'd come from, just to make sure the family would be safe. I was working with the police when they were doing all the blood tests, trying to work out where he'd come from and where he'd been all those years."

"Slug don't know about this, do she?" Lani grimaced.

"She does not..." Al sighed. "She'd hate it."

"Ae," Lani nodded. "But he was like an actual gangster, you're sure?"

"About as sure as I can be," Al admitted. He scratched his chin. "The Yakuza chapter we traced him back to had just gone through a coup, half the gang were slaughtered. The old leadership were made examples of. I think they knew it was coming… and I think the old boss got Adam a one-way ticket out."

Lani raised an eyebrow.

"Can't prove a thing," Al shrugged. "But one of the Boss' reputed closest enforcers, known only as Hogosha, fits Adam's description. His body was never found after the massacre, and no one's seen him since. If the old man knew he was about to be overthrown, and he knew who Adam really was, he might have had it in his heart to do one last honourable thing."

Lani was staring at him. Al gave her a half-hearted shrug. He wasn't really sure why he had told her all that, but maybe it was nice to just finally say it to someone – someone who actually seemed to listen and believe him. Slug, for all her kindness and patience, would never have heard him out. This was too close for her.

"Fuck!" Lani exploded finally. "Dude, that's so heavy!"

"Sorry," Al apologised. "I shouldn't have laid it on you like that."

"Are you kidding?" She punched his shoulder. "Don't pretend like I ain't a gossip bitch, cuz. I wanted to know. That's just… y'know… that's real heavy. I mean… it makes sense, but it's weird, ae? 'Course, it's weird having a hot lil cousin to watch out for too."

"Geez, Lani!" Al covered his face with his hands.

She laughed at him. "Gotta watch out for that boy, Al. Some of those other dock kids throw themselves at him pretty hard. He's not always so good at watching out for himself in that regard."

"That doesn't surprise me," Al sighed. He could imagine Adam being painfully oblivious.

"Eh, and it gives me something to do until they let me back on the track," Lani glowered, aggressively munching a cracker.

"What happened?" Al asked.

"Cheating bags of nut-waste kicked me out," she retorted. "My ride was legit. All my mods were legal. I was just better than them. Then they changed the rules and declared that I'd been riding an illegally modded racer – which was grade-A fucking bullshit. Suspended me for a year. They knew what they was doing was wrong, but it would take me more than a year to get it through the courts anyway. Just gonna finish my sentence and then storm back there and smash those pissy-trash motherfuckers outta the sky."

"Sounds like a plan," Al smiled.

"Oh, you betcha," she grinned. "Flawless."

"And those mods really were all legal...?" he checked.

"Everything above board!" Lani insisted. "Slug helped me do them, and you know what that girl's like – wouldn't break a law to save her life."

Al dwelt on that for a moment. The Slug he knew wouldn't break a law if she thought there was any risk she'd get caught, but she'd been breaking laws just to pick him up from the station on Fika. It was possible some of Lani's mods had been, if not illegal, perhaps a bit cheeky. He wasn't going to push it though.

"The whole point is to design the fastest racer anyway," Lani grumbled. "Don't know what they're complaining about. You want something to go fast, I'm your woman."

"You wanna speed up this old bucket of bolts?" Al grinned.

"Slug would flip if I rattled her girl," Lani laughed. "But, hell, you wanna get to Gilgamesh and back faster we could mod this girl out in Tupua. Just say the word."

"Probably safer if we don't," Al sighed. "Just stick to the plan. Refuel, resupply, get out quiet."

"Yeah, hopefully Slug's running Adam through a few lessons about the world before we have to go through security again," Lani grimaced.

Al pinched his lips together and ran his fingers through his hair. There had been so many good ways to handle that situation. So many options. He should have taken the guard's badge number and had him fired. That would have been the right response to his behaviour, but everything went out the window as soon as Adam had assaulted him. What a disaster.

"Maybe we just leave Adam on the ship in Tupua," he suggested.

Lani laughed at him. "Ae, yeah, okay, good luck with that."

Al rolled his eyes, but didn't push it. Lani wasn't wrong. Slug was the only one who could get Adam to behave, and trying to rein in someone who didn't know right from wrong and solved all their problems with violence wasn't an easy task for anyone. Even worse, Slug still didn't think Adam needed all that much reining.

***

In his dreams he was still trying to solve the same problem. He was calling Lin to update her on the mission. He couldn't let Adam hear him. Adam was trouble and he couldn't convince anyone else of the danger they were in, but he needed his boss to know.

He was on a ship. A different ship. Something huge. A station maybe? White halls, clean and sterile. Hospital? No gravity. He was floating, weightless. Something was beeping. An alarm? Something was wrong.

Someone was calling his name. The same someone. Always the same someone.

In his dreams he was a little girl. The ground beneath him was paved and cracked. Buildings rose up all around him. So tall. Impossibly tall. Steel and glass. The sky was so blue. So empty. He'd never seen such an empty and blue sky before. No planets. No moons. One sun. It was alien, yet enchanting. A sense of foreboding hung over it thickly, rolling in like a storm from beyond the cloudless azure sky.

Still someone called his name. *Find me.*

"Al!" Slug's voice. Her hand banging on the door.

He woke with a start, grunting and struggling. He was strapped into his bunk. Basic safety protocol. He hit the button with a groan, freeing himself and flopping from the bed onto the floor. The metal ground was cold against his bare feet and chest.

"I'm up," he lied weakly.

"Are you okay?" she called.

"Fine," he replied. That, at least, felt as believable as it was true. There was nothing actually wrong, aside from being awake, and his dreams getting weirder. His comms clattered down beside him. He'd been reading when he fell asleep.

Whatever he'd said, she clearly hadn't believed him. His door lock overrode and the door slid open. He grabbed his comms and shoved it in his pocket.

"What happened?" Slug asked, hurrying in.

"Nothing," Al laughed, struggling to his feet. "Except apparently I was tired and don't like waking up."

"You were sleeping?" She took his arm to help pull him up, but the action was mostly redundant at this point.

"Napping," he stretched. "I was reading... but I guess it wasn't that interesting. Haven't seen any decent news in weeks. Everyone just wants to talk about me."

"You're very interesting..." Slug grinned.

"Ha-fucking-ha," Al muttered.

She laughed at him, but her eyes were roaming his shirtless body. Before he could be flattered, she passed comment.

"Jesus, Al... how often do you get shot?" she asked, concern evident in her tone.

"On occasion," he shrugged, looking down at his collection of scars. "These three were stab wounds," he offered, pointing out the old injuries like they made it better.

"Don't they get you to wear, like, body armour or something?" Slug replied.

"Sometimes," he answered. "Sometimes I wear a silk dress."

"Oh, so you wear dresses now?" Slug grinned, lounging against a wall and folding her arms. "Was a time we couldn't get you near them."

"We never had dresses like these," Al grinned back, rummaging in his pack for a clean shirt.

"No?" Slug smirked. "These more like the pictures you used to keep stashed under your bed?"

Al ignored the question, keeping his back turned as he pulled a singlet on over his head. He was too drowsy to keep up with her banter right now, but he knew what she meant. Sure, he'd always had a type. Didn't everyone? Still, it felt strange to reflect on the way that what he sexualised and what he romanticised could be very different. Small fingers prodded him gently in the side. He startled as he realised she'd snuck up on him.

"Those two look particularly nasty," Slug commented. Her fingers jabbed against the fabric of his singlet at a couple of scars now disappeared beneath the garment.

It took his brain a few seconds to even register what she'd said, and then it still had to translate the memories. Usually he knew on instinct, but everything was running a little slow with her standing so close.

"Same person, would you believe," he said, as he remembered the injuries in question. "Different times, but same guy. Dude from Oberon called Eric. We have a few political differences, among other things. I don't think he likes me."

"Sounds like a charmer," Slug remarked sarcastically.

"Actually, kind of a prick," Al grinned. "Not as charismatic as he thinks he is."

"That's the definition of the profession, isn't it?" she smirked.

"Ouch!" Al put a hand to his heart. "What did I do, man?"

"Oh, I dunno… run out on the family and barely see us for seventeen years?" she shrugged. "Run away and join the army to be a big tough guy and forget how to make a comms call?"

"Are you gonna hold that over me until I die?" Al grimaced.

"Maybe," she admitted. "We'll see." She slapped him on the back with just the right amount of force to be both friendly and ominous. "Anyway, I came to let you know we're coming into Tupua. Should land within the hour."

"Already?" he said.

"Smooth trip, huh?" she grinned. "I mean, I can have Lani fly us around a bit longer if you want, but why burn the fuel if we don't have to?"

"Yeah, absolutely," he agreed. "Obviously, good that it's running so well. The faster this is all sorted, the better."

She raised an eyebrow at him, like she didn't quite believe him. He wasn't sure he believed himself. He should. Of course the faster this was all over the better for everyone. Except… it shouldn't be this easy.

Nothing should be this easy. In the back of his mind, messing with his reflexes, he could feel foreboding blue sky.

CHAPTER NINE

Tupua was a terrestrial moon like Titania, but more than twice the size and with ten times the population. It was bright lights and hot mines and compact domed environments. It was loud noises and violent scents all mixed together. Lani loved it instantly. They had organised at the docks for the *Hotaru* to be refuelled, and Al and Slug had gone off together to source supplies. That meant she could do what she wanted, and she was dragging Adam along with her. Not that she had to do much dragging.

They wound through tight, crowded station corridors. It felt like getting squeezed, but it wasn't just the space. Gravity on Tupua was stronger than back home. It wasn't crippling, but it made her feel heavy and sluggish. She couldn't imagine how Adam felt, but he barely showed any signs. Kid moved like a curious mountain.

She led the way to a dock bar. Not the first one — she looked for the loudest. Something fun and exciting. Something showing races. Everything inside was lit in blue and red neon. The dance floor was massive and packed. The bar ran along two whole walls of the square room, and smaller alcoves broke off the other sides. A mezzanine circled the entire club.

"You ready to go make some new friends?" she called to Adam over the music.

"Hai, Oyabun," he nodded respectfully.

"You what?" she raised an eyebrow. "Just dishing that title out now?"

Adam shrugged. "I don't know who's in charge..." he admitted. "You fly the ship, but it's Slug's ship, but we're only out here because of Al, but Uncle Sione's the oldest..."

"Then maybe just don't use it," she suggested.

Adam seemed to contemplate this. It took him a while. They stood in the doorway while she waited for the cogs to tick over. It was probably only a few seconds, but it felt longer. Her eyes narrowed as she watched him. He always looked so earnest. Since yesterday she had been trying to reconcile what Al had told her with the simple giant she knew. It made a lot of sense. Adam was polite and obedient. He would have been trained to follow orders, listen to the family, and take no prisoners. That didn't mean he knew what he was doing.

"Okay, we gotta sort some things, cuz," she sighed. "Whatever else is going on, you gotta stop talking like you're still in a gang. I know Slug just ignores it, but it makes Al real nervous. Also, we don't know what flies out here, and those two will be apocalyptically pissed if we start something. So knock it off."

Adam stayed quietly contemplative. He nodded again.

"Okay, Chief, can do," he agreed.

Lani gave him a wry look. "Fuck, near enough.

Come on, I'll buy you a drink."

"Arigatō," Adam smiled at her and followed her into the club.

Lani crossed the floor towards the bar, striding forcefully through the crowd. She didn't shove, but she walked like she meant business. Anyone who saw her coming saw Adam immediately after her and made space without fuss.

They hit the bar and Lani signed for drinks, swiping her chip over the reader. There were five screens behind the bar showing the race. It was a slingshot circuit around Maero, Maui's biggest moon. Not a track she'd ever come out for. It looked wild. She felt a painful jealousy gnawing at her insides, like a cramp. That's what the beer was for. Just seven more months. Just seven more… fuck. That was so long! She already felt like she was getting rusty.

Adam had barely started on his drink when a couple of girls descended, trying to coax him onto the dance floor. Just like home. He didn't take much persuading, and vanished off into the crowd. Lani grinned as she watched him go. He'd be easy enough to find if she needed to, but she wasn't his babysitter.

She turned back to the race and took a swig from her bottle. The beer was cold and sharply citrusy, with a malty aftertaste. She wasn't sure if she liked it, but figured if she drank enough she wouldn't mind. Someone sidled up beside her. She eyeballed the guy. He was hot enough to not immediately dissuade, and tall enough to meet her eye, which was part of that.

"Nice stripes," he complimented. "Ain't seen your

colours on the track before."

"Titania based," she replied.

He laughed. "Bout time the fairies got themselves a real racer."

"We've taken three of the last five Golden Circuits," she countered.

He laughed again. "That's only three of the last ten, if you count properly. Still, good to see you coming to the party, even if it's late." He nodded his head at the screens. "You not up there?"

"Not racing," she admitted. "Just visiting. Family needed to make a trip. Needed someone to fly them."

"Oh, you got your own boat?"

"Cuz is a Grade-A scrapper, so I'm testing her latest refit," Lani said, it wasn't even a lie.

"Scrappers make the best racers," the guy grinned at her.

"Ae, we do," she grinned back.

"Buy you a drink?" he offered.

She raised her bottle to show she had one, but wasn't ready to tell him to get lost yet.

"If you're still here at the end of this one…" she replied. As far as she was concerned there was no hurry, and he didn't look like he was going anywhere.

***

The fake beard itched, but at least it was only temporary. Al was on a supply run with Slug, and there was no way he was wearing his own face for it. Two weeks stuck on Oberon with Lin telling him he couldn't wear any disguises had been a nightmare. It was so nice just to be able to walk around the Tupua station without being stared at. He hung at Slug's shoulder, and no one was looking at them. They were just two people in a market crowd.

Slug was admiring fresh ingredients at a produce stall. They grew some interesting things on Tupua. Besides, regular fuel stops meant regular grocery shops. No point surviving on canned food if you didn't have to. Not that Slug hadn't stocked the cupboards with enough preserved food to feed a garrison for a month. Al wasn't surprised. Probably everyone in the family had made and packed half a dozen different things for them to take. Feeding people was one of the many ways they showed love.

It also meant that the crew didn't need much. Slug was mostly shopping out of curiosity, and a strong opinion that raw foods were an important dietary staple. Al wasn't going to disagree with her. As far as he was concerned, he was just the wallet. It was the only thing that even vaguely began to counter the guilt he felt at all the kindness everyone else had bestowed on him.

They were so nice. He didn't understand it, not really. He appreciated it. The system would be a much better place if everyone took a page from their book. But the world that he moved in, the people he dealt with, the humanity he understood… well, that was the side Sione had warned him about. People who were good at picking fights, with no care for how to resolve them.

They'd been in the middle of that when this whole

nightmare had started. He'd been part of Lin's delegation to Oberon. Their twin moon. Their ally. Al had always found it interesting that politicians seemed to take more spies visiting their allies than their enemies. He was in the tenuous position of knowing that the warm and congenial alliance was only skin deep. But he'd known that for longer than Lin had been president. It was old news, and an investigation he'd been forced to abandon after the dreams had started.

That had been unpleasant. Lin had scrambled to cover for him, once attention had been drawn to him. They'd done a good enough job, he hoped. If not, it was Lin's problem now. That was probably why she was so tight about his movements and disguises. The memory of the way President Shepard of Oberon had watched him after he'd been nailed to Lin's side still brought a pained exhaustion deep into his very bones. His official title had been Junior Aide, but everyone knew it was a lie. Now the media were digging for proof.

He watched Slug pick out a mixed collection of fruit, and swiped the bill at the counter as she packed it carefully into her satchel. What was he going to do when this was all over? Where was he going to go? It didn't do to dwell, not when there were still so many unknowns, but he could never get his life back... and that thought was like a deep scar across his heart.

Slug turned to regard him as they continued through the market, and she bopped his nose with a finger.

"You look so solemn, shin'yū," she commented.

"Sorry," Al sighed. "Just... got a lot on my mind."

"Really?" she feigned surprise. "What could

possibly be weighing on you?"

Al pulled a face at her sarcasm. She laughed and slipped an arm around his waist as they walked, snuggling in against him. It was worth the snide remarks.

"How do you stay so cheerful?" he asked, keeping an arm around her shoulders.

She shrugged against his hand. "What's the point of letting things get to you? The only person you're upsetting is yourself."

Al grimaced. "I'm not good at keeping the darkness at bay," he admitted. "Even when I know logically how I should behave, what I should think… I can't control my emotions."

"It's not about control, Al," Slug smiled. "It's about understanding. Emotions are there for a reason. They're a warning. They are your body processing what's happening to you — whether you're in danger, or having fun, or getting tired, or falling in love, or negotiating secret spy shit! They're not there to be repressed, they're there to counsel you. Even if you have to tailor your behaviour to your situation."

"That sounds like some deep Mum-Wisdom," Al commented, trying to process it.

"Yeah, well," Slug shrugged again. "My folks had to go through a lot of therapy. You know that."

It was true. Years of trying to deal with the loss of Adam had been hard on everyone. Al had been forced to live through the aftermath of that. He hadn't been around for the recovery. Maybe that was half the problem. He was so good at letting his imagination run wild. He was so good at seeing the bad. He'd been trained for it. Now, he needed to cut Adam some slack, but he didn't know how. He was still trying to control the emotions, instead of understanding them.

"Anyway," she peered up at him. "Don't they make you do a bunch of therapy in your line of work? Y'know, make sure you're not turning into a psycho or something?"

"I don't think they want to know if I'm turning into a psycho," Al grinned. "As long as I'm still resolutely loyal, they probably appreciate a bit of measured psychopathy."

"That's a terrifying thought." Slug jabbed him in the side.

"Anything for the Queen," Al sighed the old adage. The Queen was common slang for Titania, especially amongst the military. Slug didn't settle. Her eyes narrowed further.

"Really?" she pressed.

Al stopped. He froze, watching the crowd for a split second, then he dragged Slug quickly around a stall. She didn't protest, but she did cling tightly.

"What's wrong?" she hissed, taking one look at his face and knowing instantly that something was up.

"Blonde, 6'2", white jacket, 10 o'clock," Al whispered back, keeping them carefully concealed behind the stall.

Slug peered through the break in the signage and pulled a face of consideration.

"Kinda cute for a white boy," she surmised.

"Eric Maxwell…" Al muttered.

"Eric the bitch who stabbed you, Eric?" Slug's eyebrows shot up.

"The very same," Al nodded. "If he's here something is about to go very wrong, and we're not staying to find out what." He grabbed Slug by the arm and guided her away, moving carefully to keep cover between them and the man in white. He was fairly certain Eric hadn't spotted them yet, and he wanted to be damn sure it stayed that way.

"Shouldn't we warn these people?" Slug whispered, looking around the crowd as they hurried away.

"He's a spy, not a terrorist," Al replied. "They'll be fine. Trust me, Slug."

She didn't protest again, but she was still looking at him like she wanted answers as they got clear of the markets.

"What's got you so spooked about him, Al?" she asked.

He paused as he considered how to answer. He was also considering the fastest way back to the docks, how much fuel would get them to the next port, how they were going to radio the others, and if this was possibly an overreaction. It wasn't.

"Eric works directly for Bill Shepard," he said finally. "I'm confident that he's basically Oberon's version of me, just not as good."

"Not as good?" Slug raised an eyebrow. "Does he share that observation?"

"I've had to explain it to him a few times," Al shrugged. "He's a slow learner."

"You're just worried he's going to stab you!" Slug

accused.

"That's a legitimate concern, and I don't have time to get stabbed," Al countered.

"You're in disguise, silly!" Slug slapped his shoulder.

"Yeah," Al agreed. "But if he's looking for me, this won't fool him. We know each other too well, and he's good enough at what we do to pick me out of a crowd."

Slug opened her mouth like she was about to ask why Eric would be looking for him, but she pinched her lips together again in the face of so many obvious answers.

"Do you think he is looking for you?" she asked instead.

"I don't want to stick around to find out," Al admitted.

***

Things had escalated. Lani and her new friend had moved from talking to dancing. He wasn't bad. She didn't even mind that he was starting to push his luck as to where he put his hands. The air was humid with the scent of booze and sweat and perfume. She was hot and slick, blood pumping, but she was getting thirsty again. The real question was, did she need another drink, or was it time to find a room to try something else?

Convincing him they should bounce took little more than a glance and a touch. He took her hand as they headed from the dance floor. The booth by the exit had drawn a large crowd, nearly big enough to block the door. Adam was amongst the group. Lani could see him looking in, drink in hand, grinning.

Loathe as she was to stop for distractions, it was the smart thing to do. Her dance partner wasn't immune to curiosity, and they snuck to the edge of the laughing gaggle. Lani caught Adam's eye, and he indicated. She pushed inside. That was a regret she was going to have to live with. A familiar figure was nestled in the booth, holding a brightly coloured fruity drink with adornments, and surrounded by a platoon of entertained followers.

"—and he says 'Doctor, I have no idea how that got there!' and the nurse is already calling animal protection, because *something* got in there *somehow...*" Sione was recounting to hordes of howling laughter. He spotted Lani in the crowd instantly and waved her over, drawing the attention of everyone watching. "Lani! Bubba! You know this story, come help me with the ending!" He looked back at the crowd. "Lani was there, you see. She was, ohh, maybe six, seven, something like that, and she hears everything through the wall. She slams the door open – Lani, do the bit!"

She groaned inwardly, and did not oblige. It was always like this, everywhere she went. Why, God why, could she not even go to a club without her dad crashing it? Everyone loved him. They always loved him, and his camp mannerisms, and his bright floral shirts, and his stupid stories, and his fruity drinks. Goddamnit. He was the oldest guy in this place by at least two decades, and he had a bigger posse than the racers!

"What are you doing here?" she demanded.

"Having a drink," he answered like it was obvious, before turning back to his fans and continuing. "So little Lani here, tiny thing back then, with big fluffy pigtails—"

Lani wanted to die.

"—she comes crashing into the room, eyes the biggest you ever seen! And she just screams 'he put what in where?!', and suddenly I'm having to explain to my patient that my daughter is off school for the day, supposed to be the back room, and he's still standing there, undressed, with this child looking at him like he's a pet murderer—"

Lani watched the crowd, half of them weeping with laughter, and rolled her eyes to herself. Even Adam was laughing, and in the three years he'd been home there was no way he hadn't heard all of Sione's stories a hundred times. There was something about the way her dad told them that made the stupid and mundane seem hilarious – to anyone who wasn't his long-suffering child.

The front pocket of her dad's tropical patterned shirt began to light up. He made excuses as he sat his drink on the table and pulled his communicator out. The club was too loud to hear it ringing. He slid the rim to its smallest setting as he answered it and put it right to his ear to hear. Lani heard him greet someone, but she didn't hear anything else. His voice lowered in volume when he wasn't in story mode. His expression also began to fall. As bitter as she'd been to see him cramping her style, she didn't want to see him grim.

Sione looked up, catching her and Adam eyes and motioning to them. He didn't give any explanation, but he didn't have to. His face spoke volumes. Time to go.

CHAPTER TEN

The line rang two more rings than normal. For a moment Al felt a faint flicker of panic. Then the screen flared into life. He'd set up his communicator as big as it would stretch on the bench in the kitchenette. Everyone was crowded around it on stools. They were all safely back at the ship. Dawa Lin appeared in all her refined glory, but there was a touch of weariness about her eyes.

"I presume you know what the time is, Akiyama," she sighed.

He nodded. It would be the equivalent of about 3am back home. He had called her at all kinds of experimental times throughout the years. She always answered when he was on mission, and she always looked flawless. She had perfected the illusion of someone who never slept, and he'd never been able to catch her out, not that it was a priority at the moment.

"I'm checking in. This is our last call before we leave the Gan De Orbit," he told her. Everything from here would have to be done on time delayed messages, like the one Sione had been sending home this morning. Even Lin's resources couldn't defy time and space.

"You're ahead of schedule," Lin approved, glancing

around the crowd before her.

"We're leaving Tupua early," Al said. "Fuel, air, and water are all refilled. No reason to wait around."

"Indeed," Lin replied slowly, clearly aware there was more going on and waiting for him to confess what had happened.

"Eric Maxwell is here," Al told her softly, glancing around his crew.

Lin was silent for a moment. Her perfectly painted crimson lips pursed briefly in contemplation.

"Does he know you're there?" she asked.

"I don't know," Al answered.

Lin gave him an unimpressed glower. "You're getting sloppy, boy."

"I saw him, he didn't see me, and I wasn't going to fuck around risking discovery just to learn his business," Al replied.

"Al!" Slug rebuked his language in front of their President. They both ignored her.

"Your primary mission is more important," Lin agreed. "I'm not going to pretend I know what Shepard is up to, but Oberon has plenty of business with Tupua. If he's making Maxwell their problem instead of mine, I will take the blessing. However, a little more effort next time might not go astray."

"If I find anything, I will let you know," Al assured.

"Damn right you will," Lin nodded. "If this comes back to bite me, Al, I'm sending you the bill. Let us pray your little friend has other fish to fry right now."

"What is it you say, Lin?" Al grinned. "It's not

always about me."

"What I wouldn't give for that to be true right now," she sighed. "Unfortunately, I'm still dreaming about you, so I assume everyone else is as well, and our experiences with Maxwell have yet to prove me wrong. You two are an ongoing thorn in my side. Stay vigilant, Akiyama, and let me know whatever you find as soon as you find it."

"Of course," Al nodded.

Lin looked around the table again. "Thank you all for making this trip. Titania and I are extremely grateful. Everyone here is praying for your safe return."

"Thank you, Madam President," Slug gushed.

"Kia haumaru. Safe travels," Lin bid them. She didn't linger, and ended the call swiftly. Al wondered if she was busy or tired. No reason it couldn't be both.

"So..." Adam leant back, perfectly balancing to lounge on his stool. "What's the deal with this Eric guy? He kyōaku-han?"

"Sounds that way," Slug replied. "He's a spy for Oberon."

"You're worried he's here for you?" Sione indicated at Al, leaning heavily on the bench and pointing with two fingers. His round face was serious behind his short beard, and his eyebrows were raised directly.

"He and I have history," Al admitted. "We've run up against each other on jobs before. I've beaten him to the punch a few times. He doesn't like me."

"In your line of work, I'm sure lots of people don't like you," Adam shrugged.

The ladies didn't quite hide their laughter.

"You'd be surprised," Al glowered. "Eric is a special case. We had a particular falling out when I stole some sensitive information from him and fed it back to Lin. He's held the grudge ever since. I guess you could say it's personal…"

Lani had been desperately trying not to laugh the entire time he'd been speaking. Even Slug was grinning with her. Al didn't see what was so funny.

"Oh my God, Al," Lani cackled. "Do you have a nemesis? Like, an actual proper nemesis? Dude, how old are you?"

"Star-crossed rivals," Slug declared flamboyantly.

"Drama Bitches TM." Lani struck a pose.

"Whatever you want to call it," Al rolled his eyes. "There's a guy who works for Oberon, who answers directly to President Shepard, who thinks the universe would be a better place if I was dead. Most importantly, I don't want any of you getting caught up in it. Eric has no idea I have family. He doesn't know about you, and we need to keep it that way. I don't want you getting hurt, and this guy is dangerous."

"If he's that bad why ain't you put him in the ground?" Adam asked. "Isn't that what you do?"

"Not if I can help it," Al muttered.

"But he wants you dead, ae?" Adam pressed. "He's tried to put you down before?"

Al nodded.

"Why don't we just go find him, snap a few essential functions, bury him on Tupua, problem solved? No mess."

"That is the definition of mess, Adam," Al sighed.

"I'm not killing anyone if I don't have to, and I'm not risking any of you on a plan like that when we can just walk away."

"Walking away only saves the problem for later," Adam replied. "Don't let it snowball."

"Adam, honey, we don't kill people in cold blood," Slug advised, reaching out to rub his arm soothingly.

"It solves the problem," Adam insisted.

"Ae, babe, but it's wrong," Slug asserted. "We're not murderers. This isn't a game."

Lani had long stopped laughing, and she met Al's eye with brief discomfort before looking away again.

"Executive rule, no one is killing anyone," Al commanded.

"Hai, o–uh– sure, chief," Adam nodded.

Al raised an eyebrow at his change of address, but wasn't going to complain.

"Right," Lani slapped her hands on the bench. "If that's how we're playing it, let's get this shit show on the road."

"The plan says we're headed to a place called Baba Yaga next," Slug pulled out her map and expanded it for everyone to see. "It's an exo-planet between Gan De and Galileo, kinda hanging between systems."

"It's a rogue planet," Al elaborated. "Orbits the Drift, just like the suns, and caught in the gravity of both stars. It's in the middle of fucking nowhere and it's freezing cold, but the stations aren't too bad. Mostly it's just a mining town-turned-pit-stop-turned-tourist trap. It eases the journey between suns."

"I heard it's a bit of a thieves' den," Lani grinned.

"Depends where you go," Al shrugged. "We won't be visiting anywhere dangerous."

"Spoil sport," Lani poked her tongue out.

"Ae now! You heed him, Hokulani!" Sione warned. "Al is the only one of us who has gone beyond the Gan De orbit. He has experience with these places, and this trip is not about you, girl! It's not a trip for you to go out and recklessly endanger everyone by rebelling against your family! Behave yourself."

"Me?!" she echoed. "Behave myself? What about you, dad? You just casually telling a club full of people all about our business!"

"I didn't tell anyone what we're doing," Sione defended. "I didn't tell anyone who we are or where we came from. I was just telling stories – harmless stories!"

"They're not harmless, pop," Lani argued. "They're stupid, and when it turns out we've got Al's fucking spy nemesis chasing us, they're reckless, so watch where you throw your accusations."

"Woah, Lani…" Al stepped between them, hands raised. "He's just trying to watch out fo—"

"Back up, pretty boy," she warned, getting to her feet and lifting her chin at him. "You want me to fly your ship, you get the fuck outta my way."

He stood down. There was nothing to be gained from fighting her, and he didn't want to escalate this. The set of her glare told him she was in a mood. He'd been there. The fire would burn out in time. No one stopped her as she barged on down the corridor to the bridge. Al looked to Slug. She shrugged back at him. Adam patted Sione on the shoulder.

"Man… something really got up her nose, huh?" he commented.

"I still don't know how I raised such a rude and disrespectful child…" Sione sighed, rubbing his face wearily.

"She's probably just scared," Adam shrugged. "Lots of people act out like that when they get scared. Seen it everywhere, folks who just snap and get fierce – same as dogs getting threatened." He spoke casually, like someone reporting the results of an experiment they never took part in.

"Maybe," Slug chimed in. "Maybe she's just never liked being told what to do."

The engines started with a roar. Al looked around the group at the table.

"Everyone find somewhere to buckle in," he said. "Don't want her trying to shake us out."

The closest spaces with belts were the cabins, but Adam put an arm around Sione and led him back into engineering with him. Slug was headed for the bridge, and Al followed her in. The blue lights of the ship coupled with the darkness of night outside left the room with an icy atmosphere. It felt so much colder than it was. Lani finished up radioing flight control. As soon as her finger was off the button she spoke without looking at them.

"What the fuck do you want?" she asked.

Slug belted into the co-pilot's chair beside her, and Al took the seat behind his friend.

"We're just getting ready for take off," Slug answered calmly. "And coming to see if you're alright."

"Fucking peachy," Lani grumbled, her hands itching on the controls for permission to depart. Authorisation lagged. The silence of white noise intensified. Lani groaned furiously and thumped the controls. "Why is he always like that?!" she demanded. "I can't even make jokes without being dragged over the coals! I swear, Whetu and Fua never got it like I do. It's like they were allowed to grow up, but everything I do is like 'oh Hokulani don't be so reckless! Hokulani don't be so disrespectful! Hokulani don't do anything even remotely risky! Why do you shame our family so?!' Just… every… goddamn… time. I'm so sick of it!"

The console beeped. *Hotaru you are cleared for take off,* the speaker informed them.

Lani slammed the controls and the *Hotaru* screamed up into the night, racing for the sky. Al relaxed back in his chair and let the turbulence rock him. This had to be one of the best parts of flying. Everything else just melted away. People didn't try and talk when they were racing atmosphere. There was nothing but the ride. Nothing but the chaos of momentum. Then they broke gravity and there was nothing at all. That sweet moment of nothing. The first touch of the void.

Everything settled and Slug looked over at Lani sympathetically.

"You're not going to change his mind by losing your rag like that, cuz…" she cautioned.

"I know," Lani muttered. "I just can't deal with it right now though. I feel like… Fuck, Slug, I've been so stuck. These past five months I've had no idea what the fuck to do with myself, and I've just been so stuck, like spiralling, and I'm sick of it, and I thought this was going to be my chance to get back out there and then… I feel like I'm being followed. Like I'm being supervised. Like no one trusts me."

"I trust you, Lani," Slug assured. "I wouldn't have asked you to do this if I didn't."

"I know…" Lani relented. "Obviously this isn't aimed at you. I just… I felt like he sent Adam to watch out for me, but then decided that wasn't going to cut it and stalked us there himself. I mean, he was at the same club as us! Why?! What's he doing out at a club?"

"Getting a cocktail and having a dance?" Slug grinned.

"Oh, don't you start," Lani growled.

"I know you don't like hearing this, cuz," Slug sighed. "But he loves you. He's just trying to watch out for you."

"Of course you'd say that," Lani grumbled. "What about you, pretty boy? You here to cool me off too?"

"Wasn't planning on it," Al replied, watching the stars through the front window.

"What you thinking?" Slug asked, looking back at him.

Al was quiet for a moment, just bathing in the atmosphere of space travel, and barely listening to the ladies' heart-to-heart. He liked to think these things weren't his business, but sometimes he felt he could relate, even if he didn't want to.

"Your dad… other dad, Tamati," he began slowly, "when we were kids… he told us that most of the old Earth ships didn't have windows. They didn't have vitruchal on Earth, that's something from this system, so they just built ships without windows. Everything was run by computers anyway, they didn't need to see where they were going outside of camera views, and it didn't make sense to add weak points to the ships." He paused a moment, but they didn't interrupt to ask what the hell he was talking about. "I can't imagine it," he continued. "I can't imagine being stuck in a tin can, not being able to see all this… I don't think it woulda done us much good either. Humans… we like to see where we're going. We need to see where we're going, otherwise we might not get there. I can't imagine what it's like to have a kid… but I imagine if I had someone I loved that much, who liked to do crazy shit and race shuttles, I'd want to keep an eye on them too, not because I didn't trust them, just because I'd want to see where they were going. I'd want to be watching when the sun hit their wings — either to bask in the reflection or catch them if they got too high."

Al did not look over at Lani and Slug. He could feel them watching him, but his view was just fine, and he was pretty sure if he met Slug's eye right now he'd start blushing for no good reason other than his body's random compulsion to be embarrassed. Every now and again, when considering the human body, especially his own, he felt like a well-compiled argument against creationism. There was no way this system had been designed by divine intelligence, not that he was in a hurry to tell his mother, Allah bless her.

"Damn Al," Lani mused. "That was kinda hot."

"Very poetic," Slug complimented.

"I'm just looking at stars," he muttered, resting his chin in his hand and staring into space. He didn't want to be given credit for this. The worst part of the last two weeks had been all the time left on his own with nothing to do but think. At least one of the existential crises of the period had paid off. Although, he'd be the first to admit he was surprised she'd listened.

CHAPTER ELEVEN

The small girl stood alone among the tall buildings as the empty blue sky began to fill with darkness. *Al-Amir Akiyama, find me.*

Al jerked awake like he'd been falling. The *Hotaru* was steady. The engine hummed comfortingly. Just dreams. Just more weird, troublesome dreams. He missed being able to gripe about his nightmares. These days there was no one he could complain to about what he saw when he slept. Everyone else was stuck seeing him. He saw it too, like looking in a mirror of disaster. Everything else was just confusing. Beyond the mission, he wasn't sure what was real or not.

He climbed from his bed and pushed the panel on his wall that contained a small wash sink. It popped out and he rinsed his face, letting the cool water splash refreshingly against his skin. Instantly, his brain felt like it was rebooting. The water began to clear the fog of sleep from his mind, and he breathed deeply and soothingly.

The lights cut out. The *Hotaru* shuddered. Al braced himself as the ship rattled and wheezed. Everything was dark. Emergency power came on, dim and red. It reflected off the droplets in the sink, turning them into an illusion of blood spatter. Everything was too sharp, too clear, to still be a dream.

"SLUG!" Al bellowed, going for the door. "Slug! Where are you?!"

He staggered from his cabin, bare feet slapping on the metal floor. Everything listed and he stumbled, pulling himself into the main room. The A-grav was going wonky, but it was working and none of the oxygen warnings had come on, so that was something.

Her door opened next to his and she reeled out.

"Al! What happened?" she asked, grabbing him.

"You tell me," he replied, looking around.

"Must be something in engineering," she said, pushing off him and staggering towards the back of the ship. She thumped loudly on the next cabin as she passed it. "Adam! Get your ass down to engineering with me!"

His door slid open and Adam strode out, surprisingly steady and intimidatingly shirtless. He looked to Al and gave him a polite nod, before heading towards engineering. His tattoos almost seemed to move as his arms pulled him through the doorway into the back room. Al followed cautiously behind.

Engineering was a massive, two storey room that connected the upper and lower decks and housed the *Hotaru's* three engines and drive core. The core was a large, dark metal, faceted cube directly opposite the door. From its depths emerged power conduits, coolant lines, and command and control links that ran to all corners of the ship. Where the conduits and links emerged were clusters of sensors, blinking lights, and faint wafts of condensation. The core was the heart of the ship, a simmering, ion-irradiating heart.

To either side of the core, and directly beneath it, were the three largest conduits. These fed directly into the *Hotaru's* main engines, which were arranged in an inverted triangle on the rear bulkhead. Below the side conduits were two large, cylindrical coolant tanks that kept the core and engines under control, with yet more cables and pipes emerging from the top and bottom. The white noise of the engines hummed, but something was off. Al didn't know enough to diagnose it himself, especially not under the loud hissing of the coolant system and the blaring klaxon alarm.

Main control panels were positioned either side of the door; a bewildering array of dials, buttons, lights, and screens. Each monitored and controlled another key element of the ship. Along the walls on both levels more blinking lights revealed the location of the emergency battery arrays. The room was hot. Hotter than it should be, and something didn't smell right. Something chemical.

Two ladders either side of the door led down to the lower deck. Torchlight flickering through the grated platform that acted as a floor signalled where Slug and Adam had disappeared to. Al followed them down, moving like a shadow in the faint light, stalking the sound and torches. He couldn't hear what they were saying over the alarm.

Slug and Adam had already removed a wall panel and were pulling out wires and pipes. A harsh metallic odour emerged from the hole in the wall. They were focused on a large pipe that ran vertical inside it.

Slug had plugged her comms into a nearby socket and was calling out instructions to Adam. He worked with a power wrench and a charge spanner, adjusting a series of valves and circuits inside the hole.

Al stood by the ladder, poised for action. He watched as the Tanaka siblings sifted through the wiring. Adam was meticulous, obeying Slug's every instruction as soon as she gave it. She was the boss, but he knew what he was doing. A puddle had formed near the wall and it was slowly running across the floor as the gravity kept trying to pull everything off balance.

"Don't step in that!" Slug ordered him.

Al raised his hands defensively and stayed by the ladder. She didn't have to tell him twice. It looked like liquid coolant, but he wasn't going to run any tests without Slug's blessing. The *Hotaru* was not his ship to mess around with.

"Looks like the cooling system has gone full kamikaze," Slug muttered. "One of the main coolant lines to the core has melted. The backup sensors cut the power." She gestured to the dim red light. "So we're not in any immediate danger... but we're not going anywhere either."

"Can you fix it?" Al asked.

"Yeah," Slug sighed. "We can fix it well enough. It's just going to slow us down until we can get to the next station and patch it properly. I gotta work out how it happened though... it doesn't make any sense..." She yanked some of the wiring free with a ruthlessness that made Al wince. Surely that couldn't be helping... but then, she was the expert. She rebuilt the *Hotaru* from scraps, she would know how to fix malfunctions. Although it was concerning that there were malfunctions to begin with.

Yelling sounded above them. Al glanced up. Just echoes. He looked back to Slug.

"You two need anything?" he asked.

"Na, go see the others," Slug shook her head.

Al gave her a nod, but she didn't look his way. He climbed back up the ladder. Adam's voice called from beneath him.

"Ae, chief, you throw us the big wrench on your right?"

Al looked over. Sure enough, the wall had a selection of tools clipped to it. He snapped the massive wrench off and tossed it down the hole. It hit the floor with a gigantic clang.

"Arigatō!" Adam called back.

Al made his way back into the central communal space. Sione and Lani were both up.

"Ae, Al, what's happening?" Lani asked.

"Slug says the cooling system is broken, but her and Adam are patching it now," he replied.

"Is it serious?" Sione asked.

Even as he inquired, the power flared back into life. The lights all flickered back, bathing them in a soft white glow and washing the red from the room. Lani cocked her head to the side, listening.

"Engines still aren't quite right," she commented. "We ain't moving much."

"More drifting than flying," Al agreed. "One of the coolant lines melted, so that's not a quick fix. From an engineering perspective it's more than a little concerning, but it's not exactly mortal peril. Besides, Slug says she's got this, I wouldn't worry."

"Oooo, just makes me very nervous when things start to go wrong on a ship…" Sione muttered. "There are too many ways to die in space…"

"We're not going to die in space, old man," Lani sighed. "Chill. It's the coolant – not exactly fatal."

"Slug's got a reputation for solid work," Al agreed. "I know she doesn't usually fly in her own builds, but the people who do don't complain. She wouldn't let us sail around in something that wasn't up to spec."

"Honestly, it's weird that a radiator failed," Lani commented. "That's basic stuff. It's not like Slug to skip on it." She smirked viciously at Al. "Must have gotten distracted thinking about her cute boyfriend saving the galaxy…"

"Don't start…" Al growled.

"Ae, don't tease him, Lani," Sione bade. "You make him blush."

"That's not hard," Lani laughed. "It's barely teasing. We heard you yelling for her when the lights went out. You're like sweet and sour — put you together, you get a little bit sweet, she gets a little bit sour, and you both get a little bit sticky."

Al turned away. He was not getting paid to deal with that. Not without a half litre octo-shot.

"Aw, look at him, Lani!" Sione slapped her shoulder. "His face all red now!"

"Yeah, no shit," Lani laughed. "You're an easy mark, cuz."

Al ignored them both and continued making coffee. Mornings might not have been a real thing out here, but that didn't mean he liked them any better, and it was too early to put up with her sparring. Every hour of existence was too early to put up with her sparring. His coffee poured itself from the counter machine into the tall metallic mug and the lid snapped shut across it.

"Don't let her get to you, Al," Sione advised, patting his shoulder. "She just sees how cute you two are…"

"Now who's teasing him?" Lani ribbed her father.

Al took his cup and headed for his cabin.

"I'm just glad to see you two getting along again," he muttered, sipping the scalding beverage and stalking from the room without looking back.

***

Time passed as the light of Gan De moved further away. Al was sitting at the fold out table in his room, reading the latest reports on his communicator. There was nothing new. No one around Arthur was getting any new intel on the Goo. It messed with scanners, and everyone was afraid to get too close. He didn't blame them. He didn't want to go near it either.

The door opened without warning. There was no knock, and he begrudged that a little. He knew he could have locked the door, but a few manners wouldn't go astray either. Slug barged in. She stormed across and flopped down at the table opposite him, slamming something small and scorched in front of her. There were smears of oil and ash on her hands and the broken device. It was roughly the size of a candy bar.

"Adam found this in the coolant system," she told him.

Al met her eye. All traces of her usual joy had been replaced with deep concern.

"What is it?" he asked.

"Not really sure," she replied. "I just know what it does, and what is does is hack my system. Someone else must've put it there. This ain't mine. It hacked my sensor network and told the computers everything was fine, but what actually happened was the temperature regulator got smashed and the main coolant line overheated and melted. We lost a lot of our liquid nitrogen reserves. With what we have left I can only safely push the engines to twenty percent." She looked at him seriously, her frown exacerbated by the smears of dirt on her face. "Someone sabotaged my ship, Al. Someone with tech much better than any of us have ever seen. I don't know when or where or why or how, but someone doesn't want us to get to Gilgamesh. I thought you might know more about this thing than us — maybe tech you've seen before. Ain't none of us have the money for something like that."

Al picked the broken device off the table and turned it over in his fingers. It was too damaged to make out any kind of serial number or manufacturing logo. The remaining wiring was machine applied, but that didn't mean it wasn't homemade. Every nerve in his body was screaming spy tech, but he couldn't be certain.

"A spiker…" he muttered. "Who has had access to this ship?"

"Just us," she replied.

"No, I mean, since before we set sail," Al said. "Any contractors? Any of Lin's people? Anyone you didn't know?"

"Nope," Slug insisted. "Adam and I built this ship, with occasional help from the family. Besides, this thing would have wrecked our systems before the Ring of Solomon if it had been there since Fika. Our regulator was actively destroyed, Al. That didn't happen before Tupua."

Al grimaced. He closed his fist around the broken device and lowered it to the table.

"Eric..." he muttered.

"You think?" Slug asked nervously, her big dark eyes watching him. "The logs say no one else has been on the ship. No one else has the access codes."

"But they wouldn't be hard to steal," Al sighed. "If he knew what he was doing he could have hacked his way in here in two minutes — the sabotage could take under a minute. Unscrew the panel, spike the sensor, snap the regulator, boom. We left the ship unguarded. Easy enough to wipe the log and no one would know anyone got onboard."

"What? You think he did all that, wiped any trace of his crime, and then went strolling through the markets where we were?" Slug raised an eyebrow.

"The alternative is that one of us did it," Al pointed out. "I don't see any of the others pulling this off, do you?"

"Na," she agreed, shaking her head.

"And unless I've come down with a recent case of

dissociative identity disorder, I know I'm not doing it," Al looked at the fried device in his hand again. "I wouldn't build a spiker like this anyway."

"Good to know," Slug smiled. "And don't worry, you haven't been any weirder than normal recently."

"How weird am I normally?" He raised an eyebrow.

"Pretty weird," Slug grinned. "Not sabotage my ship weird, but definitely wears crotchless underwear and sniffs communal soap weird."

"What the shit?!" Al laughed. "What do you think I do, Slug?!"

"Well, you do secret weird spy stuff..." she giggled.

"And that qualifies?!" he exclaimed.

"Definitely," she grinned. "The underwear goes with all your sexy dresses, and you gotta check the soap for poison."

"Who the fuck poisons soap?" Al laughed. "You have no idea what I do, do you?"

"Of course not," she snorted. "It's secret spy stuff. But you can't tell me I'm wrong, because it's secret."

"You're wrong," he grinned.

"You're not allowed to tell me that," Slug teased.

"Soap doesn't even smell bad, I don't know why I'm fighting you on this..." he chuckled. "You know what, sure, you can think whatever you like about me."

"Arguing the truth would be treason," she assured.

"Yeah, well..." he tapped the burnt spiker against the table, watching it clunk, "maybe a bit of treason here and there would be good for me. It's not like I can go back to my job after all this anyway."

"President Lin isn't going to fire you," Slug insisted.

"It's not about getting fired," Al sighed. "I'm the most well-known person in the system right now. My face is more famous than the woman from the Lóng zhīshì commercials. I can't go back to being a spy. I…" Al grimaced. "I don't know what I'm going to do after all this. I don't know what to do with my life."

Slug reached across the table and took his hands in hers, ignoring the spiker and squeezing his fingers reassuringly.

"You'll work it out, shin'yū. You always do," she assured. "Maybe worry about it after we've survived your vengeful ex and his sabotaging attempts."

"Ugh! Slug! No!" Al pulled a face, recoiling from her insinuation. "Allah save me! That's disgusting! I'd rather sniff poisoned soap than date Eric Maxwell. That is not a thing."

"That bad, huh?" she smirked. "Then how come it's so personal between you two?"

"I tricked him," Al shrugged. "I played him and I stole from him. He didn't like that."

"How did you trick him?" Slug asked.

Al shrugged, tapping the spiker again. He could feel the judgement radiating from her. It wasn't awful, more taunting than anything, like she was egging him to admit it. He didn't want to.

"You seduced him…?" she inferred.

"Not all the way," Al defended. "Only as far as I had to go to get what I needed. Besides, he really didn't like what he found under my skirt…"

"Is that a spy thing or do you just mean your penis?" Slug asked.

Al laughed. She was serious, but it was still funny.

"Is that why the military funded your surgery?" she muttered, no longer laughing. "Y'know, as long as you stayed androgenous enough that they could exploit you."

Al stopped laughing too.

"The military funded my transition because that's a service they offer," he answered slowly. "It had absolutely nothing to do with the career path I chose. In fact, after I joined and showed promise for espionage, they tried to talk me out of it at first. They said I had too many ties to home, too many weak points that could be abused. They've never exploited me."

Slug rolled her eyes.

"I didn't know you felt that way…" Al murmured.

"I just think they get a lot from you," she said coolly. Now she was the one who wouldn't meet his eyes.

"I serve Titania, Slug," Al reminded. "It's not some cult, it's our global military. They're not stealing babies and training them up to be indebted to the cause. We choose this. I want to protect our home, I want to protect our family."

"But they stole you," she argued. "They stole you and they gave you something we couldn't and then you just never came back."

"I did!" Al protested. "I did come back!"

"No, Al, you didn't," she retorted.

He was shocked by the tears in her voice. Her bottom lip trembled and she pinched her mouth shut tightly. Al just stared, bewildered. He hadn't seen her like this since… since before he left. Since before the army. Since he said he was going.

"You would always swing in, like some hadena parrot who had somewhere better to be, who was too good for us now," Slug muttered tragically. "You never stayed. You never just came home. It's always been easier for me to believe that you were indebted to them — that you had to pay them back for helping you and that one day your service would be over. But it won't be. You wanted that. You wanted to leave and you wanted to stay away. Now you're worried about how you won't be able to go back..." she trailed off and shook her head. "But they stole you."

"They didn't steal me, Slug..." Al murmured.

"They stole you from me!" she cried. "They stole you from me, shin'yū. You were my best friend! My only real friend! And you just hopped on outta here and never looked back. Never once spared a glance at the lowly scrappers you left behind."

"You coulda come with me!" Al argued.

"And what?" Slug met his eye. "Got tough? Played make believe? Hooked up with the Oberon dude who's trying to kill us?" She shook her head. "I never wanted the things you wanted, Al. I can't be mad at you for that, but don't ask me not to feel hurt." She stood up. "I got a ship to finish fixing."

"Slug!" Al stood as well as she moved for the door. He caught her with one arm, pulling her in as she tried to leave. She didn't fight it. Her little face nuzzled into his chest as he held her tight and squeezed her. "I missed you too, shin'yū," he whispered the admission against her silky hair. "I always missed you. It was never about leaving. It was never about…" he trailed off. He didn't know what to say.

"It was never about me," Slug muttered wryly into his shirt. "I know, Al. I know that. I just wish… I wish that just once… you would choose to stay."

"Well, maybe I will…" he replied.

"You don't have to promise things you don't want, man," she scoffed weakly. "It's okay." She pulled away from his embrace. "I think I'm getting it out of my system."

"I didn't know it was in there…" Al let her go, not wholly sure he wanted to.

"Heh, maybe I could have been a spy," she joked. "At least I can keep secrets too."

Al didn't know what else to say. Her sudden revelation had come on so fast. He felt blindsided. She'd never had a go at him like that before. He hadn't known she'd had it in her. She always seemed so sweet and joyful. Another apology hovered on his lips, mostly because he hated the thought that he'd hurt her. He'd never wanted that. The words never made it out as she turned and headed out the door. She patted his arm gently as she left, perhaps to imply there were no hard feelings. And yet, it did not feel resolved. The feelings may not have been hard, but they certainly weren't soft.

CHAPTER TWELVE

Al found Lani up on the bridge. It was her usual hangout, even if she didn't need to be at the controls. Slug and Adam had fixed the A-grav, which made navigating the ship easier. In fact, everything was running as it should, just very slowly. It was probably a good idea for Lani to be keeping an eye on things for now, just in case.

Their new speed was making Al's heels itch. He'd never travelled this slowly before. He wasn't the only one. Lani looked like her favourite toy had been broken. He could relate. She had her feet on the dash and her stereo playing. The vid-screen was up and she was using it as a mirror to laser her racing stripe pattern back into the freshly shaved sides of her hair.

"Aloha, pretty boy," she called as he entered the bridge. "What brings you to this neck of the woods, cuz?"

"Yeah…" Al answered, still somewhat dazed.

"You call your boss about our bung ship?" Lani asked.

"I sent her a message," Al admitted. "Not my proudest moment to follow up a call about Maxwell with — hey boss, our ship's been sabotaged and I totally didn't see it coming."

"Yeah, you're a shitty spy," Lani laughed.

"I didn't used to be," Al groaned, sinking down into the co-pilot's chair. He kicked his heels up beside Lani's. "I didn't used to be…"

She didn't complain about his feet on the dash. She just tipped her head to get a better angle as she carefully moved her laser pen. Al tapped his fingers meaninglessly against the edge of the console. He pulled a face at nothing.

"I think I messed things up with Slug…" he announced.

"What do you mean?" Lani spared him a glance. "Did you mess with the ship?"

"What? No. I didn't do that. No, I mean her, me, us… I think I fucked it up somehow…"

"Yeah, but wasn't that like seventeen years ago?" she laughed.

Al stared at her. She gave him a dry look.

"Oh Ally… you cannot tell me you're only just finding this out now," she drawled. "Aren't you supposed to be some clever, highly-skilled, highly-trained master-of-everything? How are you so bad at this?"

"But we were always the same!" Al protested. "She was always the same! Every time I came home Slug and I just hung out like nothing had changed! I didn't know she was mad at me!"

"You're an idiot," Lani put her pen down and shook her head. "Life here didn't just pause, man. What, you thought that when you turned eighty and retired you'd be able to come home and play in the backyard with your bestie in your golden years? That the rest of us would just pause while you went off and had adventures?"

"No, of course not," Al scoffed. "I expected life to move on without me. I was always surprised that it didn't. I kept waiting to come home and find her working, married, kids, I dunno… but she just… she just never changed. She was always just Slug, just the same."

"Her boyfriends have all been dropkicks," Lani huffed. "Wouldn't have let her end up stuck to any of them."

"Can relate…" Al sighed.

Lani laughed again. "Yeah, we're all a bit useless aren't we?" she grinned. "You, me, Slug, Adam, Nara, and Tane — bloody Whetu and Fua stole all the luck in that department," she cursed her older sisters. "And our parents. Ae man, you notice how they're all so perfect and all got their shit together? It's not right. How are you supposed to follow that? They're all so good at life, and some of us just fly from one disaster to the next."

"At least you're a champion racer," Al sighed. "Can't be too hard to pull with that under your belt."

"Pull, no. Keep, yeah," Lani muttered. "Don't get me wrong, I don't want to settle down, but let's not pretend that with my dads there's no pressure. Besides, I'm a fucking disqualified racer now."

"I'm supposed to be an undercover secret agent," Al commiserated. "No one is supposed to know who I am, and I have cults popping up all over the system who think I'm some kind of messiah. Even if I had my appearance surgically altered, the attention this whole shitstorm has dragged over me means I'll never escape it completely. There are always going to be people trying to dig up what I'm doing. No government is going to want me on their payroll if it means that kind of attention directed at anything they're looking into."

"You could go private?" Lani suggested.

"Same problem," Al replied. "It's a problem for future me anyway. Gotta finish this mission first. Anything else is borrowing trouble... I just can't seem to help myself at the moment though."

"You've had too much time to think recently," Lani commented. "Been stuck in hiding with nothing to do but dwell ominously."

Al chuckled. "You can say that again..."

"What a pair we make..." Lani sighed, stashing her pen away and flicking through the stats on her screen. She grimaced at what she saw. They were absolutely crawling, but there was nothing to be done about it. Not until they got to port.

"Back before Tupua..." Al recalled. "You talked about being able to mod the *Hotaru*..."

Lani gave him a sly look.

"If we have to stop for repairs at Baba Yaga anyway..."

"I like the way you're thinking..." Lani smirked.

"I want to make up the time we're losing somehow," Al said. "We have to stop for repairs, so I'd be keen to mod her out. The faster we can get to Gilgamesh, the faster this can all be over, one way or another."

"What does that mean?" Lani asked.

"It means I've got no idea what the fuck I'm doing," Al laughed. "Some messed up dream told the three suns I've got to get to the Goo and save everyone. I don't know what I'm supposed to do. My mother tells me Allah has great plans, that I just need to be open to them, and I don't know how to tell her I'm agnostic."

Lani laughed weakly. "Shit, you really don't know, do you?"

"I really don't," Al admitted.

"Fuck..." she cursed. "I really thought that there were classified secrets you had access to that you couldn't tell us about, but that you'd crack out with when we got there."

"I wish..." Al sighed. "But, honestly, if I knew anything, I'd tell you guys."

"Ae, true that," Lani commented. "You woulda told Slug at least."

Footsteps sounded in the passage and they both turned to look. Al was half expecting Slug. Mostly he was hoping for her. Instead, Sione poked his smiling face in to check on them.

"What are you two troublemakers getting up to in here, ae?" he teased.

"We're having an existential crisis," Lani admitted.

"Ah, it's that time of day already?" he joked.

"What do you guys know about blue sky?" Al asked them, following his train of thought through the notion of existential crisis.

"Is that like a game company?" Lani asked.

"No, they make snacks," Sione countered, coming in

and leaning on the back of one of the chairs.

"I mean empty blue sky, like, y'know, the sky," Al grinned.

"Sky's blue 'cause of the stuff in the atmosphere," Lani stated.

Al rolled his eyes. "But like, on Titania there's the shimmer from the radiation shields, Pan in the sky, and often Oberon or Puck," he said. "And I'm talking really blue, I mean… really, really blue. There're no planets, no moons, nothing. I know it's possible, but it's just so rare, and the colour… it just ain't right. I've never been anywhere like it. Is there even a place where the sky is just blue and empty, y'know? Just nothing but blue sky from horizon to horizon."

"You're talking about Earth…" Sione commented gravely.

Al and Lani both looked to him. He raised his eyebrows knowingly at them, linking his fingers and shifting his weight as he leant on the back of the chair. They waited for him to elaborate, and he took the hint.

"We only have old footage of it now, ae," Sione recounted. "Earth was lost more than two hundred years ago, but she had clear blue skies, and only one moon — wasn't always visible. Tamati knows more about it than I do. He teaches Earth history."

"Earth huh…" Al mused.

"Why you asking?" Lani pestered him.

"I've been having these strange dreams recently…" he mused.

"No shit," Lani laughed.

Al pulled the fingers at her, and both she and her dad

laughed at the gesture.

"No, go on," Sione gestured at him. "Tell us, boy. What you been seeing?"

"This big city… huge, huge city, like a station with no roof, beneath a clear and empty blue sky," Al told them. "In my dream I'm not me. I'm a child, a little girl, watching the sky—"

"You sure it's not you…?" Lani checked.

"It's not me," Al shook his head. "She isn't and she never was. She's someone completely other. I don't know who. But when I'm her… I'm watching this empty alien sky… and then something comes. Something big. Something dark. It starts to close in over the sky…"

"The Goo…" Sione murmured.

"It was black when it came through the rift, wasn't it?" Lani looked to her dad. "When the rift tore open over Gilgamesh, and the Goo came through and swallowed the planet… it was like an inky darkness… wasn't it? That's what Pa says…"

"By all accounts, ae," Sione nodded. "We saw it on the news back then, same as you kids, but it came through the portal and swallowed the gate and the planet. Everything went dark, then it changed colour and started to glow. No one knows why. No one knows what it does."

"Do… do you think that's what I'm seeing?" Al asked. "Do you think I'm seeing the last moments of Earth?"

"Fuck that's creepy…" Lani muttered.

"It is not impossible," Sione shrugged. "But who

could say for certain? Earth was not empty when she fell…" A grim frown tugged his mouth behind his beard. "The ark ships came through the first rift, but that technology wasn't ours. We found it, brought it home, and turned it on. We didn't build it. Not everyone escaped Earth, so it is possible you could be seeing some horror story of the last moments… as bleak as that is. The rift was shut off deliberately so that the Goo couldn't follow us – not that we succeeded, even if we delayed it a couple of centuries."

"Humanity's finest hour…" Al muttered.

"You know what else…" Sione mused. "I forget this sometimes — Lani your Pa would scold me — but Earth was not the only planet with clear blue skies and one moon… Gilgamesh was the same. She was called the New Earth, because of all the places we found in this system, she was the closest to Earth. A little ball of green and blue, orbited by a rock called Enkidu."

"So two planets of basically the same stock got swallowed in humanity's known history… and we don't know the difference… and I could be dreaming of the end of one of them?" Al grimaced.

"Or both," Lani shrugged at him. "You said dreams, ae? As in plural? Maybe you're seeing both. The biggest cities we ever built in this system were all on Gilgamesh. When she was settled, humanity tried to turn her into the new Earth. Sure, with all the places out here there was heaps of space to go, but she was the closest and the least amount of effort. There will always be people who settle for the easy road. There will always be those who strive desperately for tradition.

Humanity's just like that. If history has taught us anything, it's that every option will be chosen by at least somebody."

Sione smiled proudly at her.

"What?" Lani demanded.

"Your Pa and I always think you never listen to us," he smiled. "But look at you now."

"Oh, don't make a thing of it!" she huffed. "Last thing any of us needs is people to start listening to me for advice."

"You were the one who suggested we could mod the *Hotaru*," Al pointed out.

"Ae, you are not modding this ship!" Sione warned.

"Sione, at this rate, provided nothing else goes wrong, and the repairs go quickly, and when we get to Gilgamesh someone hands us a cheat-sheet with the answers to everything we have to do, coupled with it being a simple day job… we're going to be lucky to get home in a month," Al told him.

The old doctor seemed to process this. His lips pursed as he mused.

"Ae, okay, so who's telling Slug that we modding her ship?" he asked.

"I will," Al offered. "I'm already in trouble, it might as well be me."

Lani gave a wicked low chuckle.

"Oh, what's this?" Sione glanced between the two of them.

"Al's just discovered he's in hot water with Slug after ditching us for the army," Lani answered.

"Wasn't that like seventeen years ago?" Sione raised

an eyebrow.

"Did everybody but me know about this?!" Al exclaimed.

"Yeah," the other two laughed at him.

"Allah be kind..." Al muttered, rubbing his face wearily. He couldn't believe he'd missed it, especially if everyone else had known. It just served to drive home his blind spots. He'd spent so long believing he was mastering the ability to read people, but when it came to his family it was like he was the one who had frozen. His understanding of the people he loved was still only sixteen years old.

CHAPTER THIRTEEN

It took another four days to reach Baba Yaga. Al was starting to go mad, at least it felt like it. He'd been on longer journeys than this. He'd been on less comfortable journeys than this. But all of those had been working a job — a real job. He'd been with strangers, and there was a certain comfort in being surrounded by strangers. They expected nothing of him. Family was different.

He couldn't escape them. The thought knotted his guts. Family shouldn't be something he wanted to escape. But they were, and he did. They wanted his time, his conversation, and there were always people in all the communal spaces. He couldn't go anywhere but his cabin to avoid people, and even then they still came to find him. It was exhausting, and the guilt over feeling drained was as bad as the depleted emotional energy. They were all such social people, it was impossible to explain.

The closest person who seemed likely to understand was Adam, but Al didn't want to go there. Adam was the only one who didn't seek his company. The silent giant was polite – if they were working together or sharing the same space he would talk, crack jokes – but otherwise he would just give Al that understanding nod and leave him be. The notion that Adam understood him was a deeply unsettling one.

Al had tried to apologise to Slug again, but it had felt like a terrible attempt and she had waved it off. Until he had told her he'd talked to Lani about installing mods on the *Hotaru*. Now he had a bruise on his ass where she'd hit him with a wrench. However, she hadn't said no. She hadn't said yes either, but there was a solid chance she was going to agree.

They had parked up at the docks on Baba Yaga. Al had never been anywhere as cold and bleak as this rogue planet, trapped distantly between two suns. The stations were all artificially lit and heated, but there was an atmosphere about the place. They hadn't tried too hard to fake what they were. Lots of stations in other places tried to generate the look of cities in lush terrestrial landscapes. Baba Yaga had stations with plenty of vitruchal windows to expose the dark, icy terrain of the planet. Nothing lived out there, and the stations seemed to want to remind people of this.

The people were a mix of standoffish bureaucrats, smug gangsters, and tourist-trap merchants. It took Al a little while to find someone he was prepared to barter with for repairs to the ship. The official who welcomed them to port was prepared to recommend repair shops, but Al didn't want a stranger working on their ship. Slug could fix it, they just needed to be able to buy parts.

She was with him now at the grungy, banged-up garage, along with Adam and a list of everything they needed to fix the *Hotaru* and install Lani's mods. This was the kind of place Al expected to get shafted at, in more ways than one. The Tanakas looked right at home.

Adam inspected things by the door, making the occasional contemplative sound when he saw gear he liked. Slug leant on the bench while she waited for the counter girl to check for pieces out back. She gave Al a curious look from even lower than normal.

"You doing alright?" she asked.

"Peachy," he responded softly, trying to keep everywhere in sight all at once.

"I only ask 'cause you've been a bit weird the last few days," she commented.

"Sorry," he sighed.

"You don't have to be sorry," she replied. "I just want to make sure you're okay."

"Why?" Al asked, catching himself and making awkward defensive motions at her expression. "Not 'why do you care', obviously — we're friends and you're wonderful, of course. Why say I don't have to be sorry? I am, I don't want to be worrying you."

"That's sweet," she grinned. "But it's okay not to be okay. It's not something you have to apologise for."

"That's sweet, but we're in this together and I don't want to make this trip harder on anyone than it already is," he countered.

"It's not exactly suffering, shin'yū," she ribbed him. "More space and peace than we get at home. Not like we're missing meals or scrapping for pay. I think what I miss most is the sky..." she looked up at the dented and scorch-marked metal ceiling above her. "I never realised I was going to miss sky so much..."

"I like space..." Al muttered. "I like being out where it's dark and quiet..."

"Ain't quiet up there with us," Slug chuckled sympathetically.

Al pulled a face. Slug laughed and stood up straight, rubbing his back consolingly. The girl from the back room reappeared behind the counter. She had her comms in hand, stretched out wide enough to see the entire list Slug had given her all at once.

"Ya, we got all those pieces," she told them disinterestedly, chewing gum as she spoke. "We can give you all that for five-seven."

"Five-six," Al countered. "And that better include delivery."

"It surely doesn't," she blew a bubble at them. It popped loudly. "Five-seven. Five-nine if you want it dropped off, and that's being nice to out-of-towners."

"There's no such thing as being nice to out-of-towners," Al replied. "Tourist scams might be how you run a lot of your business, but I'm not a tourist, so you're going to drop off everything we need to dock N-7, you're going to do it for five-six, or—" he leant in conspiratorially, "—I might just have to tell customs about the G895, the 56-T2 compressor, and the crate of quantum batteries you have in your back room."

She glared at him.

"I hear you can do time for selling those without a licence on this rock," he added. "And you and I both know this place doesn't have that licence." He paused while she considered this. He could see the cogs in her brain ticking over whether she should just shoot him. People never wanted to do anything the honest or easy way. "Look," he sighed, "those parts at any other port in the system would go for five-two. You're still ripping me off, but this way, we both get to save face a little, and I'm not going back to my boss with anything more than five-six. That bitch is scarier than either of us."

"You call your boss to transfer now," the girl grimaced. "No credit."

"Sign the goods to us with immediate transfer and I'll pay the bill before we walk," Al offered.

She raised an eyebrow, lips puckered curiously like she was sucking on the gum. Her fingers danced across the comms screen and she barely broke eye contact to do it. Slug held her comms out to meet the girl's. They swiped across. The ticked list transferred to Slug's device and the order to move the pieces went through. It hung there red, awaiting payment.

The bill flashed up on the counter. Al held his chip over it. The transfer cleared. Slug's comms went green. Now they really had the counter girl's attention, even more so than when they had blackmailed her. Al knew that look. He sighed again.

"You best tell your friends outside that unless they're carrying our gear, they're safer not following us," he warned. "We're diplomats from the Gan De System. You don't want our kind of trouble."

"What kind of a diplomat travels with a scrapper crew in a refurbished Otashii?" the girl eyeballed him like she was in on something.

"This one," Al replied, cool enough to make her reconsider. The doubt in her eyes was only a flicker. Al didn't look away as he called out across the room. "Adam, come say hello."

Adam looked over from where he was weighing up a torpedo rivetter in one hand. The tattooed muscles of his arm bulged excessively, and the tool appeared to have some weight to it.

"S'up?" he nodded at the counter girl.

Al watched her eye the tattoos with sudden apprehension. They really were coming in very useful. He had spent years mastering his 'don't fuck with me' attitude, and rather begrudged Adam the sheer ease with which he swaggered around like a giant nuclear warning sign.

"Ae, chief?" Adam called to him. "When we come back through here, can we maybe get one of these? I know we don't take a lot of hull damage, but they're real useful in repairs. Also," he practiced swinging it. "You can take a dude's head clean off in one swipe if you hit it right."

"Adam!" Slug scolded him.

"What?" he looked at her innocently, as though he hadn't casually contemplated murder aloud.

"Put it back," she ordered him, pointing at the wall.

He obediently put the rivetter back where he had found it. The girl was watching them all like she had finally realised there was more going on than she first thought, but she still wasn't a hundred percent sure what. That would do. Al knocked on the counter politely and gave her a friendly smile.

"Arigatō. Nice doing business with you." He placed a hand on Slug's back and guided her out of the store, with Adam following at his shoulder.

"What was that?" Slug asked, once they were back

in the seedy station corridor.

"What was what?" Al replied, keeping a gentle hand on her, just in case.

"All that posturing?" she smirked. "All that swagger? I didn't even know you had that in you."

"That's what I'm usually like," Al shrugged.

"Since when?" Slug scoffed.

"Since anytime you're not around," he answered. Instantly, he realised how it sounded and felt a desperate need to elaborate, but as soon as he started he wished he hadn't. "You'd never believe it, but I'm usually very suave and compelling. It's just around you that my brain seems to shut down."

"Why just me?" Slug asked.

"Maybe you're the only person around the three suns whose opinion I actually give a damn about..." Al replied, trying not to spontaneously burst into flames as he said it.

They came around a corner and Al glimpsed Adam looking back. He abandoned his mortifying admissions to Slug in favour of her brother's intel.

"How many?" he asked Adam subtly.

"Just two," Adam replied, still glancing over his shoulder. "But I caught their eye. Made sure they know I seen them." He turned back to Al, his big dark eyes concerned. "You drop that many credits that casually, people gonna notice, Chief. It ain't smart."

"It's a power move," Al countered. "Not the first time I've done it. The trick is to make sure they realise you're not the type to get mugged."

"Hm..." Adam made a dubious sound. "I seen guys

get their arms cut off for less. They think there's big money in your wrist, they'll take it, and I ain't packing much firepower to stop them."

"Just keep being you, Adam," Al assured. "Let the confidence speak for itself."

"Couldn't you just do all this without the disguise?" Adam asked. "Y'know, people keep saying you're like a saviour or messiah or something… if you just rocked up as you, wouldn't people just give you shit?"

"Maybe," Al sighed. "But it would also make us a big glowing target for anyone who might be looking for us."

Adam shook his head like he didn't understand, but he shrugged it away and followed his orders. Another block and he assured them that the tail was gone. Al believed it. They would have been weighing up whether they really wanted to risk starting a gang war. If the shop girl was smart, her message would have warned her people off after the sale. Sure, robbing someone after you sold to them was a business strategy, but Al had made it clear enough that he knew how to play the game too.

They made it back to the ship without further incident. Slug took Adam with her to engineering to get things ready and await supplies. Al went to check how the refills were going. They had used more fuel than they hoped trying to run the engines slow, but it was nothing money couldn't fix. Lin was going to slap him with her shoe when she got the bill for this mission. He didn't know how much she had already spent on Slug's work to get the *Hotaru* running in the first place.

Once the gear arrived everyone got to work straight away. Al and Sione mostly seemed to be on supervising duty and beverage delivery, with the occasional spot of heavy lifting. Slug insisted they complete the repairs before anyone started modifying anything, and no one argued with her.

Al took the down time to scan the ship for any other additions that bore similar tech to the spiker. He hadn't found anything before Baba Yaga, but now that they were parked again he was getting paranoid. He couldn't shake the knowledge that if he'd been told to sabotage this crew, it would be all too easy.

The repairs were completed quickly, which left Slug and Lani to start debating how they wanted the *Hotaru* modded. Naturally, they had started the work before they started the fight. The poor ship had multiple panels exposed in the engine room, with her guts on full display.

"You're not running that compressor there, Lani!" Slug yelled at her, wiping sweat from her brow with the back of her wrist, wrench clutched tightly. "If you fuck with my cooling system again to try and make her go faster, I will make you get out and push us to Galileo."

"If I don't have a compressor, I can't make the hard burn," Lani countered.

"You also can't fucking blow us up!" Slug argued.

Al tried not to wonder how much time was going to be saved with the mods versus how much was going to be spent installing them, but it was nice to be in the space with everyone busy and distracted. Strangely, the ship did feel more peaceful with everyone banging around in engineering. The important thing was no one needed him.

"Ae, Chief!" Adam called, sliding himself half out from under the bottom engine.

Al looked over, waiting for direction on what to retrieve or hold next.

"Don't suppose you could find us any decent beer on this rock, could ya?" Adam grimaced as he unscrewed something caked with soot.

"Unlikely, but I'm prepared to look," Al replied. "What qualifies?"

"Surprise me," Adam grunted, keeping his eyes on his work.

Al moved to Sione who was sitting on the fold-out chair by the door, taking a short rest. He patted the old doctor's shoulder.

"You need me to come along?" Sione asked.

"Na, I need you to make sure our engineer and our pilot don't start hitting each other with tools," Al replied.

Sione chuckled and nodded. Al squeezed his shoulder once more and headed out.

It was an instant relief to be somewhere alone, even the snake station of Baba Yaga. There was no schedule on his shopping trip. He could stroll. He could stretch his legs and step away from his life for a moment. Out here he didn't have to be Al-Amir Akiyama. He could be Takumi Hino, runaway thief and supreme avoider of responsibilities. It sounded like the best way to spend an afternoon.

At the second block he knew he was being followed.

He should have been mature about it, but the uncontrollable smirk that teased his lips told him he wasn't in a sensible mood. He stopped to ask for directions to the best convenience store, and the safest way to get there. The store was a recommendation he genuinely wanted. The kindly old lady's directions of where to avoid were also about to be extremely helpful. He made a point of beginning to follow her directions, before seemingly making a wrong turn.

It didn't take long to find the narrow dark passages that were more alleyways than streets. It was a good thing he was being tailed, otherwise his smile might have scared his followers off. He walked boldly in the direction of the store, turning down an even skinnier path.

They were in maintenance here. With all the pipes and steam it looked like water treatment, maybe even ice mining. It was close enough to the docks that they could be running collection from outside through here to filter into the city. He ducked quickly into the first alcove he found and waited. His stalkers were less than thirty seconds behind him. Half of him had expected them to realise this was a trap and give up. No one was that stupid.

It was the same two men that had followed them from the supply garage. He had to give them points for coming after him when he was alone rather than trying to tangle with Adam. Unfortunately for them, Al was just as dangerous, even if he didn't look it.

He melted into the shadows. The two men were nearly passed him when they realised there was no one ahead of them and hesitated. He struck. Both men were armed. He needed the surprise, and surprised they were. He grabbed the second man first, coming at him from behind. One hand closed around the man's throat, and the other disarmed him, snatching the low gun and twisting the guy's hand up behind his back. The mugger screamed as Al pinned him. His friend lost it.

The first man whirled with a yell, firing blindly. Al muttered some quiet curses as the man he was holding took two bullets to the chest. He shoved his injured captive at the first man. Both yelled as they collided, bloody and wounded. Al ripped open a small fuse panel in the wall, grabbed the uninjured man by the vest, and shoved him face first into the wiring. The guy screamed once as the electricity fried him and blasted him across the passage. He hit the opposite wall and slid unmoving to the ground.

Al clipped the panel shut again and picked up both dropped guns. He disassembled them with a sigh as the second man writhed on the ground, moaning and clutching his bloody wounds. It was almost embarrassing to think that he had been expecting professionals. This was one of the most amateur mugging attempts he'd ever seen. The man shot his own partner, for crying out loud.

"This is why you bring tasers to a mugging..." he muttered, scattering bullets over his assailants. "Anything from fifty thousand to a million volts will get your mark on the ground without frying their chip. Clean as it comes. One hit. You don't risk getting shot..." Al dropped the gun pieces just out of reach of the men at his feet. He pointed to the one that was bleeding. "You're going to want to get home and put a fuser on those before they kill you."

With no more advice to add, and still feeling a touch ashamed at their efforts, Al stepped over the muggers and headed out of the passage to the store. It was close enough he was surprised people hadn't heard the scrap. There was a security guard by the entrance, and, after a moment's consideration, he let her know that he thought he'd seen two guys get in a fight – if she wanted to radio in and get someone to take a look and help them. She thanked him and he went in to investigate beverage options.

The range was not particularly good, but it was better than he thought it would be. It warranted deliberation. Which it got, while he stood and listened to the sirens arrive outside. All things considered, Adam had probably spent most of this life drinking simple lagers, when his gang weren't celebrating by drinking the kinds of concoctions that were usually reserved for intense surgery. Which probably meant he'd drink just about anything up to and possibly including jet engine fuel. The twenty-four pack would do.

It was only when he was paying that he realised what he'd been missing. He spotted it again, just outside the store, facing away towards the alley. That white suit.

CHAPTER FOURTEEN

There was absolutely no way Al was getting out of the store through the front doors without Eric seeing him, if he hadn't already. He ducked behind a display stand and pulled out his comms. Making sure he was out of sight of all recording equipment, he opened his scanner program. It recognised Eric's device. Al had to resist the urge to roll his eyes. They changed codes and wiped so frequently, did they really hack each other so often their comms knew each other?

He made the most of it and kicked in the same back door he'd used last time. To Eric's absolutely miniscule credit, the last time Al had done this was only a few weeks ago, and there was every chance that he'd never realised because more important things had come up. Like the potential galactic apocalypse.

Al dropped through all of Eric's recent communications. Most of them from President Shepard. All of them coded. Al grimaced. It made sense, but come on, really, everything encoded? Guy probably ordered pizza in coded messages. Embarrassing.

He made quick copies of everything he could see, especially if it looked important. At this point there was no reason to assume Al's paranoia wasn't wholly justified. While the files copied he used the scanner to check the building plans. There wasn't a back door to this place that he could use without drawing more attention than the front door. While pulling the fire alarm wasn't out of the question, it was inelegant. Besides, there was a rather particular and obvious solution.

With extra care, Al set his comms back in his pocket, positioned the handle of the box of cans so that he could easily swing it as a weapon if he needed to, and strode out the door. Eric didn't move as Al came out of the store. He was standing with his back to the storefront, watching across the road as station security lights flashed from the end of the alley. His blonde hair was slicked back and he was wearing aviators. Al wanted to punch him in the face for that alone. They were on a planet with no sun, so far away from any star that even the vaguest illusion of daylight had to be artificially generated, and the douchebag was wearing sunglasses inside the station. What a complete dickhead.

"Fancy seeing you here, Akiyama," Eric smirked without even glancing his way. "I almost didn't recognise you."

"Wish I could say it was a surprise, Eric," Al sighed.

"Wish I could say it had been a while," Eric replied. "But I've been dreaming of that pretty face every night for weeks. It's getting awfully hard not to think about you every day."

"I'm flattered," Al commented, both of them standing patiently and comfortably in the lie. His grip on the handle tightened carefully. He was ready, but he didn't want to start something. Eric's hands were lost in the deep pockets of his trousers. The notion made Al very nervous. He knew from experience how many blades the other spy could stash, and how deep he could cut with them. Neither man flinched first. They both stood, politely regarding the street.

"Paying the repair team?" Eric queried. He hadn't looked over yet, but Al knew his purchase was implied.

"Gotta keep the people fixing the ship happy," he responded. "We got spiked in Tupua, of all places."

Eric gave a low whistle. "Can never be too careful. You must be a popular guy right about now."

"Only to the people who know how to find me," Al said.

Eric finally turned to him. He lowered his shades and grinned at Al over the top of them, that mischievous grin that single-handedly seemed to do so much of his job for him.

"Then I guess I'll be seeing ya," he smirked, tipping his glasses back up and gesturing at the flashing lights. "Avoid the back alleys towards the docks. I hear there are some unsavoury sorts around…" With that pointed observation, he strode away. Al was glad to see the back of him. There was no way he would have been the one to walk away first. Eric was as trustworthy as an untamed viper.

Al went in the opposite direction but left the vicinity of the store at a measured pace, as though he had simply passed comment with a stranger outside a shop. Once he was safely clear of the block, he picked up speed almost involuntarily. His feet wanted to get the hell away from Eric and anything to do with him, but he'd straight up keel over and die before he gave the man the satisfaction of running from him.

When he reached the *Hotaru* he burst into the engine room like he was announcing a fire. Everyone looked up from their work instantly as he swung in and dropped the beers on the floor by Adam.

"Shut up shop," Al ordered. "We sweep the whole ship, top to bottom, inside and out – any bugs, any spikers, any anythings you tell me. As soon as we're clean, we're out of here."

"He's here?" Slug questioned, half rising to her feet.

"And he wants me to know that he's following me," Al replied.

"The mods ain't finished," Lani warned.

"Then we'll do without them," Al insisted. "She'll fly as good as she did when we left Fika, anything else was always just a bonus."

"You sure you don't just wanna go for a walk and find this guy?" Adam asked carefully, standing so that he could address Al privately.

"If he comes at us in a fair fight we can splatter him," Al replied. "But we're not executioners. We're not hunting down a man just to kill him. Besides, I wasn't kidding when I said he's in my league, and I refuse to explain your body to your family."

"That's mighty honourable of you, Chief," Adam smiled. "But supai don't fight by our rules."

"And what rules are those?" Al challenged.

Adam weighed up the question. Al could see the kid thinking about it. His serious face considered their conversation, and Al's career, and everything that had led them to this. He dropped his gaze, dark eyes glancing over the toes of his massive boots, and posture slipping demurely.

"Nothing, Chief," he answered finally, only then able to look back up to meet Al's eye. "You want I get the big scanner to check the engines?"

"Arigatō, Adam. That'd be great," Al thanked him.

"Hai," Adam nodded politely, drawing himself up to attention and striding away towards storage.

Al watched him go. He felt like he was starting to get the hang of guiding the weapon. Slug had it nailed down to an art. She knew how to treat Adam like a person and set strong expectations. He could behave, as long as you gave him no room to waver. Like trying to raise a kid with a bad temper. Adam didn't have a bad temper, he didn't seem to have much of a temper at all, but he was a touch sociopathic. He really didn't see anything wrong with wandering into town, finding Eric, and dropping him out an airlock. Al could concede that the universe would probably be a better place without Eric Maxwell, but murdering people — straight up murder like Adam was used to — that just made them the bad guys.

***

There had been no trace of any more sabotage or infiltration. Not that Al had particularly expected it. They hadn't given Eric another opportunity like the first one, but he was glad to have checked. He was even gladder to be away from the rogue planet. Baba Yaga wasn't a bad place in and of itself. He had fond memories of jobs and layovers there. Even the attempted mugging had made him feel back to his old self for a moment, although he was starting to wonder if the thugs had been paid by Eric just to draw him out and trip his disguise.

There was no use dwelling on it now. They were safely away. The *Hotaru* was running smoothly again. Short of their ship coming under attack they were on the home stretch to Gilgamesh and some answers. With any luck he was going to be able to stop the broadcast from the station, find out what had started it in the first place, and put all this to bed.

Even better, he had Eric's messages to crack. It wasn't one of the codes he'd used before, which was rather inconsiderate of him. Al was going to have to work for this prize. He had connected his comms to the wall screen in his cabin so that he could lie in his bunk and look at the data large across the wall. He'd been poking at it for hours, and was starting to wonder if there was more than one code in place. It would explain the mess.

The door opened without any knock and Slug strode in, uninvited. Her hair was pulled back as tight as ever, but it was damp like she'd showered recently. Even her overalls had been cleaned up after the repairs.

"I brought you a coffee," she announced.

"Do you ever knock?" Al asked, lounging carelessly as she came back. "What if I hadn't been wearing pants?"

"Then it would have been an exciting day for all of

us," she grinned. "Budge up."

He deliberately hadn't moved when she'd come in because he knew she was going to do this, but if he didn't lift his legs she was going to sit on them. He shuffled up very reluctantly, sliding his back up the headboard and crossing his legs. Once he was sitting, Slug handed him a sealed mug and took a seat in his vacated warm patch with her own drink. Al sipped the coffee. It was good enough that his resentment of the invasion eased.

"What are you looking at?" she asked.

"Data I stole from Eric," Al answered.

"What does it say?" she asked.

"Don't know yet," he replied. "Still trying to crack it."

"Is it secret?"

"Hopefully not for much longer," Al smirked. "That asshole is stalking us and I want to know why. There's no good reason for Oberon to be sticking its nose in our business. Not with this. Surely they want answers as badly as the rest of us, so why the sabotage?"

"Maybe they don't want to rely on someone they don't trust to find the answers?" Slug contemplated, leaning back on Al's legs and sipping her drink.

He didn't even bother to protest the action. She'd never let him have personal space. It was one of the things that had always annoyed him about the family, but it wasn't quite so bad when it was her. She rested her head in his lap and looked up at him, her body warm through his trousers.

"Just don't let Adam get mixed up in it, ae?" she

requested. "He can be a bit trigger-happy when it comes to the theory of a fight, like he thinks he's a kid playing a video game."

"Don't worry," Al sighed. "I'm not letting him near Eric. The last thing I need is two people who think every problem can be solved with violence going head-to-head."

"Adam would never actually kill anyone," Slug insisted.

Al tried to let it go. He tried to ignore that she'd said it, tried to pretend she hadn't, but it didn't work. He couldn't do this anymore. He couldn't keep lying to her. It was no longer omission, it was deceit. He shut all his screens down with a sigh and stashed his comms.

"Yeah, he would, Slug," Al muttered. "He's killed a lot of people, he would do it again, and if he didn't have you constantly pointing out right and wrong for him, he'd probably be doing it regularly."

She sat up, leaving a cold space between his legs in her absence, and turned to him sharply.

"So you do know where he was all those years, huh?" she accused.

"I can't prove anything, and I don't want to start something," Al sighed. "But I'm confident."

"Why do you never talk to me anymore?" she demanded. "When did I become so alien to you that you couldn't even tell me you thought my little brother was a gangster?"

"I didn't think you'd want to hear it," Al defended. "I was trying to protect you, Slug. It's all I've been trying to do. I didn't want to hurt you. You got Adam back, you were so protective and defensive of him… I didn't want to say anything bad about him. I just wanted to let you all be happy. You deserve that."

"We deserve that?" she echoed. "Do we deserve having you avoid us our whole lives so you didn't have to confront it?"

"How did this become about me?" Al asked.

"It was always about you, Al," she replied.

"I thought it was about Adam," Al exclaimed.

Slug smiled sadly and shook her head.

"Of course you did…" she sighed. "Of course you thought that. You hate it when things are about you. You don't even realise how alike you two are, do you?"

"Alike?" Al repeated. "Me and Adam?"

"You're both constantly, desperately, struggling to do the right thing," Slug sighed. "You've both got something to prove and you need to be the good guy. The difference is that he knows he's wrong sometimes. He accepts that and he's prepared to ask for help."

"He's trying to be the good guy?" Al echoed. "The dude who repeatedly asks if we can go commit murder because we're being inconvenienced by someone?"

"Aren't you the one who thinks he was raised that way?" Slug countered. "I said he was trying. He always listens to you, Al. He thinks you're good people. He thinks you'll make the right call when he's not sure what it is and he follows your lead." She grasped her mug nervously, clenching her fingers around it like she wanted to warm them. "I want him to follow you. I believe in you, like so much of the system now. I know you'll try and do the right thing, but I don't want you teaching him to lie and keep secrets."

"I'm not teaching him anything," Al replied. "My secrets, insomuch as I even have secrets anymore, were all for national security. If he's been lying and hiding things, like where he was for twenty-two years, that's something he picked up from the Yakuza — not me. Truth is, I don't know as much about it as you might think, and everything I've deduced is his business. It's not mine to share."

"I'm not asking you to share his secrets," Slug sighed. "I'm asking you to trust me, and to stop lying — to yourself as much as to the rest of us. You're wonderful just being you — just being the person we all know that you are. Even Adam saw the real you and he knows he can trust you like he trusts me."

"I don't know what you mean..." Al floundered. This conversation felt like it had gotten out of his depth a while ago. "I'm just me. You know me."

"Do I?" She raised an eyebrow. "Because you were putting on at the shop, but you told me that's who you always are, except I've never met that guy."

"I just... I get weird around you..." he admitted, his chest tightening as he stared down at his coffee mug. "I... I guess I feel like every time I'm around you I revert to when we were sixteen again..."

"Cute sentiment," she smiled sadly. "But I'm worried you're just putting that on too. I'm worried I don't know you at all... even though deep in my bones I know that guy I grew up with is still in there."

Al bit his lip to hold back a curse. He wanted to say he never went anywhere, but if he tried to pull that, she would have every right to slap him. He did go somewhere. He did change. A lot. Now she was watching him try and exist between two worlds, and all that was coming up was a mess.

"I don't want to upset you," Slug sighed. "This wasn't supposed to be an attack. I don't even think it was supposed to be a criticism. I just... I just wanted to clear the air — to see the real you again. That's a hard thing to do now. You always have to prove everything. You always have to be right about everything. You joined the military because you constantly have to prove how much of a man you are, but you went into espionage so that you could play dress up with your femininity to prove your transition was healthy. You're constantly putting on fronts and hiding behind characters." Slug reached out with one hand and grabbed his, tangling their fingers together and looking at them sadly. "I don't know what you've done, what you've been ordered to do, but I really believe you're a good person. You don't have to pretend to be. You don't have anything to prove to anyone."

"How can you be so sure?" Al asked, toying gently with her fingers.

"Maybe it's faith..." she whispered. "Maybe you're right, and there will be a part of us that will always revert to being sixteen whenever we're back together... but maybe that's how I know you're good." She smiled again. "You wouldn't have come back all those times... you wouldn't be here right now, if you weren't trying to do the right thing. You wouldn't be you if you weren't inherently good."

"Why are you saying all this?" he asked, his voice strangely thick with the memories of what being sixteen with her had been like.

"I need you to know that you can talk to me about anything, that I want you to talk to me about everything, and that you have nothing to prove to me," she said.

He had an abrupt flashback to the passage outside the repair store when he'd told her that her opinion was the only one that mattered to him. It wasn't a lie, but it made him feel strange that she cared enough to come to him with all this. He had spent years distancing himself from everyone. That was the way he liked it. It wasn't Slug's way though. She had always had a big heart. That was why he cared what she thought. Her big heart and her kind smile… the compassion in her eyes that had always set his heart racing. His whole life he'd been weak to that smile. Maybe that was why he'd run from it. To pretend he didn't have weaknesses. She was asking him to stop pretending… he wasn't sure he knew how, but he could try. For her, he could try.

"Then…" he started hesitantly, tracing the inside of her fingertips with his own, "I can tell you that I don't know what I'm doing? I have no idea how to save the universe. I don't even know what kind of danger it's really in. I'm sticking a plaster over a mortal wound and praying. I can't do this, but I'm faking it."

Slug smiled and leaned in. She closed her eyes and pressed her nose against his.

"That's exactly the kind of thing you can tell me," she breathed.

"It doesn't freak you out?" he muttered, his throat starting to squeeze shut as their faces touched and her warm breath mixed with his.

She shook her head, letting her forehead rock against his. "Na, shin'yū, that's the most normal thing you've said in days."

"I'm sorry I'm not more normal," he whispered. "I just…" he paused, basking in the warmth of her sweet breath against his lips. "I spend so much time sniffing soap…"

She burst into laughter. He grinned widely at the sound, glad that she could take the joke, although he wasn't sure which one of them he was poking fun at. She placed a hand against his cheek and kissed the corner of his mouth, still giggling hysterically. His heart stopped. Briefly. More than one beat skipped, for sure. It had felt momentarily fatal. But she moved away again.

Her smile was so warm it radiated like a sun. She shook her head and sipped her drink, still enjoying his ridiculous gag. He wasn't sure what kind of a kiss it had been. It felt like it toed the line between romantic gamble and friendly peck on the cheek, just like they did, but it forced him to admit to himself a kiss was something he wanted. Merciful Allah, he had been running from his feelings for so long that when he was confronted with them his whole body froze. He couldn't move. He couldn't do anything when there wasn't a character to hide behind.

That was her point. There were things he wanted, but it was safer and easier to pretend he was above that, above feelings. Safer to be distant. Slug was asking him not to be. She was giving him an opening to ask for all the things he wanted. He should have taken it. He should have said something. Told her the truths she'd been asking for. Instead, he chickened out and went back to his drink, opening the screens again, disappearing into his work the way he had always done to hide from her.

He would try, for her he would try, but it wasn't that simple. He wasn't ready to break more than half a lifetime of habit. He wasn't ready to confront them, and that night seventeen years ago, and all the things he had run from fighting the endless battle of trying to prove his own worthiness to himself. Seventeen years, a blue and gold stripe career, and a prophesied destiny straight out of an ancient Earth legend; but he still felt like he was faking it.

CHAPTER FIFTEEN

Al was still thinking about that kiss the next day. Insomuch as days were measured out here. Time had passed. He'd slept. Badly. He had dreamt of his own face, of empty blue skies with no visible planets or shields, of a creeping darkness, of walking in on Slug in the shower and panicking but being unable to look away, and of trying to defend the way he had stared at every bare and dripping curve… the tension that had plagued him as he watched and wondered…

Sweet Allah, that had made breakfast awkward this morning. No one else knew what he had dreamt. No one else knew he was still thinking about the gentle kiss she had planted at the corner of his lips, which was growing into something wild and untameable in his mind. They weren't psychic. Still, he'd dropped his spoon three times, the bowl once, and spilt half a mug of coffee, all while flaming like a dying star and failing to verbalise an entire sentence the whole morning. It probably didn't take a psychic.

They'd been polite about it, believing his excuses that he was just tired after Sione had taken him for a medical scan to make sure he wasn't sick. It was ridiculous. He just had to remind himself of the distain Lin would show him if she could see him now. He had seduced princesses and kings! Okay, just one king, but two princesses, and five scientists, and nearly a dozen other spies. All of it flawless work. Always composed and confident.

But none of those people had been Simone Tanaka.

He lay on his bunk again, looking at the code from Eric. This time his door was locked. He didn't want the interruption. If Slug came in and kissed him again he was going to spontaneously combust, and that would be hugely inconvenient — probably for the whole system. Besides, he felt like he was getting somewhere with the code. Sections of it were starting to become clear, which meant it was definitely multiple codes, but he had managed to decipher his own name. Eric and Shepard were talking about him, not that it made them special these days.

The first full order he decoded was about him. It wasn't the most useful information, but it was interesting, and it did make him smirk. *Keep Akiyama alive.*

"Aw, Eric, you do care..." Al snickered to himself. He imagined how Eric would have reacted to receiving that order, how he would have coped with the entire ordeal since the dreams started. The notion brought him a vague sense of comfort.

The most recent messages contained repeated references to something Al had only been able to translate as 'Inanna'. He didn't know who she was, possibly another ship? Possibly Eric's ship? He made a mental note to ask Lani to scan for ships they'd been near in case they would determine which transport Eric was following them on. The problem was that everyone knew where they were going. It made it impossible to give anyone the slip, especially a trained spy.

His comms beeped as a message came through. President Lin. Al smiled to himself and clicked the recording. The President appeared on his screen, regal and glamourous as ever. He grinned at the old lady, even if it was just a time-delayed recording and she couldn't see him.

"Kon'nichiwa Akiyama," she greeted him. "I hope this finds you well. I was glad to hear that your second run-in with Maxwell went so much better than your first. I won't lie, I was concerned that two weeks of wallowing in dreams and self-pity were turning you clumsy and incompetent, but I look forward to seeing what you find in the communications you obtained."

Al rolled his eyes at the screen.

"But enough time wasted exchanging pleasantries," she waved the niceties away. "You don't need me to call to pat you on the fucking back for doing your job. I have information. Real information. The kind that we've been waiting for. The kind that makes all those delays I put you through worth it. We've heard from Merlin."

Al perked up. Merlin was Arthur's biggest moon. In a lot of ways it was considered their science capital. If anyone was going to know anything, it would be them.

"Scientists at Merlin have been monitoring the situation," Lin continued. "They are certain that the light from the Goo is dimming. Obviously, no one is sure what that means, but their best hypotheses are concerning to say the least. The Goo was an oily black substance when it swallowed Earth's solar system and Gilgamesh. It was only after the loss of Gilgamesh that it shifted to the glowing light form, which we have since surmised to be its dormant state. The dimming of the light coupled with its rippling movement suggests it could be about to awaken again."

Al whispered all the worst curses he could think of under his breath.

"However," Lin continued. "All of this only coincided with the appearance of the station and its beacon. Merlin is almost certain the station is the Inanna – Gilgamesh's biggest space station and research hub that was swallowed along with the planet. No one knows how it's moving yet, but if there is anyone alive on it, they've had twenty years to work out how to put engines on the back. If what they say is true, this is the only thing in recorded history to have survived the Goo. Nothing else has ever come back out."

Al pursed his lips in thought. Between the delay of getting information from Merlin to Titania and then back to him out here this was almost certainly half a day old if not more. Still… Eric had comms referencing the Inanna before Al did. Why? How? Someone needed their ass kicked and he wasn't sure who.

"Al," Lin implored from the screen. "I'm sorry I can't tell you more, but I need you to be careful. There were rumours when Gilgamesh was first lost that the Inanna was the one who inadvertently opened the portal back to Earth and unleashed the Goo on this system. No one could ever prove that, and with everyone dead there was no point pursuing it, but if this really is the Inanna, if it really has survived, and if there really are people on board sending this dream of you into the system… then this is more unprecedented than we ever realised. Promise me you'll be cautious, boy. I hate to think what I might have sent you into. Tell me as soon as you know something. I'll be praying for you."

The transmission ended and Al stared at the blank screen for a while, tapping his fingers against the edge of it like he was waiting for something. He was. He was waiting for answers to present themselves, and he was coming up short.

He flicked open the messages from Eric and shifted some of his translations. It was a touch easier now that he knew what he was looking for. *The broadcasting station is called the Inanna, it was an old top-secret research station that was swallowed with Gilgamesh.* Al had a strong and powerful urge to kick Eric's teeth in, but the man wasn't here so he'd just have to cool it. He wondered if this was what it felt like for Maxwell every time he'd beaten him. Al was owed this defeat, but it fucking stung. If Eric knew this shit, why hadn't he passed the information on? In theory, and some practice, Titania and Oberon were allies. Lin and Shepard certainly pretended to be, even if they constantly had people running around behind the other's back. If there was ever a time for all of them to put aside their differences and work together, surely this was it.

Instead, Eric was fucking with him, sabotaging him, delaying him, and hiding shit from him. The worst part of the truth was the tiny niggling part of his gut that wasn't sure he wouldn't be doing the exact same thing if their positions were reversed.

Al recorded a message back to Lin to let her know everything he knew, including the fact that Eric had the information before they did and was supposedly under orders to keep Al alive – although there was nothing to specify how many pieces constituted alive.

Once it was sent, he rose from his bed and went to find the others. It wasn't hard. As soon as he opened his cabin door he found the rest of them gathered around the bench at the central command console playing games. Slug had rigged the tabletop to project the board in front of them. She was laughing so hard at what was happening with the flashing pieces she hadn't noticed him come out. Whatever they were playing, they were loud and invested.

Sione met his eye first and signalled him over.

"Ae, Al, you come here boy and help me put these cheating little girls in their place!" he called.

"They ain't cheating, uncle Sione," Adam laughed at him. "You're just bad at this."

"You have to put the red pieces over the purple ones," Slug tried to guide him.

"Ae! Don't show him what to do!" Lani protested.

"Le Atua alofa mai!" Sione cried. "My own daughter! You will not help your father in his hour of need?!"

"Na," Lani shrugged at him. "Get good, Dad."

Al could see the throwdown approaching at speed, like an incoming head-on collision. Slug was trying to postpone it, but Lani was actively provoking her father again. Adam looked like he'd made sure he had a good seat to the show and could maybe do with some popcorn.

"You don't want to maybe go gentle on your old man…?" Al suggested to their pilot as he approached the bench.

"I do not," Lani sulked, shoving an entire unanumiti stick in her mouth and chewing with her cheeks out. The packet sat nearly empty beside her, and it didn't look like she'd been sharing. That was break-up binge food. She picked up the dice as she swallowed and rolled them across the screen, causing the projection to flicker. "You told me I could mod *Hotaru* to go turbo and take hoshi fuel while adding counter stabilisers, and none of that can be installed while we're flying, so now I just got ugly useless half-mods and a hold full of junk parts, which means—" She watched the dice land and moved her pieces accordingly, to pained groans from the rest of the table. "—I gotta destroy my family in Tagotakishi instead."

"Ruthless," Adam nodded respectfully, strong admiration in his eyes. He didn't seem overly perturbed about being destroyed.

"How is your code cracking going?" Slug asked, glancing over her shoulder at Al. Her dark eyes were wide and curious as they flicked his way casually, stealing a careless look that made him break out in a sweat.

"Getting somewhere," he admitted, swallowing delicately to try and keep his throat from closing up. "Actually, I got a call from Lin, who's heard from Merlin."

Everyone turned to him. He told them everything he knew, what he'd seen in Eric's messages and what Lin had told him. They took it all in stride, more curious than concerned, for the most part. Sione looked the most afraid of all of them. He was also probably the smartest. Slug, of course, was a technological genius, but was the kind of curious cat that had to be dragged back from danger before she got herself killed, Lani was similar with added bravado, and Adam didn't seem to have the sense to be afraid of anything.

"So we know where we're going now..." Slug mused, tapping the bench. "We're investigating the only thing ever known to have survived the Goo, the old Inanna research station... and Eric's helping us?"

"I wouldn't count on it," Al shook his head. "You don't sabotage someone else's ship to help them, and you sure as Allah is great don't keep vital information from them as an aid tactic."

"But you said he's under orders to keep you alive," Slug countered. "That's good, right?"

"I take it to mean he doesn't have clearance to kill me right now," Al replied. "I haven't found anything about the rest of you or anything that clarifies that I need to be kept alive in one piece. We treat him just the same."

"Then what's his actual mission?" Lani glowered, devouring another unanumiti stick. "You think he's tailing us to rob us after we come off the station? Getting you back for the stuff you stole from him?"

Al grimaced thoughtfully and didn't answer. It was as good a guess as any. Certainly solid tactics. A weary sigh escaped from Adam.

"I still think—" he started, before Slug popped a finger across her brother's lips to silence any further suggestions of homicide.

"There is another option…" she suggested carefully.

They all looked to her, and she looked up at Al, huge dark eyes still full of cautious optimism. Her full lips were pursed contemplatively, and she pressed them together tightly for a second before she began to elaborate. Al wished he wasn't watching every tiny muscle move across her face, but he couldn't look away. She blinked so softly.

"We're worried about this Eric guy chasing us and giving us grief and we want to avoid the fight, ae?" she checked.

"Yes," Al stated firmly, backed up by Sione and Lani and only moderately undermined by Adam's reluctant grunt.

"But he knows exactly where we're going, and he possibly knows more about it already than we do?" Slug continued.

Al nodded in frustration.

"But he doesn't know when we'll get there…" Slug suggested deviously. "What if we hit up Merlin, ask them if we can come see them, get all the intel direct from their stations, with Al as an official envoy, and delay ourselves long enough to learn more? If Eric hacked our original flight plan back on Tupua then he thinks we're going straight to the station even if we don't know anything about it. We could throw him off our trail by going to Merlin first?"

"And even if he thinks we're diverging he'd assume

we'd be going to Arthur!" Lani added excitedly.

"That's not a bad idea," Al agreed.

"High praise," Slug taunted.

"It's genius," he corrected, laying a supportive hand on her back. "I've met the Ambassador for Merlin, not that I know them well, but we could ask them to smuggle us in and get us an audience with the right people. Can't hurt to ask."

"I like this plan," Sione nodded approvingly. "Always best to know as much as possible."

"No complaints, Adam?" Al looked to the quiet giant.

"No new ones," Adam grinned, climbing off his stool and standing nearly tall enough to knock his head on the ceiling frames. "I just do what you tell me, Chief."

"To Merlin then?" Al looked to Lani.

"To Merlin," she agreed, shoving another snack in her mouth and heading for the bridge.

CHAPTER SIXTEEN

The bridge was dark but warm. A perfect, temperature-controlled warm as Al watched the Galileo system draw closer through the windshield. For all intents and purposes it was night. The *Hotaru's* interior lights were dimmed. Everyone else was in their cabins, presumably sleeping. It was just Al and the ship, watching the horizon, a dusty landscape of scattered stars and darkness.

He had sent a message to the Ambassador and they had already altered their course, but he was still waiting to hear back. They could always request to stop at Merlin regardless of whether or not they heard back, but he had high hopes.

The door opened behind him and he recognised the gait by sound alone as Slug came onto the bridge and shut the door quietly behind her again.

"I didn't realise you were up here alone. You still waiting for a message?" she asked.

"Something like that," he answered.

"Nice view," she commented, leaning on the back of his chair.

"It's not bad," he agreed, wondering if he could work out with his naked eye which point of light was Gilgamesh. He wasn't even sure how much the Goo had dimmed yet.

"Okay, budge up," Slug insisted, coming around to climb on him.

"There are three other seats in here!" Al protested as Slug sat on him. She clambered onto his lap and nestled back, resting her head by his chin. It wasn't even worth rolling his eyes. "If you were anyone else this wouldn't be endearing."

"Good thing I'm me then," she grinned, getting comfy between his legs. They watched the stars for a moment before she tilted her head up to look at him. "I'm glad you're here."

"I guess I'm glad I'm here too," he sighed. "Can't think of anywhere else worth being right now." He tried to make it sound like he was talking about the mission, instead of the way they were sitting, tangled together with his arms around her, holding her close.

He was vaguely aware of his own hot breath warming his lips as he rested them against her tightly bound silky hair. He wanted to freeze everything, freeze time, so that he never had to move again, never had to let her go, and never had to face the impending doom they were flying towards. He had no idea how to stop it, and the closer they got the more frightening it became. Just because Slug knew didn't mean she understood. She had faith in him. One of them had to.

"Do you think it's because we never finished?" Slug asked, her mind clearly on something else.

"What?" Al responded in bewilderment.

"You said earlier that when we're together it feels like we revert to sixteen again," she reminded. "Do you think it's because we were supposed to grow up together, but we didn't? We never finished becoming adults, so we don't know who we are together beyond the kids we were."

Al stared blankly at the stars trying to process her question. That was deeper than his brain was prepared to go at the moment. He didn't know why he felt the way he did, beyond the fact that feelings were something uncontrollable. It wasn't something he wanted to think about right now, especially not sitting here with her like this. It was safer to think of the mission, but she wasn't going to let it slide.

"I tried to get you to stay..." she muttered.

Al felt something inside him shift at the confession. He knew exactly what she was talking about, but he'd never seen it that way.

"That's what that was...?" he whispered, unable to help himself as memories of his last night at home, down at the old stone bench in the depths of the garden, began to swallow him. "I always thought it was goodbye."

"I guess it was," Slug muttered. "That's what you made it. I was trying to get you to stay."

She shifted her weight against him. He grimaced and tried to relax as he felt his blood redirect beneath her. If he didn't calm down she was going to notice, but it was hard to relax when his whole body felt like it was about to fly apart at the seams.

"That... that seems strangely out of character for you..." he stuttered, floundering for a distraction, but unable to think of anything else. "I never thought of you as manipulative. You were always so… so kind and earnest."

"Everyone's manipulative," Slug replied. "Even kids. Especially kids. It's one of the first things we learn as a survival mechanism."

He didn't argue. It felt true. It had been true for him, why not for her? Why not for everyone? He had this horrible feeling he suddenly didn't know her. It wasn't accurate. The Slug he knew was still very much there, still very real in his arms, but he'd spent more than half his life running from this conversation and now he was finally being forced to face it. She quite literally had him pinned down. At least she knew him well enough to know that was the only way to make him confront difficult issues.

"I waited for you," she said. It was an admission, but it felt like an accusation. Al felt like he was being stabbed again. "I waited and when you came home one of the first questions you asked was if I was seeing someone…" That was the sound of the blade twisting, he remembered the conversation. "When I said I wasn't, you offered to set me up with someone you met in the army…" There it nicked an artery. That was probably a mortal wound. "I should have kicked you in the balls right there and then."

"I would have deserved it," he conceded.

"Na," Slug shook her head sadly. "It's not your fault you don't feel the same. It took me a while to realise that. It took me a while for the pain to subside enough to understand I was lucky to have what I did—"

"Slug, no—" He shifted, trying to get her to turn to

face him.

"It's okay—"

"It's not! Simone…"

At the sound of her birth name, she turned. No one ever called her that. She didn't stand for it, unless she was in trouble. She shifted, twisting to face him. He caught her. His hand caught her cheek and his lips caught hers.

It was like being sixteen again. They were still fumbling around in the dark, just like they had that night. He kissed her like he meant it, he did, but it still felt like an accident. It felt like he was doing it as a means of explaining himself, because words weren't working. Surely they were better than that now?

Except they weren't.

So he kissed her. Intensely.

It wasn't just that he wanted it. He did, he wanted it so much it hurt, but he had to explain. He had to silence her defences. He had to destroy the excuses she concocted to try and protect herself from lies. Their lies. His lie that he was indifferent, and her lie that he didn't love her. That damning illusion that he didn't care. She was everything he cared about. She always had been. He couldn't bear to think she thought otherwise.

He felt like it would kill him to hear her say she thought he didn't love her with every fibre of his being. His heart would crack if she spoke those words. He kissed them away. All the words she'd been trying to say melted on his tongue. He didn't have any words. He kissed her like he was trying to make up for all the shit he hadn't said in seventeen years.

There was a confused tension in her body as she sat twisted against him, but she didn't fight it. His hand slid to the back of her neck, pulling her closer.

"Why…?" she whispered, her mouth barely leaving his to ask.

"Because it's always been you," he replied, settling on which 'why' to address first.

He wasn't sure if that was the right answer but she was still kissing him as she turned in the chair. It tilted on its pins as she straddled him, tipping her harder against him. He gripped her tighter.

This wasn't like being sixteen again. This was different. More. This wasn't something he was confused about. He wasn't stumbling and inexperienced anymore, and he knew exactly what he wanted from her.

That night in the garden she had taken the lead. She'd been trying to get him to stay. He'd been an idiot. Maybe he still was. But he was confident that however much she had wanted him, he wanted her more. He couldn't stop touching her. Everywhere his hands clutched at her body wasn't enough. He squeezed her against him, unprepared to ever let her go. She ground herself hungrily against him. Harder. Tighter. It wasn't enough.

He could hear the tremors of lust in her breath as his hands teased her through her clothes. He could feel them against his face. Her body rubbed against him and her hands were hot as they slipped beneath his shirt. He shrugged from his jacket, letting her take the shirt as he popped the clips on her overalls. Before he knew it they were undressing each other, moving as though entranced. Fabric stripped from their skin and dropped to the floor, discarded around the chair like autumn leaves.

He slid his hands beneath the tight fabric of her compression tee, pulling it away from her body and burying his face in the hot scent of her skin between her round breasts. He kissed her like he wanted to devour her. Maybe he did, but she was pulling away from his lips. She climbed off him, hauling his trousers down to his knees.

"Lani's going to lose her shit," Al commented regarding the treatment of the chair.

"What she doesn't know won't hurt her," Slug grinned. She was already stepping out of her overalls. Al stared at her, standing naked before him except for her heavy black boots. Lani's opinion of anything couldn't matter less, and he abruptly had no idea why he'd raised it. His entire consciousness was focused on the many alluring thick curves of Slug's bare skin. She stepped carefully over the chair, straddling him again. This time he barely even knew where he was, except that he was with her.

He had both hands beneath her, squeezing the cheeks of her gorgeous ass, guiding her as she rode him. She had her arms around his neck, pressing her body to his and holding on as they moved together. Her breath in his ear was musical. There were new notes he wanted to hit. They were much better at this now than they had been when they were sixteen. For a brief few seconds he was disappointed they hadn't learnt more together, but now wasn't the time for regrets.

Her thighs clenched against his hips as they rocked the chair. She was shaking, shivering, slowing. There was something freeing in her movement and voice. He wasn't ready for her to stop yet. He tipped her back, directing her gently. She caught herself on the edge of the control panel, resting her elbows either side of the mechanisms. Al held her tightly as he began to stand, holding her up as he moved in her. She moaned as he sped up, his hands supporting her body against his as he thrust faster and faster.

Slug gasped. The sound had an intensity he'd never heard in her voice. She threw an arm around his neck. Her fingers dug hard into his shoulder. They moved fiercely, rocking, rattling, like turbulence. Like take-off. Then, weightlessness. Like hitting zero gravity. That same peace. That same stillness. But better. She kissed his neck as they stayed paused, locked in the moment. He was breathing fast, still holding her up, but she was getting heavy in his arms.

Something beeped loudly from the console beneath them.

"Fuck!" he cursed, nearly dropping her.

"I didn't touch anything!" she swore, untangling herself from him and slipping from his body.

They both turned to the controls. Something was beeping and flashing. A call from Merlin. Al cursed again and Slug laughed. She grabbed her overalls from the floor and scampered out of the way, crouching down under the console and trying to stifle her giggling. He quickly pulled his trousers back up from around his ankles and opened the call.

"This is the Captain of the *Hotaru*," he answered coolly.

"Greetings, Akiyama," a woman's face smiled up at him from the comms screen. "I'm not surprised you're out in our neck of the woods, but I was surprised to hear from you."

"Evening, Ambassador," Al replied. He leant forward over the controls to try and keep everything below his neck and face out of frame, hopefully hiding the fact that his shirt and jacket were both somewhere on the floor by the chair. "Thank you for getting back to us."

"Of course. There's nothing better than hearing from Lin and the homeland, although it's morning here, so you might want to adjust your times before you land," she warned. "Based on the speed of the call, I'd say you could be here in a few hours. I spoke to the Prime Minister and they are extremely keen to meet with you."

"That's very kind of you, Ambassador," Al nodded. "Obviously this is an unusual situation…"

"It's been an unusual few weeks," she agreed. "I have been kept abreast of all the intel President Lin has been receiving. I know what's going on, and we all want it resolved as quickly as possible. Anything you need, Merlin is eager to help. The Prime Minister has already summoned two of their chief science officers to speak with you when you arrive."

"Thanks…" he replied. "We appreciate it. I'll be in touch when we're closer."

"Your ship's a refurbished Otashii?" she checked. "I'll make sure there's a landing station ready when you get here. Looking forward to seeing you again, Akiyama."

"You as well, Ambassador," he nodded, shutting off the call before he did something to embarrass himself. The screen went dark. His reflection was still surprisingly bewildered. He rubbed his face to try and remove the expression.

Slug carefully ducked out from under the console. She had half pulled her overalls back on, but tied them at her waist, leaving her chest alluringly bare. The way she looked at him was wry, one eyebrow raised in a picture of perfect cynicism. Al turned his face away, resisting the urge to roll his eyes and ask what he'd done now. She laughed like she knew the look anyway.

"Captain of the *Hotaru*, ae?" she mocked.

"I'm sorry, did you want to answer that call?" he pointed at the screen. "Tits out and everything? I'm sure Ambassador Song would have appreciated the nice view."

Slug grabbed the front of his trousers and hauled him in close, closing her mouth over the side of his neck and dragging her teeth gently across his skin.

"She got your pretty face, I'm sure that's a nice enough view..." she grinned.

"I can call her back if you want to correct me..." Al offered, tracing his fingers lightly up her sides.

"That seems unnecessary, shin'yū," she sighed, slipping her arms around his waist and kissing up his throat. "I'm just curious about when my ship became your ship…"

"We're getting possessive about the ship now?" he teased, lowering his lips to hers and halting her response with a kiss.

She laughed against his mouth and spanked him firmly. He grinned, unable to take his lips from hers even if he'd wanted to. She was open to his kiss and he slipped his tongue against hers, tasting her for a moment, before dragging his lips across her cheek.

"No thievery intended…" he whispered. "I guess I'm just feeding the needs of my fragile ego."

She laughed again. "You know what else your fragile ego needs…?"

"I'm all ears…" he replied.

She tiptoed up and softly nibbled his earlobe, brushing it with the tip of her tongue. His hand was pushing up her body, stroking the rising nipple of one plump breast. Then she pulled away. The distance between them was sharply cold as she turned her back on him, striding off. He stood, dazed, as he watched her bend over to snatch their discarded clothes from the floor. The fabric swung lazily in her hand as she moved to the door. She stopped. He was still staring. It would have been impossible not to.

Slug was grinning as she turned to him. She raised a finger and curled it, bidding him to follow. There was a mischievousness to her wide smile, somehow more wicked than ever before, and he had never been so eager to find out exactly why. He staggered after her and she laughed at him again. He didn't care. If there was ever anyone who was allowed to laugh, who had earnt the right, it was her.

His cabin was the closest to the bridge and he caught her at his door. The lights in the passage were dim and blue, like the rest of eternity was asleep. He held her firmly, pressing his body to hers as they kissed in the doorway.

"I'm sorry…" he whispered.

"For what?" she replied.

"For ever making you feel like I didn't want you," he sighed. "You were always the only person who really mattered, but…"

"But what?"

"But it's not about you," he muttered. "You… you said earlier, when we were talking about Adam, that it's always about me. That seems so stupid and foolish and narcissistic, but you weren't wrong. You're never wrong, Slug. I've been running from myself my whole life. I made decisions that would help me grow into my skin better… but I've never been able to fix myself. Not completely."

Slug laughed at him quietly, letting her lips brush his shoulder and the breath of her amusement tickle his bare skin.

"There's nothing to fix, silly," she scoffed.

"There is a voice in my head that tells me I'm broken and that no matter what I do I will never fix those cracks and I will never be good enough for you," he admitted breathlessly. "That's why I've spent my life pretending to be other people, complete people, people who don't need to be fixed."

Slug contemplated this for a moment, tracing her

fingers against his arms. Then she reached behind her and clicked the button to his cabin. The door slid open.

"I'm going to need you to come in here with me so that I can teach that voice a thing or two," she insisted.

He couldn't help but smile. "Long overdue educational experience, ae?"

"Something like that..." she grinned, dragging him into the cabin with her and sliding the door shut.

CHAPTER SEVENTEEN

They were just over an hour from Merlin. Everyone was up and gathered about the central console having breakfast. Al wouldn't meet anyone's eye, but he was managing to make it look nonchalant. Lani was heating food to take back to the bridge. Landing was still some distance away, but she wanted to keep an eye on things. Slug was bouncing between this room and her room and the bridge and the engine, like she was looking for things to fix. She seemed to constantly change what she was holding between her teeth, be it toast or the handle of a multitool, and she was trying to talk around both.

"You need a hand, Chief?" Adam asked her as she went by.

"Na, I'm good, bro," she replied, taking the multitool out of her mouth and patting his shoulder as she sped through the room again. "Just making sure the landing gear is adjusted for Merlin. I hear the gravity there is a bit iffy."

"It's light, but we'll be fine," Al told his breakfast. "As long as Lani doesn't come in too hot."

"Unfortunately for you, cuz, I always come in too hot," Lani joked. "Can't help it. This ass just don't quit!"

"That ass is gonna bounce if I don't make sure we can clamp properly," Slug laughed. "Can't rely on the gravity to keep us in place." She slowed as she passed Al, brushing by him and stealing a piece of his toast. "When you're done here, *Captain*, I'm going to need a hand in the engine room…"

"I'm never going to live that one down, am I?" he smiled ruefully at her.

"Na," she grinned, munching the toast and disappearing down the back of the ship.

Al watched her go, eyeing the saunter as she walked away. He would have loved to be able to claim that was his first mistake, but he knew better. Instinct turned his head back, so he saw everyone else staring at him before he had time to drop his eyes back to his toast.

"What was that?" Lani smirked liked she'd just caught him with his hand in the cookie jar.

"It was nothing," he replied quickly. Too quickly. Fuck. He could feel the heat rising in his cheeks instantly. Why did this only happen to him and none of his aliases? He stammered, staring at his plate and gesturing awkwardly. "Sh– we– uh– um– Slug was on the bridge with me when the call from Merlin came through," he floundered. "I was trying to sound professional, so I answered the call as the Captain of the *Hotaru*."

"Are you not?" Adam looked at him quizzically.

Sione burst out laughing across from them. "Oh Al…" he sighed.

"And the rest," Lani demanded coolly, resting one hand on her hip and leaning on the end of the bench with the other.

"What rest?" Al shrugged. "There is no rest."

"What were you doing on the bridge?" she asked suggestively.

The innuendo in her tone made him choke. He wanted to meet her eye and challenge her, but there was no way he'd survive that. Her expression was full of wicked insinuations. He could barely pretend his face wasn't flaming.

"Al-Amir, were you boning Adam's sister?" Lani demanded teasingly.

"Were you what?" Adam echoed, straightening on his stool.

Al coughed, trying to clear the crumbs from his throat. Even sitting, he had to tip his head back to see Adam's face looming down at him. He tried to pretend he was someone different, someone who wasn't like this, someone who didn't go bright red and lean back timidly as an absolute giant leant aggressively into his personal space and—

"Holy Allah, Adam, why are you so huge?" Al wheezed, unable to think of anything else as the ex-enforcer's shoulders took up his entire field of vision.

Sione was still laughing into his elbow across the table. Lani looked like she'd won something. Adam was staring down at him, his serious face deducing at speed, the same way he calculated danger and the need for violence. Al swore he wouldn't be the one to start whatever was about to happen, but the kid hadn't been dissuaded by his question. A spark flared behind his dark eyes and they widened in surprise.

"Oh my God… you did…" Adam slumped back on his stool. "You did! Chief, how could you?!"

Al was too stunned by the reaction to speak. Adam pulled his communicator from his pocket. Lani was already holding out her wrist. Adam flicked an app open and typed a transfer.

"Wait..." Al started, catching on. He watched Adam and Lani hold their wrists to the comms and approve the transfer. "Wait, you guys had money riding on this?!" Al exclaimed. "You were betting?!"

"It was Lani's bet," Adam sighed, pocketing his comms again. "I really liked my odds too, but I guess she knows you two better than I do..."

"About bloody time, honestly," Lani commented.

"I coulda saved twenty if you'd just waited until Merlin..." Adam sighed sadly, picking up his bowl and spooning cereal into his mouth.

"You were always gonna lose somewhere, cuz," Lani cackled, ruffling his hair.

"Yeah, but every stop saves me twenty..." Adam sighed. "I really thought I had that one."

Al looked to Sione. The old doctor was grinning at him like he was sitting through a comedy set. Something in Al's expression must have tipped him off, because he tapped the side of his nose shrewdly.

"The only rule was we were not allowed to interfere," he said.

"You were all in on this?" Al flushed, feeling like the butt of a joke.

"Na, boy, I'm just the cheerleader," Sione giggled at him. "You and Slug always so sweet, always so suamalie, and she like you so much..."

"Did she know about the bet?" Al asked.

"Hell na!" Lani laughed. The humour immediately fell to panic. "Why? You not gonna tell her, are ya?"

Al picked up the last of his breakfast, toasted her with it, stuck it in his mouth, and rapped his knuckles on the benchtop as he tagged out, heading for the engine room.

"Al? Al!" Lani called after him. "Tell me you're just going to fuck my cousin again not nark on me!"

Al pulled the fingers behind him in her direction as he left the room. He heard Adam protest to Lani.

"Dude, that's my sister!"

"So?" she replied.

Al finished his slice of toast as he stepped into engineering and shut the door on them. He didn't care about anything else they had to say. The whirr of a drill sounded through the grate floor. Al slid down one of the ladders to the lower level. Slug had one of the floor panels up and was half disappeared inside. He had a fantastic view of her bending over. It felt wrong to look, but he told himself she wouldn't mind.

"Remind me again what you need my help for in here?" he asked.

She grunted as she pulled herself out of the floor panel and slotted it back in place. He waited attentively as she grinned up at him and wiped grime from her hands on a rag hanging out of her pocket.

"Over there," she pointed across the room. "I want to check the stabilisers, and I figured while I was stuck on my back anyway you could do me a favour..."

"Ah..." Al smiled. "So I'm not actually useful for repairs..."

"Don't be self-deprecating, shin'yū," she grinned, climbing to her feet and pulling him in at the waist. "I think you're going to be very useful…"

"Do you actually need to check everything or are you just having fun?" he asked.

"Why can't it be both?" she smirked.

"It can," he smiled, tucking a loose strand of hair behind her ear and leaning down to kiss her. "I don't think the engine room is the right place for this though… what if Adam shows up to actually help with the stabilisers?"

"It will be extremely educational," Slug replied, kissing him back.

Al pulled away from her kiss, shaking his head like he was trying to dislodge the notion. Slug laughed at him. She still held on around his waist and dragged him over to the wall with her. One of the main control panels blinked next to them. Slug banged a large red button down with a stiff pop sound. The lights dimmed and multiple clangs signalled the doors locking. Her face was turned up to his, her lips tracing the edge of his jaw like she was waiting for him to lower to her kiss again.

"Better?" she whispered.

"Safer for our collective therapy bill," Al joked, cupping her cheeks in his hands and kissing her again. She leant into him, pushing him against the wall as her hands began to slide up inside his shirt. He slowly began to lower his hands towards the clasps on her overalls.

The speaker above them crackled as it switched on.

"Really, cuz?" Lani's voice judged them. "In the

engine room?"

Slug rolled her eyes.

"They know…" Al muttered.

"Oh do they?" Slug chuckled. "How you were ever a successful spy, boy, I will never know."

"It's just about you I get all…" he muttered, proving his point by dissolving into a tongue-tied mess and failing to complete the sentence. "Besides, they were waiting for it. Lani had a bet going with Adam. Didn't even try and hide it. He paid her while I was still in the room."

"They what?!" Slug yelled. She pushed away from him and slammed the comms button on the panel. "Hokulani! You bet what?!" she yelled down the line.

"Fucking nark…" Lani replied softly down the speaker.

Slug popped the lockdown button and unsealed the engine room. The doors clicked. Before she could take a full step everything shut down again, as though the doors had been locked remotely. Slug hit the button. The room unlocked. It immediately locked again. She unlocked it. It locked again. Each time she hit the button harder. The locks became a whirr of sound, constantly flicking back and forth.

"Enough!" Al bellowed, hitting the comms button and yelling down the line. "Stop playing with the fucking doors, ladies! You two break this ship, we're all getting out and walking to Merlin."

The doors stayed very quietly and apprehensively unlocked. Nothing moved. Al removed his fist from the comms button. Slug was glaring at him sullenly.

"She started it…" she muttered.

"Then go finish it," Al invited, motioning to the door.

Slug gave him a self-satisfied little nod and headed for the bridge. He made no move to stop her. She started up the ladder.

"Just make sure she can still land the ship!" he called after her. She gave no sign that she'd heard him, but that was fine. He knew she was responsible. More so than any of the rest of them. Besides, it was about time someone put Lani in her place. Slug was the only person on the boat she'd listen to.

***

Al contacted Ambassador Song from the central command console as they neared Merlin, and he didn't approach the bridge again until they landed. He hadn't heard any sounds of violence, but it was family business and he wasn't going to get involved. The other four took the seats on the bridge for landing; Al practically insisted on it, choosing to stay in the safety of his cabin. Partly he enjoyed the peace of coming in on his own, but partly he believed the family should be together to see Merlin for the first time.

The third largest of Arthur's seven moons was a sight to behold. Al had never been anywhere like it. The atmosphere was cramped inside the radiation shields, but it had been thin to begin with. The air was light, the gravity was weak, and the entire world seemed to hover like magic. Iridescent cotton-candy clouds covered the moon's surface, and all the buildings rose out of them like reflective pale spires and balloons. There was no architecture like it back in the Gan De system.

Al almost wished he could have seen their reactions… her reaction… coming into a world like this, but he was happy enough to know she would have seen it with the others. He felt the jolt as the *Hotaru* clamped to the station near the Parliament Towers. That was his cue. He unclipped and strode through to the bridge. At the sounds of awe still echoing down the corridor he couldn't help but smile.

"Al! Al, have you seen this?!" Slug called as he approached.

"A few times," he replied, striding into the room. "Merlin is a very beautiful place."

"It's magical…" Slug breathed, still staring out the front window at the picturesque landscape.

Al shared a nod with Sione. That was probably how it had earnt its name.

"You gotta go meet with the Prime Minister now, ae?" Sione ribbed him. "Very fancy…"

"Actually, I want you two to come with me," Al replied, tapping the backs of Slug and Sione's chairs.

"You what now?" Sione echoed. "I ain't got a shirt to wear for meeting Prime Ministers…"

"What you're wearing will do," Al grinned. "Trust me. Adam and Lani are on ship guarding duty. Everyone else, we're going to meet the Ambassador."

"What?!" Lani protested.

"Hai," Adam nodded sharply. "You can count on us, Chief."

"Arigatō," Al nodded.

"This is 'cause you're mad at us about you boning Slug, isn't it?" Lani sulked.

"Aw…" Slug pulled a face at her cousin. "Somebody's sad they're not getting any…"

"Somebody waited so long I nearly jumped him myself," Lani declared. "He's the only guy on this boat I'm not related to."

"Well, this conversation is horrifying enough that I'm glad it's safe to walk out the airlock," Al announced, turning and fleeing the bridge.

Behind him, the women laughed as Slug and Sione unbelted to follow him out. Lani reached out a cheeky hand and spanked Slug as she went by.

"Bitch," Slug turned on her.

"Hag," Lani laughed.

The two of them chuckled at each other and Slug reached back to give Lani a quick hug.

"Go have fun with your boyfriend and his colleagues, ae," Lani insisted, ushering her away.

"Ae, I will," Slug called out as she headed off. "And, oi, Adam! If she misbehaves, stab her with a screwdriver!"

"Will do, Chief," Adam called back obediently.

Sione laughed fondly at all of them, shaking his head and giggling as he followed Al and Slug to the airlock door fastened to the station tower. He tried to supress his laughter as the hatch turned and opened, but Al was deeply aware of Slug and her uncle behind him desperately not meeting each other's eyes for fear that they would erupt into laughter again.

The family, the actual real family, had a closeness that Al couldn't properly understand. They had tried to include him in it, even growing up, but whatever it was that gave them that camaraderie, he was missing it. He was broken, incomplete. He didn't fit in, so he chose to be alone. Now the choices were being taken from him and in the aftermath of forced outcomes he had to try not to mess everything up.

Time would tell if he was having any success.

CHAPTER EIGHTEEN

The door opened and they were met with a host of guards and Ambassador Song. She reminded him of a younger, taller, politer Dawa Lin. Her qipao was deep blue with pink patterns and detailing and she wore her hair pinned up. She smiled when she saw them enter the station.

"Welcome back to Merlin, Mister Akiyama," she smirked.

Al knew that look, but he decided to ignore it. If she wasn't going to bring up that she had met him under a different name, he wouldn't either.

"Thank you, Ambassador," he inclined his head. "These are my companions, Doctor Sione Faamanatu and Simone Tanaka."

Sione and Slug both bowed politely at his side, appropriately awed by the high ceilings and gleaming white architecture of the gigantic station. Song greeted them courteously but didn't stand around for pleasantries. She escorted them through the station to the Parliamentary Towers. The condensed atmosphere and low gravity of Merlin made walking feel strangely akin to swimming. Everything felt light but dense. Breathing became an odd sensation. They didn't so much stride as float across the halls, each step taking them further than they were used to.

Ambassador Song brought them to a large suite at the top of one of the tallest towers, with massive windows overlooking the majestic coloured clouds beneath. There was a long table with a central comms station in the centre and a decadent high-tea arrangement laid out. Slug and Sione kept sharing overwhelmed glances at the opulence on display. Al eyed everything carefully. So that was how they were playing it.

Song invited them to sit and Slug and Sione joined her nervously at the table. Al declined. He stayed standing and approached the windows, looking out over the cotton-candy world.

"The Prime Minister will be joining us shortly," Song assured.

"Of course," Al replied politely, still watching the comings and goings of the station from the tower. His eyes scanned the landscape for threats.

"I assure you, you're perfectly safe here," Song told him.

"You're not the one with everything but your identity code being broadcast throughout the entire system," Al replied.

"And you were such a trusting young man before that..." Song drawled.

Al flashed her a grin. She had definitely been appointed by his President. The Ambassador crossed her legs and smoothed her skirt patiently. Al risked a glance at Slug. She looked nervous and he tried to force an expression of reassurance as he smiled at her, although he wasn't sure it worked. At least the way she watched him was curious.

"You're here as a diplomatic envoy," Song continued. "No one knows about your arrival and, technically, you haven't been recorded as entering our space."

"No one knows except for everyone who's supposed to be meeting us?" Al raised.

"Naturally," Song nodded.

"And what's that old Earth saying about secrets?" Al smiled.

"Only a secret if two people know it and one of them's dead," Sione recited, leaning back in his chair. "What you worried about, boy?" He lifted an eyebrow at Al.

"Just the Goo waking up and devouring all life in the system," Al replied casually, peering at the view. "Or even just eating a single sun thereby destroying the gravitational pull of every single orbit, causing the entire system to basically turn into a meat grinder."

"Nothing major then," Slug assured.

"Nothing major," Al gave her a small smile.

He wasn't the only one. Song gave his companions a droll look too. There wasn't anything else to do. Millions of years of human existence, and sarcasm was still a reliable crutch against despair.

The door at the far end of the room opened. Security entered first and flanked the Prime Minister. Al was familiar with the tall, androgynous blonde who currently ran Merlin. Their name was Lance Pendragon and Al got a kick out of watching Sione's face as they were introduced. Anyone with any kind of an Earth education raised their eyebrows. The PM saw it too. They smirked at the room as they took a seat at the head of the table.

"Would you believe it's my given name?" they asked Sione.

"Were your parents raging nationalists?" he replied.

Lance chuckled. "It was politics or showbiz, am I right?"

"There's a difference?" Al teased.

"One has a higher likelihood of ending with a sex tape," they smiled. "But we're not here about me. Thank you for coming by Merlin."

"Thank you for having us, Prime Minister," Al replied. He hadn't moved closer to the table, but they didn't seem to take it personally.

"You're a lot more popular than your last visit," Lance commented. They gave Al a direct look. "And a lot more edgy..."

"The two are related..." Al replied.

"I bet they are," Lance nodded, leaning back. "I won't lie, Akiyama. Now that I know who you are, I am very curious as to what you were doing here when last we met."

"Official Titania business," Al replied.

"Which is my business," Lance countered.

"You were new to office, Your Honour, and we didn't know much about you," Al elaborated carefully. "That was five years ago, and I never came back."

"I don't know if I should be flattered or worried," Lance mused.

"Then at least there's one part of my job I'm still doing right," Al smiled.

"You should be flattered, Your Honour," Ambassador Song assured. She glanced down the table at Slug and Sione. "Pendragon has taken excellent care of Merlin these last five years."

"Thanks Wei," Lance smiled. "But before we make my legacy sound like a bad fanfic, let's make sure I'm going to get one." They reached forward and activated the touch screen in the table before them, waking up the control core in the centre. A comms call began to ring. It was answered almost instantly. A video link of two people in traditional lab coats blinked at them from the central projection.

"It's an honour to hear from you, Prime Minister," one said.

"It gets better than that, friends," Lance responded informally. "I have Ambassador Song from Titania with me, and she has brought Al-Amir Akiyama and his companions. Somebody work out how to save my moon."

Al did not begrudge the Prime Minister that call. He could imagine how terrifying it would be to be in charge of the rock closest to the calamity.

The scientists shared a look and then touched their own screens.

"We're here monitoring the situation as we speak," one answered. "This is Gilgamesh currently." An image was projected up onto the screens. It looked like a barren hunk of rock or perhaps a ball of cold lava.

"Fuck," Al whispered. There was no sign of light

emitting from it at all.

"Not filling me with confidence, Akiyama," Lance commented, their own face paling at the sight.

"What happened to it?" Slug asked nervously.

"It went dark," one of the scientists shrugged. "We've been watching the radiation levels drop for weeks, and they are dropping to levels reminiscent of the dark Goo that ate Gilgamesh."

Lance glanced at Al. "Fuck," they conceded. "Does Arthur know?"

"We've kept the King and the other ministers informed," the scientist answered.

"Do we need to be evacuating?" Lance demanded.

"To where?" Al countered. "Is there even any way to predict where it might go or what it might do? What if it's gearing up to leave the Galileo system altogether?" He folded his arms and stared the room down. The room stared back, but didn't answer.

"You said the radiation levels are dropping," Sione mentioned, looking curiously at the data on the screens. "But I don't see what you're measuring. Do you have comparative data?"

"You are?" the scientists asked.

"This is Doctor Faamanatu of Titania," Lance passed on the introduction.

"Doctor of medicine not astrophysics," Sione admitted. "But, even so..."

"When we say radiation..." one of the scientists began uncomfortably.

"It's not like anything else in the known universe," the other finished. "We don't even think we have the technology available to accurately measure it. When it's in its light state it emits an energy. We have been studying it for twenty years, and we have no idea what it does. Every probe we have sent has gone dark and failed to return. Now, the energy levels are dropping rapidly. It could hit the same levels it entered the system at within the day."

"What about the Inanna?" Al asked before anyone could start panicking.

"What about it?" one of the scientists shrugged. Their partner elbowed them.

"We have failed to make contact," the other elaborated. "Despite the fact that the Inanna is clearly broadcasting a signal, we haven't been able to get it to respond to any of our hails."

"And it is still far too close to Gilgamesh for anyone to consider sending a team out," the other added.

"That's where we come in…" Slug raised, watching the readings continue to drop.

The room fell silent. Al was prepared to admit he hated the way things were going. He had hoped that a meeting at Merlin would inspire him to continue, but it made him want to run away. If nothing else, he did not want to fly the *Hotaru* and her crew out to investigate.

"You have nothing to add, Akiyama?" Lance raised hopefully.

Al leant back against one of the window struts. His arms were still folded, and he could feel his brows knotting his face into an ever-tighter glare.

"You know the worst part about this debacle so far?" he muttered. "I feel like the person who knows the least about all of it."

"You're telling us you don't know anything?" one of the scientists pressed.

"Nothing," Al muttered. "I get weird dreams I don't understand of things I have no context for. It's like one of those movies where you know it will make sense on a second watch after you've seen the ending, except I don't think I'm getting a second crack at this."

Slug stood from the table. She approached him and rubbed his shoulder comfortingly. There was a warmth and confidence in her dark eyes that awed him. He didn't know how she did it. He felt ready to sky-dive out the window to escape destiny, but Slug was standing there like the process server of fate. As he thought it, something flashed behind his eyes. He winced and grabbed his head. There was a strange pressure, pulsing like a heartbeat behind his eyeballs.

He could see darkness. A white room. Bloodstains. Debris. He could hear gunfire. A crash. Massive. Monumental. Like the sound of two buildings colliding.

Slug's voice called to him. He realised he was grunting, breathing heavily, hunched over in the meeting room in the high tower on Merlin, clutching his head. Slug had her arms around him.

Al blinked the room back into focus. Everyone else was standing. They were all looking at him. Sione was approaching with a grave look on his face.

"What's wrong?" he asked.

Al blinked and gasped, shaking his head.

"I saw… I… I saw…" he panted.

"Your Honour, it's moving!" one of the scientists

called.

Everyone turned back.

"It's not!" the other argued. "It's staying put. Following orbit, as usual!"

"Right there!" the first pointed. "It's gone dark and it's pulling!"

Sione pulled Al's chin up and shone the light from his comms in each eye, watching the reaction. A med check wasn't a bad idea, but Al already knew he didn't need it.

"It's reaching," he told the room, straightening up and pulling himself from his friends' hands. "The Goo is reaching. It's going for the Inanna."

Everyone looked at him.

"What did you see?" Slug asked.

"Nothing more useful than that," he admitted grudgingly. "Come on, we have to go." He began to usher them towards the door.

"Go where?" Lance demanded.

"Where do you think?" Al replied.

He paused a moment as he realised how rude he was being and tried to get his brain back on track. Looking back he could see a room full of fear. It wasn't anyone's fault. It was just the natural reaction to the situation. He wondered if he knew how to have a natural reaction anymore, and if not, was it something he lost in training or was it more recent than that? Had it been taken from him while he was distracted by lost dreams?

"Pendragon, you're about to have your hands full with a multi-global panic," Al warned. "I know it's little consolation because I can't prove anything, but I promise you the Goo isn't coming for Arthur or the moons. It is only moving to grab the Inanna. We have to get there before it does."

"Akiyama, I need—"

"I'm sorry, Lance," Al cut them off. "I don't have time." He tried to put all his sympathy into the statement, but it didn't come at the cost of truth. There was an unrelenting command in his words as he ushered his people out and fled the wake of his apology. For the first time in weeks he knew exactly what he had to do, without knowing how or why, and the race was truly on.

Al sped back towards the *Hotaru* with Slug and Sione. He kept them in front of him so that he knew they weren't falling behind or getting lost, but he made them move at his speed. Sione was trying to ask him questions, but Al could do nothing except insist they didn't have time. It was like a broken record in his brain, like something had shorted out and all he knew was a desperate need to be somewhere else. They had to get to that station. They had to.

Slug was checking her comms. Al glimpsed her opening her messages and heard her cursing.

"What?" he demanded.

"Those idiots left the ship!" she swore. "Adam says there was a bunch of security stationed outside so Lani said she was going exploring. He thought we'd rather he keep an eye on her than *Hotaru*, given that the ship has government protection and Lani has a destructive streak."

"That's kind of him," Sione sighed with genuine

appreciation.

"They're at a bar called Light and Magic," Slug finished.

"Of course they are," Sione sighed again.

"I know where that is," Al looked over them. "Can you two make it back to the *Hotaru* from here? I'll get the others."

Slug nodded. He returned the nod. They were in agreement. Then she grabbed him, holding the side of his neck and bouncing up on her toes, almost leaving the ground in the low gravity, to kiss him. He was surprised by the action, but not displeased. The idea of just being allowed to kiss her was new, and if his brain had been working properly, probably exciting.

"See you back at the ship," he said.

The other two nodded and dashed away. Al took the turn towards Light and Magic. It wouldn't be hard to get there. Just a short detour. It was easily the dingiest bar in the area, so of course Lani had been able to find it. She had a type and she knew it.

CHAPTER NINETEEN

Adam hadn't been sure of the right call, and he had promised he would stay with the ship. It felt wrong to break that promise, but he was almost certain Slug's quip about stabbing their cousin with a screwdriver had been just that and that he wasn't actually supposed to do it. Lani was in the mood to wreck something and he wasn't prepared to put her in the med-bay just to stop her. The safest course of action seemed to be to go with her and keep an eye on her, so he sent Slug an update and did just that.

Lani had done her research, all five minutes of it. She knew where she was going and what she wanted. Adam wanted to do his best to stay out of trouble. On a scale of clubs he'd been to Light and Magic was pretty nice. Maybe it was just early. The place wasn't packed. The light was good. The ceilings high. The venting controlled. Adam sat at the bar and read a book on his comms and drank his beer and waited to hear from his sister. Hopefully the world wouldn't end first. The folk in these parts seemed awfully focused on the shifts in Gilgamesh.

He'd never taken much stock with journalism personally. He didn't like the way the media fabricated and dramatized reality for clicks. Maybe that was just because he'd been involved in so many stories growing up. He knew deeply and personally how little the self-proclaimed reporters actually knew about the events they reported on.

Someone pulled up next to him. Adam looked up and smiled.

"What are you doing here?" Al asked.

"Staying outta trouble," Adam replied. "Or doing my best, ae. Look, I'm sorry about earlier… about the bet with Lani. I know you're private about that kinda stuff—"

"Where is she?" Al pressed.

"She's upstairs, and I'm pretty sure she feels bad about it too," Adam continued. "Y'know Lani though, she wouldn't admit she was wrong if you held a gun to her head. Not the type to apologise, even if she knows she done wrong, and she knows—"

"That's not important right now," Al cut him off again.

"It is important, chief," Adam disagreed. "I'm glad you and Slug are working out. I know she's my big sister and she thinks it's her job to look out for me, but that works both ways, and her taste in guys is awful, I mean… wow. She really knows how to pick 'em, y'know? And I'm not sure if you'll be good for her, that's not for me to decide, but at least we all know you'd never want to hurt her, not on purpose."

Al paused. Adam was watching his face, trying to discern if he'd said the right thing. It wasn't always easy to know. People could be like that. You never knew what they were thinking, but you could work out what they would do. Mysterious, yet predictable.

"Adam," Al began softly. "We have to go. If we don't find Lani in two minutes, we're leaving her behind."

"Oh shit," he closed and pocketed his comms. "We in trouble, Chief?"

"No, but we will be," Al insisted.

Adam just nodded. He knew that look and tone. It was the same one that had guided him to adulthood, although from a different man. As much as he knew Lani wouldn't want to be disturbed with the guys she'd taken upstairs from the bar, she'd want to be left behind even less, and their Captain wasn't in the mood for messing around.

He got to his feet and downed the last of his drink in a single gulp before heading for the staircase to the upper accommodation. Al followed right behind him. Hopefully, picking the right door wouldn't take more than a few tries. They were still on the stairs and he was still trying to calculate how long he should leave between knocking and opening the door, when Lani came bounding down the stairs in the opposite direction zipping up her jacket.

"We're leaving," she announced as soon as she hit them.

"Ae, but—" Adam started. Al and Lani ignored him and took off towards their ship. There was nothing to do but shrug and follow. Their business was their own. At least for now.

***

Al didn't have time to look his gift horse in the mouth. He needed Lani and Adam back on the ship and he was still pissed that they'd left, but now wasn't the time to fight about it. He couldn't afford anymore delays. That Lani had been on her way back and as keen to get off the rock as him was a blessing that could warrant further investigation later. They hurtled through the corridors as fast as they could travel.

The low gravity of Merlin gave power to the leaps and bounds of his run, although he felt grossly uncoordinated. People watched him coming through the halls and moved out of his way. He saw their alarm, and their sudden recognition as he blurred passed. That was a them problem, and maybe a little bit Pendragon's problem later.

They reached the *Hotaru* and burst onto the ship. Al could already hear the engine humming as they hit the bridge. Slug climbed from the pilot's chair and motioned Lani to it.

"Everything's as we left her and there's no sign of sabotage," she informed them.

"Thank fuck for that," Lani muttered, buckling in. "Now let's hope shit stays that way and get the hell off this rock. Buckle up, bitches."

Sione was already secured with the Gilgamesh updates in the med-bay, so the rest of them belted up on the bridge and Lani took off. She was still in a foul mood and no one questioned it, not until they were clear of the moon and she changed direction.

"Where are you going?" Al demanded.

"Away from here," she snapped.

"We have to get to the Inanna," he reminded.

"We have to get away from your ex-boyfriend," she countered.

Al paused. A cold dread welled up inside him, something either more powerful than the call to the station, or something compatible with it.

"You saw Eric…?" he asked, not even bothering to fight the insinuations this time.

"Na, he wasn't there," Lani replied, firing them through space. "But he's hired mercenaries to get rid of us."

"What do you mean?" Adam asked.

"I mean mercenaries," she repeated. "Space pirates, cowboy. They got a job from Oberon's finest – hunt us down, board our ship, get pretty-boy here, and space the rest of us."

"That can't be right…" Al muttered.

"I saw it with my own eyes," Lani insisted. "This ain't no grapevine bullshit. My only saving grace is that they didn't know who I was or what I was flying, but I saw the job description. Your Maxwell buddy is paying to have you picked up and your ship and crew trashed."

Al reached to unbuckle his seatbelt. There wasn't anywhere to go or anything to do, but he had a strong urge to go out and murder something.

"Al," Slug urged him, reaching over to place a hand over his. "That's not a problem for right now. We've got to get to the Inanna first."

"Wanna bet?" Lani snarled.

The console began to flash and beep. They had company. The transponder wasn't pinging them, which meant it was safe to assume they weren't bringing tea. Another beep. An alarm. They were being targeted. The *Hotaru* was under attack. He didn't have time to move. He didn't have time to think. Everything lurched. Lani changed direction hard. Al felt his whole body pull. His brain bounced. The belts strained against his chest. Something exploded out the window. The force of the blast knocked them. Lani straightened the *Hotaru*.

"Let's do this," she announced.

He didn't have time to say 'wait'. It wouldn't have made a difference. She hit the button on her stereo. Music blasted through the ship so loud she wouldn't have to hear them yelling.

"LANI!" Slug screamed anyway.

Lani wasn't listening. Her teeth were bared and she spun the ship. Her song roared to match the engine. The *Hotaru* had flipped. Now they were barrelling head first towards their attackers.

"I can't help but feel she's taking this personally!" Adam yelled at him over the noise.

Al nodded. That was not an unfair assessment. Lani roared in fury as she fired at the other ship. They swerved her attack but didn't return fire. The *Hotaru* was a refurbished landing vessel and that… that was a Tiger 49-5GC. A mercenary gun-ship. The only reason they were still flying was because it had decided not to rip them apart.

"Lani!" Al yelled, grabbing her shoulder.

"They're going for our engines!" she yelled back, rolling the ship to keep the Tiger's target out of range. "Remember, they gotta keep you alive, pretty-boy!"

Al tried to steel his stomach as Lani went toe-to-toe with the Tiger. The other side might have had a better combat ship, but they clearly had no experience going up against a racer. Lani flew like a maniac. She twisted and spun around them, manoeuvring to keep the engines away from their guns. The Tiger rolled fiercely, trying to keep up and out-manoeuvre them. Lani corkscrewed around them like she was following an invisible ring circuit.

Hit after hit went wide in both directions. She knew how to fly, but attacking wasn't her strong suit. The Tiger got lucky. Al felt the air tear across his face as a blast ripped through the bridge. It was small, but deadly. The vitruchal screen held, but it was pierced. So was the floor. The bullet had ripped clean through. Air was torn from the room, from their lungs, as the vacuum of space claimed it.

Slug unclipped her belt and jumped, grabbing something from her pocket to start to plug the hole in the window. Al followed suit, ripping the cover off the first-aid panel and slamming it over the hole in the floor. He used emergency suture tape to seal it down. Slug was filling the window hole with a fast-sealing liquid vitruchal polymer. Lani rolled Slug's way and she finished with ease as everything else turned upside down.

Al had his mag-boots glue him to the floor, but a hand caught him by the front of the shirt and stopped him banging around. Adam looked him in the eye as everything turned right way up again. Slug bounced back to her seat.

"Turrets?" Adam asked.

Al nodded. Adam unclipped from the chair and they both took off down the corridor. Their boots kept them from falling, but the run down the length of the spinning ship involved a lot of crashing into walls. They split before engineering. Adam went left, Al went right. He hurtled down the corridor and clattered into the gunnery compartment. Part of him was surprised Slug had restocked the weapons on this thing. Then he remembered that would have been Lin's call.

He belted into the turret chair and started the console up. The screen flickered into life before him, with the Tiger dead in his sights. He took aim and unleashed. Everything spun again and his attack went wide. This was going to be harder than he thought. He set the gun to lock on to the Tiger, and steady his aim as he went for it again. The other ship wasn't bad. They knew how to avoid being hit, and they weren't aiming to kill, but it didn't feel like going easy.

Al jerked in his seat as the *Hotaru* took another hit. That was going to have to be someone else's problem. A spray of fire scattered across the Tiger's hull. Adam was having better luck than he was. He could feel the turn coming and readied himself. The *Hotaru* rotated. The turret balanced and Al blasted. He hit the Tiger dead on. It's shielding saved it from annihilation, but that was all. It gave as good as it got.

The *Hotaru* twisted away, but one side got clipped. Al felt another jerk. His chest felt bruised from the constant strain of the belts holding him in the chair. Beneath them, a torpedo exploded as Adam shot it out before it could heat-seek their engines.

"Are you sure they didn't know who you were, cuz?" Adam's voice checked over the intercom. "How'd they find us so fast?"

No one answered him, but Al accepted the validity of the question. Lani was probably too angry to reply, if she could hear them at all over her stereo.

They didn't have time for this fight. The Inanna only had so long before the Goo reached it, and once that happened it could be lost forever. The Tiger might have qualms about destroying their ship, but he had none in return.

"Lani!" Al yelled down the line. "If you can pull a Gyaku Goro I can take out their back shields! Then you can nail their reactor!"

The speaker crackled a moment.

"If I can?" There was so much contempt in her voice at her skill being doubted he was worried she would cut him off and leave him behind. But the *Hotaru* began to slow as they readied for the manoeuvre.

Al took a deep breath and brushed his thumb across the trigger. The *Hotaru* began to spin. It risked putting their engines in the Tiger's fire, but only long enough to heat blind them. Al held onto his lunch. Lani nailed it. He nailed the shot. Waiting until the last possible moment, he fired as the turret came spinning back around behind the Tiger, spraying through the seamline in the back shields.

Lani unleashed the main guns at the back of the Tiger, smoking the engines and killing the ship's power. That was all they needed.

"Leave them!" Al ordered across the comms. "We don't have anymore time to waste. Lani, I need you to get us to the Inanna as fast as possible!"

"Ae, we burnt a bunch of fuel though…" she replied.

"The Inanna, Lani," Al insisted. "Nothing else matters. If we don't get there in time, all this trip was for nothing. The Goo is waking."

There was silence down the line. A tiny hint of static.

"Ae." The answer came small and soft. The *Hotaru* blasted towards Gilgamesh.

CHAPTER TWENTY

The damage from the fight had been hastily repaired. The important thing was that no one had suffered worse than a few bruises, and the *Hotaru's* holes were all patchable. As soon as it had been safe to do so, Al had ordered everyone into their space suits. From there they had been able to shut off the oxygen and patch the holes in the ship before restoring air. It was ugly, but it was liveable.

Al was down in the cargo hold with Sione, standing over the small panel they'd just welded over the hole in the bottom of the ship. Slug and Adam were in engineering. Initial reports showed the engines were fine, but they were lower in fuel and oxygen than he would have liked. There was enough to get to the Inanna and back to Merlin. Not that Al was in a hurry to return.

He had called Song and told her to get an urgent message to Lin, as well as run the situation by Pendragon. Maxwell had put out a hit on the *Hotaru*, paying mercenaries from the moons of Arthur to take them out. He wasn't sure how his President would want to spin that politically, or how much help Merlin's Prime Minister could be, but he had told Song to tell them to get Eric's people off his back.

Slug's voice crackled over their suit comms.

"Ship atmosphere should be stable again," she advised them.

"Hai, Slug. Arigatō," Al replied. "How are you two doing?" He asked the question as he removed his helmet and strode through the open doorway into the engine room. Sione followed behind him.

"She's been better," Adam answered, appearing beside them from behind the lower core.

"She's been worse too," Slug replied, from the upper level. "She was in worse shape than this when we found her, but I'm sure we all could have done without that fight."

Al looked up as Slug clunked around above them. He could see her shadow through the grated floor as she moved about the room.

"Tell me about it!" Sione exclaimed. "I thought I was gonna have a heart-attack!"

"Al...?" Lani's voice crackled so timidly over the comms Al touched his earpiece in concern.

"You doing okay, Lani?"

"Na, man..." she muttered. "I don... I don't think we should be here..."

"I'm coming up," Al replied, boosting up the ladder and out into the central corridor towards the bridge.

The others followed him. He saw the problem as soon as he stepped through the door to the bridge. The sight made him freeze. Lani was brave to have made it as far as she did. The Inanna was close. Al could see the massive station floating before them, drifting urgently through space. It had been altered. Even from here they could see the rudimentary engines that had been attached in some kind of desperate effort to turn the station into a ship.

Behind it was darkness. A darkness purer and deeper than the edge of space. It was reaching for the station. Reaching for them. The shadow of Gilgamesh. The substance that had eaten a planet, eaten Earth's solar system. The Goo.

"She won't reply…" Lani muttered. "I been hailing her, but there's nothing. No sign the Inanna is even getting our messages. She's broadcasting a signal of some kind, but I can't tune to it."

"The *Hotaru* can't, but the human subconscious can," Al replied, slowly approaching the pilot's chair and resting a hand on the back of it.

"Scan her for heat or signs of life," Slug suggested, fearlessly following Al into the bridge.

Lani ran the scan. All three of them made curious sounds and leant over the findings. Sione whimpered from the doorway, but Adam was standing at his shoulder like a supportive wall.

"What is it?" Sione inquired hesitantly. "What did you find?"

"There are people living on that thing," Lani answered. "Huge sections are shut down, but some seem to be supporting life."

"It's possible," Slug agreed. "The station was self-sufficient. If it's been trapped for twenty years, hypothetically people could have survived onboard. The real question is why didn't the Goo eat it? More importantly, does this mean that the Goo doesn't destroy things the way we thought?"

"There are records of it," Sione countered. "Records from Earth of what happened to the solar system as the Goo approached Earth. It ate everything on the way – obliterated it!"

"The real question…" Al countered ominously, "is who got here before us?" He pointed to one of the heat signatures on the side of the station. "That's another ship, and it got here recently."

"You have some thoughts?" Slug looked at him.

"Dock there," Al instructed, pointing to an old docking bay on the other side of the active part of the station. "If that's Eric, he's not here for the goodwill of man. I want us to stay out of their line of sight. We can come at the station from the other side and see what we can find."

"You're really gonna make us get that close?" Sione muttered.

"Worse than that, Doc," Al sighed. "I'm gonna make you go inside."

***

There was oxygen, pressure, even a touch of gravity when they entered the Inanna, but it was cold. Cold and dark. Al was the first to remove his helmet, clicking it back into the suit. He hated wearing space suits. They restricted his movement and vision, even if the designs had come a long way. He'd concede it was still better than dying.

The air was freezing and stale as soon as it touched

his face. There was oxygen though. That was enough. He'd been worse places. Well, he'd been places that felt worse. They still didn't know what they had actually walked into. He had told Lani to stay with the *Hotaru* and keep the engine running. The entire situation set every nerve in his body on edge. At the rate it was going they had maybe two hours until the Goo made contact with the station.

Everyone else came with him, suited up and armed. Sione refused to carry a gun, but he'd brought his med-bag. Al wanted to be prepared for anything, and he sure as Allah was patient wanted to be ready for Eric. No one set mercenaries on someone if they weren't after the same buried treasure. If only Al had the vaguest idea what treasure they were looking for. They stalked down the dark tunnels, the torches on their suits the only light available.

"Al...?" Lani's voice came tiny and panicked over the comms.

"Hai?" he whispered.

"She went quiet..." Lani whispered back, sounding near tears. "The signal stopped. The Inanna ain't broadcasting. She just went silent."

"Well... she's been asking me to come find her for three weeks, maybe she knows I'm here," Al replied softly.

"Hai," Adam agreed gently. "Now we just gotta hope she wasn't laying a trap..."

"Don't you say things like that, boy," Sione warned. "Don't even joke."

"Sorry, uncle," Adam muttered.

They continued on down the passage, reaching a large sealed door. Al ran his fingers over the controls and inspected the seal.

"Slug, you think you can run power to this? Get it open?" he asked.

"I can take a look," she offered, coming closer. She still had her helmet on and moved fully-suited with caution. "I think the power switch is on the other side. Everything is controlled from further in. Will see what I can do though."

"We're in kinda a hurry, ae?" Adam checked. "Like, there's a hard time limit on this before the Goo eats us?"

"Boy…" Sione warned him.

"Sorry, uncle," he apologised again. "But I'm just wondering if maybe we do this one my way?"

Without waiting for a response, Adam strode up to the door. He slung the strap of the large gun he carried over his shoulder, before opening one of the containers on his belt and removing a tool. It looked like a small sturdy chisel. He jammed it between the doors, smashing it in with his fist and breaking the seal. Firmly but gently, he began to manually wedge the doors open. Al felt a breath of warm air caress his face as the doors parted. As soon as they were wide enough for his hand, Adam shoved an arm into the gap and forced the doors apart. Al swore he could see the damn spacesuit straining over his massive shoulders as he pushed the doors open. Adam looked back and jerked his head.

"All yours, sis," he offered.

"Nice one, bro," she grinned at him and patted his arm as she ducked under it into the next room. Adam gave another mighty shove and the doors clicked into place, locking open.

"Excellent work, my nephew," Sione approved, following after Slug and patting Adam's shoulder as well.

The giant turned back to look at Al.

"You don't mind?" he asked.

"Adam…" Al shook his head. "You help get us through this station and safely back home, I'll get you a medal."

"Hai, Chief," he grinned, giving Al a curt nod.

They turned and followed the others deeper. Until then, Adam had been following Al's lead, but he set his helmet back up like the rest of his family as they entered the room beyond.

"The air's better through here," Al pointed out to him.

"Yeah," Adam agreed. "But it just occurred to me that Slug's smarter than the rest of us, and the protection might be useful. Y'know, in case the Inanna takes sudden damage, or any face-huggers or tentacley-monstrosities jump out at us."

"Boy!" Sione scolded.

"Just being cautious!" Adam protested.

"Save the horror stories," Sione insisted. "When we get home you can tell whatever tales you like, ae? But not in here."

Adam glanced at Al through the visor and shrugged. Al gave him a rueful smile. The theories didn't bother him, but he could understand why Sione didn't like them. The station was creepy as hell, like an old ghost town. It looked like everything should work, but it was old, and it was empty. He'd almost expected them to have hit people by now. They hadn't docked that far from signs of life. Merciful Allah, that made Adam's notions all the more ominous. He prayed the theories would prove unfounded.

The lights flicked on. Al almost jumped out of his skin, but he was following everyone else and they were in helmets, so hopefully no one saw it. He was supposed to be better than this. He needed to keep it together. Slug was standing by the switch, and she shoved the old lever up. A warm white glow filled the space. Al blinked at the old hangar. There were old terminals and consoles all around the room, and multiple shuttle stations that stood eerily empty.

"Guys... this stuff is all still working..." Slug announced. "No one's used it in a couple of decades... but it's still functional, it's even still stocked."

"Still stocked?" Al echoed.

"Yeah," Slug nodded. "They got fuel and water and air... all looks like stock left over from before Gilgamesh got swallowed. It's still a proper station, all kitted out and everything. We could refuel *Hotaru* if we wanted."

"Do it," Al ordered, barely pausing to consider.

"Do what? Refill *Hotaru*?" Slug checked.

"Yeah," Al nodded.

"That's stealing..." Slug replied.

"It's salvaging," Al countered. "Besides, this station has less than two hours of life left. No point wasting the resources. Coordinate with Lani, take what you can, I'll take the guys and see what else we can find. I'm serious about getting out of here, and if we gotta do it in a hurry, we need the *Hotaru* to be ready for that."

Slug gave him a long look. If he'd had marines with him, no one would have questioned him, but it was hard to stay resolute against her dark eyes. She reached out and touched his chest gently.

"You all keep your suit cams on," she instructed. "That way we can see what you're seeing from *Hotaru*. You run into any problems, let us know."

"Of course," he promised. If she'd had her helmet down he would have kissed her. He wished he could have, but she just nodded and turned to go.

Slug radioed Lani directly and the two began to organise getting the ship as well-stocked and repaired as possible with the new resources. Al continued on with the others. He kept both hands on his gun, fingers tense, barrel lowered. Every creak and bang of the station felt like an imminent threat, but he was trained not to jump at the slightest sound. Fortunately, the longer he stayed here the more the training came back to him. Adam also seemed to have mastered the art of stoicism. The kid wasn't rattled by anything. He stalked the old station corridors, gun in hand, peering around every corner like he knew what he was looking for.

Sione wasn't so calm. Al could see the man's fear in his posture. He was glad the doctor had refused a weapon. He remembered his training, the way they had drilled into him what it took to be a lethal assassin, and the precision and finesse required to be classed as one of the deadliest spies on record. He also remembered his Captain teaching him a sharp distinction. No matter how hard he trained or how good he became, there was nothing more dangerous than a person with firepower they didn't know how to use. It was the difference between the right person dying and innocent lives being lost. That was how he had justified his training to himself whenever his mother had called. He was training himself to make sure he was never responsible for the wrong person dying.

This deep in the station the power was on and the doors were working. The next room they came to was an old tech lab. The walls were lined with monitors and workstations. All the computers were on. Multiple devices spread out through the centre of the room reminded Al of a med-bay. There was still no one there. Machines beeped and whirred. The space even smelled like people. There was no sign of anyone.

Al felt a cold dread oozing slowly down the bottom of his spine. His guts clenched. Something was wrong. Something was extremely wrong. He approached one of the devices. It looked like a rack, like something used to restrain a human. There were bands placed to bind wrists, ankles, shoulders, hips, and a head.

"What is this place…?" Adam muttered.

"Sione?" Al called, trying to keep his cool. "Can you make sense of all this stuff? Sione?"

There was no answer.

Al turned sharply, whirling around like a maniac at the silence. Sione was still there. He was standing at one of the workstations, flicking through files.

"Uncle Sione…?" Al approached him nervously.

"I'm here, boy," Sione answered softly as Al reached

his shoulder. He had taken two small transmitters from his bag and attached them to the computer.

"You downloading this?" Al asked.

"Ioe," he replied. "I am. It would take… a lifetime to go over all of this. If the President wants us to find out what was going on, this is where we will find it."

Al nodded. He knew that well enough. His job had been to steal secrets, even when he wasn't sure what he was stealing. Sione couldn't see the nod, not wrapped in his suit and focused on the screen, so Al patted his shoulder as well.

"Adam and I will keep looking, but we won't go far," he assured. "Let us know what you find."

Sione nodded. Al tried peering over his shoulder. It wasn't like the old man to go so quiet, and he wanted to know what had disturbed him, but the information was going by so rapidly, and most of it looked medical. Al couldn't make sense of it, but maybe it wasn't the research getting to Sione, maybe it was just the station. It was starting to get to Al, and he'd been trained for uncomfortable situations.

"Ae, Chief!" Adam called him over.

Al moved to join the other man. He was standing by the wall, with his suit cam and torches pointed down, his head tilted as he looked at something. Al was half expecting an ominous or infested grate. He wasn't expecting what they found.

Adam was staring at drawings on the walls. They looked like they had been done by a child. Multiple children, perhaps.

"What you make of this?" Adam asked.

"This station is massive," Al shrugged. "There would have been kids on it when it was taken. If there have been people living on it all this time, odds are there are more kids now."

"So where are they?" Adam asked.

Al was silent a moment as he thought. He tried to imagine he had been living on a station for two decades trapped in a ball of Goo that had eaten a planet. He'd probably be insane. Maybe not. Maybe there were enough people here that they could have kept each other sane, built the most isolated community in existence, possibly dreamt of the day they could get out. Maybe even tried to change the station into something that could escape… and then flown it out of the Goo…

It was a crazy theory, but it aligned the few facts he had currently. In that situation, he would have been desperate to make contact with humanity again. As soon as the ship docked he would have come running… so why…?

Because they weren't the first ship here! Fuck! That's what—

Alarms blared. Lights began flashing red above them and sirens screeched. Al snapped his helmet up to dull the noise.

"Adam, with me!" he yelled. "Everyone else get ready to go!"

He took off down the passages, deeper into the station. Adam stayed right on his heels. They raced through laboratories and hallways. Everything looked lived in now and Al was kicking himself for not realising it sooner. The station had been calling him for weeks, but it had no way of radioing traditionally. They had no way of knowing the ship that arrived wasn't him. They had no way of messaging for help.

There were sounds up ahead now. Gunfire. Screams. Just like the vision on Merlin. Al felt his stomach drop, but he ran towards the noise as fast as he could. Adam ran faster. The kid busted through the door like Allah himself was giving the orders. Al felt his heart break as they crashed into a new massive laboratory. The room was carnage. It looked like an explosive had gone off. Everything had been ripped apart. Soldiers had scientists and civilians against the wall and were gunning them down. Several troops were half-melted across the floor.

Adam didn't even wait to assess. He crouched behind a chunk of collapsed ceiling and opened fire on the soldiers shooting the unarmed masses. Al went wide, taking cover down the side and evaluating in seconds. His suit was telling him the room was losing air. Lani was screaming something into the comms. People were dying faster than Adam could save them. The soldiers had patches on their spacesuits. Oberon flags. Al made sure his camera caught them. If he couldn't stop them, he'd make sure someone arrested them. Even in a suit, he recognised their Captain instantly.

With an outrage he didn't know he could feel, he rushed the soldiers. The kickback from the machine gun was comforting. It felt justified. They weren't prepared for the attack. They thought they had rounded everyone up, and they were already panicked. Something had happened here. Something awful. Al gunned down more of them while Adam reloaded. There were at least fifty armoured uniforms massacring the station's survivors.

Half the soldiers turned on their attackers. Al abandoned his charge for Eric, leaping into cover as a hail of bullets descended around him. He was never going to get there in time. The room was too big. There was too much space to cross. Eric had seen him coming. Al peered over the cover, ducking back down as more people shot at him. He couldn't move. The soldiers were advancing on him. No doubt Eric had ordered them to kill him. In this suit most of them wouldn't even recognise him. Eric would have. Without a doubt that psychopath knew what he was doing.

Adam unleashed on them again, emptying another clip with practiced efficiency. It bought Al a second, but he'd never make it in time. He was about get Slug's brother killed. He could hear her voice calling to him over the comms. She was shouting. So was Lani.

"Get out of there!" she shrieked. "Get out! Guys! It's here! It's at the station! Get out now! Al?! Adam?! Can you here me?! Please! Get out! Al?!"

There was a hideous crunching above him. The floor began to tip and crack. He realised too late. They were supposed to have hours, but they were all out of time. He tilted his head up. The ceiling was gone. A darkness more profound than any he had known filled the space. The Goo. There was nothing between him and oblivion. It was right there. He could see hunger and anger in the blackness.

The station cracked. Too much of its structure had been devoured and it was breaking apart. The floor ripped, separating Al from the soldiers and their victims. His line of sight was broken as everything tilted. He yelled and grabbed for the floor, trying to keep from falling. He activated the magnets on his boots and gloves, locking himself in place, one arm jamming his gun to his side. If he got the shot… if he caught a glimpse of Eric again…

The ground tipped back, but there was no sign of him. The soldiers were already bolting. They filled the doorway. Al scanned the massacre site, searching for survivors in the carnage. Something blinked red light from the strewn bodies. Detonators. He barely had time to duck for cover. Explosions ripped the room further apart. Al could feel himself slipping towards the crack in the floor. Fuck. Something grabbed him. He panicked as he was ripped from the floor. Then a voice sounded over his comms.

"I got ya, Chief," Adam announced.

Adam half pulled, half threw him back towards the door. Al could feel the atmosphere gushing out the gaps in the station, ripping everything it could into the void of space. He wasn't sure if that was worse than getting eaten by the Goo or not. The two of them clambered back towards the door. Adam pushed Al in front of him.

A sound ripped through Al's brain. A cry of desperation so extreme he nearly blacked out. He grabbed his helmet, trying to hold his head.

"Chief?!" Adam called to him.

Al looked back. Adam was staring at him. The

closest thing Al had ever seen to panic tainted Adam's brown eyes behind his visor. Looking back, Al could see movement. The Goo was slowly oozing into the broken room, dissolving the walls as it slid down. Right in the centre of his vision, beneath a pile of rubble, a pale hand was straining.

"Adam!" Al yelled, pointing.

Adam turned. He didn't wait for instructions before leaping. The giant had his weapon stowed, and descended on the collapsed ceiling, ripping the pieces free of each other and sending them whooshing into the void. There was a figure in the debris, weak and injured, but alive. Adam snatched them up into his arms and raced back. The magnets in his boots and the strength of his body the only things keeping both of them alive.

Al reached the door, holding it open as Adam rushed to it with the survivor. He burst through. Al let go. The emergency doors slammed shut. The pressure stabilised, but it wouldn't stay that way. Adam kept the limp figure clutched to his chest. They looked like they'd been doused in something white, maybe dust or liquid. Now wasn't the time to check. Al and Adam raced back through the hallways and labs, sirens screaming at them. Al spared a breath to tell Slug they were on their way, but he didn't stop running. The only other seconds he spared were glances to make sure Adam was still following him.

The engines were running when they reached the *Hotaru*. Slug, Lani, and Sione were all waiting. They burst onto the ship and Al slammed the door behind them.

"Detach!" he bellowed down the line.

The *Hotaru* jerked as she snapped off the station dock. Al was thrown back against the wall as Lani blasted full-speed away, but he had no complaints. The vitruchal ceiling gave him a clear view of what they were leaving as they turned away. The Inanna had cracked to pieces, a solid pillar of dark ooze penetrating it like a spear straight from the body of Gilgamesh.

His entire body felt cold as he watched it, thinking about how close it had been, thinking about all those people that had just died there, and realising that he had been to the Inanna, come that close to the Goo, and he was still no closer to an answer regarding everything that had happened since the dreams began.

THE LIGHT AFTER EARTH

CHAPTER TWENTY-ONE

The *Hotaru* flew from the site of the Inanna as fast as she could. Al ordered Lani to head for whichever Herakles moon was the furthest. He didn't want to risk going back near Arthur, not if Eric was recruiting mercenaries. They needed to get as far from here as possible. As soon as they were safe he needed to send the footage of everything they had found back to Lin's office.

The first thing they had to do right now was see to their new guest. Now that they were safely on the ship, Al could see them clearly. He could see her clearly. The figure, collapsed in Adam's arms, was a woman who appeared to have fainted. She didn't seem obviously wounded but they ran her to the med-bay. Sione met them there as Adam set the woman down in one of the reclined medical chairs.

Al couldn't take his eyes off her, and the dread of the station crept back. At first he had thought she'd been doused with something, but now he wasn't so sure. She was white, not just pale skinned, she was pure white – like she'd been carved from marble. Her skin, hair, nails, even her eyelashes, all matched the tight little dress she wore. The effect gave her an oddly ageless quality. She could have been twenty years younger than him or twenty years older, no trouble. It was impossible to tell by sight.

"What's wrong with her?" Sione asked, setting up the ID scanner and med-monitor. "Who is she?"

"The only survivor of the Inanna…" Al muttered.

Sione gave him a look and set the scanner to her wrist. Nothing came up. He tried the other arm. Nothing. They all stared as Sione frantically scanned her arms.

"I don't think she's got a chip…" Adam supplied.

"Everyone's got a chip!" Sione protested.

Al felt like he was going to puke. Everyone had a chip, except whatever this strange girl was. Whoever she was. Sione checked for scars along her arms, any sign that her chip had been there and then blasphemously removed. No scars, but there was something that was worse. A tattoo on her wrist. A barcode inked on her skin, exactly like Adam's. She was one of them. One of the stolen kids.

Everything about this investigation felt haunted. He couldn't shake the image of the panicked people being gunned down by Eric's soldiers. None of them had looked like this. This strange ghost girl. They had all looked like regular humans. He wanted to call this woman a survivor… but looking at her now… he was no longer sure.

"Sione… can you run a tox-screen?" he asked, even as the doctor took the girl's hand and gently clipped her wrist into the med-monitor on the armrest. "Just… just make sure we haven't brought something we shouldn't have on board."

"She's clean, Chief," Adam assured.

"We need to check, Adam," Al muttered. "I… I'm sorry I put you in danger without thinking…"

"You didn't put me in danger," Adam replied.

"If she's got something—"

"She's good, man. She'll be okay," he insisted. "The only danger were those soldiers, they ain't here, and you weren't what put me in their firing line."

"What firing line?" Slug demanded from the doorway. "What happened down there?" She looked over the room, blinking like she was in shock. "The… the Goo… it just… it just leapt. One minute it was still miles away… the next second I blinked and it was at the station! Who's she?"

Al didn't know which question to start with. He crossed back to the doorway and pulled Slug into his arms, holding her close. Her helmet was clicked back now that they were sealed on the *Hotaru*. He clicked his own back in order to kiss her cheek.

"Al…?" Slug looked up at him with big concerned eyes.

The med-monitor behind them started beeping.

"Hm… it's not working properly…" Sione muttered. "I might need to swap it over for a spare."

"It's not the machine," Adam told him. "Spare will give you the same readings."

"Oh, you a doctor now, boy?" Sione raised an eyebrow at him.

Adam shook his head demurely. He stepped away and left Sione to swap the machines, brushing by Al and Slug in the doorway as he left the room. Sure enough, the same beeping started up from the second machine.

Sione cursed.

"What's going on?" Al asked, moving back towards the doctor with Slug in tow.

"I can't get a proper read on her," Sione muttered. "She don't seem to be contagious, so that's good, ae? But most of her vitals are shorting. The machine can't read them. And she don't have a bloody chip! You ever met anyone without a chip? Scrubbed or rewritten, of course, but no chip?!"

Al shook his head. Sione was right. Even in intelligence, where he assumed everyone he met was working with a scrambled chip, he'd never met anyone completely without one. Not unless it had been obviously cut from the body.

"Is she dead…?" Slug whispered.

"Na," Sione shook his head. "She ain't reading dead. She's reading corrupted data." He frowned and stroked his beard thoughtfully, before moving to the main medical console and plugging in the data chips from the station.

"Uncle Sione…?" Slug asked.

"I got a lot of files to dig through, but I read some while they were downloading," he replied, totally absorbed in the screen as he began to sift through his findings. "They were doing experiments in that station – human experiments."

"We rescued one of the test subjects?" Al conjected.

"You rescued *the* test subject," Sione replied. "The notes only talk about a single subject."

"And Eric shot all the scientists," Al snapped angrily. "He probably thought he'd killed her too."

"Why?" Slug looked to him in horror. "Why would he do that?"

"The same reason anyone destroys an experiment," Al muttered. "A cover up. What I want to know is how he knew what was even going on there."

Footsteps hurried down the corridor towards them, rushing over the metal floor. Lani appeared in the doorway. She looked flustered and stressed.

"What's wrong?" Al asked her.

"You tell me," she replied. "I think we got away clean, but we weren't the only ones. Took off trailing a military gun ship and they absolutely smoked us."

"Can you catch them?" Al demanded, not even sure what he would do if he could get close enough. The *Hotaru* couldn't take Eric's ship in a fight, but Al didn't want to just let him flee. The point was moot as Lani shook her head.

"Not as we are," she said. "If I'd been able to do those mods back on Baba Yaga, sure. Right now, boosting as fast as we can, we're still just trailing their fumes." She pulled a face. "They say when you're running from a bear you just need to be faster than the other guy. Well, we ain't faster, cuz."

"Then let's hope the bear isn't chasing us," Al sighed. He grimaced and rubbed his brow. The whole point of the trip had been to get answers, and he still didn't have any. Only more damned questions. So the Inanna had been trapped in the Goo running human experiments for twenty years and somehow Oberon had known about it. Now that the station had somehow miraculously escaped, Eric had been sent, presumably by President Shepard, to cover up the mess.

But what the fuck did that have to do with him?! Why was he the one people had been dreaming about?! How come he had been dragged into this unholy clusterfuck?! And what was the deal with the Goo? What was it? Where had it come from? What did it do and how did it do it?

They were supposed to have had two hours in there, but Slug said the damn stuff jumped. He thought about what he had seen and the timing of it all. The alarms on the station. That must have been first contact. That probably meant it lunged when Eric and his people started shooting scientists. Did that mean it was triggered by violence?

"So who's Snow White?" Lani asked, jerking her head at the girl in the chair and breaking Al's train of dilemma.

"Her name's Oria," Adam answered, stepping back into the room with a mug in his hand. He crossed to the reclined chair and set the mug down on the stand nearby.

"How do you know that?" Slug asked. "Did she speak to you?"

"Not yet," Adam shook his head. "But she will. Also, it's on the screen." He pointed to the monitor with all of Sione's stolen research.

Everyone looked. Sione smiled first and highlighted a patch of text. *Subject OR14*. Oria. Adam's translation was almost cute.

"And what you got there?" Lani jerked her head at the mug.

"Milk tea," Adam answered. "It's her favourite."

"Adam, do you know this girl?" Slug asked, pressing him cautiously.

"No," he shook his head. "We've never met."

"You sure about that?" Al asked, tipping her unbound wrist to expose the barcode.

"We never met," Adam answered simply. "Not yet. Not 'til she wakes up and says the tea thing."

"What do you mean?" Slug demanded gently, laying a hand on his arm like she was worried she was about to have to get him checked too.

Oria stirred. She pulled her wrist from Al's fingers and struggled groggily in the chair. Her other arm tugged at the monitor around her wrist, but not hard enough to break free. She didn't need to. Adam hit the unlock button and the monitor popped open. It hadn't been able to read anything useful anyway. She opened her eyes and blinked at the room.

At first Al had thought her eyes had rolled back, then he wondered if she was blind. Finally, he saw her gaze adjust and realised that her eyes were as white as the rest of her. Two small black pupils peered out of her marble face. Coupled with the barcode on her wrist, they seemed the only vaguely normal things about her. Everything else about her was completely, inhumanly white.

She gazed around them nervously, her strange skin clouding her expressions. Her body hunched as she shuffled up in the chair, sitting awkwardly as the new strangers watched her. She pulled her long, straight hair over her shoulder and began to toy with it anxiously.

"Hi," Adam started politely, completely unfazed. He picked up the mug and held it out. "I brought you tea."

"Milk tea…" she murmured, taking the cup and sipping it. Standard human behaviour. She sounded and behaved human, even if she didn't quite look it. As soon as she sipped the drink she smiled and looked up gratefully. "My favourite."

"I know," Adam nodded. "I remember you saying."

"When do you remember her saying…?" Slug asked.

"Just now," Adam replied like it was no big deal.

"You remembered her saying it before it happened…?" Al checked.

Adam nodded like he wasn't admitting to precognition. He gave Oria a polite nod and she smiled back. Everyone else shared a look of profound concern.

"I'm Adam," he introduced himself normally. "This is Al and my sister Slug, they're kinda the bosses around here. This is Lani, my cuz who flies our boat, and her dad Sione who does his best to keep us honest and alive. The ship is *Hotaru*. We picked you up off that station before the Goo got it."

Oria seemed to consider this for a moment. She watched Adam's introductions curiously, but when he finished speaking her gaze dropped to the mug in her hands. She watched the liquid through the clear top with remorseful eyes.

"They shot my doctors… didn't they?" she asked softly.

"Yeah," Adam nodded sympathetically. "They did."

"Why?" she looked up at him again.

"We dunno," Adam replied. "We were hoping you

could tell us."

She shook her head helplessly. Her eyes scanned them again, but found nothing familiar, and turned anxiously back to the drink in her hands.

"Would you be able to walk us through what you do know?" Al asked gently, trying to ease answers from what clearly seemed to be a traumatised young woman.

"I know the station was safe…" she whispered. "The station was safe and we were safe and all was well. After so long, all was finally well again. The doctors worked hard all the time. Constant work. Then, suddenly, it wasn't safe. There was a change. We felt it. It was wrong. Not safe anymore. I called for help… called and called… kept calling… but when… when the help came… it wasn't help…"

Al waited but she didn't get usefully specific. He decided to try a different tactic.

"Adam tells us you're called Oria?" he floated suggestively.

"Oria…" she repeated slowly. "OR14… Doctor Reynolds used to call me Oria…" Her face scrunched up miserably and she looked up with tears in her eyes. "He shot him! The blonde man shot Doctor Reynolds! They shot my doctors!" She clenched her lips together as her chin trembled and stared Al straight in the eye. "I killed them."

"You killed someone?" he replied carefully.

"The ones I could reach. The ones who killed my doctors," she said. "I was… I was so… so angry… so upset. I… I couldn't… I had never felt these feeling before. I felt things. I acted on them. I hurt those who hurt me." She looked down, touching her torso and pressing a hand repeatedly against the front of her dress like she was testing for damage. "How am I not dead too?"

"Honestly, it might have been a close-run thing," Al admitted. "If we hadn't gotten you out of there…"

"They saved you," Slug told her. "I'm sorry about your people, but I promise you, you're safe here. No one is gonna hurt you on this ship."

Al took a deep and silent breath. He loved Slug's compassion, but he really wished she hadn't said that. They didn't know what the situation was yet. Sure, if this tiny pale lady had managed to kill some of Eric's people because they shot her doctors he was all for giving her a gold star, but they didn't know the full story yet. Did he think a unit of Oberon soldiers had just gunned down a room of unarmed civilians? Yes. Did he think it was entirely unprovoked? Unclear. Did he think that the only person to survive the slaughter was potentially highly dangerous? Absolutely.

Still, it was hard to think of her as a weapon when she appeared more and more like a girl, sitting curled up on a reclined med-chair and wiping pitiably at her tears. Slug grabbed some tissues from her pockets and offered them to her, helping to dry her eyes and comfort her. Al sighed quietly to himself. One of them had to be a decent person. Sometimes he wished it could have been him.

Everyone else was still watching nearby. Lani was taking in the situation with curiosity and suspicion. Sione was keeping a half-eye on everyone while he continued to scroll through his data. Adam was staying close. He had perched himself on the side of the med-chair next to Oria's and he was watching her patiently.

"You never seen anyone get shot before, have you?" he asked.

She looked at him like she thought the question strange, but the expression quickly faded into something understanding.

"No," she replied. "I never saw a real gun before."

"You were calling for help before the guns got there, ae?" Adam checked.

Oria nodded. "Ever since the change. Ever since it stopped being safe. Long before the guns."

Al watched the two of them converse. An unsettling notion prickled the back of his neck. He felt like he was only seeing half the conversation. Coupled with the bizarre precognisant behaviour Adam had displayed a moment ago, he felt like Adam knew more about this than he was letting on. It was worth giving them a chance to get there on their own though. He wouldn't interrupt unless he had to. The kids seemed to be building a rapport.

"Do you know how you did it?" Adam asked.

The two of them looked at each other for a moment like they were communicating without words. But why Adam? Was it because he was the one who had picked her up from the rubble? Or did it have something to do with those barcodes? Al had spent so much time being worried about Adam's stint as a gangster during his stolen years, but perhaps he'd been worrying about the wrong thing. What had really happened to those kids?

Oria was struggling. She kept opening her mouth as though to answer, but reconsidering with a pained expression and closing her lips again. Distress stained her eyes.

"Hey, it's okay," Slug consoled her, rubbing the girl's shoulder. "You've been through a lot, and it's no worries if you can't answer right now. You just take your time. We ain't getting anywhere in a hurry. Drink up. We can leave you to rest for a bit if you want?"

"I can't think…" Oria muttered, kneading her temple. "Everything's so fuzzy…"

"You don't know the words, do you?" Adam asked. "I wanna know how you called for Al, but you can't explain it. Could you show us?"

"I can show…" she nodded.

Before anyone could ask her to wait, she closed her eyes. Al took a half step forward, but he was too late to stop her. A bright light flashed across his vision. He felt like the gravity turned off. Everything was white. He was suspended, floating, in an ocean of light.

Al-Amir Akiyama. You found me.

Reality hit like a freight train and he nearly fell on the floor. As the room came back into focus he could see Slug keeping herself upright using the side of Oria's chair. Lani was slumped against the doorframe and Sione was leaning on his console. Only Adam was standing without aid. He had one hand over Oria's, helping to hold her mug steady as she drooped in the chair.

"You doing okay?" he asked her.

"Tired…" she muttered.

"Ae, okay, that's fair," he told her. "You wanna have a rest and we'll come see you after?"

She nodded sleepily.

"You holler if you need anything, ae?" he instructed her.

Al realised they were being dismissed from their own med-bay, and if anyone had a problem with it, they were going to have to take it up with Adam.

CHAPTER TWENTY-TWO

It felt like evening when they all sat down to eat. It felt like dinner with the family, just somehow even weirder than normal. Slug had been reheating sapasui for everyone. Adam told them Oria was still resting, but they should save her some. Al had no problem with feeding the girl, but he was going to need some better answers than the ones they'd had so far.

"Don't worry, Chief," Adam assured him as they ate. "She'll tell us all she can, when she can."

"And you know this?" Al raised an eyebrow.

"Yeah," Adam nodded. "She's good people. I seen it. I dunno how to explain it, but I just keep seeing things and I know they're true."

"Visions of unexplainable shit aren't exactly trustworthy, Adam," Al told him. "And you're what? Seeing the future now? That thing with her name and the tea? You're the first person in this system that I've ever heard of having actual precognition."

"You sure it ain't trustworthy, Chief?" Adam asked, shoving noodles in his mouth. "I mean… what's these last few weeks been for everyone if it ain't been seeing random visions and dreams? Isn't that what got you to bring us out here?"

"He's got you there, boy," Sione commented.

Al looked over to the doctor. "This isn't scaring you, Sione?"

"Oh, it's scaring me shitless," Sione chuckled. "But I been reading about it all afternoon and it somehow makes it both better and worse, ae."

"I had a nap and I didn't dream," Lani blurted. "I actually got some fucking sleep without seeing prettyboy here."

"So it's over?" Slug asked. "We found her? We did it? Why does she need Al?"

"Na, it ain't over," Adam shook his head. "It might be different, but it ain't over. I'm still seeing stuff, even if you ain't, cuz."

"What did you read, Sione?" Al asked, trying to keep everyone on track. "What do we know?"

"Not as much as we'd like," he replied. "They were doing experiments with that girl for twenty years. All the test subjects before her died."

"Shit," Slug swore. "They were killing kids?"

"In the name of science," Sione sighed. "They were experimenting with humans and the Goo."

"They what?" Al demanded coldly. "That stuff dissolves everything it touches, and they were trying to put it in people?!"

"Don't lose your cool with me, ae," Sione warned. "I'm just telling you what I read. According to these notes I got from the Inanna, humanity has always had access to the Goo."

"What the fuck, Dad?" Lani scoffed. "The Goo was gone for two hundred years. Everyone knows that."

"Oh, well, excuse me for being stupid!" he huffed at

her.

"What do you mean we've always had Goo?" Slug interrupted, heading off the fight.

"They found it near Pluto," Sione elaborated. "They found traces — relics — of non-human technology near Pluto, back in the solar system of Earth. They gathered everything up, including roughly three litres of a strange substance they had to contain with magnets, and they brought it back to Earth."

"That was our first contact with the Goo?" Al asked.

"According to this history," Sione answered, solemnly twisting up noodles. "The technology they found was what humanity used to build the rift gate that brought us out here. They think the one they found had crashed out on the edge of our solar system. They tried to study the Goo they had contained… and they failed for two hundred years. Scientists lived whole lifetimes secretly studying it out here in the orbit of Gilgamesh. It wasn't until the Goo had destroyed Earth, traversed the gate, and eaten Gilgamesh that they were able to do anything with it." He paused for a moment, letting the noodles slide back onto his plate and shaking his head like he'd lost his appetite. "Humanity has touched something we don't understand, and we don't know how to put it back in it's box. Now, instead, they found a way to put part of their sample inside a little girl. They don't even know what she is anymore. All they discovered was that after the Goo ate the planet it seemed to settle. It became more malleable, and they could infuse it into a human without killing them. Now they have a child called 0R14, affectionately dubbed

Oria by the Chief Scientist, that seems to have two consciousnesses."

"She's not a child, Uncle," Adam told him. "She's a lady, and they knew that, even if they didn't treat her like one."

"That's very admirable of you, Adam," Sione smiled at him. "But you gotta admit this whole situation's bigger than it looks, ae? If the scientists working the project didn't know what they'd created, you really think we're going to work it out?"

"We have to," Al replied. "Someone has to work out what's going on – why was Oberon involved? What's it got to do with me? Are people in danger again? Is our system in danger?"

"All good questions, boy," Sione sighed. "I will keep reading and let you know what I find."

"Maybe keep an eye on the weird girl too, ae?" Lani suggested nervously. "Got nothing against her personally, y'know, but y'all telling me we brought Goo onto our ship in her body is making me real fucking nervous…"

"Serious butt clenching going on, huh?" Adam teased her.

"Serious butt clenching, cuz!" she shook her head. "I don't like it."

"Chill," Adam advised her. "Oria ain't gonna hurt anyone. She ain't like that."

"Thanks Adam, but maybe next time you decide to kidnap a new girlfriend, who happens to be a freaky-looking Goo-hybrid, you could run it by the crew first?" Lani snapped.

"Hey!" Slug retorted sharply. "It's not like that and you know it, so back up."

"What? He's psychically linked to the freak but you just wanna ignore that?" Lani pushed.

"She's not a freak," Adam said. "She's just different." He was trying to sit impassively, but something shifted in him as he said it. It wasn't threatening, or rather, it didn't want to be, but silence reigned and everyone froze nonetheless. He looked Lani in the eye, and it was clear she instantly regretted speaking, despite his patient tone. "I didn't kidnap her. Chief said to bring her, so I brought her. We weren't gonna leave her to die on that exploding station. You don't get a say in that. It's his call to make and he made the right one. That's why Al's in charge – he makes good choices. Oria's good people. She deserved to be saved."

No one disagreed. Someone swallowed loudly.

"That was very well said, Adam," Slug praised.

"Thanks sis," he nodded.

Adam stood and Al could feel himself draw back, along with nearly everyone else. He wanted to justify to himself that it was simply a space thing. Adam was someone who expanded when he moved, and you didn't want to be in the way. It wasn't because it felt like if you did the wrong thing he could rip your head clean off your neck.

"I'm gonna take her some food now," Adam announced. "We good?"

"We're good," Al assured him. "She's our guest. You let us know if you need anything."

"Hai," Adam nodded obediently. He dished up an

extra bowl and headed off to the med-bay.

Al watched him go. So did everyone else. He didn't need to explain to them that they had to take the situation gently. Gentle might not be in Lani's nature, but they all knew what was required here and drawing attention to it was just condescending. Watching Adam now, thinking about the Inanna, he couldn't help but remember what Slug had said about the similarities between him and Adam. He hadn't liked hearing it when she said it, and the notion was even more uncomfortable now, but he couldn't help but notice that Adam followed orders like he was in the army.

That military style training was drilled in. It made perfect sense, even if Al hated it, but he felt like he understood what she'd meant now. In his own way, Adam had been raised in a private army. He knew the rules, knew the discipline, knew what it took. There were similarities. It was nice to have someone around who followed orders and did as they were told, who trusted him unquestioningly. It had felt strange but comforting to have Adam tell Lani that Al was in charge because he made the right calls. Now he just had to live up to it.

***

She reminded him of a yuki-onna. Some of the elders had told stories of old myths, leftover bygones of Earth culture that no one had truly given up. In the winters and out along the ice mines, the old men had talked about the snow women. That's what she made him think of, an icy maiden that would melt in a bath or vanish in a gust of wind. Her fingers were cold to the touch, but Adam told himself that had more to do with the minimal clothing she wore and the fact that she'd been lying still for hours than because she might actually be made of snow.

Besides, she was devouring hot sapasui and wasn't melting. Yōkai weren't real. He knew that. Mostly. It wasn't something he'd had to try and convince himself of since he was a kid though. Not since cold nights staring into space through a tiny port window, sore and exhausted from hauling ice out of the asteroid mines, and wondering if the things he saw in the dark really were snow women hiding in the ice.

It didn't help his superstition that she had turned down a blanket or jacket. He'd asked if she wanted anything but she had shaken her head and declined, shoving noodles into her mouth like it was her first meal in weeks.

"This is so good!" she praised enthusiastically, noodles trailing from her mouth to the bowl as she held it near her chin. "It's even better than soup! Soup was my favourite, but this is the best food I've ever had!"

"Yeah, I don't imagine there was a lot of variety on that station, ae," Adam smiled patiently. "Self-sustaining is one thing, but you guys were cut off from the rest of the galaxy for a couple of decades. If you didn't have it, it figures you did without."

Oria looked up at him with big eyes, blinking slowly. She reached a hand up and wiped her chin with the back of her wrist. There was something hypnotic about her eyes, and she always looked at him like she was waiting for him to elaborate. He wasn't used to being the one who had to carry the conversation.

"This ship…" she began, but trailed off, struggling. She squeezed her eyes shut and lowered her face, scrunching it up like she was fighting to remember something.

"You okay?" Adam asked, placing a hand on her shoulder.

"I don't know," she muttered into her nearly empty bowl. "Food good. Mind…" She shook her head.

"Food good, brain not so good?" Adam supplied.

She looked up again, her pale features softened by a rueful smile and accompanying nod.

"There's no pressure," he assured. "You know that, ae?"

"There is," she insisted. Her eyes met his intently. "We're running out of time."

"For what?" he asked.

She pinched her lips together in frustration. He could see the strain squeezing the corners of her eyes. She didn't know what. He could understand how aggravating that could be. There was nothing as infuriating as knowing there was something important you couldn't remember.

"Hey, you can't force these things," Adam sighed, relaxing back. "Eat up, do something else, have a rest. You'll wake up in the middle of the night and remember. That's always the way."

She sighed deeply and finished her noodles. The slurping was accompanied by more noises of appreciation that made Adam grin.

"I think this batch is my mum's recipe," he told her. "All the aunties have their own take on it."

"So good," Oria gushed, wiping her chin again as she finished. "I could eat that for every meal."

"Wait 'til we get you on pai fala," Adam grinned.

She nodded eagerly and looked around. Her eyes drifted to the window, entranced by the view beyond. He knew that look, knew that awe. It made sense. They hadn't talked about it yet, but Adam was confident that stars were new to her. She had been living in a station inside a ball of glowing Goo for twenty years. She hadn't even had sky.

Just like that he could see something again, something not yet real, but that might be. His visions didn't make any sense. He could see the stars, although it wasn't immediately obvious where. He was looking at them through the visor of his spacesuit. *Hotaru* felt solid beneath him, but gravity was non-existent. Only the pull of magnets kept him clamped to the ship. Oria was with him. She was staring at the sky, without a spacesuit. It couldn't be real. Not with her exposed to space like that. She was smiling at the stars. It felt like the other visions. There one second, gone the next. He didn't know what to make of it.

"What do we do now?" she asked. Her voice seemed wiser than it had a moment ago, and he wasn't sure if she was asking in reality or in the vision. The two still felt like they were mixing.

"I dunno…" he muttered, waiting for reality to fade in properly. He blinked, totally and completely back in the med-bay. She was watching him curiously and he felt like he needed a better answer than that. "I could show you around the ship if you want?"

She nodded. He motioned her up and led her from the med-bay. They dropped off her bowl at the kitchen, and voices down the hall indicated everyone else had migrated up to the bridge. He pointed out the cabins and the bathroom, drifting towards the bridge. He wanted the others to get used to her, and the view was the most impressive from there.

Oria was distracted though. Her bare feet crossed the metal floor soundlessly as she wandered slowly around the console towards the back corridor. Adam followed her. He knew he should get her some mag-boots to help keep her steady on the ship, but he also knew she wouldn't take to them. He didn't know how he knew that. It was just one of those things across time that bled into his system.

"You wanna go that way?" he asked, watching Oria drift to the engine room door and press herself against it.

"What's in here?" she asked.

"That's engineering," he answered, tapping the button and letting her in. "This is where I earn my keep on the boat."

She stepped lightly across the grated floor. He followed her in gently. Oria went straight to the core. Her thin, ghostly fingers reached out and touched it tentatively. She dragged her fingertips across its edges, tracing patterns seemingly only she could see. He watched her duck agilely around the massive conduits.

It was almost too late when he realised what she was about to do.

"Wait, don't!" he yelled, chasing after her.

Oria pressed herself against the back of the engine. Adam swore, trying to get around the core and the coolant lines to reach her. He couldn't get through the crawl spaces. Those were Slug's domain. Oria was still holding the engine. Adam paused mid-struggle and watched. She wasn't burning. She held the side of the engine like she was hugging a copper statue. Her cheek was pressed against it and her opaque skin stayed pristine and undamaged against the metal.

"Listen..." she whispered over the rumble of the engine. Oria smiled, eyes closed, pressed to the ship. "She's breathing..."

Adam stood there mutely. There was nothing to do but nod. Yeah, sure. She was.

"Constant breathing... never faltering..." Oria murmured, holding the engine and listening to it like creation's biggest shell. "She knows what she's doing."

"That makes one of us..." Adam muttered.

She opened her eyes again and looked at him.

"You know what you're doing, Hogosha," she told him.

It felt like a long time since he'd answered to that name. He didn't mind, but he didn't want Slug to know.

"Call me Adam," he replied.

"Adam Tanaka," she nodded. "But you are still, and never stopped being, the Guardian."

"Is that why I'm here?" he asked, braced by the core. He watched her intently as she let go of the engine and stepped away again, completely unharmed. There was a wisdom in her eyes that hadn't been there when they entered the room, but it was pained. He knew that look. He'd seen it so many times, in so many faces. It was the look he had seen in the face of Oyabun the last time they had met. But this was not goodbye. "You don't know," he alleged.

"I don't know what I don't know," Oria muttered, slipping back through the coolant lines towards the core. "And I don't know what I do know. Everything is different and confusing. I am… broken."

"Everybody's broken," Adam told her as she reached him, her face barely reaching the middle of his chest when they were both standing close. "That don't make you special."

"What is it?" she asked, tilting her head back to meet his eye, "when everyone is broken?"

"Seikatsu," he answered.

She blinked at him. He stepped back, relaxing his stance and giving her space to move. She followed him to the edge. Her head stayed tilted and her eyes stayed on his.

"What you're feeling is normal," he told her. "All of it. You're dealing with trauma. You're dealing with exploration, and the overwhelming struggle of the new. Life happens to everyone. Sometimes it's chill, and sometimes it hits you over the head like getting clipped by a speeder bike. If you don't feel like you're drowning every now and again, you ain't doing it right."

"What is drowning?" she asked, swinging herself curiously against the security rails and peering down at the lower level.

"It's when you suffocate," he replied. "When you get liquid in your lungs and you can't breathe."

"How do you fix it?" she asked.

"Actual drowning you get the liquid out, use a tube or CPR, get someone breathing again," Adam shrugged. "I think this is more metaphorical drowning."

"The tube CPR doesn't work on the metaphor?" she checked.

Adam smiled. "Not literally, you'd have to extend it." He knew he'd lost her before he said it. She was confused again. The uncanny intelligence that had blossomed in her eyes when she had been touching the engine was gone. The girl from the med-bay was back.

"What is metaphoric CPR?" she asked.

"I got no idea," he admitted, his metaphors running out.

"What is not-metaphoric CPR?" she asked.

"It's a medical emergency procedure," he answered. "Chest compressions, you push on someone to restart their heart, usually with mouth-to-mouth, uh, fake breathing or whatever the docs call it. Your mouth breathes into their mouth to give them air and get their lungs working."

"How... rudimentary," she commented.

He laughed and gave a rueful nod. "You ain't gonna need it, Oria," he promised. "We got you."

She shook her head, smiling gently.

"You have undeveloped technology still," she chuckled and poked him in the chest with one sturdy finger. "I got you."

Her wilful certainty felt for a moment like arguing with a child, but the sensation passed as he realised with a strange insight that it actually felt like haggling with a friend.

CHAPTER TWENTY-THREE

The hum of the engine filled Al's subconscious. It was a strangely comforting drone as he lay there warm and naked in his bunk, Slug snuggled up beside him. She was still asleep and he wished he was. He'd dozed for a moment, but peace was eluding him. The stress of the last few weeks felt like it was beginning to crack his sanity. Maybe it had been foolish to believe everything could be over so easily once they reached the Inanna, but he didn't know what else to do. His entire life had been supernaturally upended, and for what? What possible reason could humanity's greatest sin of experimentation have to call out him specifically?

Slug shifted in his arms, mumbling slightly in her sleep. Nothing intelligible. He held her slightly tighter, not wanting to wake her, but enjoying the feel of her skin on his and the way she sprawled contentedly across his body. He traced his fingers along her side, trailing the curves of her stomach and hips. She stirred.

"Sorry," he whispered.

"Don't be," she smiled sleepily. "I wasn't sleeping..."

He laughed at the lie and she scrunched her nose up reluctantly at being caught.

"Ae, okay, I wasn't dreaming..." she muttered.

He hadn't dreamt either. Lani was right. That nightmare was over. But Adam was right too, whatever was actually going on was far from done. Al just didn't know how it involved him anymore, despite feeling like he was chained to the centre of it. Slug nuzzled his shoulder.

"What's stirring your brain, shin'yū?" she asked.

"I don't know what to do..." Al sighed.

"What do you mean?"

"I just... I just feel like I'm waiting," he muttered. "I'm waiting to hear back from Lin. I'm waiting for orders. I'm waiting to get where we need to go. I was stuck on the *Hotaru* waiting for days just to get two hours on the Inanna, which was cut short before we could find any decent answers. I feel like I should talk to Oria, but I don't want to push a potentially dangerous and unstable traumatised kid. She and Adam seem to know each other, and there's every possibility they do, but they're both denying it. I tried going over some of the notes Sione stole — hoping that we miraculously picked up the key — but most of them are so technical I'm not sure he can make sense of them, I've got no chance."

"I get it's frustrating," she sympathised, kissing his shoulder. "But that's what travel is, shin'yū. That's what life is, isn't it? You talk like all the answers should come out of a bottle. Things ain't ever been that simple."

"I get that," he sighed. "But I've never had this much down time. I'm lost and I just want to know what's going on."

"You're living your life," she told him. "For the first time ever, you're just having to live as you, on a regular human timeframe, with a regular existence. No orders, no instructions. You're fumbling around in the dark like the rest of us."

"I don't think flying through the system trying to stop a giant planet-eating entity from waking up and destroying all life is all that normal," Al countered.

"But is that what you're doing?" she asked. "I know you're trying, Al, and I believe in you. Whatever it is, you'll get it done. But I'm listening to you and what I'm hearing are the same complaints I used to spout when you were gone, when I was stuck between jobs, or stuck working a scrap I hated. If you're ambitious, driven, then life ends up being a lot of waiting around feeling stuck and helpless and like you're not getting where you need to be fast enough — even if you're doing everything you can."

He lay in bed and stared at the ceiling. She wasn't wrong. He had felt that way before in his career. He could imagine it being the same for her. Patience was hard. It didn't come to him naturally, not for things like this. It was strange how he could be so patient working a job, stalking a target, building a confidence, yet when it came to his own life, his own progression, all that patience vanished. Poof, up in smoke. He didn't have time for himself.

"I don't know what to do…" he whispered, turning into her shoulder.

"You could do me again," she grinned.

He wasn't sure if she was teasing or inviting, but it

sounded suspiciously like both. She drew into him as he kissed her. He scooped an arm under her, pulling her close.

The speaker above the bed crackled.

"Ae, Captains, you boning?" Lani called down to them.

Slug started to laugh and Al rested his face against her neck with a grimace. Reluctantly, he reached up and hit the button by the comms.

"Not helping, Lani," he replied.

"Finish quick and get up here," she ordered. "I got something you need to see."

"Send it down," he countered.

"Na, Al," she replied, and her tone was deadly. "I'm serious, cuz. Get some pants on and come see this."

***

Adam had never had to explain himself before. No one had ever been interested. Well, no one he'd been prepared to talk to had been interested in him. Police didn't count. He'd had to explain his actions before. That he could do. But that was something he knew. He always knew why he acted — why he'd stolen that item, why he'd killed that person, why he'd changed that coolant line. All those things had a reason. They made sense.

Oria was fascinated by him, and he had no idea what to do with that. He was fascinated by her too, but that was simple. He stuck by her, looked out for her, and listened to her. That's what you did for people you cared about. The lady had nothing, and she didn't deserve that. It was their responsibility to look after her now.

Sione was running more tests on her. That was fair, she was game. Adam was happy to sit with them, in case either of them needed support. Uncle Sione could be like that. He wasn't the kinda guy who was any good at hiding how he felt and, try though he might, Oria made him nervous. He was good at his job though, good bedside manner. Adam liked to watch it.

He didn't mind distracting Oria while she was scanned and injected. She was good about needles. Must be used to it. Sione was trying to get some kinda data from her barcode. She saw Adam's. Now she was interested. Something about being the object of her attention was strangely dreamlike, like being fussed over in a spa. Her little fingers traced up the ink on his arms like she was trying to read it. The craziest part was that he felt like she could.

She started at the barcode on his left wrist. Same as hers, or near enough. She looked at it, tracing over the lines with a finger like she knew what it meant and how it had been done. The lines were blurry with age now, but she could run the edge of her crystal white fingernail against them like she knew exactly what it had once been.

Her hands traced the other designs like they were connected. They weren't, except under her scrutiny he wasn't so sure about that anymore. The lines of the barcode bled into a waterfall and koi wrapped around his forearm; the water shifted as it went up into sakura branches holding an oni mask on the side of his shoulder. Her fingers followed the tattoos like braille until she came to the oni. Her hands rested either side of the mask and she brought her face close, staring it down like a real creature. He would have sworn, ink or not, it was the demon that blinked first.

"Okay missy," Sione called. "I'm gonna need your arm for a bit."

Oria held her arm out straight behind her, refusing to break her staring match with Adam's shoulder. Sione gave Adam a wry look over the girl's head, but Adam met the look expressionlessly. He didn't know how he was supposed to react, so he didn't. He just watched as Sione took two small vials of Oria's blood. Sione slipped the needle in at the crook of her elbow with gentle and practiced hands. She didn't move or flinch as he worked. The blood that came from her veins was as red as anyone else's. Adam didn't know why that surprised him. Maybe it was just the shock of the stark red against her abnormal skin.

She turned as Sione finished. Before he could seal the tiny puncture, she was touching it. Oria squeezed the hole with her fingers, smearing them with blood. By the time Sione turned back to her, after setting the vials in the compound reader, she was already drawing on her own shoulder with her blood.

"Ae, no! No, no, no, no, no, no!" he bid, hurrying back over and trying to pull her hand away. "That's not good. None of that, girl!"

"But I'm red," she insisted. "I'm the red one." She looked between them both and back to the roughly smeared demonic face on her shoulder. "Adam is blue. I'm the red one." With a very deliberate finger she dragged a mark down the bloody drawing, like a tear track on the oni's face.

Sione quickly medi-sealed the tiny needle puncture on her arm so that she couldn't make anything worse. He had that serious frown doctors wore when they were worried they were dealing with the severely mentality ill. Adam slipped off the edge of his seat and grabbed a couple of sanitary wipes from the dispenser, carefully taking Oria's hands in his and beginning to wipe her fingers clean.

He could feel her big white eyes watching him. It was uncanny, the way she could stare. He wondered if that was how people felt when he watched them. She didn't blink, not like real people did. Those eyes were waiting for approval. She was the red one. The oni who cried. He knew the story of the red and blue oni. He knew she knew too. Almost like the ink on his skin had told her. He was the blue one. That was how she saw him. He could live with that.

"You're not a monster," he assured her gently. "But if you need help, I got you."

She nodded. With permission, he cleaned up the mark on her shoulder. She thought she was the red one. She needed his help to befriend humanity. Wasn't that a joke. Or, maybe, that was the whole point.

They both looked up as the screen behind them beeped. Two small beeps, twice. Message incoming. Adam felt a faint twist in his stomach at the thought of Oria listening to the things Al's people might say about her, but when the message popped up it was from Tamati. Sione didn't wait to open it. He clicked the link and Tamati's smiling face appeared on the large screen.

"Everybody wave!" Tamati called, the camera jiggling as he held it up so that everyone in the background could wave and call out their greetings.

Sione smiled as he watched it. Adam recognised most of the family in the shot. They were all calling and talking over each other, sending their blessings. Oria hopped off the chair and approached cautiously, watching the video message with undivided fascination. Adam smiled slightly as he watched her. She'd probably never seen a call like this one. She'd probably never seen a family like theirs. At this distance the message would be at least ten hours old, but that didn't stop the others from being glued to the screen.

"Whetu sends her love," Tamati assured, walking from the loud kitchen out the door and into the quiet garden. "She's having a lie down at the moment. You know how it goes. Pregnancy is not treating her kind and her ankles have all swollen up. She looks like a balloon, ae, and she slaps me every time I say it," he laughed. "I miss you, aroha. Next time you go off to save the galaxy you gotta take me with you, yeah? These girls are running me ragged. I can't go five hours without someone reminding me I ain't the doctor and I don't get a say. Ah, I bet Lani's giving you just as much grief. Where'd we get such mouthy daughters, my love?"

Oria was watching the video like she was reading a book. Her mouth had almost opened in shock at the sight of the garden and her eyes were struggling to take everything in. She scanned the moko on Tamati's arms whenever it appeared in shot like she had read Adam's just before. He wondered what she could see, or even if she was just taken aback by the simple content of the message. That was always the first thing that had struck him about the family.

Even after these last years, he still found the simple way they loved each other inspiring and baffling. Oria struck him as the kind of person who probably hadn't seen a lot of love in her life. He could relate. The guilt of it was palpable, in so much as he could even feel it. These days he was surrounded by people who loved him, but he had no idea how to reciprocate. Protection was all he knew. It was all he could do for them. He was the blue one. He could take one for the team so that the other monsters could befriend the humans.

Maybe that was what was important. Maybe he could never truly feel like he belonged amongst other people, never quite fit in, always be left with a few screws missing, but he could still help. He could help the red one. He did his best to follow Slug's lead, Al's lead, keep his head down and be good. He could learn to be good. What was important was that they made him a better person. Oyabun had always said surround yourself with people who make you a better person. It was the best advice he'd ever got.

***

Al had decided he didn't want to know how and why Slug could dress herself completely in the time it took him to stumble into pants. He assumed most of it was overalls. Fast and easy. The rest of the why… no. No, he really didn't want to know.

They both clanked down the hall, boots hammering the metal floor as they hurried to the bridge. Lani was sitting at the controls and her face was grim. The horizon was dark with spots of bright lights as they headed for civilisation, but Lani had a screen open in front of her and the prognosis wasn't fun.

"What the fuck is that?" Slug demanded, leaning down beside her cousin to get a better look at the screen.

"Gilgamesh," Lani answered tightly. She pointed to a dusty cluster. "That's the Inanna."

"So what the fuck is that?" Al asked, knowing full well what the answer was but hoping desperately that someone might say something completely different.

"That's the Goo," Lani answered, exactly as he'd known she would. "It's moving. Pulling, drifting… something." There was a horrible pause as they considered this, followed by Lani's even more horrible hypothesis. "It might be following us."

"It might be?" Slug echoed.

"Yeah, it might be," Lani repeated. "It's pulling away from Gilgamesh, it's moving in a direction, that direction is the same as ours. It's coming our way."

"How far and how long?" Al demanded.

"I mean… not sure exactly," Lani muttered. Her voice was strained and he had a feeling she'd been sitting up here cursing to herself about not being paid enough to deal with shit like this. "We don't seem to be in immediate danger," she hesitated. "It's a good way behind us and not moving fast, but… y'know… that shit could change quick. Also, at this rate it's going to end up in Arthur's orbit…"

"Fuck!" Slug cursed in exasperation.

"How long do they have?" Al asked.

"I'm thinking a week… unless things change…" Lani answered with less conviction than Al had ever heard in her voice before.

"Fuck indeed…" he muttered. He pulled his comms device from his pocket and strode from the bridge. He still hadn't heard from Lin, and this was getting out of hand. He scoffed internally. Like it had ever fucking been in hand. He opened the link to send a new message. Nothing. Just static. No line. Something was jamming him.

"Lani!" he called back down the hall. "Do we have any—"

There was an ear-splitting crash. The noise and the force blew his consciousness from his body. There was a flash of pain. Then nothing.

CHAPTER TWENTY-FOUR

The first sound that came back was the ringing in his ears. Then there was pain. A lot of pain. Al blinked weakly. Warning lights were flashing red all through the corridor. Droplets of blood floated in front of him. Shit. They didn't have gravity and the blood was probably his. What the fuck had happened?!

"Lani…?" he called weakly, hoping that the comms were working, or at least that his voice might still carry to the bridge. "Slug?! Slug, are you okay?"

He tried to turn, to move. A sharp and sudden pain through his leg almost made him scream. He looked down. When the ship had crashed his mag-boots had stopped him from flying off and colliding with the wall at fatal speed, but his left leg was very obviously broken. Right one didn't feel fantastic either. Very tenderly, he reached down and switched the boots off, letting himself drift off the floor and easing the pressure on the break. He took a deep and steadying breath.

"Guys…?" he called out, clutching at the wall and slowly pulling himself back towards the bridge. "Slug? Can you hear me? Simone?!" He could hear the panic rising as his voice got deeper and his cries became yells.

They weren't the only sound. His concussed brain

didn't register until it was too late — until the door to the airlock cracked open as he neared it. The pressure stayed intact, but the end of a crowbar was visible.

Al instinctively reached for his weapon. Except he wasn't armed. He wasn't even wearing a shirt. Fuck! He pushed himself off as hard as he could with both arms, aiming for his cabin door across the hallway.

The mercenaries broke through as soon as he opened his door. He heard them yell, knew they'd seen him. They were fast. He threw himself into his room, praying he could hold them off. The gun was by his bed and he snatched it up, turning in mid-air and trying to brace himself against the bunk.

He fired through the doorway. There was a shout. A ricochet. He silently begged Allah not to let him miss. The next shot sounded more successful. Except it earned a counter. Al grunted as he took a bullet to the shoulder. His arm protested the new injury on top of the unaccounted damage he'd already sustained. He wheezed in pain, trying to keep hold of his gun. His eyes were watering with pain. Someone was storming the room.

Al fired again, but it didn't slow the armoured thug coming for him. He tried to push away again. They snatched for him. He dodged, swinging back to fire again. He never got the shot off. They grabbed him by the left ankle and pulled. Al screamed. He couldn't help it. The pain seemed to flare through his body. Everything went black again.

***

It felt like seconds, but he woke in the cargo bay. The A-grav was back on. He could feel it pressing on his injuries. His body hurt so much he was trembling, and his arms were bound behind his back. The bloody hole in his shoulder felt hot. The rest of him felt cold, except for his left leg which didn't feel anything except pain. It was throbbing, like a giant twitching heart he was half kneeling on.

"Al!" Slug's voice sounded right beside him. "Oh my god, Al!"

He'd never heard her so upset. Not even when he'd told her he was leaving. Fuck, he was so dizzy. Everything swam in and out of focus. He blinked desperately at the room. They were all there. His whole crew, all on their knees with their hands bound. He blinked again, eyes darting. Seven mercenaries. If he hadn't been injured it would have been a cinch. As it was… he started praying for a miracle. Allah hadn't let him down yet. He was choosing not to count the success of his last prayer. For all the good it had done, he was confident he hadn't missed.

Two of the mercenaries were wearing battle armour. Proper military grade shit. The kind that got made out by the Giants. The other five had armour vests under their clothes at least, if not full protection. Two had quick-AG helmets. One was wearing a conspicuous hat. These were no amateurs. They didn't work for chips. Eric's bounty. For one very strong and shining moment of agony, Al absolutely regretted not just taking Adam's advice and killing Maxwell when he'd had the chance.

Diplomatic fucking immunity. The good of the galaxy. It would have been too. Then all Oria's people might still be alive.

Someone else came stomping in from engineering. Another mercenary. That made eight.

"Checked the whole ship, Captain," they announced. "No one else here."

"Good work." The one who replied wasn't one of the armoured thugs. No. The one in the hat. Of course. Cliched, useless, stereotypical, garbage-eating, mother-fucking, space pirates.

Al knew he was going to die one day, but he would rise from the grave before he went down to toenail-munching donkey-breeders like these. Even as he thought it, someone grabbed him by the hair and pulled his head back. He discovered a wound on his scalp he hadn't noticed before. His teeth bared in a grimace as his whole body shook with pain.

"This the one we want then?" the mercenary holding him asked.

"Looks it," the Captain nodded. "We take him for the bounty. Space the others."

Al ripped at his bonds. The only way anyone was getting spaced was over his dead body. One hand nearly tore free. Everything in his torso pulled. His vision went black. It almost worked. He'd been so close to grabbing the gun pointed at his back. Blood from his shoulder was floating in little droplets before him, slowly growing in number. He heard his own breath falter. The room swam again. He kept nearly blacking out.

"Al!" Slug called his name again, more desperately this time. "You're killing him! Ah—!" Someone silenced her protests with a blow to the face.

"There must be some kind of arrangement we can come to," Sione pleaded.

A few of the mercenaries shared a shrug.

"We could sell them?" one suggested.

"And put up with their trouble until we get to a slave port?" the Captain countered. "I said space them."

Al willed himself to act, despite his broken body. It didn't work, but it didn't have to. Someone else had better luck breaking free.

For the first time in his life, Al couldn't imagine anyone he wanted on the *Hotaru* more than Adam. The giant grabbed both captors behind him, moving at phenomenal speed. Al could hear bones break as their skulls collided. Two mercenaries dead instantly. The others rounded on him, but he held the bodies as human shields as he charged the gunfire. He threw one corpse hard enough to knock over one of the armoured units, and took the gun from the other.

Adam shot like an enforcer. Al almost admired the skill. Whatever sides of the fence they'd grown up on, he could appreciate someone who knew how to kill for a living. At least, he could now that it was on his side. There was a blank yet primal bloodlust in Adam's eyes that spoke to a psychopathic proficiency in the art of murder.

Brains splattered the walls as Adam efficiently killed another two mercenaries. Now there was yelling. The Captain was screaming at their people to put down the dogs. Adam casually shot another thug dead as he moved to shield himself behind the second armoured captor.

Then one of them got a lucky shot. One lucky shot was all it took. Adam's hand flew to his neck as a bullet tore through his throat. Blood gushed between his fingers into the air like a spray of mist. Slug was screaming. Lani and Sione were screaming. Al wasn't. He knew as well as they did that a wound like that was fatal in a fight like this. That meant it was up to him.

A sound like a banshee split the air.

Al barely had enough brain power left to wonder what alarm had been triggered. He felt like his ears were bleeding. Only the Captain and the armoured mercenaries were left, but the Captain had their hands clamped to their ears and they were going down. So were the others, they just didn't know it yet. Al felt his heart skip a beat when he saw her, though from terror or awe he'd never know.

Oria stepped forward. He would have sworn she'd been bound with the rest of them but there were no signs of any bindings. Her skin changed colour like ink poured into milk. The darkness spread through her limbs and hair and eyes until she looked like a walking shadow of nightmares. She descended on the remaining mercenaries like a screeching animal. The horror of her savagery was almost enough to stir a tremor of pity.

All she did was touch them. Bullets sprayed through her like nothing, vanishing into her body like a pool of water. Her hands snatched at the helmets of her attackers and she smashed them together against the

Captain with the force of a much stronger creature. It would have hurt, but it was nothing. A feat that was utterly forgettable in the face of what happened next.

From the point of contact, her darkness spread. Just like the Goo, where her inky black hands had touched the armour, the vitruchal began to dissolve. It spread to metal and cloth and flesh without mercy. The mercenaries barely had time to scream as the darkness disintegrated them to dust and then to nothing.

Oria was already turning, dragging her fingers across the bodies of the fallen, reducing them to oblivion as she scampered like a feral beast across the ground. She was going straight for Adam. Al didn't even have time to yell to stop her. She reached him, pausing, crouched and hesitating as he lay on the floor where he had fallen, his hand still clutching his throat as his life bled out.

The change started in her fingertips this time. The slow bleed of light spread back, rushing through her hands and staining through her body. It wasn't just a change in tone, it was bright. Like starlight. Al saw her reach out, slipping her fingers under Adam's to press against his neck. Then the light became too much and he was forced to look away. The light was blinding, but warm. It eased his tremors, his pain. He could feel his head clearing and his thoughts steadying.

When the light died down she was just the weird pale girl again, kneeling on the metal floor of the cargo bay like nothing had happened. There was no sign of the mercenaries. There was no sign of Adam's injury, save that he was gasping on the floor holding his neck like he had no idea what had just happened.

Al ripped himself free of his bindings. It didn't even hurt. His shoulder wasn't bleeding. He stood, and his legs straightened with ease. For a moment he wondered if his mother had been right all along. No prayer for a miracle had ever been answered so conclusively before. He almost wanted to ask what had happened, but the question felt stupid. The answer was obvious, if impossible and horrifying.

Oria seemed to know that. She flinched to her feet, turning to face Al and meeting his eye in a panic. Before he could say something, before he could do anything, she spooked and fled. On quiet bare feet she threw herself up the stairs and vanished into the upper deck.

"Wait!" Adam yelled after her, scrambling to his feet and following. "Oria!"

Al just blinked and looked over at Slug. She was holding the side of her face, rope loose around one arm, and looked like she was in shock. Al did not blame her.

CHAPTER TWENTY-FIVE

Hotaru wasn't a big ship and Adam didn't have to chase Oria far. He knew where she was going. When he reached the med-bay doors he paused. They were wide open and his hands caught the doorway, slowing his pursuit. The place was a mess after the crash, clutter strewn everywhere, but at least the important things were secured. He watched curiously for a moment.

Oria paced back and forth by her reclining chair. Her long white hair drifted weightlessly around her, like the A-grav didn't work on her properly. It was like a processing glitch, like the simulation hadn't caught up or didn't know any better. She was fizzing. He could see her freaking out. She clutched at herself, muttering, whimpering.

"Hey," Adam called to her softly, stepping in as lightly as he could. "Hey, you're okay."

She shook her head, trauma written all over her face. Adam approached her cautiously and coaxed her nearer. Her hands flailed urgently and she shook her head, but she came closer.

"I'm the red one…" she gasped.

"No, no you're not," Adam assured. He pulled her gently into a hug, holding her close and rubbing her back comfortingly. "You're not a monster. You did good."

"They attacked!" she choked. "They attacked first!"

"Yeah, they did," he agreed. "You didn't do anything wrong."

She shook her head against him furiously, clearly too worked up to accept that right now. It sounded like she was sobbing, but Adam wasn't sure if she could produce tears. A faint glow emanated from her body again, but weaker this time. It stuttered and flickered, going out.

"Tube…" she gasped. "Need tube…" She tried to pull away from him, but he held her in firmly, worried she was about to fly off the rails.

"Oria, it's okay," he insisted. "Trust me. Just… just calm down, yeah? Just breathe. Y'know, deep breaths…"

"Can't breathe! Need tube!" She pulled away and patted her chest urgently. Her distress was absolute and he realised she was having a panic attack. He kept hold of her shoulders and crouched to meet her eye, trying to speak as slowly and soothingly as he could.

"You're gonna be just fine, ae? I promise. Oria, I need you to take a deep breath. You can do that, yeah? One deep breath. Come on." He breathed deeply, trying to show her how.

She screwed up her face behind her hands and he swore he heard more mutterings about red oni. Now he was taking the deep breath to calm himself. He stood again, trying not to roll his eyes, and brought her with him. He pulled her in tightly, one hand almost encompassing her tiny back as he held her close. She hung gently in his arms, her feet dangling by his knees, and her face buried in his shoulder.

"You ain't a monster, okay?" he insisted. "I seen monsters. I've been one. I know what that is. You ain't it, lady. Not by a long way."

"Drowning…" she whimpered.

He sighed, trying to work out a new way to explain it before she hyperventilated herself into unconsciousness. She saved him the trouble. He only realised what was happening a second before it did. She pressed her lips to his urgently. He kissed her without thinking. It felt like the only natural response. She was wrapped in his embrace, her hands clutching his cheeks, and her kiss was so insistent. He couldn't bring himself to refuse. Her trembling eased and her breath steadied. He could feel the panic ebb from her sigh as it entered his mouth. He slid a hand through her hair, holding her closer. She tasted like… nothing. Like air and starlight.

When she pulled away he didn't want to let her go, but he couldn't help himself as she slipped from his fingers. Now he was the one gasping. She set herself back on the floor. Two gentle fingers pressed themselves to his lips.

"It works…" she whispered, like she was surprised. "Rudimentary, but effective."

Adam decided now was a bad time to tell her that he had not explained CPR very well, and that she still had no idea what it was or how it worked, and had not actually used it in any way. He was glad she was feeling better though. It was easier to settle for a nod. Besides, he was not wholly unhappy with the way things had turned out. He was trying to work out how to explain that he wanted to kiss her again when he heard footsteps crashing outside the med-bay.

Slug and Lani appeared in the doorway as he let go of Oria and turned to meet them. They looked shaken. Unsurprising, given what they had just been through.

"Adam!" Slug gasped as soon as she was in the doorway.

"You guys okay?" he asked. He could hear Sione hurrying up behind them.

"Are you okay?!" she demanded, bursting in and grabbing him. "You got shot!"

"I'm good, sis," he assured, patting her back. "Oria here fixed me up like it never even happened."

Slug paused and looked behind him to the tiny ghostly woman who was miraculously half floating in his shadow. Sione reached the doorway shakily as Lani decided to enter, and the two of them came cautiously closer. Oria blinked curiously at all the attention.

"You just saved all of us..." Slug said to her slowly. "We'd all be dead without you..."

Oria pressed her lips together nervously. "They shot first..." she muttered. "They shot *Hotaru*."

"You did good," Adam assured again, publicly this time, resting a hand on her back.

"You did better than good," Slug nodded. She reached out gently and took Oria's hand in both of hers. "Thank you, Oria. You saved our lives — you saved Adam's life — we owe you."

"Life is not an owe," Oria disagreed. She took Slug's

hands in both of hers, mimicking the sincere gesture. Then she looked up at Adam and smiled a smile he swore was almost smug. "I am the red one."

He rolled his eyes. There was no persuading her.

"Ae, if you wanna be," he shrugged. "I don't think you're no monster though."

"You're not," Slug agreed. "You're not a monster, Oria. You're a hero. Arigatō."

"Ae, next time can you Goo them before they board us?" Lani asked.

"There will not be a next time," Sione barked. "No next time! Never again. It's over. Let's leave it at that and get home, ae."

"It's not over yet," Oria murmured, turning to look across the room.

Adam followed her gaze, but she was staring at a wall. More staring at something beyond the wall, he realised. She frowned. It was a micro expression, but he saw it all the same. Not a sadness, but a reluctance in her eyes. It was coupled with Slug's immediate fear. He knew that look. She was worried about Al. Before she could ask, Oria answered. There was no fear or grief in her tone. Just a resignation. She understood the necessity.

"Now it is over," she sighed.

***

The mercenaries had been flying a modified lightweight Washington-CR3. It was a bigger ship than the 02-Otashii, but not by all that much. There had been three other people on board, including the pilot. Al didn't know what they had heard, or not heard perhaps, over the comms when Oria had obliterated the rest of their crew, but they hadn't been expecting him. He got the drop on every single one. There wasn't much to be done about the blood and brains plastered to the walls, but as he released the airlock and watched the bodies drift out behind the ship into space he knew he wasn't going to have to explain any corpses to his people.

He scoured the ship top to bottom, hacked into its logs, and made damn sure there were no other survivors left to cause them any trouble. Finding the bounty from Eric just drove home Al's anger. A quiet and intimate fury. This was beyond personal now. It hadn't been that long since Adam had verbally placed his faith in him, and Al had just watched the kid get his throat shot out. If it weren't for the weird magic girl they'd picked up, Slug's brother would be gone, for real this time. Adam had said Al made the right choices, but staring down the bounty and mulling things over, he just wasn't so sure he could stick to that anymore.

Those heavy thoughts brought him back onto the *Hotaru*. His boots clomped against the floor as he came back into the hallway. Slug was coming towards him from the other direction. He wished he knew how to express the relief he felt at seeing her safe and well, but he couldn't even smile. It still felt too grim.

"Hey…" she greeted him, her tone utterly understanding, like she already knew. She snuck over, legs shaky and one hand out to steady herself against the wall. Her dark eyes were sympathetic, but touched with fear. The sight of it made him feel sick with guilt.

"Do we know the damage?" he asked, unable to find the words for anything else.

"She took a big hit," Slug sighed, reaching him. "They knew what they were doing. Shot out our main engine. We're honestly lucky we didn't explode. They musta known how to disable a ship with a single shot without destroying it."

"Their stealth tech is particularly good," Al conceded. "We never would have seen them coming. It's a solid tactic — for pirates. Easy enough to sneak up in the jet stream and target right through the engine gap. Total annihilation would be rare, and even if the other ship wasn't completely crippled they'd be hobbled enough to catch easily. We got lucky."

"That was more than luck, Al..." Slug shook her head, allowing herself a small smile and reaching out a delicate hand to rest against his chest. "That was some kinda miracle."

"Do you know where she is?" he asked.

"With Adam and Sione in the med-bay," Slug answered. "I think she was a bit spooked by it all, including what she did. Sione wanted to check her over and Adam's looking after her. After what she did for him I imagine it feels like the least he can do."

Al nodded. He tried to think of something to say. He wanted to say sorry, but it felt redundant. He felt like he needed to apologise, but knew the apology would just be for him. Slug would scold him for thinking it was his fault. She wasn't looking for blame or accountability, she wasn't that kind of person. She looked for solutions.

"We… uh," he swallowed uncomfortably. "We need to get the *Hotaru* up and running again. I… I don't want to pressure you… but you're going to have to take the lead on repairs. Maybe take Lani and raid the *Washington*? I don't know about you, but I'm not interested in trying to sell it or haul it. I say we scrap it for parts and call it a day."

Now it was her turn for an uncomfortable silence. One of her fingers traced a small pattern on his chest and she wouldn't meet his eye.

"… We could just abandon it," she muttered quietly.

"We gotta get the *Hotaru* working again," he countered. "That means finding repairs for a whole engine, and going nowhere, risking life support, while we do."

She nodded. She knew he was making sense. He didn't begrudge her the reluctance to go anywhere near that ship though. That made sense too. The two were not mutually exclusive. He raised a hand to touch her face and leant in to kiss her cheek.

"I swear it is completely safe over there now. Scrapper's honour," he promised.

"You're not even a scrapper, shin'yū," she teased.

"Assassin's honour," he corrected.

She didn't try and argue. She leant in and kissed him softly. Lovingly. The kind of kiss that told him she knew and there was a good chance they might never talk about it. His hands caressed her arms, eager to hold her close, but understanding that there was a time and a place, and that neither were now.

"I need to see Oria," Al sighed. "Chat to Lani. I think everyone will do better if we work together on this, but we gotta get our girl fixed."

"Yeah, we do," she agreed.

She kissed him again before they parted ways and he was grateful for the affection. It helped settle his nerves, if only to help convince him she was going to be alright. He wouldn't have wished that horror story on anyone, least of all his loved ones. They didn't deserve this.

When he got to the med-bay he found Sione alone. The doctor's round shoulders sagged beneath the bright floral pattern of his shirt. Every air about him was at odds with his joyful attire. Al watched him from the doorway for a moment. Sione was leaning on the bench with his back turned and it felt wrong to interrupt him, until Al realised he was just standing, almost unresponsive. He strode into the room loudly, making sure Sione had time to react if he wanted to. He didn't.

"Uncle Sione?" Al asked softly, approaching him. "You alright?"

Sione began to nod slowly, but he didn't turn immediately. There was a sag of resignation as he did. Al saw his traumatised eyes as he turned to look at him. That was a truly haunted gaze.

"I'm alive, boy," he sighed. "You hurt?"

Al shook his head. "Not anymore. I got caught in her blast and I think she stitched me up as good as Adam."

Sione nodded again. "Ain't she a little miracle?"

"Something like that," Al agreed, still not completely sure what she was. "Slug said she was in here with you?"

"I let her go off with Adam," Sione shrugged, half turning back towards the bench. "I put a monitor on her so that we can record the radiation and vitals as best we can, but there's nothing much else I can do with her. I've run all the tests I can think of — she is beyond what human technology can understand."

Al nodded. That seemed fair, if daunting. He sighed and rubbed his face like he could shift some of the mental exhaustion. It nearly worked.

"How about you?" he asked Sione. "How are you holding up?"

Sione shook his head and looked away. Al understood that look. Sione was still partially in shock. After everything that had happened, Al didn't blame him. The old doctor stared across the room with distant and sickened eyes. He raised a hand, fingers visibly trembling, and rubbed his short beard, massaging his quivering chin.

"It's okay not to be okay…" Al offered.

Sione gave a small scoff. He recited that to patients all the time. He needn't be told.

"I'm serious," Al insisted. "That… that shouldn't have happened. None of you should have gone through that. I should never have let you end up in that kind of danger. You didn't need to come with me…"

"Well, someone had to, ae," Sione snapped. He pressed his lips together, his nostrils flaring as he took a deep and calming breath. "Someone had to tag along, Akiyama. You think I was just gonna let my daughter — my reckless baby girl — and my sister's kids run off into the depths of space with a spy?!"

Al bit his tongue. He deserved that.

"Tamati and I talked it over..." Sione sighed, rubbing his face in frustration at the memory. "We knew we couldn't just let the kids run off with you in a spaceship. Someone had to stay with Whetu. He woulda been better here... but I had medical skills. It was easier for me to get the time off. He still got classes... but he... he's so much stronger than I am... he wouldn't..." Sione trailed off, his lips constantly distorting into distressed frowns. Tears stood out in his eyes. He grimaced painfully as he tried to hold them back.

"It's not about strength, Sione," Al murmured. "You never should have been in this position. I've been through shit, but I signed up for it. I've been shot and stabbed and poisoned and captured — all in the name of Titania — but I've never been as scared as I was in the hold just before, when you lot were in danger — when Slug was in danger. You guys are my family. The job has always been to keep family hidden and out of the way. I told Lin. I told her I didn't want this, I didn't want you in this and she had to find other people."

"What did she say?" Sione asked.

"She said I don't trust anyone else," Al admitted.

Sione snorted. "You don't trust us either. This only happened because you never told us what we were walking into — because of your rivalry with that boy! You two duking it out in life or death Chess for your puppet masters. That's all it ever is, and us little people get caught in the crossfire."

"Eric's a psychopath," Al argued. "Don't lump me in

with him like we're two sides of the same coin."

"Aren't you?" Sione challenged. "See… for all your training and experience, boy, they only trained you to be experienced in what they wanted you to be. I don't think you can see the bigger picture. They tricked you into wanting to be a hero — all nationalism and righteousness and that stubborn brainwashing that gets folks killed — like something out of a goddamn story."

"This isn't a story," Al snapped. "I'm out here with no fucking idea what I'm doing, trying to hold it together with a bunch of civilians who think I should have the answers, stuck doing fucking nothing while we sail between message points that should have been fucking phone calls! We never should have been out here in the first place, and Eric should never have been able to place the bounty that he did. Oria's the only reason any of us are alive right now, and I'm the only reason she's alive after what Eric did to the Inanna. So don't try and make this some superhero spiel about how we're reflections of each other or some bullcrap about good and evil. Ain't no one got time for bullshit stories."

He turned to go, already aware that he shouldn't have lost his temper, but half surprised that it had taken this long after all the time the crew had spent stuck on this ship.

"Sit your ass down, boy!" Sione ordered.

Al stopped. It was instinctive. Something primal from his childhood. He turned back and perched on the side of one of the medical chairs. For all that Sione had claimed his husband was stronger than he was and better suited to this job, he did an awfully good impression of him. Al swore that he had just flashed back more than twenty years to the back of Tamati's classroom. Maybe it wasn't intentional. Maybe people just inadvertently adopted each others mannerisms over time.

Sione shook his head wearily again as he looked at Al. He folded his arms and stared him down.

"Look, Al," he began firmly. "I dunno what's going on. I don't know what's happening with this girl we rescued, or this information we recovered, or how the Goo comes into it all, or how you got mixed up in it, but I do know there's a story here. There always is. That's what humanity does, no matter where in the galaxy we go. The one thing that always stays consistent is how we weave our tales of existence. You are in the centre of one right now, and you don't get to say you don't have time for it. Stories are important. Every mass bloodshed in human history was because of a story. We are on the brink of one right now — I can feel it in my bones. If that girl really is tied to the Goo, and you really are connected, then every civilisation in existence is going to come knocking, and you're going to have to know where to take the legend from there."

Footsteps sounded in the corridor and Al turned. Lani appeared in the doorway. She looked them over and gave Al a sympathetic grimace.

"You getting a lecture, cuz?" she asked.

"Something like that," Al replied. He felt like Sione had actually been on the edge of something. He also knew there was a piece missing.

"Dad, are you doing Pa's spiel about stories dictating the fate of humanity?" she accused.

Sione looked away, his face tightening around his eyes and mouth again. Lani slowed, reaching an absent hand up and anxiously scrunching her mohawk curls.

"Dad...?" she inquired softly.

"You know what he'd say to me now?" Sione sighed, a slight tremble in his voice. "Your Pa, he would say it was not about victories won. Na, na, na, it's never about the win — it's about resilience. Always has been. Humanity's tale is not one of victory, but of perseverance in the face of insurmountable odds. That is what we do. No matter what is done to us, we always get up and keep going. We began on one little blue planet far away and endlessly lost... look at us now."

Everything about his expression spoke to his desire to embody that resilience, but it was easier said than done. He looked over to Lani as she stood in the doorway. She watched him with concern, but couldn't maintain the tenderness. As their eyes met, her wry shield returned and her shoulders slanted with attitude.

"Ae, we gotta get you home," she commented cynically.

"How's that coming?" Al asked.

Her face said it all. He almost didn't want to ask, but he didn't have to.

"So, I got more bad news..." Lani muttered.

CHAPTER TWENTY-SIX

The immediate repairs had been surprisingly easy. Slug had been worried about trying to repair an Otashii with pieces from a Washington, but it wasn't impossible. The damage to the engine was the kind that needed to be cooled down and patched, rather than replaced. They must have been hit with some kind of stun weapon designed to incapacitate engines without destroying them. It was much smarter than what she had initially imagined which was the pirates rolling a dice on blowing up the ships they attacked. Part of her wanted to steal it.

The notion of scrapping the Washington was mellowing in her mind. Once she'd actually seen the place it was less scary, and the fear all but vanished when she got to work. When she could get in the zone everything else faded. Adam was out helping her. Apparently, Sione didn't need to do much with Oria and the girl was tired after her bout of magical heroism. Adam had left her to rest while he helped Slug get the ship working again.

They had finished welding the new panels on. Slug was magnetised with both feet and one hand to the side of *Hotaru* as she opened another hatch to check the wiring. It looked good. Thank god.

"Right, bro, we're good here. Let's close her up," Slug told him.

"Hai," Adam answered, letting her move back before he clipped the hatch shut. He took the wrench from his belt and began to bolt it shut properly. The first bolt went in easy. Slug didn't see what happened with the second. She was thinking about what to check on next, and whether they should head in and see if they could get all the engines running again.

The first thing she noticed was the wrench beginning to float away. Instinctively, her hand lashed out to grab it. It was too far. Her fingers knocked it and sent it spinning. She demagnetised her hand and stood upright to get the reach she needed, nabbing the wrench.

"Adam!" she exclaimed, looking down again as soon as she'd caught it.

He was still hunched over, primed for work, but he was completely still. Slug couldn't see his downturned face through his helmet. She crouched down and grabbed his shoulder.

"Adam?! Adam, what's wrong?!"

He didn't answer. She peered at his face. His expression was stunned but blank, unblinking. She stashed the wrench in her belt and hit the health display on his suit. It sprang to life in a bunch of glowing, blinking stats. At the same time she felt him move again, saw his breath fog his mask.

"Adam!" she called. "Are you okay? Your heart's racing like crazy, did you get a shock or something?"

For a moment all she could hear over their comms

was his breathing. She checked his expression again. He still looked stunned, but he was blinking.

"Where am I...?" he muttered numbly.

"You're outside *Hotaru*, we're patching her up..." Slug reminded slowly, trying not to panic. "You just... you just froze up. Adam, what's wrong?"

"Nothing..." he muttered, shaking his head. "It's nothing." He stood upright, but the zero G exacerbated an unsteady wobble and he couldn't keep back a quiet, "woah..."

"It don't look like nothing," Slug argued. She grabbed onto him and pulled his arm around her shoulders. "Come on, we're getting you back inside."

He didn't fight her. Given the dazed look in his eyes she wasn't convinced he was completely there. The thought was bone-chillingly terrifying, but she couldn't panic. She just had to get him inside and Sione could take a look at him. He'd be okay.

Every time the memory of Adam getting shot flared in her mind she felt like she was going to puke. It was hard not to think about it. The work had helped. It had felt normal. Almost normal enough to stop her shaking and blank her trauma. But now this... Adam fading in and out... Fuck, he'd nearly died!

"Just a little bit further," she coaxed, dragging him with her.

"I'm okay," he gasped as she pulled him back inside the ship. "I'm good, Slug. Really."

She sealed the doors and let the airlock stabilise before clicking back her helmet. He followed suit, much slower. Now that she could see his face her anxiety eased slightly. He still looked wild-eyed, but he also looked present in his body.

It was all well and good for him to assure her, but she wanted Sione to give him the all clear before she would let him outside again. Besides, she might as well test the engines now while she got her brother properly scanned. The others would be eager to get real power running through this place again. Bare minimum wouldn't cut it for long.

****

Al was having one of those moments when he knew deep in his bones that some asshole on this ship had mused after the shooting that things couldn't get any worse. He rubbed his weary face, busying his hands so that he didn't try and punch something. Lani had forwarded her display down to the med-bay and Sione had it up on the big screen. The three of them were all staring at it. Al could sense their dread emanating from them. His was pushed down to make way for frustration.

"It's chasing us…?" Sione whimpered.

"I'm not sure, Dad," Lani admitted. "But it sure fucking looks like it. At least, it's starting to look like it. There's a big spike coming right in our direction, trailing all the way back to Gilgamesh. Also, see this," she zoomed in and played through a small section of video. "It jumps. By my count it was when we were about to get spaced. When Oria melted those dudes and saved us."

"How big is that jump?" Al asked, not really wanting to know the answer.

Lani gave him a look. Fuck, he really didn't want to know the answer. It was crucial, and he had to know, but he didn't want to.

"It jumped about fifty million ks faster than our monitors could follow," Lani finally answered. "And it's moving faster now than before the jump. It's spread through Arthur's orbit. If it doesn't move, they're gonna hit it within a week."

"Fuck!" Al cursed.

Lani and Sione flinched from his anger. He pinched the bridge of his nose, grimacing.

"That's a whole planet and seven moons they have to evacuate in under a week," Al muttered, half to himself. "Where the fuck are they going to go?"

"That's for the United Planetary Systems to work out," Lani countered, flicking another window up on the screen with multiple tabs of media coverage displayed. "Obviously the news has it already. Everyone's been watching this shit since before we got to it. Arthur was the best source of info on the Goo and Gilgamesh, so it makes sense that they're freaking the fuck out now. We gotta work out what we're going to do to stop it from catching us."

"This jump," Al pointed at the screen. "That proves the Goo is connected to Oria — that it's got a link with her."

"Not exact proof," Sione muttered. "But a very high probability..." They all stared at it in silence for a moment before Sione voiced their thoughts. "That girl saved our lives, Al," he reminded.

"Yeah, she did," Al nodded. "And she might need to save a lot more people than just us." He grimaced again. "Lani, how much time have we got before that shit catches up to us?"

"I can run the numbers," she offered. "But even if we get moving again I still think we're talking hours, not days."

Al resisted the urge to curl up in a small ball and cry. He could do that after he fixed this situation, or died trying.

"We have to go speak to Oria," he sighed. "Anyone know where she is?"

"With Adam," Sione reminded.

"Na, Adam's out helping Slug fix *Hotaru*," Lani disagreed. "I think he left her to take a nap in his bunk. Ship might be able to sustain air and water for a good few people, but we didn't kit it out with all that many rooms. Not really sure where to put her — and I figure Adam owes her for saving his reckless ass."

"Adam was trying to save our asses," Sione pointed out.

"Let's just… go see if we can find her," Al sighed, trying to head off the impending argument.

He led the way out of the med-bay and around the corner to Adam's room. The door was shut, but that was hardly a surprise. He knocked and called her name. No answer. Lani gave him a shrug. The door wasn't locked so he hit the button. It slid open. Inside, the lights were on and something had managed to build a nest of blankets and pillows on the bunk.

"Oria…?" Al called.

The pile of bedding slumped sideways with a muffled groan and a long snore.

Sione gave a small chuckle, softening his state of intense distress. He cupped one cheek and shook his head as he looked on.

"Sometimes it's hard to see her as anything but a little girl, ae?" he commented.

From down near the airlock a call echoed down the corridor.

"Uncle Sione!" Slug's voice rang out.

"Ae, ae, what's happening?" Sione turned first, with Al and Lani following his attention.

They all saw Slug half dragging Adam past the kitchen towards them. She looked frantic and he was trailing behind her, dazed as a stunned moose.

"Something happened out there," Slug called to them. "Adam blanked on me. I dunno what's wrong. Can you check him?"

"I'm fine, sis," Adam protested wearily. "You don't gotta freak."

"You don't get to make that call," she insisted, hauling him down to the others.

"Come with me," Sione motioned to him as soon as they reached them. "Tell me what happened." He put a hand on Adam's back and guided him to off to the med-bay as soon as Slug dragged him within reach.

"Don't tell me she's bad?" Lani grimaced to her cousin.

Slug shook her head. "We got her patched. Might as well test the engines and see if she'll run. Adam got his work done before he blacked out. I dunno what's wrong with him, but after what happened down in cargo..." she trailed off anxiously.

"Dad will fix him up," Lani assured, catching Slug around the shoulders and squeezing her comfortingly. "But if you wanna know more about what she did to him, Al's about to interrogate sleeping beauty here."

"We do, unfortunately, have more pressing concerns," Al admitted, stepping into Adam's room and approaching the bed.

As he neared, Oria's little face poked sleepily out of the nest, hooded in blanket.

"Hey," he greeted her, striding over and crouching down to face her. "Sorry to disturb you, but we've got some problems I'm hoping you can help us with."

"Is Adam okay?" she asked. "Does he need air?"

"I'm sure Sione's got it covered," Al reassured her.

"I think... I think I was dreaming about him..." she muttered, scrunching her face up and massaging her sleepy eyes.

"That's... very cute. You two can catch up in a minute," Al brushed over that. "Oria, the Goo, that big gooey thing that ate Gilgamesh, the one that destroyed the Inanna, it's following us. Do you know anything about that?"

She blinked at him innocently and shook her head.

"Are you sure?" he pressed. "This is really urgent, Oria. That stuff jumped massively when you saved us from those pirates. It's only a few hours away. I know your doctors were running experiments on you with it. It seems like you're connected to it, and if it catches us, there's a good chance we'll all die, so I need to know everything you know and I need to know it right now."

"I don't know anything…" she murmured. "I… I'm not sure…"

Al shook his head at her and stood. "Sorry, Oria, but I'm going to need better than that."

Behind him, Slug was giving Lani a startled look.

"It's only a few hours away?!" she exclaimed.

"Maybe more than a few, but it's gaining pretty rapidly," Lani grimaced. "I dunno what to do."

"We start by getting *Hotaru* going," Slug ordered. "I took what we need from the Washington, everything else we cut our losses on. Cut her loose and take off."

"What if *Hotaru* craps out on us?" Lani countered.

Slug shook her head. "Not worth it. My baby's gonna be fine and we gotta put as much distance between us and that dead ship as possible. Don't want anyone connecting us and them or pinging their identity as us. Ditch 'em and ride."

Lani nodded curtly and hurried off, racing down the corridor to the bridge. Slug half moved to follow, but paused and looked back at Al and Oria, choosing to stay.

"I don't got better," Oria looked up from her blanket nest.

"What is it? What does it do?" Al demanded. "You turned into something like tar and disintegrated eight bodies in seconds — just like that stuff did when it took Gilgamesh. Then you go all glowy and heal all of us? I'm guessing that's tied into the Goo, yeah? So, how does it work? Can you talk to it? Can you make it stop chasing us and go back?"

She shook her head fiercely.

"Oria, people are going to die," Al warned her. "That spike trailing after us is right through Arthur's orbit. Billions of people are in danger right now. I need to know how to put that thing back in its box. You are the only clue we have."

"I don't know!" she protested. "It just… it just wants the pain to stop…"

"What pain?" Al asked. "What pain? Is something hurting it? Can we fix it?"

"It…" she screwed her face up and buried it in her hands. "I don't know. It… it wants to be whole again."

"Be whole again?" Al echoed. "What… what is that? Whole? Is that about you?"

"No," she shook her head. "It's nothing to do with me. I… I can barely feel it. I… I think I felt it when it jumped. When I changed. I… I felt something… but that's gone now. It's all gone."

"Oria," Al knelt again and grabbed her blanketed shoulders. "It can't be gone. You have to get it back. The entire system could be riding on this."

"But I… but I can't…" she muttered.

"Too. Fucking. Bad," he told her. "You told the entire damn galaxy I was going to be the one to fix this, so now you're going to help me fix it. That's it. There is no plan B. If we don't do this, everyone dies and you ruined my life for nothing!"

Oria flinched from him, but he only tightened his grip. She wasn't getting away from this. In the depths of the ship, the *Hotaru's* engines roared into life. They started to move. That might buy their crew more time, but it wasn't helping anyone in the Galileo orbit.

"It's not about you," she told him.

"It's a bit late to decide that," he sneered. Oria struggled in his hands.

"I can't help you…" she insisted.

"You don't have a choice," he countered. "You didn't give me one, so I won't give you one. What does it want? How do I stop it?"

"I DON'T KNOW!" she shrieked at him.

He didn't flinch from her. There was nothing to flinch from. No one with his training had ever been fazed by a raised voice. Not even the one that followed it.

"Hey!" Adam yelled, storming his own room. "What the hell's going on, Chief?"

Al let go of Oria and stood, glaring down at her. The look she returned was sullen, but there was no point trying anything else with that gorilla standing over her. Fresh from the med-bay, Adam had his space suit tied at the waist and every ugly inked face on his arms seemed to glower at Al like he was the one in the wrong. He gestured at Oria.

"We got Goo trailing right on our tail and your girlfriend can't even summon basic advice to help us, despite being the only connection to it humanity ever discovered."

"She'd help if she could, Al," Adam told him. "She ain't holding back on us."

"What I wouldn't give for your faith," Al replied cynically. He watched with tired frustration as Adam slowly, but painfully obviously, placed himself between Al and Oria. Al eyeballed them both. "When that shit hits this ship and kills us all, don't say I didn't try."

"That ain't gonna happen, Chief," Adam insisted.

"Why? Because that would be bad?" Al snapped. "I don't know if you've noticed our luck since setting out, Adam, but this is just the icing on our disastrous cake! You think everything's going to magically work out? The only shit that did was thanks to her, so unless she's going to pull another stunt without warning, we're screwed."

"Yelling at her isn't gonna get you what you want," Adam countered.

"In case you missed it, we're under a bit of time pressure, and asking nicely wasn't getting us anywhere either," Al argued. "What would you have me do instead? Sit and wait? Séance? Pray? I'll light some incense and beg Allah — let you know if he writes back."

Adam was unmoved by Al's scepticism. Al was aware that it was the kind of disparaging comment that would have gotten a rise out of his parents, not these members of his would-be family. Adam didn't give a shit about Al's faith or lack thereof. It was probably for the best. Al turned to go but paused for a moment as he crossed the room.

"Whatever this is about to turn into, Adam, when the shit hits the fan, I don't want to find out that the only thing that turns the magic on is shooting you." His tone left no space for doubt about the warning.

Adam all but ignored it. He kept his position in front of Oria, arms folded, until Al traipsed from the room. Slug was still waiting just outside the door. It shut as soon as he was out, but he wasn't sure if the switch had come from inside or outside. He honestly didn't much care.

"Adam wasn't wrong…" Slug began coolly.

Al sighed and crossed to the bench in the centre of the room, leaning on it wearily and staring into the blue light of the central command console. Slug gave his despair a dark look.

"What was your next step, Al?" she demanded. "Slapping that poor girl around until she made up shit you wanted to hear?"

"Don't be so dramatic," Al scoffed at her. "That really who you take me for, Slug?"

"I dunno," she shook her head. "I just dunno with you sometimes. It almost feels like you're two different people. I mean, she did ruin your life, right?"

Al felt himself sag under the weight of the accusation, rolling his eyes helplessly in the face of it.

"Don't do that…" he ordered.

"Do what?" Slug countered innocently.

"Don't make this about us," he said. "This is about the mission and the Goo and Arthur. Don't try and drag our personal shit into it."

"I'm not dragging anything," Slug retorted bitterly. "You said it. Verbatim, that is what you said to her a minute ago — she ruined your life."

"What do you want, Slug?" Al grimaced, pinching the bridge of his nose. "You want me to pretend this is what I want? Huh? You want me to pretend that my idea of a good time is flying around the edge of extinction with your family hoping we don't get killed by half a dozen different things queuing for the chance?"

"I dunno, Al," she countered painfully. "Maybe I just don't want to have to listen to you so casually describe the event that brought you back to me as the thing that ruined your life…"

"It's not like that," he sighed. "Don't make it like that."

"I'm not making it like anything," she argued. "It is what it is. I just… I just thought that maybe it was better than it was…"

"Fuck," he swore, rubbing his face despondently as he heard the tears in her voice. "This isn't about you, Slug. This isn't about us."

"Yes, it is," she disagreed. "It is because this is something we're never going to get around. I love you, but you… you never would have come back if Oria hadn't sent out that beacon. You'd still be off galivanting across the system, living your glamorous life and never thinking about us."

"Fine! Yes!" he exclaimed. "Yes, yes I would! So what? Like you said — it is what it is! We can't change any of that now. Who cares what would have been? I'm trying to make sure we get to live with what is."

"And that is so characteristically heroic of you," she commented, a weeping tremble in her voice. "I just… I'm allowed to be sad that you didn't choose me… and that if you'd been given the choice you never would have."

"What the fuck…" Al stared at her.

Slug turned away, shaking her head and fiercely blinking back her tears. Al grabbed her by the shoulder and turned her back to him.

"No, what the fuck?!" he demanded. "Didn't choose you? You think I didn't choose you? You think me leaving wasn't me choosing you?!"

"How the fuck could it be?!" she yelled at him.

"Because it was always about you!" he bellowed. "Because it was always about what was best for you! You think I was going to be good for you?! I'm an asshole! I am a selfish, narcissistic, piece of shit. I am a horrible person, Slug. It's why I'm such a good fucking spy! You deserve better, you always deserved better! You were going to go to university and become an engineer and raise a family! You think I could have been a part of that?! You think there is any place for me in that scenario?!"

"Of course there is!" she answered.

"No! No there fucking isn't!" he replied. "I'd be a fucking terrible husband! I'd be a worse dad — if I could even be a dad! You know what my odds of having kids are after my surgery? It's bad, Slug. It's very fucking bad. Medical science can do anything except, oh, that." He shook his head, running his fingers through his hair and resisting the urge to tear it out in frustration as she stared at him, dumbfounded. "I never wanted your dream, Slug. I'm broken. I did everything I could to fix me, and, you know what, it still wasn't enough. I'm still fucked. I don't want what everyone else wants. I don't want kids, I don't want a cute life with a family. I don't understand the appeal, and I never wanted you to wake up one day without everything you wanted, stuck with some cranky old asshole who had nothing to offer you. I left to help you — to make sure you didn't waste your life on me. Fat lot of good that did either of us."

She was still staring and he couldn't stop talking. If he stopped they would just be standing there, wallowing in the aftermath of his outburst. He felt like he'd lit a fire in his chest and after all these years he finally just had to get it out.

"I… I never wanted to hurt you, Slug," he begged. "That was the last thing in the universe I ever wanted. Just being there… growing up around the family… it never worked for me, and I know you know that. I never really belonged. It never felt right, not just me in my skin… all of it. I can fake so much… these days I can fake whole lives. I can lie and cheat and steal and kill. I can take a bullet, and crack a safe, and hack a console, and manipulate interplanetary leaders, but I cannot make small talk with your family. I can't talk shipping and scrapping and I can't bear people being interested in me. I don't know how to talk about myself. I don't know which person to be to make myself interesting to them. Especially to people who remember what I was, who know me as that weird quiet antisocial kid that didn't really fit in. That struggled… struggled so much just with existing…" he trailed off as she placed a hand on his arm.

Slug finally lost her battle with her tears, and the first one fell glistening and wet down one cheek. Her hand on his shoulder was warm and soothing, rubbing his sleeve gently like she could wipe some of their collective pain away. There was a tight and agonising clench in his stomach that made him want to puke. She swallowed thickly, trying to find her voice. It didn't come. Instead, she slipped her arms around his waist, her hands apologetic and tentative as they inched across his sides. He pulled her in and held her close. Her breath trembled against his chest and she tried again.

"How'd we mess this up so bad…?" she sniffled.

"I dunno…" he replied. "… we might just be idiots."

"How do we fix it?" she asked.

"I dunno…" he answered. "Maybe… maybe we don't." Her body shook with tears in his arms. He held her tighter. He didn't want to make her cry. He didn't want this to be how their fight ended. "Maybe… I dunno. Maybe we learn to live with it." He sighed deeply, squeezing her reassuringly. "Maybe no one actually gets the life they want. We don't get to hand pick them. Maybe neither of us gets anything perfect… but maybe, if we live through this, we could see if having each other is enough?"

"That's a lot of maybes…" she muttered into his chest.

"Yeah it is," he agreed. "Maybe we'll see if we can get through some of them."

CHAPTER TWENTY-SEVEN

As soon as the door was closed, Oria crawled out of the blankets and tumbled from the bunk. Adam turned to her, but she picked herself up and brushed herself off before he could help.

"Hey, you okay?" he asked. "I'm sorry about that."

"He's angry..." Oria muttered, rubbing her shoulders where Al had grabbed her.

"He's scared," Adam elaborated. "None of us want to die. He thinks it's his job to fix it."

"It's not about him..." She shook her head.

"He doesn't know that," Adam countered, resting a hand on her shoulder. "Humans always think everything is about them, and you told everyone it was about him. Can't blame him for getting stuck on himself."

Oria pouted, but leant into his touch. She began to curl into his arms and he was abruptly reminded of the vision that had possessed him outside. It hadn't seemed right to share with anyone else, but maybe she should know. Maybe she already did. He didn't really know how the sight worked. He didn't know when in time he'd been, but it had felt too real not to be. She had felt too real.

"I think I dreamt of you…" she murmured, nuzzling into his chest.

"What kinda dream?" he asked.

"The good kind," she answered simply, eyes closed as she rested against him.

He gave the ceiling a wry grimace. That could mean so much, or it could be as simple as she made it sound. But he'd been here before, in this room, with her, at the same time he'd been out bolting *Hotaru* back together. He didn't know how to explain it to her, but he had to try.

"I think I dreamt of you too…"

"Was it a good dream?" she asked.

"Yup," he nodded. "That's not a bad summation, ae." He pulled away from her with a sigh and sat down on the edge of the bed. She kept hold of his fingers, peering curiously at his hand like she was trying to read his palm. He watched her look, his eyes tracing the soft and inquisitive lines of her face, before travelling down her neck, along the deep collar of her dress. "Oria…" he began carefully, "I need to tell you something…"

She turned her pale eyes up to his. They were nearly the same height when he was sitting. The constant polite inquisition with which she looked at him set off a strange tension in his lungs. It rattled him. In her eyes he saw everyone he hadn't done right by, and a chance to fix it. It wasn't her problem, and he had no right to change that. She wasn't here to redeem him. That ship had sailed. But he wanted it, with a strange desperation he'd never felt before. He turned his hand to clasp hers gently. It was crazy how small she could be for a grown adult. Her tiny hand vanished in his massive grasp.

"What happened in the med-bay, after the fight…" he muttered. "That, um… when you needed air…"

"Your CPR?" she asked.

He chuckled despite himself, tangling his fingers in hers and watching the massive difference between them.

"That, uh, that was not CPR," he admitted. "I didn't say anything at the time. I didn't wanna freak you out and, honestly, I just didn't wanna say it. Didn't wanna put you off. I didn't need to breathe for you or start your heart again, you were just having a panic attack."

"Panic?" she asked.

"Yeah," he nodded. "I mean, it's fair. You'd just been through some shit. I haven't known you that long, but you seem to have been through quite a bit of shit since we met, like, I dunno, a day ago?"

She didn't say anything. Maybe she didn't have anything to say. Maybe she was trying to work it out. Maybe time had as little meaning out here to her as it did to him.

"Look, I just gotta say, in the med-bay earlier, I kissed you. That's what that was. That's what people would actually call what we did. You were confused, and I took advantage of that, and I shouldn't have done that, and I want to be sorry…" he paused, trying to find the words. "Fuck, Oria, I want to be sorry but I don't know how. More than being sorry, I'd kinda like to kiss you again, but it's cool if you're not interested."

There was caution to her curiosity now. Her eyes were narrowed but the interest wasn't going anywhere.

"'Cept I gotta feeling you kinda are..." Adam continued.

She was already drawing closer. Adam slipped his hands from hers and pulled her in slowly. His fingers traced the curve of her back through the fabric of her dress. She moved into his touch, not the least bit concerned where his hands went. Her fingers traced his cheeks, clutching his face like she'd done the first time.

"Kiss...?" she checked hesitantly.

"Yeah," he replied, turning his lips closer to hers.

She brought her mouth to his again, without the desperate urgency of last time. He missed that, but this was good too. There was an uncertainty to it now. He didn't blame her, but he wanted more. He pulled her in tighter, sliding one hand around her backside and squeezing, opening his lips to her kiss. The enthusiasm seemed to encourage her. She kissed him back harder, letting him guide her. He leant back against the wall behind the bunk and she followed him, climbing onto his lap and straddling his hips. Her tongue brushed against his mouth. He slid his hands up her thighs, pushing the short skirt of her dress all the way up. Her breath shivered on his lips.

"Kiss...?" she whispered, like she wanted to know if it was working.

He could feel his blood pounding as the crotch of her underwear brushed against the strained fly of his suit. It was definitely working. He dragged his lips hungrily along her jawline, kissing down the side of her neck. She still tasted like starlight. He hadn't imagined it.

"I want to do a lot more than kiss you," he admitted.

She wrapped her arms around him and tangled her fingers in his short hair. He realised that his sentiment was too vague for her. She was the kind of woman he was going to have to be direct with. That was cool too. He paused, pulling his lips from her skin long enough to meet her eye.

"I wanna take your dress off," he told her.

She nodded. He reached under the hemline, pushing the tight fabric up and over her body. She raised her arms as he tugged the dress off over her head and tossed it on the floor. He quickly followed suit with his own singlet and pulled her back in against him. She didn't quite feel real. There was something about the feel of her skin that was almost synthetic in its smoothness. Not that he felt in a position to criticise a single thing about her.

He pulled her higher in his arms, gently kissing between her breasts. She was just as pale without the dress, like some alien god had sprayed her with colour – or an absence thereof. He could feel her shiver as he kissed her. Her chest trembled and her breath quivered as he drew his mouth across one marble nipple. One arm kept her pulled firmly against him, but he began to move his other hand between her legs.

"I want to touch you," he told her quietly. "I do anything you don't want me to do, you tell me, okay? I'll stop. Anytime. Just say."

She nodded weakly. "Okay…"

He took her permission and slid his hand inside her panties. She gasped as he traced his fingers gently across her clitoris and down her vulva. Her arms tightened around his neck and she clutched him with the desperation he had missed from their first kiss. That felt right. He began to kiss and suck at her breasts again as he stroked her. She was gasping, trembling. She blurted his name. He paused.

"You alright?" he asked.

"It's warm…" she whispered, her voice shaking.

He smiled. It was more than just warm. His middle finger teased the opening of her vagina where he could feel her growing wet. Everything felt hotter and brighter than before. That wasn't an illusion either. She was starting to glow. He could see the light coming off her skin, her hair. He realised she had been glowing in his vision too, when he'd been with her, riding her in this bed. He wanted her on him, like this, just the way they were. Wanted that escalation. There was no reason not to do both. It was strange, knowing that she'd be okay with it, remembering how much she'd wanted it, in a future that he was eager to make the present.

***

It felt like the end of the world. It felt like sitting in a ship with dead life support, watching the temperature drop and waiting for the air to run out. Al sat on his bunk, half dressed, leaning back against the wall and watching the Goo grow nearer on the screen. Slug lay with her head resting peacefully on his lap. Lani was boosting them away as fast as their repaired engines and stolen extra fuel would take them. It wasn't enough. Sure, it was buying them a few more hours, but in the long run that wouldn't cut it. He was all out of ideas.

Someone knocked at the door. Al looked over to it, but felt no desire to answer it or even call out. Slug clearly didn't feel the same. She got up and crossed the room to open the door. Sione was waiting patiently on the other side.

"Comms all seem down still," he commented.

"I thought it was just a signal blocker — that once we got away from the Washington everything would unjam…" Slug mused. "I can take a look—"

"Got something to show you first," Sione motioned to them, deliberately peering into the room and catching Al's eye. The invitation came with a look of sharp insistence.

Al hauled himself reluctantly from the bed and followed them into the main room. Lani was already there heating up drinks while the autopilot flung them towards Herakles at speed. She handed one to Adam, who schlepped from his room with a yawn like he'd been casually napping without a care in the world. Lucky for some.

Sione moved straight to the central console and began opening some of his files for everyone to see as they gathered around. Al scanned his eyes over decades of statistics from all over the system, details from around every sun.

"What are we looking at, old man?" Lani asked, slurping her drink.

"Research," Sione announced. "Decades and decades of research. Some of it taken from the Inanna, but most of it just found in public health records from all over the tertiary system."

"Nice," Adam offered encouragingly.

"Why do we care?" Al asked, watching the room with his arms folded and knowing that Sione's point was buried somewhere in all that data.

"Did you know," Sione pointed between them and the numbers instructively, "that Arthur and its moons have consistently been the healthiest civilisations of any terraformed nation for the last twenty years?" His question was met with silence. No one had known.

"Good for them," Adam offered.

"Very good for them, ae?" Sione glanced up at the giant. "There are several hypotheses out there about the quality of their air, energy, and agriculture."

"But you've got a new one," Al caught on. "You propose it's something to do with them being the closest lifeforms to the glowing ball of Gilgamesh?"

"I'd say it begs the question, ae?" Sione replied. "We all saw what that one little girl did to Adam. We all felt the power of that light. Scientists have been trying to measure the radiation coming off that Goo ever since it got here, and we never obtained conclusive data. Now, it's possible we never actually managed to read it properly because our tech just can't do it yet. But it's also possible we just didn't know how to read it. No one ever expected anything good to come out of that stuff. But if we take these findings, coupled with what we've learnt from Oria and the Inanna… Look at this, yeah? We could be talking regenerative radiation when light, destructive ooze when dark. Original records state that it was dark when discovered and the only time the light has ever been reported was twenty years ago in the aftermath of Gilgamesh. Oria said it wants to be whole. What if Gilgamesh was the first time it was whole again since humanity discovered it?"

"Sione!" Slug exclaimed. "That's brilliant!"

"I try," he flashed her a grin, but couldn't maintain the jubilation. "Problem there is that we've broken it again, or, at least, the Inanna did. Everything began when the station broke orbit. That seems to be what woke the Goo from its regenerative, dormant state."

"Fuck…" Al muttered, catching on and hating where this was going.

"What's wrong, Chief?" Adam asked, sipping his drink and clapping Al's shoulder. "This is good news. This is what you've been waiting for. Just put the thing back together and it's all good again."

Al couldn't bring himself to meet Adam's eye. The kid did not seem to realise what he was saying. He stayed silent, hoping the others would catch up, hoping he wouldn't have to be the one to say it.

"So, it's that easy?" Lani asked. "We just got to put it back together and it will be fine?"

"It will be better than fine," Sione replied. "It will be curative."

"That means that Arthur and the moons might not have to evacuate," Slug added. "If we can switch it back, it's possible things might be able to pass harmlessly through it, like the escaping Inanna."

"How do we put it back together?" Al asked, tired of waiting but hopeful he could nudge the others there.

"We have to talk to Oria," Sione admitted, touching the display to move new data to the front. "The spike following us is still picking up speed, but my monitor tells me she's gone through twenty-eight radiation spikes in the last two hours." He zoomed in on a graph that looked like the erratic heartrate monitor of someone with a life-threatening condition.

"Yikes," Slug commented, looking at the spikes of radiation. "And we're sure this is safe?"

"I scanned Adam before talking to you," Sione replied. "There's not a sign of any degenerative tissue. I don't know what this is going to mean for medical science going forward, but he's the single healthiest man I've ever seen in my life."

Slug cursed and looked back at her brother. "Well damn, bro! You been looking after her all this time, got anything to add to Uncle Sione's findings?"

Adam took a long sip of his drink as he contemplated that question. His eyes stayed on the graph and, finally, he gestured his mug at it.

"Yeah, she… uh… she glows when she comes," he added.

Lani seemed to have caught on a second before he answered, and had buried her face in her arms as she began to cry with laughter. Everyone else stayed frozen in shocked silence for a moment. When the moment broke everyone tried to talk at once, but Slug beat them all with volume.

"WHAT?!" she demanded, rounding on her giant sibling. Adam stared down at her, startled by her reaction. He had, after all, merely answered her question honestly. Slug looked like she was going to beat him around the ears with her shoe. "Adam, tell me you did not have sex with the weird alien girl!" she bellowed.

Adam glanced between everyone else, aware that this was a trap. Lani was worse than useless as she howled with laughter. Sione looked like he was barely keeping it together himself. Al privately felt a massive well of doom opening up beneath him as, somehow, things actually managed to become worse.

"Why...?" Adam countered Slug hesitantly, clearly unsure why he was in trouble.

"Adam!" she yelled at him.

Lani had elbow crept her way along the bench and grabbed Slug by the shoulders, holding her back and propping herself up all in one go. She was still laughing.

"Oh, come on, cuz!" she cackled.

"No, nope, no, this is not funny," Slug warned.

"Funny? Are you shitting me?" Lani pointed to the graph and stared Adam dead in the eye. "You see this shit? Twenty-eight spikes in two hours?! What the fuck did you do to her?!" She smacked him on the shoulder.

"There's small ones. Some of them stack..." he pointed out modestly.

"Oh my God, Adam!" Slug yelled at him, smacking his shoulder with every word. "You can't just stick your dick in the alien girl!"

"Why not?" Lani countered with a maniacal chuckle. "She clearly don't mind."

"Reason would argue in your favour, Slug," Sione agreed. "Common sense would beg one to make some considerations, but it certainly doesn't seem to have been bad for him, ae?"

Slug rounded on Al to help come to her defence, but the wind went out of her sails when she looked at him. That caught everyone's attention. He was still standing, staring at the data projected before them. His arms were folded across his chest, but he had one hand raised contemplatively to his mouth, the back of his thumb brushing against his lips as he pondered. The room was full of smart people and none of them seemed to be getting there on their own. This was one of the things that had always annoyed him about the family. They could be so silly when they were all together. They didn't focus on the important things.

"How did the Goo break…?" he asked slowly, trying to force them to consider it. "What part of it went missing?"

Before anyone could answer, the door to Adam's room slid open and Oria stepped out. Everyone turned to stare at her. No one was laughing anymore and Al finally felt like they were catching on. Oria paused as they stared and regarded them all curiously.

"Oh no…" Slug whispered.

"Sione," Al addressed the doctor softly. "Is there anything in the stolen research that talks about what was done to her and how to reverse it?"

"Uh…" Sione muttered, a sick sweat beading his shiny head. "I can look! I, uh, I haven't found anything yet… but, but I can—"

"Can you find it and perform any procedures required in under an hour?" Al asked.

"Al!" Slug exclaimed. Everyone knew that was going to be impossible. "Al, what are you saying?"

"You're kidding, right?" Lani checked weakly. "You're… you're not gonna ask me to turn this boat around…"

"No," Al shook his head. "The Goo's coming to get itself, and I'm not risking the crew like that. I have other lives to think about."

Sione went pale, even slightly green. Slug covered her mouth with her hands.

"Oh my God, Al!" she exclaimed breathlessly. "Al, you can't!"

He ignored them all. His eyes were fixed on Oria, and she was meeting his gaze. Her expression was sombre, but he couldn't tell if she understood. Still, if he was going to go through with this, he owed it to her to look her in the eye when he did it.

"Al, she saved our lives!" Slug was still protesting. "You can't do this."

"I'm sorry," he replied. He said it to the room, but he was still looking at Oria when he spoke.

She broke his gaze as she looked at the console in the centre of the bench, wandering over and reaching out to touch it. Her fingers brushed at the data — at the rate the Goo was catching up to them and her own statistics.

"It's sad…" she told them. "It's broken and it hurts…"

"We gotta put it back together," Al replied grudgingly. Oria nodded at him. He grimaced. "I'm sorry," he apologised to her again.

"It's not after me," she said.

"That data disagrees," Al said.

"It wants itself," she explained patiently. "Not me."

Al grimaced. He didn't have to explain it to anyone else. It was obvious to them.

"Oria," he said as gently as he could. "It's been chasing us since the Inanna, and you are the only thing we took from there. You are… well… you're a part of it now."

The damning truth hung over them like a guillotine.

"I'm sorry," he told her a third time. "I truly am. You don't deserve this. You never asked for it. All of this was done to you against your will… but it's the way things are, and I think you called me all this way, whether you knew it or not, because you knew I'd have what it took to make this call."

"Al, no…" Slug begged.

"We don't have a choice," he sighed.

"There's always a choice," Adam countered. He loomed impassively, and had been dangerously quiet during Al's elaborations. Now, his dark eyes stared down the room as though daring it to breathe. "Oyabun said there's always a choice."

"Hai," Al nodded slowly. "But if the choice is the death and displacement of billions of people or one person, I know what we have to pick."

"This ain't right…" Lani muttered, hugging herself.

"No," Al agreed. "But this is one of those situations where there is no right answer. There are only great evils in play. We can't outrun this thing. It's going to catch us in an hour or two anyway. If I want to save all of you and all the people around Arthur, this has to happen. Go to your rooms, shut the doors. I'll let you know when it stops."

"If it stops," Slug snapped disgustedly. "If we do this, we deserve to get eaten."

"No," Sione shook his head. "Al… Al is right… this is basic triage, Simone."

"This is murder!" Slug blurted.

"That's why she called me," Al sighed. "I haven't been able to stop wondering why the fuck I was the one singled out. Sure, I bet there are thousands like me, but if this was the final call that was going to have to be made… Allah knows I've made some tough decisions before. This one takes the cake, but it's what has to be done."

Oria was still standing there like she had no idea what they were talking about. She was glancing between their upset faces curiously. Al was all too aware that Adam was standing between him and her.

"There are other options," Adam said, coolly as you please. "This isn't one."

"Sorry, Champ, but you sacrificed your chance to get a say in this," Al sighed, moving to step around him.

Being hit in the face by Adam felt not too dissimilar to getting hit by a bolt gun. It was fast. So fast Al hadn't realised it was happening until he was stunned. Enough of his brain was aware that people were screaming, and it was possible he was in pain. Excruciating pain. He felt the second punch. He didn't feel the third.

CHAPTER TWENTY-EIGHT

He was home. He was sitting on the floor of the kitchen, looking up at his parents standing at the bench. They were talking and laughing while they prepared food together. Rajiya was finely dicing something, the rocking of her knife against the board making a rhythmic sound like a heartbeat. Takashi was hand stirring a large mixing bowl beside her. Neither were paying him any mind.

He began to cry. A high, stuttering, baby wail came out from his mouth. One of those primal sounds. An infant screech that feared abandonment. His mother turned instantly, laying down her knife and silencing the heartbeat of the kitchen.

"Oh Alya!" she crooned softly, sweeping him up off the floor. "Whatever's the matter, baby?"

Then he was safe in his mother's arms again, and it was fine. He wasn't going to get forgotten about. He wasn't going to drift off into space. He wouldn't die cold and alone in a ship rattling bleakly between suns. Things would be okay.

His father turned to him, smiling. "Who's my little Al?" he asked, and bopped him on the nose with the mixing spoon. Al pulled a face as he felt the cold wet muck from the spoon stick to his soft skin. He made another half-hearted, protesting wail. Takashi laughed and kissed the spiced mixture from his nose.

Al could feel the affection across time and space, like he was every baby being teased by their parents since creation. A universal truth.

He was still in Rajiya's arms, but now he was standing on his own feet, so much taller than her, and she held him pinned to her side. He kept his arms draped around her. It was so much better than letting go.

"Where are you going now?" his father asked.

"Nowhere," Al replied. "I'm staying right here."

But here wasn't the kitchen anymore. Here was the back garden, down by the old stone bench. His parents never came down here. This was the abandoned section of the Tanakas' garden. His father was sitting on the bench. He wasn't sure his father had ever actually sat on that bench, not in Al's lifetime. This was where Al hid with Slug. That was their bench.

Al's face began to flush as he thought about everything that had happened on that bench, and every mistake he'd made since. Merciful Allah, there had been a lot of them. It was insane how, after all his successes and all of Lin's praise, he could still look back on his life and feel like he'd simply been stumbling from one mistake to the next the whole time.

"It's because you're learning," his mother whispered.

Al looked to her, then he looked back to his father. Takashi was sitting on the bench with Al's sixteen-year-old self. He recognised that scrawny body and soft face. Just pre-surgery. Maybe only by hours. His father was rubbing his back comfortingly. That hadn't happened here. That had been at the hospital. Al grimaced at his old self with a sick self-loathing. He could feel his mother's hand on his back, mimicking the supporting gesture of his father on his younger self.

"I don't want to learn," Al replied. "I just want to know."

"It doesn't work like that, my darling," she sighed. "Nothing comes for free. Someone, somewhere, must pay the price."

"But look at me…" he whispered sickly. "Look at how… how insecure and foolish and fragile I am. It's embarrassing!"

Rajiya chuckled. Takashi looked up from the bench, met his eye, and smiled. Al despaired of it. His parents had wise smiles, and kind eyes, and all the answers all the time. How were you supposed to live up to that? The standards were so impossible to reach, while at the same time patiently acknowledging that there was no expectation to meet them. Yet, they'd still made him want to run off and do something completely different instead of attempting and failing.

"Being embarrassed by your teenage self is good," his father offered gently. "It shows you have grown as a person and developed maturity." He paused with that wise smile. "However…"

Al had known there was going to be a 'however'. There always was with his dad.

"However," his mother continued instead, "one day

your older self will miss that beautiful disaster child."

Al was all ready to scoff at their wisdom, but the words died on his lips. They weren't... wrong. His mother's hand tightened on his shoulder warmly.

"That person," she indicated his younger self, "who did so much struggling and learning so that you can be who you are. You lie awake at night still, even now, and you judge and stew in old embarrassment. Old resentment. Cut them some slack. They were still learning. You are still learning. You will always be learning."

He didn't want to always be learning. He wanted to be good at things — to excel beyond expectation. He wanted to be impressive and special, because then, finally, he might actually belong. He might finally fit his skin, that skin he'd never been able to cut to fit his body. He might finally stop hating himself long enough to believe the people who said they loved him, and feel for a moment that he wasn't tricking them somehow, because they were kind and caring, and he was not those things. He knew he wasn't. Nothing came for free. Someone, somewhere, had to pay the price. The family had taken him in, but he couldn't love like they did. Not the same way. He didn't know how. The price had to be paid somehow. He had to make himself valuable to compensate.

His father stood and joined him and Rajiya standing. He reached them like he had when Al had been with his mother in the garden last time he'd seen them. He placed a hand on each of their shoulders. This time, instead of turning to each other, they both turned to him. They all rested their foreheads together, and Al could feel a hand on each of his cheeks. One from each parent.

"You are enough," his father told him. "Just as you are, my boy. You are enough."

Al was crying. He was screaming. He knew that his parents felt that way, that they had always felt that way, that they had always loved and accepted him. Everyone in the family had. But he had never been able to accept that before. He wasn't sure if he was accepting it now. He was weeping like a shrieking baby. The problem was not with them. It was with him, and he had always known that. Always.

That didn't mean he was any closer to fixing it.

"You can't run from who you are forever, my angel," his mother whispered, louder than his cries, that somehow extended through every conception of himself since birth, with every voice he'd ever had.

The cries were softening, despite the pressure in his chest building. He felt like he couldn't get them out, like he was slowly getting dialled down to mute.

Then he was waking, weakly, struggling beneath a bright light. He hadn't been screaming, but he wanted to. He hadn't been able to. His face was wet with tears. He blinked in the harsh light of the med-bay on the *Hotaru*, lying back in one of the reclining chairs and staring at the ceiling.

"Ae, he's stable," Sione's voice floated across the room. "We got brain activity."

That was promising, Al thought. Brain activity. That meant he could think again. Did that mean that he had stumbled across his most profound understandings without his brain, or just that no one had been monitoring it then?

The glow continued to die down as he blinked, his thick, dark eyelashes fluttering rapidly over his eyes. Everything still felt hazy and sore. An inhumanly pale face came into focus in front of him, and he realised why the glow had been fading. Her glow. Her fingers seemed to be hesitating around the edges of his face, reluctant to touch him, but careful and curious.

He raised his own hands to his face and she backed off. Everything felt normal. No tubes or machinery. He hadn't been fixed by medicine.

"Did you just... save my life...?" he asked thickly; his mouth tasted dry and his tongue was heavy.

Oria flicked a glance between him and Sione repeatedly. No one else was around.

"Uncle said your brain was showing," she told him. "I put it back to how it was."

Al tipped his head to look at Sione. It all felt like it was working properly. Sione was trying to convey the severity with his eyes, and they spoke with an intensity no words could capture. It sounded more like resurrection than recovery.

Al sat up from the chair slowly, wincing and touching his head. There was still some pain.

"Careful, ae," Sione warned, hurrying over and sliding a hand over his back to help steady him. "You might still have a concussion, Al."

Given that it sounded like his skull had been caved in and probably pierced his brain he thought he was doing rather well. The poor brain, back from the dead, or close to it, was having to work extra hard now as well, just to catch up. He pulled back all the memories leading up to Adam punching his skull in.

"How much time do we have?" he asked, with no idea how long he'd been out.

"Just under three thousand minutes," Oria answered automatically.

They both looked at her. She blinked back.

"It was only an hour or two behind us," Al countered. "That doesn't stack."

"It's not following us," Oria replied. "It doesn't care about us. It wants to be whole."

Al was all ready to start kneading his newly reformed face when Sione chimed in.

"She's right, Al," he said. "It's already bypassed us."

Al turned to stare at him. There were no lies in his eyes. Which meant…

Al did knead at his face. It was surprisingly soothing. When he looked up Oria was still watching him. Her expression was always so blankly curious. Of course. She was, in her own way, a lot smarter than he was. She was always trying to learn.

"I'm so sorry," he told her. "I don't know how I can make it up to you, but I will try."

"For what?" she asked curiously. "You didn't do anything."

"No, but I would have," he said. "If Adam hadn't stopped me, I would have done something unforgivable, and I would have thought myself right and justified."

"But you didn't," she repeated.

"The intent matters," he insisted.

"Yes, it does," she smiled.

He paused for a moment, considering that. Somehow, they were making the same point.

"I never wanted to kill you," he blurted. "I never wanted to hurt you. I just wanted to protect my people, and I was scared. But… but that's when humans do their worst. When they're scared." He glanced at Sione. *Every mass bloodshed in human history was because of a story.* Yeah, the ones we tell ourselves. "We do terrible things and then try and justify it. It doesn't make it okay."

Oria nodded at him. He swallowed back the horrible truths.

"I trained myself to be better than that," he muttered. "I trained hard not to give into that fear… to surrender emotions to logic."

"Triage," she stated, and looked up to Sione. He gave her a nod and she smiled proudly. Then she turned back to Al. "That's not good for you, to run on triage all the time. It's unsustainable."

"It wasn't…" he muttered, trying to understand how he'd fallen so far, but he already knew. He knew that training himself to be calculated at work was one thing. It had to be paid for somewhere. So he left his emotions at home, where they would be safe until he could get back to them. To her. It could never be work, never be safely and impassively triaged, while she was there. He couldn't be cold around her. It just didn't work that way.

"What… what do we do now…?" he asked weakly, hating himself for even asking the question. He wasn't supposed to ask that. He didn't ask for help. He was the one who helped, who had all the answers. Who was he if not that person?

"We go talk to Lani," Oria said, taking his hand and helping him off the chair.

His head still hurt as he stood, and he was grateful to have her to hold on to as the room seemed to move — beyond the natural speed they were travelling at, which should only have manifested as gravity anyway.

Sione came with them as Oria walked Al out from the med bay and down to the bridge. He couldn't help but notice the silence and the emptiness. There was no sign of the others. A small red light, no bigger than a pinhead, marked a lock on Adam's door. It shone in stark contrast to the otherwise blue light of their shared space. He didn't have to ask.

Lani turned from the controls as they all traipsed into her space. Her eyebrows shot up towards the curls of her mohawk as she saw them enter.

"Holy shit, pretty boy, you're still pretty," she commented, only just managing to aim her mouth with the cracker she was munching.

"You don't need to sound so surprised," Al told her.

"Ae, sure," she agreed, standing up and giving him a quick hug. "Aloha, cuz." She whispered the words in his ear, like she couldn't bring herself to tell him she was glad he was alright. Even the hug was too gentle and swift a gesture. It was the most unsettling part so far. He looked out the window as she let him go again, striving for some semblance of normality, and finding that things just got weirder.

"Where are we?" he asked. The view from the bridge looked like an asteroid field mixed with a graveyard. There was a haze of dust and particles, beyond which the shadows of larger rocks and lost ships loomed. There was only one place Al knew that looked like this. Only one place where the dregs of space collected, spinning endlessly in the crushing pit of gravity between the three suns. "Lani..." Al muttered slowly. "Are we... in the Drift?"

She scrunched her mouth apologetically, which, again, was more alarming as her behaviour went than anything else happening.

"Look," she replied, clearly starting an explanation she'd been practicing. "You said that stuff was chasing us — that it was chasing her! But then you were... like... nearly dead... and Slug was— and Adam was... and... and I'm sorry! I know it wasn't my call to make, but no one else was around to make it, and, like... if that stuff was actually chasing us... I couldn't drive it towards Herakles! We'd already put Arthur in danger, I figured... y'know, I figured the Drift would be the safest place to lead it, ae? Maybe even drag it away from Arthur's orbit? Which, totally moot now, I mean... thing didn't even come after us at all... Totally bypassed us. Shot straight by Herakles, thank god. But it got close."

Al contemplated silently, vaguely staring both at her and the carnage beyond the window.

"You didn't even flinch?" he mused. "You just shot

off for the Drift?"

"What else was I to do, man?" she shrugged. "Seemed like the best bet."

"There were a million options, Lani..." Al smiled softly. "What you did... that was a surprisingly selfless act. You put the wellbeing of billions of people ahead of your own."

"Not something you really expected of me, ae?" she challenged.

"Na," Al admitted. "But that says a lot more about me than it does about you."

"Damn straight," she muttered.

Before any of them could continue, the sound of mag-boots stomping up the hall echoed loudly through the bridge, followed by Slug's voice.

"Ae, Lani, I think I finally sorted these comms and removed the jammer. Can you give us a hard reset—" She stopped dead as she came through the doorway and saw them all standing around. Her eyes fixed on Al like she was seeing a ghost. He'd never seen her look that way at anything before, but he wondered if that's how she'd looked when Adam had finally come home after mysteriously vanishing for twenty-two years. It wasn't a good look on her. Her usually joyous round face was pinched and tight. Her eyes were full of grief. Before anyone could work out what to say, she leapt at him and buried her face in his chest. He held her tightly, squeezing her against his body and feeling her tremble in his arms. She was muttering tearful curses into his shirt.

"Hey, hey, it's okay..." he murmured against her

hair, holding her as close as he dared.

"It's really fucking not!" she wept, muffled into his chest.

He didn't want to let her go, he couldn't even bring himself to relax his grip. He held her to him like he feared a slight breeze in the hall would snatch her away. Behind him he could hear Lani rebooting the comms system. Sione was asking about it.

"Is it working yet?" he demanded. "We got to call your Pa, can we get through?"

"Give me a sec, old man, sheesh," she muttered, flicking the systems back on. "Slug and I been doing the best we can."

"When was the last time you heard from President Lin?" Slug asked, pulling her tearstained face from Al's body.

"Before the Inanna," he replied. "I don't know how long we've been blocked or how many messages got through, but I imagine she'll give me a bollocksing when she finds out we're still alive and how long we've been out of touch."

"It gets worse…" Lani hesitated.

"How in Allah's name can our situation get worse?" Al demanded. "Are we about to run out of air?"

"Not us," Sione said grimly. "Home."

Al gave him a confused look. He couldn't imagine how a terraformed moon was going to run out of air.

"The Goo shot right by us," Slug told him painfully. "It's not aiming for us. Maybe it never was. Thing is… we ran some calculations… given the direction and speed… it's going to collide with Pan…"

"Pan?" Al echoed. "The planet Pan? Titania's Pan? Our Pan?" He didn't know why he was asking. Everyone on the bridge looked like they'd been told their house was about to be bombed. Almost everyone. Al rounded on Oria, but he knew better than to get mad at her this time. "What do we do?" he asked her. "How do we fix this?"

"We have roughly three thousand minutes to make the Goo whole again," she replied simply. "That's all it wants. Just for the pain to stop."

"But how do we do that?" Slug asked. "Al wasn't wrong before, the only thing we took from the Inanna was you, Oria. We don't wanna have to give you back to it, especially when it's not even coming after you…"

"It's not about you…" Al murmured, staring at the luminescent alien girl.

She met his eye and smiled.

"Yeah, we worked that out," Lani scoffed.

"No…" Al shook his head and pointed at Oria. "It's not about you… you said that… to me…" He turned his own finger back on himself. Finally the pieces began to slot into place. All this time… he'd been parading his own narcissistic trumpet. Oria, the Goo, the Inanna… they had called to him, singling him out, and he had been more than happy to decide that made him a martyr. He had been so insistent on playing the self-sacrificing hero… it had never occurred to him that this wasn't about him or his actions. "I'm an asshole…" he muttered.

"Glad you've finally worked that out," Lani drawled. "Maybe next time we could skip the trauma and buy you therapy?"

"Shut up, Lani," Slug snapped. "Shin'yū, what's wrong?"

"Eric. Fucking. Maxwell," Al growled. "I should have known."

"He took something!" Sione cried. "He got there first! He took something! The Goo is chasing him!"

"I'm betting it's not just something," Al sighed. "You told us about what they did to Oria… that means the Inanna had a supply of Goo on hand inside the station. Probably the same one they took from Pluto centuries ago."

"You're shitting me!" Lani exclaimed.

"It makes sense," Al shrugged. "That one small sample… it ended our first solar system. The Goo ate everything between Pluto and Earth — possibly more, we'll never know — just to try and get that part of itself back. Then it ate Gilgamesh and the Inanna. Once the Inanna was inside it, that must have counted, and it fell dormant. Once the Inanna broke out…"

"The whole cycle started over…" Slug murmured.

"And now it's chasing itself to Oberon," Sione hissed. "And endangering everyone else along the way!"

"Then we have to stop it," Al insisted. "We need to call Lin, we need to rally everyone we can, and we need to get to Eric before he gets to Oberon. We have to get that sample back and return it to the Goo."

"I don't wanna be a bummer, but, like, how…?" Lani asked. "Sorry fam, I know it's on me, but we're kinda stuck in the Drift. Also, we straight up not fast enough to catch that gun ship."

"You still got the supplies to mod the *Hotaru*?" Al replied.

"You're talking the fastest mod job in the universe and then it would still be tight even blasting us so fast we might feel like we're gonna liquify," she said.

"But can we do it?" Al pressed. Everyone looked to Slug. She shook her head slowly.

"You can," Oria stated like it was basic arithmetic. "It is possible."

"I'd need Adam's help," Slug admitted. "I'd have to let him out."

"Then we let him out," Al stated, turning and barging off before anyone could stop him. He knew they wanted to, but they'd already wasted so much time being wrong about things on this journey. They were all out of time to waste, and this needed to be something he did anyway.

Everyone else chased him to Adam's door. He could hear the family clamouring behind him in nervous hesitations, but they didn't have the nerve to stop him. They knew he was right. Luckily, Oria seemed as unfazed as he was, and it helped to keep him calm as he unlocked Adam's door and slid it open.

Adam was sitting hunched on the bunk. He looked up at the group gathered in the doorway. His massive body was tense and there was solemn regret in his eyes. He stood when he saw them, and began to approach slowly.

Al felt his loved ones draw back slightly behind him, and he suddenly felt what it must be like for Adam to always have people drawing away from him, even unconsciously. Match that with the rest of his life, no wonder he was the way he was. No wonder he liked Oria, who didn't seem to harbour natural human caution.

Adam stopped in the doorway and looked down on them.

"Gomen'nasai," he said. "I'm sorry I hit you, Chief."

"Hit me?" Al echoed. "Adam… I think you might've killed me."

"Na, I didn't," Adam shook his head. "I knew she'd fix you. I just… I couldn't let you space her, Chief. I couldn't."

Al nodded. Maybe it was the dreams, the lessons, the urgency of their situation, or maybe just the satisfaction of finally feeling like he had all the pieces of the puzzle after so long. He could accept Adam's argument. He knew, deep in his own soul, that he couldn't have been persuaded in that moment. He had believed Oria was a danger to those he loved, and he had not had the mental or emotional space to hear reason against it.

"You did what you had to," he conceded. "I understand that. I'm still learning, and that was an important lesson." He paused a moment, appreciating the recoils of horror he sensed behind him, before he tried to stare Adam down. "But maybe, in future, bring up this example instead of hitting me again. See if the reminder works first."

"Hai," Adam nodded curtly.

"Now, get out here and help me help Slug to get this ship ready to win an interstellar race," Al ordered.

CHAPTER TWENTY-NINE

The modifications were an all-hands-on-deck mission. Sione stayed inside as mission control, but Al suited up with Slug, Lani, and Adam to help out. They shut the *Hotaru* down to basic functions. However, the engines were still hot, and waiting for them to cool enough to make adjustments to them added to the stress. Not to mention that the time pressure only served to exacerbate the claustrophobia of the situation.

Al's breath steamed his mask as he slowly helped Lani guide a piece into place. Adam was already waiting, and began to weld the new section in as soon as it arrived. Al helped hold it in place until he was done, and then straightened to look for Slug. He was about to ask her what she needed help with next when Sione's voice crackled over the comms.

"You lot all good?" he asked. "Who's coming in?"

"No one," Slug replied, checking the heat radiating off the main engine ruefully. "We're all still working."

"Then what's in the airlock..." Sione trailed off with a sharp gasp as he checked the systems. "Oria! Oria's coming out! She don't have a suit!" he yelled.

Al turned tail, but Adam moved faster. He didn't even put his welding tool away, just bolted with it in hand. His mag-boots went off to allow him the extra speed, and Al felt his heart skip a beat as he watched Adam throw himself across the side of the ship anchored by his tether alone. He still wasn't going to get there before Oria spaced herself.

Which didn't seem to matter. Oria, with no suit to keep her safe or boots to keep her secured, wandered barefoot over the hull towards them. She smiled and waved, her long hair drifting serenely around her body as she signed 'I came to help'.

Adam was stopped dead in front of them all, presumably staring at her, as they all were. Slug reacted first, her voice crackling numbly over the comms.

"Oria, honey, you're not wearing a suit," she said.

"She can't hear you, cuz," Lani replied in the same stunned monotone. "She don't got comms."

In the darkness of the Drift, standing almost naked on the side of the ship, she looked the least human Al had ever seen her. The subtle glow that radiated from her was stark out here, compared to inside the ship where it was possible not to notice. She was still smiling helpfully, and she pointed to the extra thrusters and cooling lines they hadn't been able to install around the hot engines. She signed at them, offering to help install the pieces.

Adam signed back that the engines were still too hot to be safe. She replied that the heat wouldn't harm her. She could do it. She began to move towards the engines.

"What the fuck…" Lani breathed. It was an accurate summary of the situation.

"Yeah, so…" Adam muttered, activating his boots again and clamping onto the hull. "I dunno. I guess…

you coulda spaced her after all...?" No one said anything. "Glad you didn't," he added, hurrying to catch up to her.

"What's going on out there?" Sione demanded.

"Oria's out here," Al told him. "She's decided that physics and the laws of nature don't apply to her, so she's going to help us mod the *Hotaru*."

"Ae?"

"Trust me, it makes even less sense if you can see it," Al muttered.

Adam led Oria around to the space they were working on, signing instructions as they went. She walked across the side of the ship like she was walking across the bottom of a pool. She didn't even seem to need to breathe. Al watched for a moment, but after seeing her bounce between items with no kickback, he turned away. It was just too unnatural. The sheer impossibility of it nauseated him.

A call rang through his comms. Now that Slug had unjammed everyone and the Drift had spun them near enough to Gan De that he could receive messages, something was coming through. Not just something, of course. Lin. Al muted himself on their crew line and opened the call.

"Nǐ hǎo—" he greeted her, barely able to get the words out before she cut him off.

"Where the fuck have you been, Akiyama?!" she screamed down the line at him.

He winced and raised his hand automatically, but he couldn't touch his ear through the suit.

"Mostly dead, boss. Thanks for asking," he replied.

"Oh, you better be!" Her voice was practically quaking with fury. "I told Simu, I told him, I said: Akiyama's only excuse for leaving us in the dark without an update is death, and if that boy up and died on me, so help me God I will go out there and fucking kill him myself!"

"That's very kind of you, Madam President," Al drawled.

"Shut up!" she snapped. "Where are you?"

"In the Drift," Al answered. "We're trying to get our ship fixed so we can save the system."

"Save the system?" she echoed. "What are you, some kind of superhero now?"

"Someone has to be," he smirked. Her scoff was instantaneous. "Lin," he cut her off urgently, before she could yell at him again. "It's worse than you think."

She fell silent. Even her breathing became soft, no longer edged with indignation. He assumed she knew the Inanna was gone, the Goo was stretching through the orbit of Arthur and every other planet in the Galileo orbit, aiming straight for Pan and endangering everything else in Gan Dee's orbit as well. The entirety of human civilisation was staring down the collapse of the tertiary star system they called home, with no real idea why. He could understand her compulsion to swear at him.

"It's Oberon," he told her. "I can't be certain that the orders came from President Shepard, but Maxwell's the one leading the Goo, whether he realises or not, so we have to assume someone in Oberon's government or military is pulling his strings."

"How?" Lin asked warily.

"Eric stole an old sample of Goo from the research base at the Inanna, just before he slaughtered the scientists," Al said. "I tried sending you the details, but I think our comms got jammed before we were attacked by mercenaries he hired. I'll double check and resend everything after this call." Her silence echoed in his breath between sentences. Once he started, it seemed stupid to stop, despite her bewildered stillness. He told her everything, in as much detail as he could manage, and laid out what they were about to do and what they needed from her. He left out the part that he had been waiting to try calling her again until after he'd helped to fix the ship, figuring he could make contact while they were travelling. As logical as his priorities were, he didn't imagine she'd appreciate them.

"Send me your evidence, Al," Lin bid him once his story was done. "If even half of what you say is true, and you have the footage and messages to corroborate it, I can call out Bill Shepard publicly, on behalf of everyone in the Gan De orbit. The people deserve to know what is happening and who is putting them in danger."

"I'd appreciate it," Al replied. "Anything we can do to slow Eric down or make him turn around will help save lives right now."

"Yes, well..." Lin sighed. "Unfortunately, Eric Maxwell is not the type to cave to threats and pressure, but, with any luck, his bosses might be. We will have to strike carefully if we hope to avert this disaster without also starting a war."

"You have other people in Shepard's staff?" Al checked. He could almost hear her rolling her eyes. It was uncanny.

"Of course I do," she scoffed. "Not that it's any of your business."

"No, Ma'am," he grinned.

"Send me the files, Akiyama," she ordered. "And get your ass back here before I'm forced to save the system myself."

"Yes, Ma'am," he responded.

"Good boy," she finalised, in that abrupt way that she had, managing to make her endorsement sound affectionately grandmotherly instead of condescending. There was a pause as he reached for the button, but she spoke again before he could press it. "Al…?"

He hesitated, his finger hovering over the 'end call' symbol.

"Al, I'm glad you're okay," she told him softly. "I was worried about you."

"Thanks Lin," he smiled. A small bud of awe stirred inside him. She must have been practically grieving to have admitted that much.

"Of course," she said. "Now, quickly, boy! Gǎnkuài! Time is running out!"

"Yes Ma'am," he obeyed immediately, shutting the call. He unmuted his comms to let the others know what had happened.

Oria was walking casually over the glowing hot engine to run new coolant lines through it and Al decided the team didn't need his help anymore. With

Slug's blessing, he left them to it and joined Sione inside. The two of them double checked the files and sent them through to Lin. This time they went through clean and Al got a notification of receipt.

He tried not to notice the open chat that Sione had beside him, messaging back to Tamati. It was hard to ignore, but the glance he couldn't help but give it showed nothing confidential trickling back home. He hated himself for thinking that way, but old habits… Whether or not he was green-lit, he was still a spy. This was still supposed to be classified.

Sione noticed him noticing. Al sighed.

"You can call him, if you want," Al caved. "Tell him everything."

Sione shook his head. He reached out and clasped Al's fingers tightly in his hand, squeezing them heartily.

"No," he replied softly. "We do this right, I'm home in two days. We mess this up, there's no home to get back to. My family are in Fika. We do this proper, ae. We get them safe. I can talk to them then."

Al nodded understandingly. "Then let's do it proper." He opened the comm chat. "Slug, babe, we're done in here. What else can we do?"

"Get down to engineering," she called back through faint static. "I need you to see if you can link the grav boosters to the couplers, then use the atomic power units to route them through the new thrusters."

Al shared a look with Sione. Neither of them had any idea what she meant.

"Sure thing," he replied. "Might have to call you from engineering for a few more instructions when we get there."

Slug laughed like she understood and her line went quiet as she got back to work.

"When *we* get there?" Sione checked.

"What?" Al shrugged. "That sounded like how you talk about people. *Hotaru's* just a big person, right?"

Sione gave him an unimpressed look.

"Al-Amir…" he sighed. "I'm glad you're still alive, boy. Now get your ass down to engineering and do what your lady said. I'm still running the shop up here."

Al half wanted to tell their doctor that if anything went wrong they had Oria now and he could come help like everyone else, but that was mostly just because he didn't want to get stuck sounding stupid down there alone. Unfortunately, there were more important things to consider than pride.

***

Adam and Oria were the last ones to finish up outside. He still couldn't get over the casual way she exposed herself to space. When he'd had the vision of her out there, just looking at the stars with nothing between her and them but the void, he'd assumed it was a dream. Nothing was anymore. Not like it used to be. With Oria, dreams were reality and reality was a dream.

The airlock secured behind them and repressurised. She stood there looking around curiously, that way she always did, completely unaffected, like some kind of doll. He waited for the room to stabilise and clicked his helmet back. Her endless curiosity turned to him.

"So, I gotta ask…" he began, fully unclipping his helmet and starting to struggle out of his suit, "you don't actually need air at all?"

"Not the way you do, it would seem," she replied, moving to help him. "I spent my whole life on that station, in Reynolds' labs, always just being whatever they told me I was." She slipped her hands under the shoulders of his suit and helped strip it fluidly from his upper body. "I've been learning a lot about myself since I left."

Her hands stayed on his arms and she stood so close their bodies nearly touched. He wanted them to. He wanted to lean into her, the half a breath it would take to feel the warmth of her chest against his stomach, but he stayed perfectly still, as though she was a wild animal he didn't want to spook. She was running the tips of her fingers over his tattoos again, watching them, tracing the path of the koi upstream and into the sakura branches of his left arm. On his right, a snake curled through flowers on his forearm, twisting into a dragon coiled around a samurai on his shoulder. Her fingertips followed the scales.

"I… get the feeling… I did something bad…" he whispered. It wasn't a feeling he got from her, but he knew it was the reason he wasn't touching her now. The feeling like he shouldn't, couldn't, until he'd washed the blood off his hands. "I shouldn't have hit Al… That… I think that was wrong."

Oria sighed. She leant into him, resting her forehead against his chest and her hands against his biceps. She was warm and small and he couldn't stop thinking about the way he'd had her earlier. The way he'd held her and moved in her, gently, worried he might break her because she felt so fragile in his arms, until she had pushed back into him with a strength that told him he didn't have to worry. He wanted that again, but he didn't feel like he could ask for it after the brutality he'd shown.

"I'm really good at killing people..." he muttered thickly, aware that she should at least know what she was getting into.

"So am I," Oria whispered into the front of his singlet.

"I... I like to think I only do it when necessary..." he defended. "But..."

"But you're the blue one," she finished. They both stood in silence as he considered that. He'd been so confident before, trying to convince her they weren't monsters, but he only said it because he knew that's what you were supposed to say. It's what Slug would have said. She was good people, and he liked to think that made her right, but in this case... who were normal people to decide what he and Oria were? Maybe she was right. Maybe this beautiful, luminescent alien was right. She tipped her face back, staring up his body at him. "You're the blue one," she repeated. "I'm the red one. The one who cries."

The blue oni made the red oni cry, Adam recalled. He didn't want to make her cry. Except. The red oni cried with gratitude. With joy.

They moved at the same time. Oria caught him around the neck as he scooped her into his arms, catching her legs around his waist. They were kissing again and he didn't know which one had started it this time. He held her on his hips as he staggered to the edge of the room, pressing her up against the wall. She didn't need to breathe, but she was breathing like she needed him, gasping and kissing him hungrily. He could taste the electricity and emptiness on her tongue as he took it into his mouth. He pushed against her harder and she gave a trembling moan, her grip tightening everywhere she touched him.

Suddenly, she was pulling away. He had her pinned, but he could feel her resisting, even as her lips left his to drag down his throat.

"What's wrong?" he panted.

She shook her head, failing to answer in words and struggling to untangle herself. He let her go. He didn't want to. He didn't understand. But he put her down, shaken and confused. He hadn't quite taken his hands off her when his comms beeped. Oria pressed her lips together anxiously and Adam grimaced, letting her slip away and leaning ruefully against the wall.

"Hai?" he answered, trying not to sound as frustrated as he felt.

"Adam, where are you? Are you back on board?" Slug demanded.

"Yeah," Adam sighed. "We just repressurised."

"Well, get your asses up to the bridge, bro," she ordered. "We gotta set off!"

She was right, of course. She was always right, but he really begrudged her that in this particular moment.

Oria wasn't even looking at him. She was already

opening the doors and following Slug's instructions. Adam allowed himself a rough sigh as he tied the arms of his suit around his waist and followed Oria up to the bridge.

Everyone else was already in there and there were only four chairs. A sullen part of him wanted to make an argument that there wasn't actually room for him and Oria in here and everyone else could call them later if they needed them, but he stayed dutifully silent. He knew things were about to get hairy, and possibly painful. They were going to be travelling as fast as the human body could go, and it was more than likely Sione would have to drug them just to help them survive it.

"Okay, we're all in," Slug rounded them up. She stood behind Lani's chair and looked over her shoulder. "Everyone is going to have to buckle in."

"Imma follow the churn of the Drift," Lani announced, starting everything up. "Use that to sling us out the side towards Gan De, and give it both barrels, but you best believe that is gonna suck. You wanna be belted in tight for this. It's gonna hurt."

"No," Oria shook her head.

"Yes, hunnybun," Lani gave her a look and pointed to the monitor. "Look here, we're aiming for half speed, and with the crazy shit you added to our engines that's going to feel like 5Gs. It's going to feel like Adam is lying on your lungs — and not in a good way."

"That's too slow," Oria told her. "You have to go full. It's the only way we'll make it in time."

"I go full and we all die," Lani explained patiently. "Sorry, babe. I crack this baby as fast as she'll go and we will literally liquify from the pressure. No can do."

"You'll be fine," Oria insisted. "You have to. It's the only way."

Lani heaved an exasperated sigh and looked around like she was hoping someone else would explain science to their resident alien. She made impatient eyes at her dad, and Sione pursed his lips in thought as he approached Oria. Oria ignored him, but Adam was certain it wasn't intentional.

Oria moved into the middle of the room and sat cross-legged on the floor. Adam stepped toward her cautiously.

"Oria…?" he hesitated.

"Make them go fast," she said, closing her eyes and settling like she was about to meditate. He could already see the glow building. He could already feel it. She was getting brighter and brighter, her light filling the bridge, but he couldn't take his eyes off her. Everyone else was staring at her too. If he didn't look away eventually he'd go blind.

Finally, she became too bright and he had to tear his eyes away. He looked over to Lani, blinking back stinging tears of idiotic pain.

"You heard her, cuz!" he called over the sound of *Hotaru's* booting engines. "Let her rip!"

CHAPTER THIRTY

Al couldn't work out if it was a nightmare or a miracle, and wondered if it was possible to be both. He had sat down and buckled in, even though Oria assured them they didn't need to. The problem was that no one in the history of humanity had ever gone this fast before. This was the definition of terminal velocity. They should be dead. He kept trying to forget that. It was a difficult thing to forget.

No one knew how Oria's magic — and he was calling it magic, for lack of a better term — was keeping them alive. Sione had hypothesised that she was healing them faster than the speed was killing them, which was hypothetically possible, and profoundly disturbing.

Slug was sitting in the co-pilot chair next to Lani and keeping an eye on everything through the displays. She had a concerned grimace that suggested if something went wrong at this speed they might be dead before they could fix it, but that she also might not be able to get down to engineering and fix anything if she needed to because Oria's glow almost certainly couldn't extend that far.

Al and Sione had taken the chairs behind them, and Al couldn't help but wonder if buckling in was habit or simply a comfort blanket in the face of disturbing impossibility. Oria sat like a serene, glowing Buddha in the centre of the room, and Adam hovered protectively around her. He stood or sat or just generally loitered about her like he was waiting for her to need him, like he needed to be ready to catch her when she fell. Hogosha. Of course.

By the time they blew past Maui, Al was starting to feel a little sick. Whatever they were doing, magic or not, it couldn't be good for them. His comms beeped and he opened it publicly, grimacing with the effort of not puking or melting.

"Hai?" he clipped out.

"Akiyama," Lin greeted him. "Where the fuck are you? The Goo has picked up speed and will be descending on us in a few hours! Also, there is a goddamn projectile coming at Oberon faster than an asteroid—"

"That's us," Al grated. "That's us. We're the projectile."

"That's not possible," she snapped.

"Deal with it, old lady," he gasped. "I have to, you have to."

"Al!" Slug turned in her seat, she was looking a little pale. "You can't talk to the President like that!"

"You would be dead at that speed," Lin told him.

"Don't remind us!" Al barked. "You wanted a miracle, you got a miracle. We can still beat the Goo, but it's going to be close. Where's Eric?"

"Puck," Lin answered curtly, apparently deciding that explanations for the impossible could wait.

"President Wattana came out to mediate between myself and Shepard after I exposed your evidence against Oberon. Al…" she sighed at him, "you didn't skim those files very carefully. There were direct messages from Shepard in there. He is involved."

"Whoopee for him then," Al grated. "His government should turn on him."

"His government is ripping itself apart," Lin sighed. "Which, ordinarily, I would be grateful for, but right now Shepard is still in charge, and he still has Eric, who — to the best of my knowledge — still has the Goo sample. That gives them the upper hand. For all we know, they could be planning to deposit it somewhere on Titania — turning the Goo into a weapon that could wipe out any civilisation they choose."

Silence reined in the wake of her statement. Al sat in it, feeling his body vibrate with speed and trying not to vomit or think about Titania being eaten by the Goo.

"Al," Lin addressed him again. "Maxwell's warship is scheduled to dock at the Puck Station. Come find us there." She paused a moment. "I guess I don't need to tell you to hurry."

He laughed as the line went dead. He couldn't help himself.

"Lani?" he called.

"Yep, I heard," she called back. "I gotta slow us down, fam. If we hit the Ring of Solomon at this speed I'm not sure I can weave all those asteroids." She did not have to add that if she hit an asteroid at this speed they would be little more than dust, and the fate of Pan's moons and the entire system would no longer be their problem.

He thought he would feel better when they slowed, but his version of slow and Lani's version of slow didn't seem to be measured on the same scale. His entire body clenched as they fired through the asteroid belt. Everything moved at an insane blur. He tried to remind himself that the rocks were massive distances apart, and this was a tiny ship, and they would be completely fine, but Slug kept making alarmed yelps any time they came close to one until she finally covered her eyes with her hands.

Sione had his eyes closed and his hands clasped, visibly sweating and praying. But this was Lani's bread and butter. She raced obstacle courses. She lived not just to dodge danger in a fast ship, but to beat everyone else on the track while she did it. Somehow, it helped to hear her crow triumphantly as she spun them wildly through the field. Adam and Oria seemed to ignore the ordeal and Al felt a little jealous as his stomach churned.

He let himself close his eyes and try to breathe gently. He could actually feel *Hotaru* continue to slow. Oria's glow didn't waver, and when he wasn't looking at it, he could feel the way his body responded — growing stronger and steadier in her aura. It was a nice feeling. It began to ease the nausea.

"Oh shit," Lani cursed.

Al's eyes snapped open.

"What?!" he demanded, looking for the problem. The green orb of Pan was starting to fill their horizon. Three little moons hovered in its orbit and Al felt a twinge at bypassing Titania for the smallest rock of the bunch. Puck Station was growing larger in front of them, but that was exactly where they were supposed to be heading. "What, Lani?! You can't just say 'oh shit' when you're the one driving!"

"That," she pointed to the monitor.

Al blinked a couple of times before he realised what he was seeing. It looked like a needle stalking their ass on the display. The reality hit him like an electric shock. The Goo. It had warped in its travels. The ball of dark ooze that was Gilgamesh was still all the way over by Galileo, and it was a holy miracle that it hadn't pierced through anything important yet as this snaking tendril reached between stars to take back what was stolen from it.

"It's right behind us," he blurted stupidly.

"We don't got much time," Lani agreed, hailing Puck Station. Fortunately, Lin must have told them to expect *Hotaru*, and there was already a spot waiting for them.

Oria slumped as they pulled in. The glow stuttered out, but Adam was there to catch her. He bundled her up in his arms, holding her close as soon as she wilted. Al didn't hear what she whispered, but Adam murmured in reply. He held Oria gently against him, kissing her temple and telling her how good she'd done. They were a giant killing machine and a ghostly weird alien, but it was almost cute.

It seemed redundant to note anything was wrong when they docked, given the situation, but things were still wrong. Al knew it the instant they disembarked. Lin had sent her aide Wu to meet them. Al recognised the traditionally garbed woman instantly as he stepped off the ship. The other woman standing at her side must have been a chief official of the station, Al assumed from the uniform as well as the posture.

"Where's Eric?" he demanded as soon as he reached them.

"Puck," Wu answered bitterly. "President Wattana had Lin and Shepard come down to the Capitol Building in Buri to meet with her, and Maxwell followed after Shepard as soon as his ship docked."

"He killed one of the guards who tried to stop him," the official added with a grimace. "Now our station's in disarray because the Goo is bearing down on us and we've already had a distress call from a ship that got caught by it."

"Someone got hit by the Goo?" Slug asked, the others all coming up behind Al.

"A mining ship returning from the Ring," Wu admitted. "The Goo came up too fast and they couldn't dodge it. It took out half their engines. If they try and turn on what they've got left they'll only push themselves further into the stream melting their ship. They need to be rescued, but all the rescue ships here are trying to move the station out of the Goo's path."

"That won't work," Al muttered. "They'll never drag it away fast enough. I need a shuttle to Buri."

The official shrugged. "Good luck. All the shuttle queues are overflowing."

"Idiots!" Al cursed. "No shuttle from this station has the range to get anywhere safe. If these people want to live, I have to get to the Capitol Building, and unlike Eric I don't want to have to kill anyone to do it."

Both Wu and the official paused a moment, sharing a glance, then gave sharp nods to show they understood and were prepared to help.

"I might be able to buy us more time..." Oria muttered. She was barely standing and Adam still held her close to keep her propped up, but her pale eyes were steady as she spoke.

"Who are...?" Wu began, trailing off like she realised a better question might have been 'what are you'.

"You sure?" Adam asked Oria, gently adjusting his hold on her. She nodded.

"I might need a little help..." she admitted.

"I got you," he assured. His eyes were patient but unrelenting as he turned to the ladies who had met them. "We're going to slow the Goo down." He told them.

Neither seemed in any hurry to argue with him.

"We could go back for the mining ship..." Slug volunteered. Everyone looked to her.

"Yeah, why not?" Lani shrugged. "Someone oughtta. Those people are dying. I got a doctor, an engineer, and a ship that's fast enough to get there."

"That's very generous of you," the official said. "But that ship is already half destroyed. It's still stuck in the Goo. Any ship that goes to its aid risks falling into the stream themselves."

"Not with my Lani at the wheel," Sione countered, clamping a proud hand on his daughter's shoulder. "She already outrun that muck more than anyone in history. She thinks she can do this, then she can."

"Shucks, Dad..." Lani muttered, rolling her eyes.

"Adam," Al looked up at the giant, "take Oria and help her slow this shit down. We need every second we can get. You three, go rescue those miners." He paused mid-orders, worried that he was going to have to justify them, but he should have known better. "I'm going to go stop Eric."

"Al!" Slug exclaimed. They all knew it was right, but no one liked hearing the announcement. She bounced forward, grabbing him by the front of the shirt and kissing him. He shouldn't have been surprised by the cliché, but he was a little. Still, he would have regretted it more if she hadn't.

"Thanks cuz," Lani drawled. "Now we're all going to die."

"Shut up, Lani," Slug snapped. She whirled around and led her cousin and uncle straight back into *Hotaru*.

Wu and her companion led Al, Adam, and Oria deeper into the station. The official took point and led them straight to one of the shuttle bays. She flashed her badge and commandeered the shuttle. Al was all set to fight the crowds looking to argue, but one look at his face and every single person settled into stunned silence. Of course. The dreams. He still wasn't used to that. In the haze of everything that had happened, he'd nearly forgotten how it had started. The thought made him turn back to Oria, but the look in her eyes told him there was no time for questions. If he wanted answers, they had to survive this first.

Al thanked Wu and the official who helped them before diving onto the shuttle, locking her up, and aiming straight for the tiny moon below.

***

Adam wasn't going to tell Oria he didn't like her plan, but he was pretty sure she knew. Watching her admire the vastness of space with naked eyes while they had worked on *Hotaru* had nearly been fun. This was nearly enough to make him nervous. He could hear his breath in his ears, reverberating through his helmet. The tether cord keeping him bound to the station pulled at his back, and it felt very fragile. He and Oria were roped together as well, but he still kept his hands on her. It felt necessary.

They drifted gently away from the station, floating in an ocean of nothing. Even compared to the ice mines, nothing had ever felt so claustrophobic. There was nothing but space, his own breathing, his hands on the woman in front of him, and her sure and steady path towards a spike of darkness so severe it wiped out the stars.

Yup. What could go wrong?

***

Al let the shudder of the shuttle soothe him as it came in to land. He had to admit, after a week in Lani's hands, he was not a good pilot. But he could land a shuttle. It came down heavy on the landing pad of the Capitol Building and he felt his brains rattle, but he was fresh and strong from a journey in Oria's light, and he was ready to do whatever he had to in order to fix this. He was ready to do what he was good at.

He staggered out and security met him immediately. That was hardly a surprise. They had guns raised so he came out with his hands up. If any of the poor bastards had run into Eric first they would be in a jumpy mood.

"Presidents Lin and Shepard," he called out. "I have to find them!"

"Fire!" a guard ordered.

Al cursed every stupid person who'd ever wasted oxygen as he dove behind the shuttle. Gunfire erupted around him. He hunkered down as bullets ricocheted off the shuttle. His comms beeped in his ear.

"Yeah?!" he bellowed into them.

"Akiyama!" Lin yelled back. "I can hear the gunfire, where are you?"

"In the middle of it," he admitted.

"Of course you fucking are," she sighed. Her voice became more distant. "Lawan, cease fire! That's my man you're shooting down there!"

"Those aren't my guards!" another woman's voice called back.

Al risked a peek. Stupid! He should have noticed before. The uniform matched the people who had shot up the Inanna. Al felt his mouth set firmly. At least he didn't have to worry about hurting Puck security.

"Lin, I'm on my way," he told her, hanging up the call and drawing his weapon.

***

Slug buckled in with Sione and Lani. Her heart was racing and she would have sworn there was more adrenaline than blood in her body right now. The sheer exhilaration and terror of what they were about to do was maddening, but it was the right thing. She just wished Al and Adam could have been with them. Lani must have been having similar thoughts.

"Are we insane?" she asked as she started the engines.

"No," Sione shook his head. "Or if we are, it's too late now. This is equally as sane as our mission when we left home."

"And this time we know that there are people who need our help," Slug added.

"But we're about to fly straight at the Goo…" Lani muttered. "And it's so fucking close now!"

"I'm not worried," Sione assured, squeezing her shoulder without a trace of fear. "I got the best pilot in the system."

"Dad!" Lani protested.

"You think I don't mean that?" he checked. "You think I don't believe that with every fibre of my being, whether or not I'm your dad?"

"No, I think you've spent my whole life telling me to cool it and stop being such a high-speed disaster!" she snapped.

Sione undid his belt and leant forward, taking both Lani's shoulders in his hands and grasping her reassuringly. He whispered by her ear.

"Hokulani, baby girl, don't you think for a moment that I haven't been proud of you every single day of your life." He gave her shoulders an emphatic squeeze. "I only get mad because I worry, and because you know how to hammer down every one of my buttons like you're mining for exasperation, but you best believe me and your Pa are as equally inspired by you as much as we are aggravated." He giggled and she couldn't quite hold back a smirk at that. Sione kissed her cheek and sat back in his seat. "Now, go! Go! Go!" he encouraged, buckling up again.

Slug gave her cousin a warm smile. Lani rescued her glower.

"Fuck you both," she growled, pulling away from the station. "Now we're definitely going to die." It was as close to an 'I love you' as they were going to get from Lani.

Slug grunted as Lani boosted away from Puck with enough speed to hurt. It wasn't a sharp pain, but after travelling under Oria's light the G's came with a kick. Slug scanned the radio for the mayday, settling on the frequency and calling them back.

"*Waitoreke*!" she called down the crackling line. The other end didn't sound good. "*Waitoreke*, this is *Hotaru*. We're coming to get you. Get all your survivors to the airlock furthest from the Goo stream. We'll be there in three minutes."

***

Eric's soldiers were still descending on the shuttle. It was fast turning into a smoking wreck, but that worked to Al's advantage. He could use the cover. Al took out the closest soldier first. It gave him a clear line to use the body as a shield and take their weapon. The guards weren't expecting one of their own to fire at them. That took care of three more. By then bullets were running out and he was moving in.

The first living soldier he reached got an elbow to the throat. Al snatched their gun and smashed them over the head with it. They dropped. He snuck through the last dregs of smoke, but there were still half a dozen guards behind him, and he really didn't want that to be a problem for future Al. They were still looking through the shuttle wreckage like he wouldn't have had the sense or skill to escape. Insulting, really.

He lined up his shot carefully and mowed down half of them with a single bullet. Their guns were bigger than his, and he appreciated the armour-piercing ammo they'd come after his shuttle with. Automatic too. Weapons of choice for mercenaries with more money than skill. The rest were dead before they finished turning around.

Al checked his comms. There was a message from Lin. *Sakura Hall. Third floor.* He bolted for the building. Inside the Capitol Building the security was all President Wattana's, thankfully. A few guns were raised on him as he came racing over, but as soon as anyone saw him they knew to lower their weapons.

He went for the stairs, taking them three at a time in massive strides as he raced the clock on their demise. No one else had contacted him since they'd split, but he couldn't stop and think about that now. He couldn't worry about Slug racing off on a suicide mission. Not that he was behaving any better.

Sakura Hall was signposted as soon as he reached

the third floor. His footsteps slowed automatically. His gut twisted. If Lin hadn't called again it meant she couldn't. This wasn't going to be some dramatic showdown. Nemeses or not, that wasn't how they were going to end.

His hand tightened on his gun and he stepped carefully to the edge of the corridor, peeking around the corner. The doors to the Sakura Hall were shut tight, but there was no one waiting outside them. Al was grateful for that. That meant Eric didn't have enough people with him to post extras. Still not wise to bust in alone.

A guard posted outside would have been useful for that, but looking around he was going to have to settle for a cleaning supply droid. It deserved better, but it was also going to be a lot easier to mend than he was. Al kicked the door to the hall open and shoved the droid through. It was met with a hail of bullets. He charged in after it, aiming right where the fire had come from.

Al shot the first of Shepard's guards through the throat. Someone grabbed his gun. Not someone. Never just someone. Eric grabbed his fist with both hands and slammed it against the nearest conference table. Al dropped his weapon but took the opportunity to punch Eric in the face. The two of them tackled each other to the floor, a whirl of fists and feet.

He could hear women screaming across the room. Probably Lin and Wattana. There was a small collection of guards positioned about a shallow barricade of tables who were staying out of this fight. Their jobs were to protect their respective presidents.

The only other person in the room was Shepard. He was sitting at one of the tables on the opposite side of the room from the other presidents, save that he had half risen from his chair when his guard was shot. Al could see the canister on the table in front of him. That was it. The magnetic containment of the Goo sample.

Eric punched him in the ribs. Al stomped him across the knee, dislocating his patella. Both of them were trying to grab the other by the face and gouge their eyes out. Al could feel Eric's fingernails scratching at his face. He tried to hold him down with one arm and punch him out cold. Eric writhed beneath him, squirming free. He lunged for the gun.

Al snatched him and slammed his wounded leg. Eric grunted in pain. Al tried to go over him, but Eric grabbed his belt and brought him crashing to the floor.

"For God's sake! Just kill him!" Shepard yelled.

Al brought his knee straight into Eric's ribs. Eric pulled a switchblade. It was such a classic Maxwell move Al knew he should have seen it coming. He knew exactly what had happened as soon as he felt the knife pierce his side. But he'd got his fingers on the gun. He snatched it off the ground, rolling off Eric, and scrambling up. He grabbed his side where he could feel hot blood pouring from the wound.

Eric rose to meet him, knife in hand and smirk at the ready. This wasn't the first time they'd done this. It was a dance they both knew, and had performed countless times. There was one small difference this time. A difference in Al. Eric didn't see it coming. His expression was almost surprised as he paused, brains splattering the table behind him and bullet hole through his forehead. His body hesitated a moment, eyes glazed, before toppling over. Al wasn't surprised that his new willingness to kill had caught Eric off guard; he'd asked himself — what would Adam do?

"Assassin!" Shepard bellowed, snatching the canister and hunkering behind the table. "Stop him!"

No one left in the room was on his side. The other guards were putting their weapons away. Al assumed from the positioning that he had interrupted a stand-off. He could see Lin and Wattana now, both presidents huddled together behind their bodyguards' barricades. Lin met his eye with alarm and concern, her hand pressed to her heart. He had no idea what he looked like, battered and bloody and homicidal, but it must have been a sight.

Al turned on Shepard. The President of Oberon was so pathetically ordinary. Another average middle-aged man, still going grey and pudgy despite obvious and extensive aesthetic surgeries. He cowered as Al descended on him, clutching the canister to his chest. Al grabbed him by the collar and jammed his gun under the man's chin.

"This is how it feels!" he roared in the quivering man's face. "This, right here, is the feeling you just gave to everyone else who lives around the three suns! This is what you cost them! Give me that," he spat in disgust, trying to haul the canister from Shepard's arms.

"No!" Shepard pleaded. "No! You can't! This is it! This is what we need to control it! All the tests… all the research! Hundreds of years of research have come out of this! It's all we have to work with, to understand—"

Al punched him in the face and ripped the canister from his grasp. He was dripping blood all over the man's pristine suit, and the pain in his side caused him to pause. Of all things, in that moment, he heard Sione's voice. He looked down on the fool at his feet, the man who truly and absolutely believed that canister was the answer; who had greenlit horrific, unspeakable atrocities to get it, because he *believed* so completely the story that it was the only way.

"This thing," Al held it up above him. "This thing is what destroyed Gilgamesh, and Earth — the entire solar system we came from! This tiny piece of goop and people like you — people who stole this and risked everything just for the chance to possess more power! You! People like you killed our home!" he roared with an anger he didn't realise he'd felt, a grief he'd never realised he'd known, but that had settled numbly in the bowels of humanity since they had fled Earth. "We were supposed to be better," he proclaimed. "Losing Earth was supposed to be a lesson in hubris. When we lost *everything* why didn't it teach us to be better? Why, two hundred years later, are we still making the same mistakes?"

No one answered, and he didn't actually expect them to. The wound in his side stabbed painfully and he winced. Foolish. He didn't have time for grandstanding. He tightened his grip on the canister, holstering his gun and clutching his side as he staggered from the room.

CHAPTER THIRTY-ONE

Hotaru crept up on the *Waitoreke* like a cat burglar in the dead of night — save that she had announced herself. Lani had lined the ships up and latched on as gently as a dawn kiss. Only half the mining ship was still intact and it was drifting further and further into the Goo, which roped towards Pan like a tentacle of pure darkness.

Slug was suited up and carefully guiding people onto *Hotaru*, beckoning them across. She could see the Goo out the vitruchal windows, and trying not to look was failing utterly. It almost seemed to throb, slowly growing wider and thicker, like a seeping trail gushing from a distant bleeding heart.

They were down to the last few survivors when something deep in the *Waitoreke* went crunch. There was a heart stopping pause as everyone shared a glance. Then the ship began to rip apart. Slug leapt forward to grab the last passengers. She could hear them screaming as the hull tore open and everything was sucked towards the vacuum of space. Two of them she caught in her arms, and the last man grabbed her sleeve. She clamped her boots to the floor to stop them all from being sucked away, but the strain was vicious and the floor was tipping already.

"Lani!" she screamed into her comms as the floor of the *Waitoreke* began to fall away underneath her. Slug grabbed the handle of the tether from her belt and threw it back towards *Hotaru*.

Sione appeared in the doorway, catching the handle and clamping it to the wall of the airlock. Slug disconnected her boots and hit the button on the tether. It began to reel them inside even as Lani began to unlatch from the other ship and back off.

Slug and her passengers crashed into the hallway and Sione slammed the airlock closed behind them. She stayed on her hands and knees for a moment as the room repressurised around her and Sione checked over the *Waitoreke* survivors. She was shaking. Part of her felt like she could still hear herself screaming.

Then Sione was kneeling in front of her. He clicked her helmet back, exposing her to the light and air of the room. It was stale ship oxygen, but somehow still better than her suit. She was gasping, maybe even crying, but he squeezed her shoulder and she started to steady. She was alive.

"Guys...?" Lani called hesitantly over the comms. "Guys? Are you all good?"

"Yeah," Sione called back, patting Slug as she calmed down. "Yeah, bubba, we're good. Everyone's on board. We got them."

"Swell work, fam," Lani breathed a sigh of relief. "Heading for the station. Let's hope the rest of the team's having as much luck as we are."

*****

Adam was starting to weaken. He could feel it. There was no pressure, no weight, but he was tense. More tense than he'd ever been in his life. He had stared down death before. It was easy enough when it was just another person, when it was you or them and only one of you was gonna walk away, and that was okay because it made sense.

This Goo didn't make any sense. He didn't understand it at all. He didn't know what was going to happen to him when it touched him, and he didn't want it to hurt Oria. He didn't want anything to hurt Oria. That was important. She deserved better.

He held her tightly around the waist as she reached out. The Goo reaching back. It was aiming straight for Puck and seemed to have every intention of going directly through the station to get there. He could hear the overlapping station alarms through his comms. They were freaking out. He didn't blame them. If he was honest he was freaking out a bit too. The Goo was so close you could reach out and touch it.

Which was exactly what they were doing.

He could feel her body straining in his hands, naked to the emptiness of space save for her dress. She was glowing like a small star, hands outstretched. The point of the Goo had reached them, and she held back the end of it like she was guiding the nose of a shark. It hovered curiously in her hands, seemingly recognising itself, or its progeny, the tip of it pulsing and growing like an incoming tide.

But she was fading. He could see her glow waning,

could feel the effects dwindling. They weren't gonna make it.

"Guys?" Adam called weakly into his comms. "Anyone still there?"

"Adam?!" Slug's voice crackled back. "Adam, babe, where are you?"

"We're outside the station," he panted, listening to his breath echo in his helmet. "We, uh, we're not doing so flash. I don't… I don't think she can hold this much longer, and this station ain't evacuated."

"Don't worry," Al's voice cracked across the line. "I'm on my way. Just give me two minutes."

"Al!" Slug cried so loudly Adam winced. "Al! Where have you been?!"

"Some assholes blew up my shuttle," he replied. "Had to steal theirs. Hold up, coming your way."

Adam felt his hands steady. She could do it, he was sure. A couple of minutes. They got this.

***

Al felt the bump and rush as the stolen shuttle crashed away from Puck's gravity, shooting for the station. Boom. Weightlessness. He could never get sick of that feeling. The radio chatter told him that *Hotaru* had completed a successful rescue and was on the way to Puck Station. Adam and Oria were hanging in there. It was going to be okay. He stroked the canister in his lap with the side of his thumb. There was a lot of blood on it now. There was a lot of blood leaking out of him.

"One minute to impact," the shuttle told him.

"Hear that, Adam?" Al asked. "Two minutes down to one. What did I promise?"

"Hai, Chief," Adam replied. Al could hear the strain in his voice.

"Impact?" Slug echoed. "Al, what does it mean 'impact'?"

"I gotta get the sample back into the body," Al told her carefully. "Gotta do it fast."

"Al… tell me you are not crashing your shuttle into the Goo!" she demanded.

"I am not crashing my shuttle into the Goo," he promised.

"What are you doing?" she asked.

"I'm crashing Eric's shuttle into the Goo," he grinned, feeling rather satisfied with himself. The wound in his side stabbed painfully. He winced and pressed on it again. There was so much blood. He was starting to feel dizzy. He was glad Slug couldn't see him like this.

"AL-AMIR!" Slug screamed at him so loudly he winced. "That shit just ate through an entire mining ship!"

"So keep *Hotaru* well away from it," Al winced. "I'm counting on you to take care of my ship, Slug."

"Your ship?!" she challenged.

"Yeah," he grinned. "My ship. What's yours is mine, remember?" He could practically hear her fuming down the line. "What's mine is also mine," he added, before softly supplying with a pained grimace, "but that's okay, because… because I'm yours. I am, Slug. I always have been. I need you to take care of *Hotaru* for me, ae? And Adam, because, come on—" he chuckled weakly as the dizziness intensified. "That guy clearly can't take care of himself."

The shuttle began a ten second countdown. Nine. Eight.

"Al, are you injured?!" Slug called. She sounded like she was crying. Seven. Six.

"Na, I'm okay," Al lied, hearing the grimace in his own voice. Five. Four.

"Al—" Slug choked. Fuck, she was definitely crying. Three. Two.

"Take care of her until I get back," Al insisted.

The shuttle collided with the spire of inky blackness. Everything went dark.

***

Everything went dark, but it did not stay that way. Al felt himself drifting in the light. Everything was bright and white, and he was warm and safe. Nothing hurt here. He could feel someone holding his hand. When he looked over he was not surprised by who he found, although he would also have had other first choices if there had been an option.

"Hey…" he greeted her.

"Hey," Oria smiled back.

"Did I do it?" Al asked. "Did I do what you wanted?"

"Everything I asked of you and more," she replied, her voice resonating with a soft bell-like quality, like distant wind chimes.

"Good…" Al rested back in the soothing warmth. "That's good."

They stayed like that for an unmeasured length of time. Al was confident that this was not a place where time was kept. This was a realm where time was left wild, limitless, and free range. He basked in it, comfortable and content. They were not feelings he was particularly familiar with, but he felt like he could get used to them.

"I have a question for you," he stated finally.

"Only one?" she teased.

"Rude," he retorted.

Oria laughed, and he smiled at how many of the family's mannerisms she had managed to adopt in such a short time. Unless, of course, they were simple human truths that just came naturally to their species. Or, just as likely, she wasn't actually there.

"Ask your questions," she invited, patting his hand.

"Why me?" he asked.

"Humans have been asking that question since they developed the capacity to consider themselves as individual entities," Oria sighed.

"Yes, we're very self-involved," Al conceded. "Now answer the question."

"Why you?" she asked.

"Yes, why me?" he demanded.

"Why you what?" she asked.

"Why did you pick me?" he insisted. "You could have picked anyone in the system. You could have picked Adam directly, if that's what you wanted. He would have come out with Slug and Lani and Sione and rescued you. They were the ones you actually needed. You could have picked someone from Arthur to pop straight over, rescue you and the scientists, and push the sample and the Inanna back into Gilgamesh! Why in Allah's holy name did you pick me?"

"Because it had to be you," she told him. "For the pieces to align, it had to be you."

He stayed silent in response. Her answer was annoying and weak, and she must have known that. Here, he was perfectly happy to wait for eternity until he got a better answer. Oria sighed patiently.

"Let's not pretend that I was making the decision alone," she reminded.

He understood. Oria, fundamentally a person, wasn't actually capable of transmitting telepathic thought throughout an entire star system. It was something the Goo could do, whatever it was. She had become linked to it, and the two of them together had used each other to do whatever it was that they thought had needed to be done.

"If I had called Adam..." she mused. "If I had sent out the call I did, the call I had to make, and begged for Adam Tanaka... he is lovely, but he was not the right person for this role. He would not have known how to make the right decision. Besides, if I had alerted all life to his presence, the gangs would have found him again before he could get a ship."

Al pursed his lips in thought. That was valid.

"All your crew... they are good people. You needed them. I needed them, but none of them know enough about the things you know to do what had to be done, to do what you did," Oria tried to explain. "And I could have called someone from Arthur… but that wouldn't have stopped them. We both know that."

Now it was Al's turn to sigh. "It was about me after all."

"I needed someone who could stop the thieves," she said. "Although, I will be the first to admit I didn't always know what I was doing or why. I was being guided by a power much more advanced than I. We. We needed someone to stop the thieves, not just your adversary and his employer, but the ones who would have followed."

Al nodded. He was starting to catch on. Maybe it was because he was just lying here, soaking it all up, or maybe he'd always understood it. Hence Oria's choice and his grandstanding to Shepard.

There would always be humans who would steal, to the detriment of humanity, for their own selfish desires. There would always be the politician who would run their nation into the ground, just to expand their own private wealth. There would always be the scientist who would create the artifice to destroy mankind, just to see if they could. There would always be the village lunatic who would press the button to destroy the world, just because they were curious.

If Oria had organised for the rescue of the inhabitants of the Inanna, Oberon would have come for them — for their knowledge, for her, and for the Goo itself once they realised what it really did. People would always come to steal pieces for themselves, unless the threat was real. Unless the entire system had nearly been wiped out, in which case a few decades of caution could perhaps be bought.

"Will it work?" he asked.

"Who can say?" she sighed, and he could tell from her tone that it was impossible to know, but that she hoped her choices had led to the most optimistic outcome.

"What do we do now?" he asked.

"Wake up, I'd guess," she shrugged. "Just whenever you're ready."

Al wasn't sure he was ready but, just like the village lunatic, he was too curious to resist.

When he opened his eyes everything was still white, but somehow blurrier. It took a few dazed blinks to bring the room into focus. He glimpsed a haze of white walls and monitors and clean sheets, before someone collapsed on him.

"Al!" Slug breathed into his ear, her voice thick with emotion. She had her arms wrapped around his neck before he even knew where he was, and he wasn't unhappy with the feeling of her warm and heavy on top of him.

"I'm not dead…?" he mused.

"No, shin'yū, but you will be," she threatened lovingly, heart in her throat. "You will be."

Faint memories of his call to her as he had crashed into the Goo stirred in his mind, and he realised that even if she didn't make good on this immediate threat there was a good chance he was going to get his ass kicked once he was well enough to tolerate it.

"Don't let her bully you, Chief," Adam advised,

appearing at the side of his bed and smacking his shoulder. "We didn't go to all the effort of saving your ass just so she could spank it."

"I think that's between them, Adam, don't you?" Sione teased cheekily, checking the monitors on the other side of the hospital bed.

Al grimaced as *Hotaru's* crew piled into his hospital room and Lani grabbed his shins, shaking him enthusiastically like she thought he hadn't been through enough. The last one through the door was Oria. Al watched her step inside the room but hang back from the others, gifting him a private nod.

"You are the luckiest son of a bitch I ever met," Lani praised.

"Hokulani!" Sione reprimanded. "You cannot talk about Rajiya like that!"

"Shut up, Dad. I know you're proud of me," Lani grinned, bouncing over to her father and kissing the top of his bald head.

"What happened?" Al asked blearily. "Where are we?"

"We are in a hospital suite on Puck Station," Slug announced, still lying in the bed beside him. "And *you*," her tone dropped accusingly, darkening with every word, "flew a shuttle straight into the Goo spike and Oria had to go in there and fish you out so she and Adam could reel you back into the station."

Al listened to the story like he knew he was going to be grounded at the end of it. It didn't sound so bad. He'd survived the Goo.

"It's gone all glowy again, Chief," Adam told him

helpfully. "You fixed it. Everyone's safe."

Al resisted the urge to add 'for now' and checked under his blanket for the condition of his wound where Eric had stabbed him. There was nothing. Not even a scar from this one. He looked up at Oria again.

"I got you to thank for this?" he asked.

"It was a joint effort," she replied, looking to the window and smiling. "You helped us, after all. It's nice not to hurt anymore." She touched her temple gently, like an ancient headache had finally vanished.

"So what now?" he asked.

"That is the question of the hour," a voice announced regally from the doorway.

Al looked over as Lin, dolled up in her finest crimson, stepped into the room, flanked by two guards, both of whom immediately shot Adam nervous looks. He didn't seem to care. Al chuckled as Slug hurriedly straightened up in the presence of the old lady. Lin smiled her scarlet lion grin as she approached the bed.

"You put on quite a show for us, young man," she said pointedly, perching by his feet and patting his leg. "I'm afraid that whatever you want to do next, anything anonymous is probably out of the question for you."

"Yeah," Al muttered ruefully. "I don't imagine anyone's going to forget those dreams for a while."

"Forget the dreams, Akiyama," Lin waved that away. "President Wattana had cameras in the Sakura Hall. There is footage of you threatening Bill Shepard all over the interstellar web."

Al took a second to let that sink in.

"On the bright side," Lin continued. "There is also

footage of him endangering the entire tertiary system, so you're probably safe. But keep me in the loop. I have some lawyers on standby just in case."

"What happens to Shepard now?" Al asked. "I imagine your job's about to get very interesting."

"My job has always been interesting, Al," she smirked at him. "You were only ever the cherry on top. As for Bill? He was always a soggy fucking trifle of a man. I imagine he will plead a case with his government behind closed doors. Although, he will have to work his goddamn ass off to stop them from handing him over to the United Planetary Systems."

"What about Al?" Slug asked nervously, sucking up her courage in the face of the President.

"I think that there are less than a handful of people around the three suns who would be brave enough to try and come after him now, save the paparazzi," Lin shrugged. "But, like I said, if he needs lawyers, he has my best."

"No, she means 'what about him'?" Adam clarified, knowing Slug was too intimidated to correct her and having not even the remotest notion what that felt like. "She wants to know what's going to happen to him. Where he's going to go."

Lin shrugged and looked at Al. "What do you want to do, Akiyama?" she asked. "Where do you want to go?"

"Yeah, come on, cuz," Lani teased, clapping hurriedly at him. "What do you want to do with the rest of your life? Chop, chop!"

Al pulled the fingers at her and she laughed at him.

"I don't want to make that decision right now," he answered. No one pushed him. He looked around the people gathered about his hospital bed. They were safe, for now. The system was safe, for now. He was safe, for now. That was enough. He slid an arm around Slug, holding her close and casting a glance her way. "I want to go home first. At least for a little while. Got a few things that need growing into there."

Lin smiled at him, that really annoying knowing smile that so many people he knew seemed to have, like she'd been waiting for him to decide to go back and grow into his skin for years.

"I look forward to hearing about your future aspirations once you've had some time to think about them," she smiled, her eyes just a little too smug and her lips just a little too wise.

"Me too," Al countered, trying to match her confidence. "I'm liking my options. They're nice and varied."

No one had to agree verbally. Their expressions said it all. Out the window the Goo was curling, slowly winding itself back to Gilgamesh in a lazy drift through the stars. The future was looking bright.

Did you enjoy this book?

Please consider leaving a review for it on Amazon or Goodreads. Every positive review allows me to spend more time writing books for you to enjoy!

OTHER BOOKS BY KATE HALEY

Welcome to the Inbetween

The Vincent Temple Trilogy

Gateway to Dark Stars

Tomb of Endless Night

Fortress of the Shadow Reich

The War of the North Saga

Footsteps into the Unfamiliar (short story collection)

1. Steel & Stone

2. Magic in the Marshes

3. Forest of Ghosts

4. Women of the Woods

5. Spirit & Sand

6. The Prince and the Witch

7. Gods & Dragons

ABOUT THE AUTHOR

Kate Haley is a speculative fiction author who works predominantly in fantasy and horror.

While currently content to fill their days with writing and table-top RPGs, their grander plans involve world domination. Something akin to the tyranny of the greatest city atop the Disc would be an acceptable standard. They believe a super-villainous overlord would be an upgrade, given that our current villains lack style and imagination.

After all, super-villainy requires Presentation.

If you like their references, consider visiting their website www.katehaleyauthor.com for short fictions and merchandise, and join the mailing list for early access and exclusive cool stuff.

You can also get in touch through the website regarding their work, your position in future slave armies, or a general interest in all things nerdy and wonderful.

www.ingramcontent.com/pod-product-compliance
Lightning Source LLC
Chambersburg PA
CBHW031828310726
48972CB00005B/1205